Praise for *Beyond The Red*

"Ava Jae's *Beyond the Red* is a sand-swept fantasy of court politics, rebel attacks, and forbidden romance. While reading, I had flashes of *Star Wars*—a new planet, a fascinating culture, a fresh look on a ruler struggling to keep her power—and I had to know what happened next. Dangerous, exciting, and fast-paced, *Beyond the Red* is a story not to be missed."

—Francesca Zappia, author of *Made You Up*

"Packed with political intrigue and smoldering romance, *Beyond the Red* left me craving more of Kora's and Eros's story and the unique, fascinating universe that Ava Jae has created."

—Sarah Harian, author of *The Wicked We Have Done*

"*Beyond the Red* is a sweeping, compelling romance in a complicated and gritty world. Intrigue and heart on every page—I couldn't put it down. I'll be following Ava Jae to see what comes next!"

—Kate Brauning, author of *How We Fall*

"I loved this book! I couldn't put it down! What a fantastic debut, perfect for fans of *Firefly* and Star Wars. Ava Jae's *Beyond the Red* packs a punch, a total thrill ride that will keep readers turning the pages. I stayed up all night reading it. From page one, I was sucked in. Jae's writing style is a perfect mix of stop and go, and her world comes to life within the first few pages. The action was power-packed, and the star-crossed romance had me begging for more by the end."

—Lindsay Cummings, author of The Murder Complex series

Book 2 of the Beyond the Red Trilogy

INTO THE BLACK

AVA JAE

Sky Pony Press

NEW YORK

First Edition

This is a work of fiction. Names, characters, places, and incidents are either the
products of the author's imagination or used fictitiously.

Sky Pony Press books may be purchased in bulk at special discounts for sales
promotion, corporate gifts, fund-raising, or educational purposes. Special
editions can also be created to specifications. For details, contact the Special Sales
Department, Sky Pony Press, 307 West 36th Street, 11th Floor, New York, NY
10018 or info@skyhorsepublishing.com.

Sky Pony® is a registered trademark of Skyhorse Publishing, Inc.®,
a Delaware corporation.

Visit our website at www.skyponypress.com.

10 9 8 7 6 5 4 3 2 1

Library of Congress Cataloging-in-Publication Data

Names: Jae, Ava, author.
Title: Into the Black / Ava Jae.
Description: New York : Sky Pony Press, [2017] | Series: Beyond the red
    trilogy ; book 2 | Summary: When The Remnant abducts Eros, rightful heir
    to the world throne, ex-queen Kora tries to stave off those who would
    seize power, including a new charismatic candidate, Lejv.
Identifiers: LCCN 2017025332 (print) | LCCN 2017039129 (ebook) | ISBN
9781510722361 (hardcover : alk. paper) | ISBN
    9781510722378 (ebook)
Subjects: | CYAC: Science fiction. | Kings, queens, rulers, etc.–Fiction. |
    Inheritance and succession–Fiction.
Classification: LCC PZ7.1.J384 (ebook) | LCC PZ7.1.J384 Int 2017 (print) |
    DDC [Fic]–dc23
LC record available at https://lccn.loc.gov/2017025332

Cover design by Sammy Yuen
Map design by Kerri Frail
Interior design by Joshua Barnaby

Printed in the United States of America

*To the fighters, the resistors, the rebels
holding on to hope and making their voices heard—
this one's for you.*

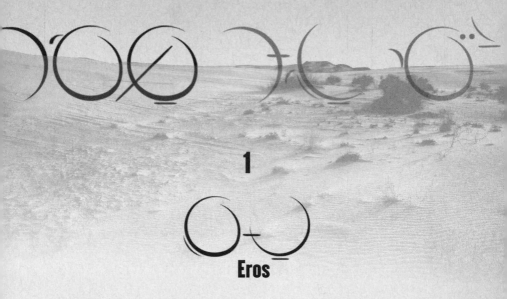

1

Eros

"In the end, we all become the same: dust, stars, and sand."

Those were the words Nol said to me when I was five as he bandaged my bruised ribs. I didn't understand what he meant then, with my mouth tasting like sand mud—bitter, thick, and chalky—my tears drying on my red-dusted face, and my ears ringing with words gathering in the back of my throat like broken glass.

Half-blood.

Alien bitch.

Mutt.

But now as crackling orange flames lick up the pyre and the people I love burn to dust and sand and stars, it's Nol's words tattooed across my mind. It's my nephew Aren's face lighting up like a sunrise when his father and I came home from a patrol—it's every moment we had together curling into smoke and reaching to the stars where I can't follow.

Mal shifts beside me as he sniffles and rubs his eyes again. He lowers his head until his rusty hair cover his eyes.

"It's—" My voice comes out tight and raspy. I clear my throat and try again. "It's okay to cry. You don't have to hold it in."

Mal squints at the pyre and doesn't answer. I don't push.

Not so long ago, before Kora's soldiers attacked our camp, there were 236 of us. Not so long ago, I had a mother and father, and a brother with a young, happy family.

Kora's raid brought our numbers down to just over one hundred. Now I count fifty-three. And of my family, Mal is the only one left.

What happens now? What am I supposed to do with a kid, who at thirteen, just lost everyone and everything? I'm not his father. I'm as lost as he is.

The crackle of flames fills my ears. My skin prickles with the weight of stares from the silent mourners. Their gazes flicker to me through the shadows of the burning pyre.

Gray begins the funeral song. His low hum reaches through the stark, flame-casted shadows. Others join him, maybe half a dozen, their tones of sorrow and ache twisting together into a melody of pain. Of wanting. Of remembering. Tonight, we're united in our sorrow, but tomorrow, with Serek's echoing words—a dying world prince—broadcasted over the red, they'll expect me to act.

There is a man with royalty in his veins, a man whose birthright outweighs Roma's.

I know my birthright: my neck beneath an executioner's blade. I know what my blood carries: a lifetime of scorn and hatred. I'm not royalty destined for the throne—I'm a guy exhausted to my bones; I'm ready to curl up in the sand and sleep until eternity takes me.

Mal squeezes my hand. I squeeze lightly back. The flames burn and burn, dancing over people I loved.

Eros, please return to Asheron.

How can I return to a capital that cheered at my would-be execution? How can I face a girl who I trusted long enough to hurt me? Who kissed me before reminding me I'm not worth the sand beneath her feet?

The territories—and your people—need you.

Who are my people? I thought they were the people who spat in the sand as I walked by; the peers who pressed my face into the dirt with my arm pulled tight—too tight—behind my back, so close to snapping. I didn't scream, didn't cry, but stars, I wanted to.

Today those people whispered *thank you* as I washed up Mal and sat with him on a dune at the edge of camp, facing an endless desert horizon. They didn't apologize. But for the first time, my name—not *half-blood*—slipped from their lips.

The fire crackles and pops; the heat of the flames licks at my skin. The moon-dotted sky paints us in cool, silvery light as the funeral song's hum settles on my shoulders. The smoke curls and rises into the deep purple night, blocking out swaths of stars.

I join quietly, humming just loud enough for Mal to hear. This was always Nol's job—carrying the tone for the family—but with everyone gone, it's the least I can do. For everyone I've lost. For the only one I have left.

Serek thought people would overlook the truth of my blood, the truth that I shouldn't exist. Serek thought birthright would triumph over hatred, over generations of murder and slavery and the unchallenged belief that humans and Sepharon will never be equals. That mixing the two is akin to bestiality. That half-bloods like me don't get to take a first breath.

But people aren't that forgiving. Hate isn't forgotten overnight. Generations of *half-bloods are an abomination* can't be erased with a few pretty words and a genetic test.

Going back to Asheron would be brainless. Going back to Asheron intending to take my *rightful place* on the throne would be laughable—in that they'd laugh while dragging me back to their half-destroyed arena for the last time.

I inhale deeply and focus on the song, on the snap of flame, on the pressure of Mal's hand in mine. The truth is I'm not scared; I'm fucken terrified. The truth is I want to walk into the suns until the pain disintegrates into stardust, like me.

Of course, doing that means leaving Mal, who has no one left. It means abandoning the mourners looking at me for hope of something better. And it means turning my back on Kora, who maybe deserves it even if I care when I don't want to, and Serek, who literally used his dying breath to legitimize me.

I have too many people's lives on my shoulders.

Mal presses his palms against his eyes and I put my arm on his shoulder. He keeps shaking his head, his dark orange hair glinting in the firelight, so like Jessa's. He has her freckles, too, scattered across his light brown skin like thick grains of sand. I don't tell him it'll be okay. I don't say they'll be with him wherever the stars reach. I don't pretend his hurt is anything less than agonizing.

Nol would want me to go. He'd give me that thin, grim smile and tell me to try. He'd say my whole life had been leading to this moment, this impossible decision, this thing

I never could have imagined happening. This thing I never would have wanted to happen.

I touch the bracelet Aren gave me, not so long ago. *It's a protection bracelet, so nothing bad can happen to you when you wear it.* My eyes sting and my vision blurs. Inhale, exhale. Breathe. The song ends, and only the pop of the flames fills the night for a beat, two, more. Then like a wave, the whispers wash over us, again and again.

"Go to the stars."

"I love you."

"Go to the stars."

Mal pulls his hands away and blinks hard, squinting into the darkness. He blinks again and again, his body shaking as he—

He's shaking. "Hey," I say softly. "Mal—"

"I can't see right."

His words come so quietly I'm not sure I heard right at first. I frown. "What do you mean?"

"There's something wrong with my eyes." He turns to me, squinting, but though his amber eyes are clear, his gaze is unfocused. "I can sortuv see, but . . . it's like . . . after what happened . . ." He presses the heels of his hands to his eyes, takes a shaky breath, and makes a pained noise like—crying. He's crying.

Dammital.

"Okay." I crouch in front of him and touch his hands. "Okay. Don't worry, I'm here. Look at me."

Mal sniffles, wipes his eyes, and squints at me through tears.

"Can you see me?"

"Yeah," he croaks. "But you're blurry, and I'm sleepy all the time and my head hurts. And everything around the edges is even blurrier and dark even during the day and there are black blotches . . ."

My stomach sinks. Mal has never had vision problems—at least, Day never mentioned any, but maybe . . .

It could be temporary, right? Based off the awful head pain everyone described, best I can guess is the nanites attacked people's brains. So maybe he's still recovering, or it's from when he collapsed, or . . . or maybe it's more serious.

I won't know unless Mal gets medical attention. And he's not going to get the help he needs out here in the desert.

Mal rubs his eyes again and again, then squints at me some more. Whether I want it or not, everything points back to Asheron.

"It could be a concussion," I say. I think concussions make people sleepy. They definitely cause brainblazes. "Maybe you hit your head when you fell. It's okay, look, we'll go to Asheron together and I'll make sure as sand a medic sees you. They've got blazing good docs there—super high tech stuff— they'll figure out what's going on and fix you right up. Okay?"

Mal leans his forehead against my shoulder and whispers, "Just don't leave me."

My stomach swoops as an ache spreads behind my lungs and claws up the back of my throat. I slide my arms around him and pull him closer. "Never."

Mal doesn't cry anymore and neither do I. I don't have any tears left to give.

Camp must've been preparing to move when the nanites attacked and everything went to the Void, because Mal's things are already packed in what was once Day's bag. I give our passed family's things to Gray, who disperses them among the remaining survivors. There used to always be a family who could put the deceased's things to use, but I wouldn't be surprised if we have a massive excess now that we've lost so many people.

Then again, a lot of people lost everything to the fires that consumed camp during Kora's raid, so maybe not.

The deep purple sky turns dusky pink, orange, and red. I fold up Day's bedroll and add it to Mal's pack. He's still asleep, so I let him get a little more rest—it's going to be a long set for both of us.

I've already made the mistake of leaving my family behind once. I've already depended on camp to keep them safe, and it didn't. And maybe it would be different this time, maybe camp is safer than Asheron is, but Mal asked me not to leave him, and even if he wanted me to, even if my sole purpose for going wasn't to get Mal the best medical care on the planet, I wouldn't.

I may have failed everyone else, but I won't fail Mal.

I slip out of the tent and dig my toes into the cool sand. The suns have barely started rising and it's already warming up quickly; it's going to be hot, like every set this time of year. I retrace my steps to the edge of camp, where I left Serek's bike after crashing it into some perimeter soldiers, but everything is sand. It wasn't breezy last night—there are still footprints everywhere—so I can't imagine the sand would've buried it already, and yet . . .

I walk all along the perimeter. I came in from the east, but maybe my sense of direction is off this morning? Or someone moved it? But even after completing the circuit, no bike.

I run a hand through my hair and turn back to camp. Guess I'll have to find Day's old bike, which Gray would've kept because we don't have ports to spare. But Serek's bike was at least five times faster, which means it'll take all set to get back to Asheron. Doable, but still.

A patch of shiny black and gold dust catches the corner of my eye. I kneel beside the pile and run my fingers through the powder—it's colder than the sand and a little slippery, almost like metal.

I take a closer look at the footprints near the dust. A long wake leads right up to the patch, like something dragged through the sand. Prints are everywhere, some grouped together and leading back into camp.

This has to be it. This is where I came racing in. This is where I crashed the black and gold bike. Black and gold like this powder.

Did Serek's bike . . . disintegrate? Is that even possible? He did say it was nanite-made, but if there was a risk of it literally turning to dust, wouldn't he have warned me? What if that had happened while I was using it?

Sighing, I stand and turn back to camp. If I were superstitious, I might take the whole thing as a sign I shouldn't go. If I were religious, I might think something out there was messing with me. Which is what Gray seems to be thinking when I tell him about the fate of Serek's bike.

"Dust?" He arches an eyebrow. "What, like, poof? You're sure?"

I show him a handful of the stuff.

He shakes his head and brings me to Day's old bike, kept with the camp junkers. "Damn alien tech. They think they're so advanced, but at least our *primitive* shit doesn't melt under the suns."

I grimace and turn away, but Gray grabs my shoulder. "Hold on."

I stare at him. He smiles apologetically and releases me, wiping his hand on his pants like he's been contaminated by touching me. Old habits.

"I just—we hadn't really . . . left off on the ride foot before. And that's on me—I was a deck, and I'm sorry. But I just . . . hope you know you're the first and only chance we've ever had."

And here it is. What everyone's been saying through their glances and whispers. The truth no one wanted to say outright: the half-blood they treated like garbage is now someone they need. So now they'll be polite. Now they'll use my name. Now they'll treat me like a person, like someone deserving respect.

Almost like a human.

My voice comes out flat. Tired. Sick of the falseness already. "You're unbelievable."

Gray frowns. "Eros—"

"No." I step toward him, my blood boiling under my skin. "You all treated me like trash my *entire life*, and yet I stuck my neck out for all of you again and again. I'm going to Asheron to get Mal help, and I don't fucken know what will happen after. But I don't owe *anyone* a damn thing and you don't get to ask me for shit. You don't get to guilt me into risking my life for any of you ever again."

Gray's gaze falls to his feet. I clench my fists. "I've been telling you I'm one of you all along, but you didn't want to hear it until you could get something from me. I'm not going to forget who I am, and I'll never forget my home, but whatever decision I make will be because I choose it. Not because you had a change of heart and decided to treat me like a person eighteen years too late."

Gray's sharp eyes are soft when he finally looks up at me. "For what is worse, I'm sorry."

I don't humor him with a response. The suns have risen, and if the trip is going to take all set, then it's time to go.

I don't know what will happen when we get to Asheron. But this time, I won't be coming back.

After riding hard for hours, we stop to stretch, piss, drink, and gnaw on dried meat strips. Mal hasn't said a word—and still barely looks at me—but I don't want to push him. He just watched his family die; I can't expect him to be his cheery, chatty self. Maybe I should be trying to talk to him, but . . . I don't know what to say.

I'm sorry I wasn't fast enough.

I'm sorry I wasn't good enough.

"I'm sorry," I say softly.

Mal stares off across the sand.

We sit in silence for a while before I stand and stretch my arms over my head. "We should—"

"I'm scared." He squints at me and picks at his fingernails. "I know I'm not supposed to say that—I mean, I'm thirteen—but the aliens . . . they don't like humans. What if they don't help? Or make me a slave?"

Despite the heat of the twin suns on my back, something inside me turns to ice. Of course Mal is scared—after everything he's suffered at the hands of the Sepharon, why wouldn't he be? *I'm* scared, and I've lived with them. Mal's lost everything, and now I'm dragging him across the desert to a city full of his enemies. A city full of people who will never see him—or me—as an equal.

Am I making a mistake? The people of Asheron aren't going to accept me. How do I know they won't try to arrest us both as soon as we arrive? But I can't second-guess myself, not now. Not when Mal needs medical attention before his eyesight gets worse. Not when the only way to fix him is to take him to the very people who tried to kill him.

It's a risk. But I'll die before I let them hurt Mal. And Kora—she may have turned her back on me, but I have to believe she'll be willing to help Mal. Even if only because she fucken owes me after I saved her life *twice*.

"I'll keep you safe," I say. "I promise I won't let anything bad happen to you. I swear it on the stars."

Mal's eyes widen for an instant—an oath you make on the stars isn't one you break on penalty of condemning yourself to the Void, if you believe that stuff. Mal does, and it's enough. He nods.

I ruffle his hair and help him up. "Let's go. The sooner we reach Asheron, the sooner we can get you better."

We climb back onto Day's bike and kick off. Mal's tight grip on my waist keeps me focused as the hot, dry air races past my face. Mal will be okay. Mal *has* to be okay. This isn't a big deal, right? It's not like his vision has gone totally black—things are just a little blurry. He's fine. He's *fine*.

I'll make sure someone looks at him, and I'll make sure they do it right. I don't care if he's human—I'll make them listen.

Mal is my responsibility and he's dealt with too much.

A deafening rumble like a thunderclap rolls under us and then—

A blast of sand as tall as Asheron's Spire jets into the air in front of us, exploding into a massive red cloud filled with smoke and flame—

I throw the bike down, slamming Mal and me into the sand as Day's bike skids ahead. Mal shouts something—I cover his body with mine—and sand hammers down on us. It weighs on my back, fills my ears, becomes the air in my lungs.

A beat, and a building is sitting on my back.

A mo, and my lungs ache.

I spit sand and more takes its place. I clamp my mouth shut. Mal and I will suffocate if I don't move. I need to get us out.

My muscles strain against the sheer weight of sand on my back as I force my body to uncurl. I drag one arm above my head, but the sand is resisting, pushing back against me until—air. I lean toward the surface, stretching my head up—

A hand grabs mine and yanks up. I clench my arm around Mal's waist as something—someone—drags us up and into the hot, free air. On my hands and knees, I sputter sludge and blink sand mud from my eyes. My whole body shakes as I spit up sand and catch my breath, taking in huge gulps of scorching air.

Mal. Is Mal okay?

Someone pulled us up. Someone—

I stagger to my feet. Mal is on his hands and knees, coughing violently, but he's okay. My vision is blurry and red. I wipe my eyes again, clearing the sand mud.

A man is standing across from me. Human, dark skin, shaved head, dressed in some kinduv sand-colored uniform.

We're surrounded. Two dozen people, all armed. A couple of them have beards. Where did they come from? The desert was empty—I *know* it was empty—and we're too far from camp . . .

"Eros, right?" The man takes half a step toward me—I stumble a step back. He raises his hands in front of him and offers a small smile. "We're not going to hurt you. I'm Shaw, of the Remnant. We want to talk before you go to Asheron."

The Remnant? Am I supposed to know what that means? I'd never heard Day mention them—does Gray know who they are?

"What makes you think we're going to Asheron?" I help Mal to his feet and keep him behind me—not that it matters, with people standing behind us, too, but . . . "How do you know my name?"

"Everyone knows your name and where you're headed," Shaw says. "The former *Sira* broadcasted it to the entire planet."

I grimace. "Fine. Talk. Starting with why you tried to blow up me and my nephew."

"Ah." Shaw runs his hand over his skull and laughs lightly, glancing at the others. A soft chuckle rolls around us. "Sorry—we did'n' mean to—well. You were never in any danger—we targeted it precisely. We needed to stop you and it seemed a better option than shooting at you."

"Or," I say, "you could've not hidden in the sand to start with and—"

"Tactics aside, this isn't the best place to talk—we're too exposed. We need the two of you to come with us."

A cold tingle nips at the base of my skull and slips down my back like a trickle of water. "Come with you?"

"That's what I said, yes."

"To where, exactly?"

He smiles. "Somewhere safe."

Uh-huh. "And if we refuse?"

"I wouldn't recommend it." Shaw lowers his hand to his holster at his hip, where a gleaming black phaser is ready, all while keeping that easy smile. "There's no need to make this unpleasant. We don't want to harm either of you—we'll just have a quick discussion, after which you're free to go."

"Then let's discuss here."

His smile tightens. "I'm afraid that's not possible."

"And why not?"

"Because the one who wants to speak with you isn't here. Look, I'm asking out of courtesy. It'll be easier—and less traumatic"—he nods at Mal—"for everyone if you cooperate."

I don't like any part of this—the way they nearly killed us, then saved us, just to corner us. We haven't been gone from camp a set and Mal's life is already in danger—is this what every moment will look like for him at my side?

But I guess none of that matters, because right here, right now, we don't have a choice. Not if I want to keep Mal safe—not if I don't want to risk him getting hurt.

So with their phasers surrounding us, with Shaw's hollow smile and his fingers drumming his holster, I say, "Fine."

Shaw's face bursts into a bright smile. "Perfect. I knew you'd be cooperative."

"One discussion, then we're leaving."

His grin doesn't falter. "Of course." He places his hand over his heart and bows his head slightly, with that infuriating smile glinting in the suns. "You have my word—you'll be on your way in no time."

I don't bother pretending to believe him.

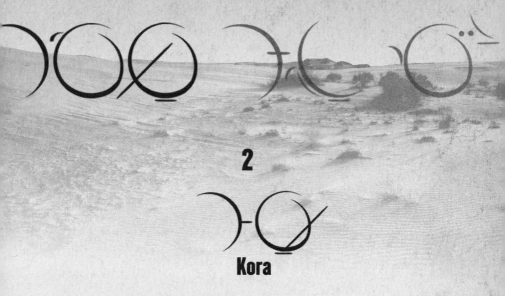

2

Kora

Six guards stand outside my bedroom chamber "for my own safety."

They don't technically suspect me of anything, not since the Spire's built-in recording played back the footage of Serek's murder—but this is the consequence of attacking eight guards to break into the Spire and shut down the nanites ex-*Sira* Roma had programmed to kill the redbloods. Without the footage, I would've been imprisoned—most likely executed. With, they still don't trust me . . . but I can stay as Eros's representative. And when he arrives, I'll help him secure his place and prepare for the throne. I can do some good yet.

At least, that's what I'll argue if anyone questions me.

Of course, I'm not the only one being monitored by warriors; Asheron's streets are full of them keeping order and smothering the panic before demands for answers turn into an outright riot—the consequence of a necessary military takeover. It's eerily familiar to my final terms as *Avra* back in Elja, failure of a territory ruler that I was.

I dab sweat off my forehead with a towel then do my best to comb my fingers through my damp hair. My dominant arm is tucked against my chest in a makeshift sling—and using my left so much is somewhat unfamiliar because I'm out of practice, but like most Sepharon, I'm ambidextrous. Adjusting to using my left while my wrist heals shouldn't take long.

Except, of course, wrapping my scarred left arm in its black covering is much more difficult when every movement with my right flashes with pain. If I were in Elja, I'd slip into one of my many single-sleeved tops, but I'm not, and I don't have help, so I grit my teeth and bear it. One agonizing breath at a time, I cover my mottled, pink skin with black.

With the destruction of the nanites came the loss of so many luxuries, like cooled air and sand screens on the windows. Thankfully, however, not *everything* was built on nanites—power planet-wide comes from the light of the suns, our communications systems are completely separate, and while there was once a movement to integrate nanites into the plumbing system to make it more effective, it was never incorporated, thank *Kala*. We've likely lost some high-tech transportation—newer port units were created with Serek's coded nanite technology—but the majority weren't nanite-built.

That said, the luxuries lost are nothing compared to the more serious loss of vital technology, like disease prevention and most of our medical care—the reason my wrist hasn't mended—and crop assistance, and *Kala* knows what else.

I can deal with the heat and my aching arm. What's much harder to swallow is the Sepharons' worldwide suffering. How will we heal the gravely injured without nanites? Or feed the southern nations when the crops growing in the desert, no longer protected by nanites, cannot be flash-grown and wither and die? We're on the brink of global panic, and without a *Sira* to guide the nations, the tentative peace won't last.

We need the nanites. If leadership in Asheron doesn't get sorted out quickly so we can figure out a way to restore them soon, I don't know how Safara will ever recover.

I push the double doors open and step between my narrow-eyed guards. "It's sunrise," I say, answering the question in their eyes. "The Emergency Council should be arriving, *sha*? Has the rising meal been served?"

I walk right past them without waiting for an answer. Steady footsteps follow me, but no one tries to stop me. My bare feet pad over the smooth, cool stone of the polished hallways. Black and gold banners hang on the walls with Serek's name sewn into every other banner—preparation for his funeral and the first sign of the commencement of the official mourning period, which will go on for eight sunsets. Or it would, anyway, if the nanites were functioning and able to preserve his body, but as they aren't, and we live in the desert, the mourning period has been accelerated to three sets, with the final five sets left for contemplation *after* his funeral. The acceleration adds insult to injury, but the alternative is even worse.

In contrast, no one speaks of Roma—the brother who killed him. Roma isn't dead, but he might as well be; Serek programmed the last of the functioning nanites to put him in a deep sleep, permanently. They're keeping him alive in the medical ward, always under supervision of armed guards, until the next *Sira* decides what to do with him.

I hope the next *Sira* sentences him to death. He deserves nothing less after attempting genocide and murdering Serek.

I hold Serek's name in my thoughts long enough to pay

my respects, and then force his smiling face out of my mind. Thinking of him much longer is too painful right now. If I start remembering his contagious smile, or the glint in his eyes as he looked at me, or his kindness, even after I admitted my feeling for Eros—

Stop. I clench my fists and take a slow, painful breath. I can't do this right now, not again. I need to focus on the task at hand. I need to make certain someone isn't appointed in Eros's place before he arrives.

But what if he never returns? After the way we treated him—like he wasn't worth the breath in his lungs even *before* his near-execution. . . After the way *I* treated him—earning his trust enough to make it hurt when I turned away from him . . .

My quiet footsteps echo in the vast hall; the warm, polished rock unyielding beneath my feet. The truth is, I don't know why he'd return. I can't say I'd return, in his place. But Safara needs a ruler now more than ever, and Eros—compassionate, daring Eros—is everything I imagine his father wanted when he and Eros's mother decided to have him.

Asha and Eros's redblood mother created a half-blood *kaï* intending to change the world. And as much as I fear Eros has no motivation to return, I can only pray he does.

Because Safara doesn't need another ruler who will sow more generations of hate; Safara needs *Sira* Eros, who would break the cycles of injustice. And I need him, too.

The dining hall is empty save for black-clad Sepharon servants setting out the food—Asheron never used redblood servants—and armed guards lining the walls. The banquet set out—platters of fruit, large carafes of colorful juices, flat *kata* wraps beside bowls of spreads and spiced meats, fruits, and vegetables—are far more than any one person could ever hope to eat, but the banquet isn't just set out for me.

The Emergency Council will be arriving soon. The former *Sirae*, world rulers, and *Avrae* will arrive from Shura Kan, the sacred city where all former rulers live after passing down their thrones to their children. This Council hasn't been called in centuries; we never imagined their presence would be necessary. And I alone will face them.

A disgraced *Avra*.

A failure.

A woman.

But there's no one else to do this. No one else who'd want to. And without Eros here, I'm the only one fighting for him. So I'll stand and face them for him. For all of us.

Please return quickly, Eros.

My chest tightens as I awkwardly prepare *kata* wraps with *ushri*—my favorite orange savory spread—and a selection of meats and vegetables. Truthfully, the last thing I want to do is eat, but I'll regret it later if I don't. I'll need my strength when I face the Council.

It's so quiet here. You'd think the palace was deserted.

Satiated and humming with anxiety, I suck the spicy juices off my fingers and inhale deeply. I flex my fingers on my good arm and try to still my shivering center. I'll have to show the Council the footage first—Roma murdering his brother, and Serek's desperate message to Eros and the world—which they've already seen, but the repetition should help my position. I'll show them the genetic testing Serek conducted before Eros's failed execution. One cannot argue Eros's claim to the throne, not with Asha's blood running through his veins. Surely Asha's father, the former *Sira*, will see that. Asha was rumored to be the favorite son, after all . . .

Or, more likely, the evidence and Serek's final message won't matter, because Eros is a half-blood. Because the suggestion of putting a half-blood on the high throne won't be acceptable to a council full of former leaders. I'd said so myself to Serek not so long ago: *the people would never accept him—not in his court and not in the public eye.*

Of course, what Serek said was true, too. *Denying him his inheritance would dishonor Asha's memory.*

Though Asha's reign was short-lived, he was a truly good *Sira*. Firm, but not blood-thirsty; ambitious, but not power-hungry; and, like Eros, compassionate. The people loved him—he was young, but spoke with wisdom and passion that hushed Jol's Arena without raising his voice. I listened to recordings of his speeches as I studied with Mamae. He'd said he wanted to do things differently; he wanted to make Safara a place of balance and love.

Looking back, his vision is probably what got him killed—just not before he started his plan to change Safara, not with a directive, but with Eros. A boy who isn't fully Sepharon or fully redblood, but both. A boy, who on the throne, could change everything.

But will honoring Asha's memory matter when the alternative will be unthinkable to the Council?

Footsteps echo behind me, each step like a phaser burst ripping through the absolute quiet. A man with dark hair pulled back, dressed in the typical black and gold high-collared uniform of Asheron officials enters the room. He doesn't even glance at me as he approaches the table and serves himself. I eye him and wait a breath as he piles fruit into his bowl, but he still pays me no mind.

I clear my throat, settling my gaze on him as he glances dully at me at last. "Do you need something?"

Rude. "I'm Kora Mika—"

"*Sha*, I know who you are." He returns his attention to his bowl and adds a dollop of thick, dripping cream to his fruit. "But unless you *need* something, I haven't time for trivial matters."

My face warms. I hold a breath in my chest and swallow my irritation. "And you are?"

"Currently in charge, at least until the Council arrives." He lifts a slice of blue *ljuma* with a bit of melted cream dripping off it and wrinkles his nose. "The lack of refrigeration is going to be a nuisance." He lowers the bowl and claps twice—a servant tidying up in the corner hesitantly steps forward.

"You," he says. "Figure out a way to keep the fruit and cream chilled. The last thing we want is to present lukewarm food and melted cream to the former leaders of our world."

My mouth drops open—the last *Sira* just killed his brother and committed an act of genocide. There was an explosion in the capital, nanites—the foundation of our economy—have been destroyed, military rule is barely keeping the peace, and he's concerned about *cream*?

But now, with this ridiculous display, I know exactly who he is—Niro d'Asheron, *Sira* Roma's former advisor. Though I'd never met him myself, I'd heard stories of his . . . let's say *lavish* behavior. Despite his arrogant reputation, he's supposedly a brilliant strategist and works closely with Roma's top military commanders. Now, without a *Sira*, it seems he's taken over keeping things running, at least until the Emergency Council arrives.

"The cooling systems are down." The servant lowers her gaze. "None of the nanite-run technology has worked ever since—"

"I'm aware, which is why I'm assigning you the task of figuring out an alternative method of keeping the food cool. I will not dishonor the greatest city in Safara by presenting our leaders with *melted cream*. Understood?"

"*Sha, ve*," she says quietly.

"Good."

I watch, stunned, as the girl hurries out of the hall. He notices me staring and lifts both eyebrows. "Is there a problem?"

Stating the obvious isn't going to do me any favors, so I try a different tactic. "What preparations are being made to receive Eros?"

He stares blankly back at me. "Eros?"

"*Sira* Asha's son. The one *ana da Kala* Serek appointed." I use the honorific with Serek's name to respect the newly dead during the eight-set mourning period—*Kala's* heart, meant to indicate even *Kala* is in mourning over his passing.

"The half-blood, you mean."

"The next in line to take the throne, *sha*."

"Well, *ana da Kala* Serek's claim will need to be confirmed, of course, by our best geneticists. They've found the genetic test Serek ran on the half-blood and are analyzing it. But assuming the former young *Sira-kaï*—all respect spoken to him—ran his analysis correctly, it'll be up to the Council to decide what to do, assuming the half-blood returns to Asheron at all, of course. As I understand, he took off right after the explosion at Jol's Arena—"

"After we tried to execute him."

Niro waves his hand and shrugs. "The circumstances of his disappearance are less important than the fact that he is not in the capital he is trying to claim as his own. Not the most resounding exemplification of strong leadership, if you ask me."

Heat gathers in my chest, dissolving my body's trembling into something still. Something sharp as a sun glare and hard as stone. "And I suppose you would have hung around the capital after narrowly escaping your own execution, then?"

He scoffs. "Well I certainly wouldn't have *abandoned* the city of my heart."

"Then you'd have been caught and killed and we wouldn't be having this conversation." Niro's right eyelid twitches. I suppress a smile. "Eros hasn't abandoned anyone. He'll return and take his rightful place on the throne."

"Whether it's his place to take will be up to the Council to decide." He pops a slice of *ljuma* in his mouth and chews it slowly, his lips glistening with sticky, blue juice. "But as far as I'm concerned, if he's not here to make his claim, there's little point in discussing it. The Council won't appoint someone who has fled from his responsibility, no matter how legitimate his credentials are. Of course, you already know that, being a former *Avra* yourself." He smirks and lifts his eyebrows. "Speaking of which, what *are* you still doing here? You no longer have a throne or any claim to one, and while I understand you had a relationship with *ana da Kala* Serek and you're no longer welcome in Elja, this isn't a refugee center."

I was prepared for this question. I *am* prepared for this question. But the reminder that I'm not wanted anywhere, that I've failed so miserably, stings nonetheless. "I am Eros's representative in his temporary absence. As such, I've the right to stay as long as his claim is being considered."

"Not long then." Niro smiles and turns away, walking toward the door with the bowl in his hand. But not before he adds one more parting gift: "By the way, how is Elja doing these days? I hear your brother has *quite* a situation on his hands. It'd be a shame to see such a respectable territory crumble under weak leadership."

And with that, he smiles at me and slips out of the room, his words like knives in my gut.

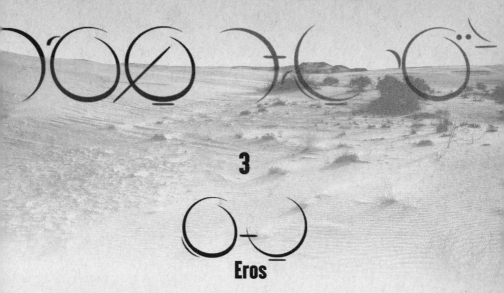

3

Eros

Mal's fingers dig into my ribs as we ride back west, away from Asheron, backtracking all the progress we made today. For the first tense seg, it seems almost like they're taking us back to camp, and I imagine us riding into camp like this, a circle of armed Remnant people on sand bikes with Mal and me stuck in the middle. Someone looking in might think they were protecting me like some kinduv ragtag security detail, but this is not that.

This is much worse.

My sweaty palms slip on the bike's handles as the suns beat stars onto my back. I take deep, even breaths behind the headscarf I tied around my mouth and nose to filter out the kicked-up sand, trying to calm my erratic heartbeat. I need to focus and clear my mind—I can't let my nerves make me jumpy and dull. But the truth is I'm terrified this is going to go every bit as wrong as it could. That they'll try to hurt Mal, or take him away from me, or use him to get me to do what they want, or, or—

Enough.

I have two knives strapped to my legs, and one strapped to Mal's just in case. I don't know where they're taking us, but

I know these sands and how to handle myself. I'll do whatever's necessary to keep us safe.

I'll stop at nothing to protect Mal.

Another seg passes before the first real landmark drifts onto the horizon—a towering cluster of spiky rocks like enormous sharpened stakes, with a plateau in front and a group of dark shapes scattered across the base: Devil's Eye, and the abandoned city Kora called Enjos.

My stomach twists as we race closer—just five sets ago, I made this exact same route alone, whispering *hold on* under my breath as I pictured Kora dehydrated in the desert. But she was in more danger than even I expected. When I got there, she wasn't alone.

And the men who cornered her weren't interested in a chat.

I lean forward, focusing on the pressure of Mal's fingers on my sides; on the fresh, arid smell of the world baking under the suns; on the hot wind pressing against my face; on the powdery sand coating my cheeks, mixing with my sweat and dripping down my skin in blood-like trails.

I won't think about what happened last time I was here.

I won't think about Kora.

I won't.

We pass the bodies left to rot in the sand—most of them have been eaten, their bones picked clean by *kazim* or ugly as fuck predatory birds. We pass a guy who still kinduv has half a face, with shriveled skin on the left side, gaping holes where his eyes were, his skull and jaw visible on the right side of his face. Another with his midsection busted open, ribs scattered across the sands. Mal rests his forehead against my back, but no one else seems surprised by the corpses;

they ride past them like they're just rocks or prickleplant bushes.

We stop in the center of the ruins that were once a city. And it's like the universe is taunting me, because out of all the places we could have stopped in this dead city, we stop right in front of an old building with a low, sharply peaked roof and stone with faded, shiny blue paint. It's the building where Kora and I . . . whatever that was. That building.

I bite my lip and try to help Mal off my bike, but he shakes his head and stumbles off himself, crossing his arms over his chest. Pretty sure he's telling me not to baby him.

Shaw smirks. "You know where we are?"

Why is he smirking?

Wait.

Fuck.

Does he know?

"Enjos," I say evenly.

His lips quirk and someone chuckles behind me. "Sure," he says. "Enjos. Look any different from last time you were here?"

Well, of course he fucken knows—why wouldn't he? My chest tightens and fists clench. I scowl. "Fuck off."

He laughs and gestures for us to follow him as he starts toward the building. "C'mon."

I swallow my irritation and rest my hand on Mal's shoulder.

"What was that about?" Mal whispers.

"Nothing," I mumble. "He's just being a jerk."

I glance around, but our circle of *escorts* make it hard to see much of anything. Snippets of a building here, a sand dune there, a crumbled home, a patch of tube-like prickleplants, a dried-out fetcher skeleton. Nothing to indicate any kinduv camp out here, nothing to hint that a group of heavily armed humans live here, somewhere.

But that time out here with Kora, I would have noticed if someone else was here, wouldn't I? Unless—there was a mo, a blink where I thought I saw someone, but it passed so quickly I figured I'd just imagined it. But what if I hadn't imagined it? What if someone was out here, watching us when we—

You know what? I don't want to know.

But apparently we aren't just walking *near* the building Kora and I defiled, because Shaw ducks into it. Great. Out of *all* the buildings out here, and there are more than I can count. One after another, our escorts duck under the crumbling doorway. Mal and I enter and more file in behind us.

It's dark inside, the ground covered with a thick layer of sand. This entrance room is small—too small to fit all of us, but it opens into a larger room twice the size of Kora's Asheron bedroom, which is to say, ridiculously big. This can't have been someone's home, unless someone was disgustingly rich and wanted to be able to house, like, two hundred people. But as big as the room is, there isn't much left of it. The ceiling has collapsed in spots, leaving large piles of rubble buried in sand. The walls are tiled with some kinduv blue, pink, and purple metal spotted with patterns I guess were once filled with something valuable because the patterns have been stripped off, probably looted.

Mal squints at everything, but continues silently forward with his arms tight at his sides, fists clenched. Shaw leads the group to the very end of the room where some kinduv stage is elevated but also buried in sand and debris. He walks to the center of the platform, crouches, and starts clearing away sand with his hands. A man and woman join him to help dig until Shaw reaches down and pulls a dirty metal handle out of the ground.

He leans back as the man and woman grab the handle too, then together they pull, straining as a low groaning noise fills the room and they open a black, metal door out from under the sand.

And it hits me like a humiliating kick to the stomach: their base isn't just in the city where Kora and I had that moment I wish we could take back.

It's in the fucken building we made out against.

"In you go," Shaw says.

I walk up to the edge of the hole in the ground where the door once was. It's dark—too dark to see the bottom—and there are ladder rails in the wall that reach all the way to the bottom. I frown—is Mal going to be able to do this?

I glance at Mal. "It's a ladder—"

"I'm not dense," he says quickly. "I guessed, just go."

"Are you—"

"*Go.*"

I'm probably embarrassing him. He's young, but he's not a little kid, and messed up eyesight or not, he's not going to want to be treated like one. I lower myself into the hole, gripping the first cool, rough handle. I descend slowly, keeping my gaze up until Mal climbs in after me and starts descending. He's trying to act brave, like this is fine, like he isn't completely blind in this tunnel, like he's okay. But he's shaking and I can't blame him. This is unnerving to *me*; to him it must be even worse.

We move lower and lower, and the deeper we go, the cooler and darker it gets. I don't know how long we climb, but it feels like forever, and by the time my foot hits solid ground, my breath is rattling in my lungs and I can't see a fucken thing. I hold the edge of the ladder and move out of the way until my back hits a wall. Mal's feet pat against the cold floor next, and I find his hand on the edge of the ladder then pull him back against me. He doesn't protest and stands shivering in my arms.

A thump, and Shaw's voice echoes through the blackness. "Now, that wasn't so bad, was it?" He laughs, and then a cracking noise makes me jump as a glow bursts through the darkness. Shaw shakes a thin, glowing green tube, says, "Heads up," then tosses it to me.

I catch it and frown at the bright green light. It's not warm like I expected, and the light is coming from some kinduv liquid inside the tube.

"You know what that is?" Shaw cracks another against his leg and shakes it, grinning.

"A light," I answer dully.

He laughs. "Yeah, but it's not just any light—it's 100% bond and fie human made. Crazy old *Earth* tech, can you believe it? The Old Ones called them glow sticks. Took us forever to figure out a Safara-equivalent formula for the liquid, but we managed it."

I guess this is supposed to impress me, and maybe it would if he hadn't fucken kidnapped Mal and me and forced us to be here. But instead I just stare at him.

Shaw whistles and nudges a guy next to him, snickering. "Tough crowd."

Is this guy for real? Does he think we're just going to warm up to him after blowing us up and threatening us to get us to go with him because he gave us a fucken glow stick? Does he really think I'm going to laugh and enjoy his jokes when we're effectively his prisoners?

"Lighten up." He nudges me as he passes. It takes everything in me not to nudge him back. With my fist. In his face.

The detail forms around us again as we follow Shaw down a narrow, black tunnel. Shaw spins the glow stick in his hand as we walk, making jokes to the guy next to him all the way down the fucken tunnel until we reach a heavy, circular door made of some kinduv thick, black metal. No handle, just a sleek, dark wall.

Shaw raps on the door with the light stick and laughs. "Sis, we're home! And we've got a very special guest. Isn't that right, Eros? Oh, and, uh, what's your name, kid?"

To his credit, Mal glares at Shaw instead of answering.

Shaw just laughs and shrugs. "And a *real* tough kid who's too cool to give us his name."

A loud click echoes around the tunnel and Shaw takes a couple steps back as the door swings open. He grins at Mal and me, his teeth glowing green in the artificial light. "C'min, now, don't be shy. Grumpy guests first."

I grip Mal's shoulder as we enter the open doorway. Mal trips over the lip, but I hold him up and then we're in.

It's dim in here—wherever here is—but it's not pitch black, which is a step up from the outer tunnel and ladder. White lightstrips are embedded into the ceiling and walls, which all seem to be built out of sand and rock. I have no idea how deep we are, but if the cool temperature and damp air is any indication, we're deep, and the thought of being so far from the surface makes my chest tighten. The suns can't reach us down here, and the air must be pumped in somehow because they'd all suffocate otherwise.

I glance at Mal, and I'm not sure if it's a trick of the light, but his brown, freckled skin seems pale. Hopefully he's not imagining this whole place crumbling under the weight of the world and burying everyone down here alive, like I am.

"Not bad, yeah?" Shaw smiles at us. "Of course, you haven't seen the *really* impressive stuff yet, but still."

"You run your base underground," I say.

"Yup." Shaw steps ahead of us and starts walking. "But you'll learn all about that in a mo. C'mon."

He leads us down yet another tunnel that branches off on both sides into at least ten other tunnels on either side before turning right. This tunnel isn't as empty as the first was—people in identical red uniforms walk down this hall, stepping to the side and pointing their right hands to their right temples as we pass; some sortuv salute, I guess.

This herding is uncomfortably familiar—a couple terms ago, Jarek, not Shaw, led me through foreign halls with the threat of my life hanging over my head. And given how well *that* ended, I can't help but worry this won't be any better.

Difference: I'm armed this time.

Difference: Mal is with me.

Difference: These are humans at least trying to play nice. While holding us at phaserpoint, of course, but I guess it counts for something that they're pretending we're on the same side.

Or maybe not. At least in Vejla, I knew where I stood and no one insulted my intelligence by trying to convince me otherwise.

We weave through a ton of turns—third right, second left, right, sixth right, seventh left. This place is a labyrinth, and Shaw's probably taking us a roundabout way to try to confuse me. But if Shaw thinks I'm going to forget the route back just because it's complicated, he's underestimating me.

Finally, we stop at another circular, handle-less black door, but this time Shaw doesn't need to knock and it doesn't swing open—it rolls to the side, disappearing into the thick sand wall.

And this time, Shaw doesn't gesture for us to go in first—he waltzes in with his shoulders back and head held high. The detail moves forward, and I give Mal a light squeeze before we step inside.

"Lip," I whisper as we step into the doorway—Mal steps over it and mumbles something I'm pretty sure was supposed to be thanks. I'll take it.

Unlike the bare halls we just spent a good ten mos strolling around, this room is packed with people and tech. And unlike Shaw, a lot of the guys down here are bearded, like some of his detail—and many of them are so pale they look ill. The sandstone walls are lined with monitors like giant glass tablets, multicolored lights flicker on and off around us, and at least twenty people are seated in rows with their backs to us, looking at the many screens covering the far wall as they work on their own personal glasses. It's some kinduv security room, I guess—every glass has a different image of various hallways and rooms, and different views of the abandoned city above us. How did they get all this tech? I'd never even seen a glass—let alone a giant screen—until I lived in Kora's palace complex. But these people are overflowing with technology the nomads only ever whispered about.

To the left are more screens, these with what are probably Sepharon news sources. I scan them for something I recognize and find the high palace in Asheron right away. Text

scrolls on the bottom of the screen, both the Sephari cres-
cent-like letters and blockier English letters, but I never got
a handle on reading either language so I'm not sure what it
says.

Shaw walks past the seated people to a tall woman standing at the front. They hug and speak quietly while the detail
stands silently around us and the murmur of low voices works
through the room.

Then the woman stiffens and looks at me, eyes wide for
just a mo before she smooths her expression. She's even
darker than Shaw—her skin a smooth, rich black. She's thin,
but strong—and of course, no Sephari markings. Because
she's human. Like everyone here but me.

She runs a hand over her shaved head, pats Shaw's
shoulder, then walks toward us. "Welcome." Her voice cuts
through the murmur of conversations like a blade. "It's good
to see you, Eros. We've been waiting a long time."

I don't know what to say. They've been waiting a long time
for what? *Me?* I still don't know who these star-crossed under-
grounders are—or why I've never heard of a group called the
Remnant, or why if they were here all along they didn't help
my people when Kora's army destroyed everything.

She steps up to me and extends her arm. "Rani."

At camp, they clasp arms and shake once, and it looks like
that's what she's offering. But that's something you do with
companions, or new acquaintances—not people who have
abducted you and your nephew at phaserpoint. I stare her
down.

Rani smiles and drops her arm. "Right, well, I suppose
you have a point—these circumstances aren't ideal. You must
be confused and scared . . ."

I arch an eyebrow.

"... or irritated, more like. You've probably been through worse, given ... everything."

I don't answer. She glances at Mal and blinks, like she's noticing him for the first time. She smiles at him. "What's your name?"

Like last time, Mal mimics my stony silence. Rani laughs and looks at me. "Well he's too old to be your son, but if I didn't know better, that's what I would guess."

"What are we doing here?" I finally say. "You didn't drag us out of the desert at phaserpoint for friendly introductions. What do you want?"

Rani smiles weakly. "I know we've butchered our chance at an amenable introduction, and for that I apologize. But my brother assured me no one was injured—"

"You nearly buried us alive," I answer. "Had I been riding any faster, you could have blown us up."

Shaw looks at the ceiling and sighs heavily, like *he's* getting fed up. The asshole. "That wouldn't have happened. Like I said, we calculated everything and—"

"I don't fucken care," I cut in. "The only reason I'm here is because you threatened our lives, and I, for one, would like my nephew at least to live a long life."

Shaw opens his mouth, but Rani lifts a hand and he shuts up. "I'm sorry about the tactics we had to use to get you here—you have every right to be angry and defensive. If anyone had threatened my family that way, I wouldn't be in the mood to play nice either."

"So get to the point," I say.

Rani nods and turns to the seated people. "Put Asheron on front and center."

A moment later, the screens blink black, then together they form the feed I was looking at before, except blown up wall-to-wall so it almost looks like we're standing right in front of the palace.

"Right." Rani turns back to me. "So you were headed back to Asheron to take your rightful place on the throne, like your father intended eighteen years ago. We're not trying to stop you—in fact, we *want* you to succeed. But it was vital we made you aware of our presence first, because we need to be working together from here on out."

I snort. "And I suppose you abduct all the people you want to work with?"

She smiles weakly. "It's not usually necessary, but our time was limited. We had to work quickly or risk losing you."

"Losing me? You never had me to begin with."

Rani's mouth opens and closes. She bites her lip, then nods. "I understand it seems that way to you."

My eyes narrow. "What's that supposed to mean?"

"We've been watching you for a long time, Eros." She snaps her fingers. "Footage RQ-465."

The screens blink black again, then fill with a new image. Nol, leaning toward the screens, his light brown face wrinkled in a frown. My chest aches and heat lodges in the back of my throat and crawls up into my head, stinging my eyes. Nol is dead, I *know* Nol is dead, and his blond—not white—hair confirms this is an old recording. Really old, at least ten years judging by his smoother face.

He's unwrapping a bandage, unraveling a long strip of white as his warm voice fills the room. "In the end, we all become the same"—Mal's head jerks up at the sound of Nol's voice—"dust, stars, and—"

"Turn it off," I say loudly. My voice is thick with the pain gathering in my throat, in my chest, in my eyes. Rani waves her hand and the screens go black again. But everything I see is red.

I clench my fists. "What is this? Why do you have that recording?"

"Like I said," Rani says softly, "we've been watching you for a long time."

I am ice. I am fire. I am every explosion replacing my heart and setting my blood ablaze. They've been *watching* me? Which means— "So, what, you've been *spying* on me?"

"I wouldn't call it spying—"

"No? Then what would you fucken call this? You've apparently been *watching* me somehow my whole life—with what, hidden cameras or something?"

"Not cameras, exactly, no."

"Then?"

She hesitates. "We lost track of you a couple sets ago. This is the last footage we have."

New image on the screen, and a voice—my voice, no my *scream* fills the room. Something is blocking whatever camera they're using—two large, dark blobs—oh, hands.

My hands.

Sephari shouts layer over mine, then a bright light washes out the screen. It's hard to hear what's going on, between my agonized screams and the Sepharon yelling at each other, but then the screens go black and I know what happened.

That was when Kora's medic, Neja, shot me. When I had a reaction to the nanites Kora's people injected me with and they nearly blinded me. Because I already had nanites in my system; nanites turning my gold eyes green.

"The nanites," I say. "That was you."

She nods. "It was. The nanites were multipurpose—they disguised your eyes so no one would recognize you for what you were, and they allowed us to keep tabs on you and make sure you were safe by letting us see what you were seeing and hearing."

Her words sink into me one layer at a time.

She was behind the nanites that changed my eye color.

Nanites that fed every moment of my life up until a few terms ago to these strangers in an underground bunker.

Strangers who apparently knew who I was all along.

"You don't have the ring." Rani frowns at my left hand. My stomach twists tighter—she must mean the ring of *Sirae*, which Serek took from me for safekeeping. The ring I never got back when I had to run.

But how does she know about it? They've been watching me all along, apparently, but I hadn't discovered the ring until well after the nanites were filtered out of me. Only Kora and Serek knew I had it, unless—

"Who are you?" My voice comes out hoarse and quiet; the words drag against my throat as her admission sinks deeper and deeper into me.

She hesitates. "My name is Rani Jakande."

"No." My voice grows stronger, filling my lungs, freezing over the heat burning in my chest. "You said my 'rightful place on the throne, like *my father* intended.' And—and you've been fucken *watching* me my whole life and injected me with the nanites and . . ." My heart pounds. My breath catches and catches and this isn't—she's not—

"Yes," she says softly. "I knew your father, and I administered the nanites myself when you were an infant."

My mind is a whirlwind. My heart is a storm. My breath is a downpour.

"I'm your mother, Eros."

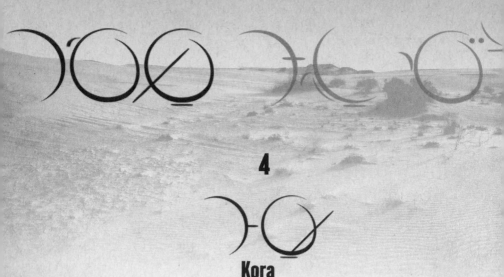

4

Kora

The first royals to arrive are, of course, the last I want to
see. *Avra* Druzja's eldest son, Jolek da Sekka'l, arrives in his
bronze hovercraft in front of the palace shortly after my conversation with Niro. The thin, silver-leafed *unaï* trees bordering the side courtyard dance in the wind kicked up by the
craft as it lowers to the white sand. His men pour out of the
sleek aircraft in their customary shiny bronze uniforms, and I
brace myself for the slight certain to come.

The royals of Sekka'l are extraordinarily chauvinistic—
which was why I avoided sending an invitation for courtship
to his younger brother, Rumen, back when I was *Avra* and
had to find a mate. Jolek won't be a part of the Emergency
Council, however—that would be his grandfather's role, if
his grandfather were still alive. Unlike most of the territories,
Avrae da Sekka'l don't immediately pass on the throne when
their eldest turns fifteen; Jolek is in his twenties and still waiting for his father to concede the throne. So, it's not surprising
Sekka'l's former *Avra*, who would ordinarily be on the council, has already passed away. Instead, Jolek must be here to
mourn and petition for Eros's spot on the throne.

Niro steps forward and bows to the *Avra-kaï*, welcoming him to Asheron and asking him how his trip was—unimportant pleasantries as the men step past me without so much as a glance in my direction. But if they think they're going to get away with ignoring me, they're wrong.

I step in front of them and nod at Jolek. "*Avra-kaï* Jolek, how are your wife and son? Well, I hope?"

Jolek's gaze rolls over me as his lips twist into a grimace. Unlike most of the nations who use tattoos to emphasize *Kala*'s mark, the Sekka'l burn the markings into their pale skin, leaving raised, white or pink scars in their wake. Jolek's marks curve around his mouth and under his eyes, and the back of my neck and my scarred arm prickles. I know all too well how painful burns are; while I understand the significance and honor of getting them, the thought of burning yourself intentionally—and on your face no less—churns my stomach.

Then again, the process of getting markings isn't much more pleasant, so I shouldn't judge.

But rather than addressing me, Jolek looks at Niro. "What is she doing here?"

Niro opens his mouth to answer, but I cut in instead.

"I'm here representing *Sira-kaï* Eros—and I can speak for myself, thank you."

Jolek's face contorts like he's just smelled something dead, but he finally turns to me. "That half-blood isn't a *Sira-kaï*—and even if he were, you certainly wouldn't be worthy of representing him. It's incredible you weren't executed alongside him."

Heat rages through me, but I keep my expression calm. "Eros wasn't executed."

"He would have been had those redbloods not inter-fered." Jolek steps around me, then pauses and smirks at me. "Maybe it *is* fitting you two banded together—trash with trash, and when you lose, you'll be burned together."

"Of course," I answer. "Burned like your traitorous uncle, right? Or was it brother? Sekka'l family history is so compli-cated with all that disloyalty—was it both your uncle *and* your brother?"

Jolek's face darkens, and he turns on his heel and storms off, Niro tutting after him.

I smile and turn back to the horizon, the heat in my blood ebbing away to pleasure.

I can't make too many enemies here—not when Eros will need all the support he can get. But that doesn't mean I'll let the prejudiced royalty who would never support him anyway trample me.

One royal handled, many more to go.

By mid-set, most of the royalty have arrived, including much of the Emergency Council, which includes surviving former *Avrae* from Ona, Inara, Daïvi, Kelal, and A'Sharo. Only the former *Sira*—Asha, Roma, and Serek's father—Ashen, has yet to arrive. Which is just as well, as he's the last person I want to see.

What am I supposed to say to the father of the man I helped make comatose? And the father of the man I nearly killed by accident, then could do nothing to save as he died in my arms? And what will he think of Eros? Ashen wasn't a cruel ruler—not like Roma—but he was much more like Roma than he was Asha and Serek. I can't imagine he's going to accept Eros, even if I hadn't been involved in Serek's death.

Then there are the *kjo* like Jolek arriving to presumably place their bid for the throne. After Jolek da Sekka'l, Lejen d'Inara—a religious man from our most pious territory—arrives with his detail of light blue and white-clad guards. Shortly thereafter, two men with piercings in their eyebrows, nose, lips, and all over their ears arrive: *Avra-kaï* Simos d'Ona and his husband, Ejren. A pang goes through me as they enter, hand-in-hand—as terrible as Dima was to me, I wish Eljans were as accepting as the Onans so my brother never felt the need to hide. But it's nice to see Simos and Ejren's open happiness nevertheless.

After them, *Avrae-kjo* Sulten and Deimos d'A'Sharo arrive in the black and red colors of their nation, which is interesting—surely they don't expect to place *two* bids for the throne? The men speak quietly in the dining hall as servants fan them with large palm fronds, though it does little to cool the oppressive heat.

I glance at the door, swallowing the tension in my throat, the edge of panic whispering *Eros is late*. Whispering *maybe he isn't coming*.

I awkwardly pour myself a lukewarm glass of blue *ljuma* juice one-handed as I glance over the table of Serek's favorite foods—the second set of mourning requires serving all the favorite meals of the dead. I can't help but smile faintly at some of the choices: apparently Serek was a big fan of sweets, because many of the options include fruits soaked in pucker-sweet glazes. My breath trembles in my chest as the ache blossoms deeply, stinging my eyes; it's been only two sets since he passed, and I already miss him dearly.

I hate being so alone here. I'd grown used to having some-one at my side: first Anja, then Eros, and eventually Serek. But I made mistake, after mistake, after mistake, and now . . . Kala, please let Eros return. For Safara, but also—

I'm terrified to even think it. But I don't know what I'll do if he runs from the throne and I can no longer represent him. I can't go home. I have no one to turn to. This is the only thing I have left to cling to; I can't lose it.

Nearby, the candidates close their circle and continue to ignore me. Continue to pretend Eros isn't in contention, like he doesn't have even the remotest chance to take the throne he's inherited.

They speak like Eros doesn't exist at all.

"I doubt Kel'al will participate," says Sulten. "*Avra* Shura's children are too young to be considered, which only leaves his sister."

Simos smirks at his husband, Ejren. "As if that would stop them? I'd be amazed if *Avra* Riza da Daïvi didnt send one of her sisters, not that any of them have a chance, realistically . . ."

Jolek snorts. "Can you imagine? A *woman* as *Sira*?"

"I can imagine it easily," Ejren answers. "Just perhaps not in our lifetime as men like you still hold power."

Someone snickers behind me. I start and spill sticky juice over my hand as I face a handsome *kaï* with trim stubble and a shock of thick, dark hair. Deimos d'A'Sharo, who evidently didn't join his brother Sulten in the exclusive circle several paces away.

Deimos smiles at me. "Now, what'll *really* be interesting is when one of the Daïvi sisters arrives. I'd pay good money to see *Avra-saï* Aleija come head to head with Jolek. Or my brother, for that matter."

"It *would* be entertaining," I muse, looking him over. "You know, if I didn't know you were brothers, I'd never have guessed you and Sulten were related."

Deimos laughs, his face lighting up with the sound. "I know—Sulten inherited our mother's pale northern Invino genes." He steps closer to me and lowers his voice. "Don't tell him I told you, but he has to *color* his hair dark—ordinarily it's a sickly yellow he *hates*. Meanwhile, I inherited all the dark and handsome genes." He grins and winks at me—I can't help it; I laugh.

"Seems you inherited the charming genes, too."

"Naturally. My brother wouldn't know charm if it stripped naked and danced the *balaika* in front of him." I laugh and Deimos smiles easily. "My *mamae* likes to tell people the only part of Invino I inherited is my right eye." He points to the eye, which unlike the left—a mix of light orange, to brown, to deep green—is light blue to gray. That's not the only asymmetrical part of him; judging by the markings on his arms, those on the left side of his body are rigid and maze-like, with sharp edges and straight, intersecting lines, whereas those on the right are smooth curves with pointed edges, like engraved, pointed teeth.

"A unique trait," I say. "It suits you."

"Thank you. I agree." He smiles. "I'd introduce myself, but I suspect you already know who I am."

"I do. And I think it's quite clear to everyone who I am, as well."

"That it is." Deimos glances at the men gathered several paces away. "I'd wager we're probably the only reasonable ones in this room, save for Simos and Ejren."

"Excluding your brother in that estimation, I see."

Deimos snorts. "Sulten is many things, but reasonable is not one of them."

"Unfortunate."

"In this context, perhaps, but it makes me look excellent in contrast, so I can't say I usually mind it."

I laugh. "How generous of him to remove from his personality to bolster yours."

Deimos laughs. "Well, from what I've heard, you seem quite familiar with handling unreasonable brothers."

My smile drops and so does my stomach. I sip my juice, focusing on its sweet bite.

"I'm sorry," Deimos says quickly. "That wasn't—I didn't mean to—"

"It's fine," I answer stiffly. "You're not wrong."

I step away from him just as two new royals enter the room—and this time, even thoughts of my brother aren't enough to wipe away my smile. Tall, beautiful, and dressed in the deep blue and white garb of their nation, *Avra-saï* Aleija and her wife, Jule, walk into the hall with their heads held high and determination set on their faces. Aleija looks much like her *mamae*, former *Avra* Lija, who is on the Emergency Council, but with partially braided light brown hair and dark eyes. Jule looks much more traditionally northern, with near-white hair in an intricate braid and paler skin. But both women are equally stunning, and they carry themselves with confident power and pride.

While the Emergency Council will meet to choose and confirm the next *Sira*, as well as establish a baseline rule until the new *Sira* is crowned, the rest of the royals will gather to bid for the throne and eventually to throw their support behind a candidate that the Emergency Council will take into consideration. Due to their royal status, all they must do to be permitted to stay as the selection process begins is "be of some use," even if that use is just to share their opinion with whoever represents their territory on the Council.

But for the most part, royals are always free to come and go as they please, capital to capital, and Asheron is no different. Especially now that there's interest to bring them here—and not to mention Serek's funeral, which would bring royals from all over Safara even if the *Sira* spot weren't open.

"Oh, excellent," Deimos mutters beside me. "It seems I might just get my wish after all."

And he's not wrong—if any more royals had to arrive, I'd choose Aleija over anyone else.

But the fact remains the one who isn't here is the one I need most.

If Eros doesn't arrive soon, there might not be a place left for him to take.

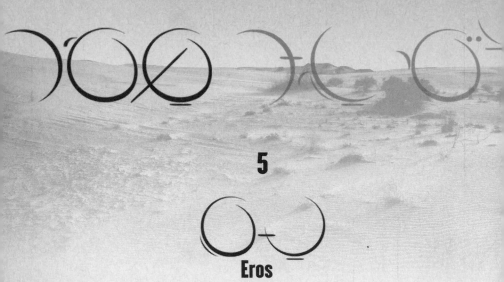

5

Eros

Mal lies curled up in a cot, rubbing his eyes again, and again, and again, until he gives up and just closes them.

"Any better?" I ask helplessly, but the answer is obvious even before he shakes his head and presses his face into the mattress.

"I hate this," he whispers.

I touch his shoulder, but he pulls away from me, curling up closer to the wall. It stings, but the truth is I'm unequipped for this. I can barely handle my own grief—how am I supposed to help Mal deal with his? And to deal with the scary reality of losing at least part of his vision on top of it . . . I can't begin to imagine what he must be going through. I don't know how to help him.

I sigh and glance around the small room. The woman who says she's my mother calls our cell a bedroom. After I stormed out, she said we needed time to digest before we "get to business," whatever that's supposed to mean. And we can't leave until we do. If I'd been thinking clearly, I would've demanded we "get to business" right away so Mal and I could go, but all I could think about was this stranger calling herself my mother—which would make that asshole Shaw my uncle—and those screens playing my life for all to see like some—some Voiding entertainment. There was drumming in my ears, and the air—too hot, thickening—in my throat was gathering in my lungs, broiling me from the inside out.

So. Yeah. Our cell/bedroom. Four black stone walls, cool and slick to the touch. An identical stone ceiling, stringed with one dim light hanging overhead. Two clumpy beds stacked on top of each other on metal stilts. It doesn't look safe. It looks like it'll collapse under my weight the moment I climb onto the top bunk, but Rani insisted it's safe and knocked on the top bed's rail, claiming it'll keep us from rolling off.

Mal is afraid of heights, and his vision problems would make it riskier for him up there anyway, so there was never any question who was going to end up on top. It's not the most comfortable thing I've slept on, but it'll do.

As Mal settles down on the bunk below, I stare at the smooth stone ceiling. If I let my vision blur, it almost looks like a starless night sky. Like I'm not lying stars know how deep beneath the sand, far from four moons and twin suns and a glittering horizon. Like a woman I don't know—a woman who ordered my abduction and has been spying on me for most of my life—didn't just say she's my mother.

She's not my mother. She may have given birth to me, but a mother doesn't drop her kid off with a group of strangers and walk away. I had a mother, and though we didn't share blood, it didn't matter. Esta took care of me. Esta hugged me after Nol patched me up, and she whispered stories of a boy so loved his heart contained galaxies into my hair. Esta promised me I'd meet someone who loved me with everything and never, ever turned away. She made me believe on my darkest nights I wouldn't be alone, I'd have my own family, I'd live in peace with someone who made me so happy my smile sparkled like stars.

And then Esta died and my hope died with her. But there's no question she was my mother and Rani is not.

Someone knocks on our thick, metal, blast-proof door. The door with guards standing on the other side to *keep us safe*.

I've been a prisoner enough times to know what this is. At least in Asheron's dungeons, they'd had the decency to call it what it is.

The door opens, and Rani enters with another woman with lighter brown skin and long, black hair. The new woman smiles and extends her arm. "I'm Tana, one of the docs here."

I don't shake her arm, but I nod at Mal. "He's been having trouble with his eyes ever since the nanite attack."

"Ah, right." She sits on the edge of the bed and nods. "We've heard about that from the feed and refugees. Horrific, but they say the former *Sira*'s brother put a stop to it . . ."

"A little late," I answer flatly.

"Yes, well, let's take a look." She smiles at Mal. "Hey, hun, can you sit up and look at me, please?"

Mal hesitates then sits up and faces her.

"Eros," someone says softly. Rani. Rani Jakande. Who says she's my mother. I look at her, and she nods to the open doorway. "A word, please."

I glance at Mal.

"He'll be fine," Rani says. "We'll be right in the hall. We're not going far."

"Mal?" I ask.

"It's okay," he answers softly.

I nod. "I'll be right back. If you need me, just shout."

Mal nods.

I step into the long hall with Rani, the lights flickering above us. She sighs and runs a hand over her head. "Look, I . . . I think we started off on the wrong foot."

I stare at her. Started off on the wrong foot—as if that even begins to scratch the surface of everything blazed up about this.

"You're angry—I understand, and you have every right to be. All of this must be a shock to you, and you need some time to process—"

"No." I step toward her, scowling as my pulse hammers in my ears. "What I need isn't *time to fucken process*. What I *need* is to get out of here and get to Asheron so Mal can get some *real* medical attention."

She purses her lips. "Unfortunately, I doubt you'll be able to get him comprehensive medical care in Asheron."

I ball my fists. "I'll make them look at him. I don't care what it takes; I don't care that he's human—"

"You're misunderstanding me. I'm not saying you won't be able to get him medical care because they'll refuse—though they might, but I don't doubt you'd ordinarily find a way anyway. I'm saying you won't be able to get him medical care because they won't be able to give him medical care. If our techies are right, they're unable to give *anyone* the kinduv medical care you want right now. They don't have the tech."

I shake my head. "You don't know what you're talking about; their tech is way more advanced than ours."

"It was, yes. But our techies think when Serek stopped the nanite attack . . . he didn't just stop them from attacking."

I stare at her.

"He stopped them completely. We think he executed a universal kill command, and not just to the nanites attacking the humans."

A chill washes over me as her words trickle down my throat one syllable at a time. ". . . a kill command."

She nods. "It was effective—there were topside human survivors, and I doubt that would've happened without interference. But it also means, as of the moment the command went out, the nanites are ineffective."

"What are you saying?"

Rani sighs. "All the nanites are dead, Eros. And with them, the foundation of their technological advancement. Some human slaves are running from their Sepharon masters for the first time—their tracking nanites have been deactivated and we've taken dozens in, free for the first time in their lives. Crops are wilting, technological luxuries eradicated, and their medical care has just jumped back two centuries. They'll be no more capable of helping your nephew than we are—in fact, given their reliance on nanites, they're likely *less* capable right now."

Her words are everything I don't want to hear. They sink into my stomach and grip my lungs and nip my skin, traveling over my body in waves. If she's right, the nanites are gone. And if the nanites are gone, no one can help Mal. No one can stop whatever's happening to him.

"That can't . . . their society is built on nanite technology."

She nods. "The whole planet's on the brink of panic. There've been riots all over—most of them put down, but the ones in Vejla are ripping the city apart. Royals are gathering in Asheron to make a decision about the throne and take charge before the planet goes to shit. Everything is changing;

we're on the edge of revolution, and we need you to tide us over."

"I'm not your spokesperson," I say stiffly. "I don't even know you. I hadn't even heard of the Remnant until you nearly killed us."

"And that's my fault. I should have reached out to you sooner, but it was essential to your safety no one knew who you were—"

"Stop." I press my palms against my eyes and inhale deeply. Calm. Drop my hands. Glare at her. "If you're *really* my biological mother—and I'm not convinced you are—then you don't get to stand there and pretend you were somehow protecting me by abandoning me. And you don't get to call yourself my *mother*, either. You weren't there—Esta was. But you were *never* there."

She winces, but nods. "You're right. I wasn't there. But I couldn't be; you weren't safe here. I brought you to Nol and Esta knowing they'd take care of you better than I could. I know life with the nomads wasn't easy, but you were safe. I didn't have to worry about someone . . ." She sighs. "Forget it. I'm sorry I wasn't there—it wasn't an easy decision for me, either. But I don't regret bringing you to the nomads. They took good care of you."

Heat clenches my lungs and climbs up my throat. "You're unbelievable."

"Am I wrong? I'm not saying it was easy, but—"

"Well, apparently you've been *watching* me my whole life, so you tell me: was it safe? Did you really not worry some-one might lose control and not stop beating the stars out of me? Did it not occur to you maybe one day they'd turn their backs on me just like you did? Did you not realize the nomads didn't stay in one place because they were literally running for their lives?"

"Eros—"

"I haven't been safe a mo in my life. Maybe it made you feel better to pretend otherwise, but you're living in a dream world if you think that's true."

She frowns and hesitates, then: "I'm sorry."

I shake my head and turn back to the door, flames simmering in my lungs. "Save your apology for someone who cares."

"They would have killed you if you'd stayed with me."

I pause at the door but don't turn around.

Rani takes a shaky breath. "I control the Remnant now, but I didn't then. My father was in charge, and he didn't take well to the news I was pregnant with Asha's son. He called me a traitor; they nearly kicked me out. Not even Shaw could convince him otherwise."

I turn around. "If you're trying to make me feel bad for you—"

"I'm not. I just want you to understand why I made the decision I did; it wasn't because I didn't want you, it was because I couldn't handle the responsibility of raising you and I didn't have a choice—not if I wanted you to live. When you were born and Asha was killed, my father told me to leave you in the desert or he'd end you himself. I knew Nol from some of our negotiations and trades in the past, so I did the only thing I could to save your life. And it wasn't perfect, it wasn't easy, but you're alive. You're here. And you wouldn't be if I hadn't left you with the Kits."

I cross my arms. "But you still went back to them."

Rani frowns. "I did."

"You could have joined the nomads yourself and raised me with them. You didn't have to leave me there alone. If you really cared, you would have stayed."

She bites her lip. "That's not fair."

I laugh. "Isn't it? Why didn't you stay?"

"I—Eros, I have a responsibility to the Remnant."

The heat rages through me, slamming into my chest. "No." My words shudder with the weight of my fire. "You had a responsibility to me. Your son. And you decided the Remnant—the people who wanted me *dead*—were more important to you."

She winces. "It's not like that."

"No? What's it like, then?"

"If I'd stayed with you, I never would have been able to take over the Remnant. Someone else would have taken my place; I wouldn't be able to make a difference like I can now. This is so important, Eros, now we can make a real change for humans everywhere."

I almost laugh at her twisted logic; everything inside me burns and burns and burns. She can try to justify the choices she made all she wants, but she doesn't get to look me in the eye and pretend her actions don't have consequences. She doesn't get to have a happy reunion where I make her feel better and tell her everything is okay.

Fuck that. Fuck her.

"No," I say. "You wouldn't have taken over the Remnant. You would have been a nomad, and maybe you would have died in the raid, or in the nanite attack after. Maybe I would have watched your ashes join the stars, and maybe I would have mourned you. But before that, you would have been my mother. You would have been with me as I grew up, and you would have been there for me when I needed you."

Her eyes widen and shoulders go stiff like I've hit her. "Eros—"

But I'm not done. I step closer and meet her gaze. "You weren't there. You chose a movement over your son, and maybe you can live with that. But you gave up your right to call yourself my mother when you left me behind with Nol and Esta. You're not my mother. You're nothing to me. I don't know you."

She purses her lips and crosses her arms over her stomach, but I turn away before she can try to guilt me, before she can try to make me care. I yank open the door to our bedroom-cell just as the doctor stands and smiles weakly at me.

"Good timing," she says. "We just finished up."

I take a shaky breath and force calm into my voice. "Is he okay? What's going on with him?"

The doctor hesitates. "He *will* be okay, once he adjusts to his limited vision. His eyes are physically fine; my best guess is the nanite attack damaged portions of his occipital lobe—the part of the brain that interprets vision. Some other refugees had brain damage from the attack, as well. It'll take some time for him to get used to it, but I don't think his blindness should progress any further."

The room warms as I glance at Mal, turned away from me, curled up on his bed. "Get used to . . . you mean there's nothing you can do? We can't—there isn't a cure?"

"Short of brain reconstruction—which is impossible without nanites and dangerous even with—no, there's no way to restore his vision to what it was before the attack."

I don't want to process her words; I don't want to hear my barely-teen nephew will be partially blind the rest of his life because of the attack. Because I didn't get there fast enough. Because we didn't stop Roma before he did something irreversible—before he slaughtered my family and—

I pinch the bridge of my nose. Take a deep, shaky breath.

"I'm going to let you two process this privately," the doctor says. "I've left a bottle of painkiller for him for his brainblazes from eyestrain—just have him drink a capful whenever he needs it. If you need anything, just tell the guards outside your room. They'll make sure you get whatever you need."

She starts to walk past me, then pauses. "He *will* be okay," she says softly. "I know it's a shock right now and not what you wanted to hear, but this isn't a death sentence. He'll adjust, in time."

I don't answer. My eyes sting, and my nephew is blind. Even if the nanite thing is true, Mal's best chance is being in Asheron when they get the nanites up and running again. So we need to leave, but we're stuck here until we talk business or whatever and dammital—I should have brought that up with Rani. Why didn't I bring that up? What is Voiding wrong with me? I wasn't thinking—*again*—I let her get to me—*again*—and now we're not progressing, not moving forward, not changing a damn thing.

I keep fucken this up. I keep getting distracted when I'm supposed to focus. I've been just as useless as I've ever been and I hate it.

I hate it.

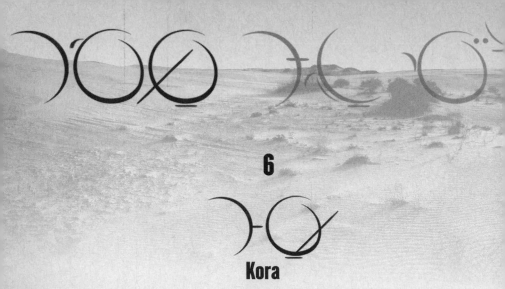

6

Kora

The scrape of utensils on plates grates against my ears. Despite the protests in the street, despite the worldwide footage of riots—both put down and active—on every screen in the palace, despite the unbearable heat, and wilting crops, and the serrated edges of panic coating the edge of every word, we are eating a feast for royalty.

Today's meal: *keta-mel*, an A'Sharan special, a stew of sorts cooked overnight with three different meats, loads of vegetables, and a thick, spicy broth served on a flat wrap over a layer of rice. This is a surprising choice, as I would have assumed Serek's favorite evening meal would be of Ona origin, but evidently not. I suppose it makes sense: his *mamae* was A'Sharan. With the *keta-mel*, there's *azuka*, six different vegetable sides, and a host of various desserts, one to represent Serek's favorite from each nation.

All in all, it's more food than any of us can ever hope to eat; every dish is rich, celebratory, pretending the world isn't crumbling around us. And I understand it's to honor Serek, as is tradition, but if I'm being honest with myself, I expect they'd have an equally lavish meal prepared either way.

The men laugh riotously at a joke Oniks d'A'Sharo—Deimos and Sulten's father—made. I've stopped listening; the whole meal has tasted like blood and glass, every joke a knife down my center. Safara is teetering on the edge of a precipice, but no one here seems concerned about the plunge.

Well. Maybe not no one. Aleija and Jule have barely touched their plates, and while Deimos is on his second glass of *azuka*, he hasn't laughed at a single joke or so much as smiled during the whole event. His gaze meets mine, and he grimaces and drinks another deep gulp.

Sulten claps his little brother on the back, his face red with laughter and drink. "Deimos, tell them about our visit to Ela'Tik two cycles ago; you recount it best."

Deimos shrugs away from his brother. "I'm not in the mood."

"Not in the mood! Please." He smirks and leans conspiratorially over the table to the still-snickering regents. "Little Deimos is the most theatrical of our family—if you ever want a good story—"

"Truly," Deimos says loudly, cutting Sulten off. "There won't be any stories from me tonight. In fact, I don't anticipate any stories at all until we've restored some peace and order to our panicked people. *Also*, I don't appreciate the insinuation I'm *theatrical* because—as most here know—I'm *lijara* and prefer men."

The room goes quiet and Sulten flushes. I'm not sure how many royals already knew about Deimos's sexuality, but it's news to me, at least.

Ejren is the first to break the silence. "It *is* an over-characterization of *lijarae* men."

"It is," Deimos agrees. "And I won't sit quietly while my own brother perpetuates it."

"That's not—" Sulten takes a breath and sighs, lowering his voice. "I apologize."

Deimos nods stiffly. "Good."

"You're right," Aleija adds. "This display of shared humor seems inappropriate, given our dire circumstances."

"They're hardly dire," Tamus d'Ona, one of the elders on the Emergency Council, says. "When former *Sira* Ashen arrives, we'll begin the selection process for the next *Sira*. All will return to normal shortly—there's nothing to worry about."

"Nothing to worry about?" I say. "Have you forgotten about the riots in our territories? The people are afraid—and they *should* be. We need to prepare for a famine in the Southern nations—our crops will die without the aid of the nanites, and we'll need resources shipped from other nations until we can determine an effective, alternate solution to nanite-aided desert farming."

Aleija nods. "Daïvi is already stockpiling surplus to send to those in need. What about the rest of the central and northern nations?"

The youngest on the Emergency Council—Hala d'Inara—shakes his head. "These would be legitimate concerns if we didn't hope to restore the nanites with the installation of the new *Sira*, but that's not the case. It'll take some time, of course, but Asheron's best technicians are already working on the restoration and building of a new supply of nanites—"

"It took fifty cycles to build the nanites up to the comprehensive network we had in place the first time around,"

Deimos says. "We don't have fifty cycles to wait around while people starve."

Hala waves his hand and Sulten laughs. "Don't worry so much, little *eran*. Everything will be taken care of soon."

My stomach churns; I push my untouched plate away and walk out. Down the hall, turning again and again, the empty patter of bare feet on smooth stone, one breath and one step after another until I slip into the warm night air, ignoring the rhythm of guards behind me. The quiet hum of the not-so-distant marketplace carries through the darkness. Smooth, golden glow lights marking the edge of the higher security area—where only approved royals can enter—hover like stars above the white sand.

But as beautiful and calm as it is out here, the edges of panic wrap around my heart and bury deeply into my chest. My breath shivers on my lips. Eros is running out of time, and he isn't here, and he needs to be here.

"Maybe he isn't coming," I whisper; the words taste like sand on my tongue.

"I'm starting to wonder the same," a voice says behind me.

I gasp and spin around, heart hammering as Deimos raises both hands.

"Sorry for startling you." He smiles weakly and lowers his hands. "I sometimes forget how good I am at tailing people unnoticed."

"It's fine," I say softly. "You don't mean me any harm."

Deimos nods and runs a hand through his thick hair. "I'd half-expected Eros to be here with you when I arrived, but I suppose the desert's a big place."

I grimace. "To be true, I was hoping he'd be here before anyone arrived, as well. Assuming he reached his people, his journey was less than a set's ride into the desert . . . but I understand why he wouldn't have come immediately."

"Even so . . . seems worrisome he isn't here yet."

I glance at him. "Shouldn't be worrisome to you—I imagine it'd be good news, given you and your brother are campaigning for the throne."

Deimos's face contorts like he just bit into something disgusting. "I'm not campaigning for the throne."

"*Nai*? Then why are you here?"

He lifts a shoulder. "To support Sulten, and . . . other reasons."

I arch an eyebrow. "Other reasons?"

"I may have been a bit curious about the man *a'da Kala Sira-kai* Serek declared the true inheritor of the throne." He uses the shortened version of the honorific—the A'Sharan people tend to shorten and mash words together as part of their dialect.

"Ah." I frown. "Well . . . with *Kala*'s grace, you'll get to meet him."

"Suppose it won't matter anymore if I don't meet him soon."

I glance at him. "Why do you say that?"

Deimos shakes his head. "If he doesn't arrive to claim his place quickly, he'll have nothing to come back to. It'll be too late."

I bite my lip. "That's true. I just . . . hope nothing's wrong."

"Wrong?"

"It's possible he isn't here because he doesn't want to be—we didn't exactly give him a lot of motivation to return to Asheron—"

Deimos laughs. "What, the chance to rule the world isn't enough motivation?"

"Eros didn't want power." I sigh. "And even if he did, I can hardly blame him for not trusting us. We tried to execute him in Jol's Arena—his head was literally on the block when the explosions happened that allowed for his escape."

"*Shae*, I watched the streaming." *Shae*, another A'Sharan variation, this one a casual version of *sha*.

I nod. "Before that, he and I were framed for *ana da Kala* Serek's attempted assassination—Eros risked his life to save mine and allowed my brother's guards to catch him so I could escape. He was tortured for sets and never gave me up; *ana da Kala* Serek stepped in and pulled Eros out of my brother's interrogation. And before that I . . ." I sigh. My stomach sinks. "It's . . . not something I'm proud of, but before that I ordered a raid on the village he lived in. Much of his family was killed, and he was made a slave during the ordeal. And all of *that* was before the nanite attack that must have affected his surviving family and . . . I understand why he may not want to return."

Saying it out loud, it feels even worse. And that doesn't even account for all the crimes Eros has suffered—doesn't even mention the way I treated him, the way he saved my life in the desert and I . . .

I'm so sorry, Eros.

Deimos whistles. "That's a lot to account for."

"I know."

"It's a wonder you expect him to return at all."

I bite my lip. "Eros is an honorable person. He knows we need him, and he could do a lot of good for his people, too, if he claimed his position . . . but maybe that's not enough. As he told it, his people didn't treat him well either."

"He may still want to fight for his family," Deimos says.

"Assuming they survived the nanite attack . . . maybe." I turn away from the city. "But if that were the case, he would be here by now unless something happened to him."

Deimos looks at the city with me, standing at my side. The blue and white and gold glow of night flowers in the museum's garden ahead of us spots the shadows with beautiful light. The endless hum of the bustling complex washes over the breeze. After a pause, Deimos says, "You'll never know if something did happen to him. I doubt anyone knows where to start looking for him, even if they wanted to."

"No one is going to look for him," I say. "It's in their best interest for him to disappear. As far as they're concerned, if he doesn't arrive, it just means he wasn't meant for the throne after all."

"Which is exactly what they want."

I nod. "It makes the decision easy—they don't have to consider him if he isn't here."

Deimos quirks his lip. "Sounds like someone should look for him."

"Someone should," I agree. "Someone who knows what's at stake if he's overlooked."

He glances at me with a glint of mischief in his eyes. "Someone who knows where to start looking to begin with."

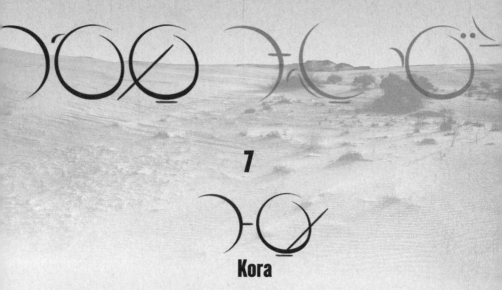

7

Kora

"Tell me if you want me to stop."

Eros's taste is on my tongue, his hands setting fire to my skin, his body pressed hard against mine. My back digs into the rough sandstone exterior of the building behind us, my fingers grip his muscled back as my legs pull him closer, closer, nowhere near close enough.

The world is fuzzy, blazing, dark, sharp as glass. He kisses down my neck, pulls my bottom lip into his mouth, kisses, and touches, and I'm sorry, I'm so sorry for what I'm about to do, for all the pain about to come. I'm so sorry for everything that's my fault and everything that isn't. I'm sorry, I'm sorry, I'm—

Eros is standing a few paces away, his back to me. Enjos is silent around us; the marks of the temple pressed into my back burn me to the core.

I try to scream *I'm sorry* but instead I say, "Eros, we shouldn't stay here."

He turns and frowns and shakes his head—and shakes his head—and shakes his head—like a glitch in a recording, again, and again, until I blink and—

He's several paces closer. His mouth is painted with sand the color of rebel blood, and his hands are wet with actual blood, and he says, "Sorry. I thought I saw—never mind."

"I thought I saw—never mind."

"I thought I saw—never mind."

What did you see? I want to ask. *Why are you apologizing? That word is mine. Sorry. Sorry. I'm sorry. I'm so sorry. You have nothing to apologize for, why are you—*

What did you see, Eros?

What did you see?

But I say nothing, and the world fills with sand—sand in my mouth, sand in my nose, sand in my lungs, and I can't breathe, and the world presses heavier, and heavier, and heavier against my shoulders, crushing me into the dirt, and I don't fight.

I don't fight for escape because I don't deserve it.

The echo of the dream lingers on my tongue and whispers over my skin as I look at my supplies.

A bottle with a cold-water generator in the cap (though the *cold* part doesn't work without nanites); light wraps to protect me from the suns; enough travel food for three people for eight sets, not that I expect to need anywhere near that much but I'm never going into the desert unprepared again; nutrient mixes for the water; a glass to keep connected; three changes of clothing; refresher spray to keep me clean; a seeing glass to scan the desert. Now I'll just need a bike and face-mask to protect me from the spray of the sands when moving at full speed.

It's doable. I don't technically have access to the *Sirae* transportation, but I should be able to convince someone to let me borrow a sand bike, which will be made easier by the fact that no one wants me here. And with *Kala*'s grace, I'll be able to figure out how to drive one without using my injured wrist.

I seal my pack and hoist it over my shoulder. Today is the set former *Sira* Ashen is due to arrive as well as Serek's funeral on the accelerated schedule. The decision to leave today isn't an easy one; just the thought of missing Serek's funeral pricks my eyes with new tears, but I can't put this off any more. And maybe I'm making a mistake by not being here—maybe I'll regret leaving on the set the most important man in this decision makes his entrance—but none of it will matter if Eros isn't here anyway.

It's possible Eros doesn't want to return. He could have decided he's had enough, which is his right. But maybe he hasn't, and maybe something is wrong, and maybe he needs help. I don't know which it is, but I'm not going to sit around and hope someone else answers the question for me. I'm not going to wait for an act of *Kala* anymore. I'm not going to wait until I'm out of hope, and options, and end up on the street.

I may very well regret this decision, but at least I'm making a move.

It takes me a while to find the garage—the palace grounds are huge, and it's only after searching for close to a segment that I remember to access a map on my glass with my authorization. Which I should have done in the first place.

I approach the entrance to the large, underground garage, which, of course, is guarded by six men—as if the two following me around everywhere weren't enough. I wipe sweat off my forehead and force a smile as I near the scowling guards, all six of which eye me suspiciously before glancing at the guards behind me. One I recognize from the tower aftermath; he's one of the men I stunned and was the first to wake and find Serek. There isn't a chance he hasn't told the story to the others, so I suppose I can only hope he hasn't held a grudge.

"*Ora'denja*," I say lightly—our customary morning greeting. "Ordinarily I'd use my own transportation, but as I traveled here with *ana da Kala Sira-kai* Serek, I don't have any."

"*Naï*," the guard says.

I blink. "I haven't asked—"

"You don't need to ask. The answer is *naï*."

The heat of the twin suns drips down my back and sinks under my skin. I swallow my irritation. "And how am I supposed to leave the palace grounds without transportation?"

"I don't know," the guard answers. "And I don't care. That's your complication—not mine."

"*My compli*—" I stop myself, swallow the boiling words, straighten my shoulders, force a breath, and calm my tone. Control—I can control my emotions. "If you're worried I won't return, the—"

"The answer isn't changing, no matter how many ways or how many times you ask. *Naï*. Or, how is it the redbloods say it? Perhaps you'd understand that better, as you seem to like them so much—I think it goes *no*."

"You *kafrek sko*—"

"Wow!" someone laughs behind me. "Kora, there you are, I was looking all over for you." Deimos steps next to me and smiles at the guards. "Silen, Tomae, Alden, good to see you all—and I don't think I've been acquainted with you three?"

I stare at Deimos—how does he know their names already? Could he really have introduced himself to half the guard in the short time he's been here?

Then again, he *is* impressively charismatic . . .

"Kea, Rimo, and Bjule," the guard I was arguing with—Silen—answers.

"Good to meet you all," Deimos answers with a charming smile. "I'm Deimos Zielo Azani *Avra-kaï* d'A'Sharo." The men nod at each other and Deimos smiles at me. "Looks like we're ready to go." He gestures to his own bag slung over his shoulder and looks at the guards. "We'd like to access my bike, thank you."

Silen blinks, glances at me, then looks at Deimos and nods. "Certainly, *ol Avra-kaï.*"

And just like that, they move out of the way. Unbelievable.

"Thank you," Deimos says brightly. We step between the guards and walk down the smooth tunnel in silence until the guards are well out of earshot.

"What are you doing?" I hiss. "Why do you have a pack with you? How did you know I'd be here?"

"Well, I believe *we* are headed into the desert to find Eros and bring him back to Asheron. My pack is full of supplies, of course—we don't want to go into the desert unprepared. And I knew you'd be here because I'm not dense and it was obvious after speaking to you last night that you'd go looking for him."

"You can't have known that," I snap. "I didn't even know until this morning."

"And yet, here we are."

I narrow my eyes at him.

"I know it's hard to believe someone as handsome and charming as me could *also* be so intelligent—"

"—Deimos—"

"—but don't let this dreamy body fool you. I'm quite possible and in fact completely handsome and real."

"You already said handsome."

"Why, thank you for noticing, *sha* I am."

I open and close my mouth then settle for shaking my head. Deimos snickers and smiles at me. "Don't worry, this will be fun. And besides, you could use my help."

"That's a rather grand assumption."

"But it's not an assumption if it's true; then it's a fact. But I don't say that because I underestimate your abilities—I don't. I, in fact, find you quite impressive and don't doubt you'd find him on your own. However, with my help, you'll find him faster."

A bold claim. "And what makes you think that?"

He opens his mouth.

"If you say it's because you're so handsome, I'll be severely tempted to hit you."

Deimos laughs. "That *would* be like me to say, but *naï*, that's not why."

"Then?"

"Are you ready to be astounded?"

I roll my eyes. "Go on then."

"I'm not just an *Avra-kaï* with a pretty face; I'm a bounty hunter."

My mouth opens and closes. I may have guessed many answers from Deimos, but *bounty hunter* wouldn't have been one of them.

Deimos grins. "Astounded?"

"Surprised," I admit. "Do you ordinarily track people through the desert?"

"I've tracked all over. People will run just about anywhere when they're desperate."

It's an unusual choice of profession for a royal, to say the least. Most who aren't set to be rulers join the military, or religious services, or stay in politics in lesser roles—what I would have done, if I weren't raised to be *Avra*. But Deimos has no reason to lie; after all, he has nothing to gain in joining me to find Eros. Of course, I don't know him, but the little I *do* know—that he's the youngest of the A'Sharon *Avrae-kjo* and that most have a positive opinion of him—tells me I needn't worry. Given that I need to find Eros quickly . . . I suppose I can't think of anyone more useful to have at my side. "Hmm. Welcome to the search party then."

Deimos snickers. "Well, seeing how we're taking *my* bike, I was already invited, but thank you anyway."

"You're welcome."

I glance around the dim garage, gleaming transports of every shape and size, each as luxurious and shiny as the last, are lined in long rows in the large, open room. We walk to a glass embedded in the wall just beside the entrance, and Deimos presses his palm against it.

The glass lights up red, and a voice says, "Welcome, *Avra-kaï* Deimos Zielo Azani d'A'Sharo. Your transport is on its way."

"Thank you," Deimos says happily.

Moments later, a low hum fills the room, and then lights crest over the hill of the sloping tunnel as a sleek red sand bike drifts over to us. Deimos smiles and pats his bike before opening a compartment at the bottom and pulling out two red and black helmets. "I suspect this will work better than a headscarf."

"You're right." I shove my supplies back into my bag and take the helmet. "Thank you."

"Sure. I can take your bag, too."

I pause but hand it over. He opens a second compartment behind the first, then pushes our bags inside, seals both compartments, and smiles. "So which way are we headed?"

I hesitate. The truth is, I don't know exactly where Eros is; the nomads move all the time, so assuming he's still with them, they could be just about anywhere in the desert. But their last location was near one landmark, and something still pulls me there.

It's a gamble, and I might be wrong, but it's the only place I can think of to start.

"South," I say. "To Enjos."

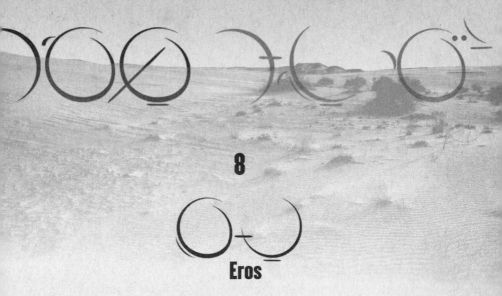

8

Eros

Can't sleep. Not sure I want to. And yet, after those sets in Dima's dungeon, when sleep was the only thing I wanted and the one thing I couldn't have—

—the screaming the pain the—

—sleep was a rebellion. But no amount of pushing my palms against my closed eyelids, no amount of listening to Mal breathe softly in the bed below me, no amount of staring into shadows wipes their faces from my mind. Their screams. Their writhing, and burning, and crying, and worse, worse: their silence.

Their silence is the most haunting of all.

Held hands and children huddled around their mother; an older sibling holding his silent baby brother. Crying and whimpering and alive, still alive, but just.

How does Mal sleep with the memory of lying in the sand, surrounded by his dead family? Does he wonder if he could have done something more? It's the question I wrestle with every blazing mo. Does he dream of his last moments with them like I do? Of Aren pushing a bracelet he made with his own hands onto my wrist, of rolling my eyes at Esta's kiss, of arguing with Nol, and fuck, I want it to stop. I don't want to remember, not anymore, because it *hurts*. It hurts so fucken bad and there's nothing I can do to change it.

But if I'm being honest with myself, if I had the choice to forget, I wouldn't choose that either. Because if I forget my family, if I forget the only people on the planet who ever cared, who were there for me all along, then what do I have left?

I'm a shell without them now.

Eventually I roll out of bed and slip out into the hallway. It's impossible to know what time it is—underground, so far from the suns and moons, the sets are determined by artificial lights and schedules, by people who decide when to turn on those lights.

I'm guessing it's still late—or really early—though, because the lights are dim when I step out of my room, and the withering look the guards give me says everything they don't speak.

"Can't sleep," I answer. "I want to go for a run. Is there somewhere I can do that?"

The guards glance at each other, and then one lifts a shoulder and nods to the left. "There's a track on this floor. I'll take you."

"Okay," I say, trying to pretend he's taking me because I don't know the way and not because he doesn't trust me, not because I'm their prisoner. We start down the hall, but I hesitate and look back at the guard staying behind. "If Mal wakes up, send someone to come and get me."

The remaining guard nods. We continue down the hallway. This walk is a little less confusing—only five mos or so, left, right, right, left. Easy enough to remember, not that I'll ever need to because they'll never leave me alone anyway.

We pass a few people who are probably civilians—they aren't wearing a uniform, at least—who I guess are early risers, too. I spot one woman with a shaved head and the edges of a tattoo peeking out from under her sleeve. I don't know her, but I'd recognize that tattoo anywhere because I have one, too. She must be one of the ex-slave refugees Rani mentioned taking in. Her dark gaze follows me as we pass, and I nod at her, tapping the identical band inked on my arm. We share a pained smile before she walks away.

The track room is large, with some kinduv spongey, stiff, and bouncy floor with a thick blue ring bordering the room. The walls are deep red sandstone, and the ceiling is so low if I jumped I could reach it. Like everywhere else down here. Closed in. Underground. So far from the suns and free air and life.

I shudder and try not to think about it.

The guard points to a white line across the ring. "You start there. If you had a comm linked up the system, it'd give a running count for you with all sorts of statistics, but you'll just have to count for yourself."

A comm linked up to the system—did they track everyone with nanites, too? Somehow I doubt everyone's privacy had been invaded like mine. Somehow I doubt watching my every move through my eyes, and recording it, and viewing it like observing an animal all without my knowledge is standard operating procedure.

And yet, she treated it like no big deal. Like I was overreacting. Like it's unreasonable that I was blazed as a supernova after learning the only private moments I've had my *entire* life began when Kora's panicked medic filtered all nanites from my system a couple terms back.

But I guess I don't have the luxury to hold on to that anger, because I'm here, and I have to deal with them, and there's nothing I can do about it.

I take a few mos to stretch out, then step up to the line, and when the guard moves out of the way, I run. It's nothing like running in the desert, nothing like the sand in my toes and the slight slip of every step as the powdery sand pushes back, back, like sinking just for a breath with every step. It's nothing like the morning rays of the rising suns painting the skies orange, red, purple, and gold. It's nothing like filling my lungs with warm, free air that smells like home; it's nothing like ignoring the Sephari buildings in Kora's palace complex and pretending I'm back at camp running, running, running.

It's not comforting, and it's not familiar, but it is moving. It's pushing my legs until they ache—then harder. It's taking steady, cool breaths until my lungs burn—then more. It's pumping my arms and sweat dripping down my temples; it's the tingling of my tiring body; it's knowing the harder I push, the more it hurts, the faster and farther I run, the sooner I can clear my mind and focus on nothing but air and ache. But not the ache of guilt churning endlessly in my gut, not the ache of a hurt I can never fix; it's the ache of muscles, and it's good. It's good.

I have to believe that. I have to believe there's still some good left.

And I have to get to Asheron. For Mal, mostly, so we'll be there when the nanites are fixed but also . . .

I slow to a walk, heaving air into my lungs in long, shuddering breaths. I have to be realistic. When I get out of here—and I *will* get out of here—if I don't go to Asheron, where else would I go? I'm not welcome anywhere. Humans are just as likely as Sepharon to kill me. Serek wanted me to claim my spot on the throne, but I . . .

I don't want that. Not really. I don't want the responsibility of billions of people—most of whom will probably always hate me. I don't want the hopes of every human weighing on my shoulders, praying for something I might not ever be able to get them as long as prejudiced Sepharon stand in my way.

I don't want it, but I'm not sure I really have a choice, either. Not when the other option is starve on the streets with Mal until someone kills us. Or worse—staying here. But with time slipping by, my window for getting to Asheron before they choose someone else to rule is closing.

The guard watching me is leaning against the wall, arms crossed over his chest, head dipped toward the ground. Sleeping—or falling asleep, at least. But an escape isn't an option, not really—there are too many checkpoints and cameras and guards and levels, and even if I somehow managed to get Mal, get my bike—wherever they hid it—and get to the surface without being detected, they'd run us down easily. I can't outrun anyone on Day's old junker; I was already pressing my luck trying to get to Asheron on that old thing as it was.

Which means the only way I get out of here is if they let me. And they haven't asked, not really, not yet, but there isn't a chance in the Void they're going to just let me walk out of here without doing something for them first.

I don't know what that something is, but I can't imagine it's going to be anything good.

Still, I need to talk to someone and figure out how I'll get out of this fucken place. Mal can't get the help he needs here, and maybe he won't be able to right away in Asheron, either, but they're sure to build new nanites quickly, and when they do, the first with access will be the *Sira* and whoever is in his inner circle.

It's not a good plan—chances of actually becoming *Sira* are slim, and chances of the new *Sira* liking me enough to help Mal are slimmer, but it's all I have. And even if it's a shit plan, it's better than being a prisoner here and accomplishing nothing.

The guard is practically using his blond beard as a pillow for his chin as I step up to him—and then a thought kicks me in the stomach: a lot of the guys down here are bearded and pale.

Pale like the bearded assassin who tried to kill Kora when I was her bodyguard.

"I want to talk to Rani."

The guard jerks up, blinking rapidly and adjusting his posture, like I didn't just catch him sleeping. "Um," he says. "Rani?"

"Yeah. Your leader—the woman who—"

"You mean Commander Jakande."

"Whatever," I say. "I want to talk to her."

He frowns and nods at a blue number on the wall. "You realize it's four in the morning."

"Then later in the morning, but I want to talk to her today."

"I can put in a request for you, but it's not that simple—"

"It *is* simple, actually," I say. "Your people abducted my nephew and me because they wanted to talk. I'm here, and I'm ready to talk. Make it happen."

He hesitates, then nods. "I'll see what I can do."

"You tried to kill Kora."

I'd had another intro ready—a better, less aggressive and accusatory one—but the realization is too much for me to ignore and it sets my blood boiling. It all makes sense; the assassin was pale because he lived underground where some of the people are light-skinned, and he was bearded because apparently that's not an uncommon custom down here. The Remnant is anti-Sepharon, so it'd make sense they'd want to kill Kora, though why Kora over any other royal, I don't know, but I'm going to find out.

Rani arches an eyebrow and gestures to a seat in front of her desk. Her office is small—just a dark room with a ton of little lights, a propped-up glass, and stacks of what I think are supposed to be books but aren't nicely bound like the ones in Kora's library were.

"Please sit," she says.

"I'm good."

"Suit yourself." She leans back in her seat and looks at me. "I don't know who Kora is."

"Hodgeshit," I say. "If you're paying half as much attention to Sepharon politics as you claim to be, you know who Elja's former *Avra* is."

"Oh. That Kora." She shrugs. "Yes, we accepted a deal to try to assassinate her. What of it?"

My mouth opens and closes. Rani smiles at me nonchalantly, like she didn't just admit to attempting to kill a royal. "You—*a deal*?"

"The second from Eljan royals, actually. They were pretty determined to get her out of the picture—looks like they finally succeeded on their own."

It takes a lot of self-control not to gape at her. "From *Eljan royals?*" Is she saying Kora's *family* hired them to try to kill her? But then—Kora said Dima had saved her from an assassination attempt when she was fifteen. Why would he do that if he was behind it? Unless . . . "Which royals?"

"First was the *Avra* at the time—the explosion at her coronation was supposed to kill her . . . but got him instead." She smirks. "Oops."

Kora's own father. What in the Void was wrong with her fucken family? "And the second time?"

"That was not long ago—her brother contacted us that time." She smirks. "It was a win-win for us. Further destabilize their government and get paid in weaponry, tech, and credits."

I scowl. "And meanwhile, they got to blame the violence on us—on *humans*—because apparently it *was* us."

Rani shrugs. "Doesn't bother us; we're not trying to get along until we've changed things."

"No? It didn't bother you, then, when they used the coronation explosion as an excuse to hunt down my camp, kill my family, and nearly kill *me* in the process?"

Rani grimaces. "That was . . . an unforeseen consequence, and I'm sorry you had to go through that. But you made it out—and when they brought you to the arena, we made sure it didn't go too far."

Didn't go too far? My head was literally on the fucken chopping block—I was *breaths* away from execution. My fists shake, and everything inside me screams this is wrong, this is *wrong*, but she doesn't care.

"You're welcome, by the way," she adds. "For saving your life."

I force out a laugh—because if I don't laugh, I might do something regrettable. Like leap across her desk and strangle her. "Doesn't count as saving when you're the reason I was there in the first place."

Rani purses her lips. "You would have been discovered one way or the other. You're not just a half-blood, Eros, you're the son of a *Sira*. I hate to say it, but a quiet life was never in the stars for you."

Every part of me blazes to tell her off. To say I'm not just a pawn in her plan for power—but maybe she never saw me as more. Maybe that's all I've been to her all along, since the moment she agreed to have me.

And maybe it doesn't fucken matter how she wants to use me, because I'm my own person and she needs me way Voiding more than I need her.

I just need to get out of here first.

I take a deep breath. "You said you abducted me because you needed to make your presence known before I went to Asheron, so we can work together from here on out. So, what's it going to take to let me go?"

She smiles. "You know, I'm glad you came back to talk, I was waiting for the right moment to finally have this conversation. I still think we can salvage this butchered introduction and work together." I stare her down. She laughs and runs a hand over her buzzed head. "Okay, so, we want you to go back to Asheron and claim your place on the throne. And once the dust settles and you've been fully accepted—"

"If you think I'll ever be fully accepted as *Sira*, you're deluding yourself."

"That's true; I more mean once it's official and you're *Sira,* that's when I'll contact you."

"And then?"

She crosses her arms and a slow smile slips over her lips. "Then we'll tear it all down from the inside. Start a revolution with the *Sira* at the helm."

I frown. Tear it all down? A revolution? "What's that supposed to mean?"

"Exactly what it sounds like—you'll dissolve the current monarchial setup and start over. Create a representative government with humans and Sepharon alike spoken for equally. We can work together, Sepharon and humans, once we've thrown out the old system, but we need to start at the government level or nothing will change."

I stare at her. Laugh. "Seriously. This is what you and Asha had planned?"

"Well, no, but things have changed in eighteen years. Asha is dead, humans are persecuted now more than ever—"

"We can't just rip the government apart. I'm not even sure they're going to *let* me be *Sira* to begin with, and even if they do, there's no way I'll have enough support to make such a drastic change. Humans in the government—that is *never* going to happen. At least not in our lifetimes."

"I don't believe that," Rani says. "Two decades ago, we would have said a half-blood *Sira* was impossible—but here we are and you're a real candidate—the *only* legitimate candidate."

"I won't be for much longer if you keep me here."

"I need your word you'll help us with this."

I run my hand through my hair. Search for the words. "Look, I want rights for humans as much as you do—and *if* I manage to become *Sira*, you can bet I'll do everything I can to make Safara safer for humans. But what you're asking for isn't a reasonable solution—you're demanding *anarchy*. We can't just throw out generations of tradition and try to force something new on them. They'll kick me out of the capital and off the throne in a heartbeat—no, worse, they'll throw me back into the Arena and then there won't be anyone around to stop them."

She grimaces. "I doubt that; as much as I'd hate to lose you—and I would—we'll still be around regardless."

"That's not the point—there are ways to make changes without triggering a global war by throwing out the government that's kept them peaceful for generations."

Rani shakes her head. "The system will never be balanced as long as it's run by a single ruler—a ruler who more likely than not will be fully Sepharon again at some point even after you're on the throne."

"If I'm *Sira* and my heirs take over after me, they won't be completely Sepharon."

"No, but unless you marry a human—which, let's be honest, is unlikely—your heirs will be even less human than you are. And *their* heirs will be practically Sepharon. And *their* heirs for all intents and purposes *will* be Sepharon, and we'll be back to square zero again."

Less human than you are. The words sting even though I should be used to it by now. I hate the term *half-blood* and everything it implies: that I'm less than human and less than Sepharon. That I'm not a whole anything. And there she is, my own mother affirming she thinks I'm lesser, too.

The sting runs deep and twists bitter and black in my gut. But as much as I want to call her out on it, focusing on the current conversation is too important.

"You're assuming the world will be in the same in two generations—or my great-grandkids will be biased against humans."

"It's not exactly a far-fetched scenario."

"It's not, but . . ." I sigh. Glance around her tiny, dim office. Try to compose myself to say this the best I can. "Look, I can't see into the future—I don't know what the world will be like in ten, twenty, fifty, a hundred years. Maybe things can change now, but it's not going to change for the better if we try to overthrow their government. All that'll do is establish humans as enemies; it'll show the Sepharon they were right to hate us all along, and if they respond in kind again, I don't know we'll survive it. Any of us."

"Which is why we have to win. We have to strike fast enough that they won't see it coming and hard enough that they won't be able to get back up again."

"Which is impossible. Even if you *did* manage to take control of Asheron—which I'm seriously doubting—there are eight other nations, each with their own powerful army you'd have to convince, too. Asheron's army is strong, but it isn't strong enough to fight off eight nations at the same time."

"You're not seeing the big picture—"

"I am, but your *big picture* is suicidal and will only make things worse for everyone. I'm willing to work with the humans, of course I am, but I'm not promising to help you make such a boneheaded move."

She shrugs. "Then I hope you've made yourself comfortable. Looks like your stay's just been extended."

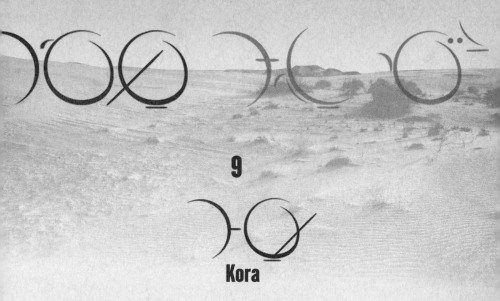

9

Kora

Holding on to Deimos with my uninjured arm as we race over the sands feels like a time I wish I could go back to. A time when the purring beneath me wasn't a machine, but an animal—my dearest *kazim*, Iro. A time when I was steering in the front, bent low over Iro's back, his powerful muscles moving beneath me. A time when Eros was sitting behind me, his arms wrapped around my middle, laughing as the sand whipped around us and the world sped by.

A time before Serek, before the assassination attempt on his life, before I ran, and Eros was tortured, and a band of criminals found me, and I broke Eros's heart and nearly got him killed again, and Roma murdered his brother, and I put Roma down.

A time before so much pain, so much fear and anger and hurt and death. A time when all that mattered was the heat of the suns and the expanse of the desert.

That time is long past, and the feeling whirling through my blood isn't freedom or a moment of peace; it's the churning of fear, hot and ever-present in my gut. It's the heavy knowledge that if we don't find Eros, and quickly, and if we don't convince him to return to Asheron, it's over. Sulten, or Simos, or Jolek, or someone else will become *Sira*, and Eros, and his people, and anyone like him will remain at risk. Because while nearly everyone agrees what Roma attempted with the nanites was awful, none seem interested in making amends or trying to make life more equitable for the redbloods.

The bike slows to a stop, and Deimos sits up and glances around. Near us is a patch of blackened rocks and what was once a prickleplant bush, but has now been ripped apart, also with blackened edges.

"Huh," Deimos says.

"*Kazim* didn't do that," I answer.

"*Naï* they didn't." He gets off the bike, walks over to the bush's remains, and lifts a black leaf. It crumbles between his fingers. "Burned."

I walk over to the rocks and pick one up. Half of it is black—with streaks of darkness racing over the surface and a chunk of it broken off. Deimos steps beside me and touches the rock—some of the black smears off on his fingers.

"Soot," I say.

He nods. "Those marks, though . . . and something to break the rock. It looks like part of an explosion."

I glance at him. "An explosion in the middle of the desert."

He smiles wryly. "*Kazim* didn't do that, either."

"You don't think . . ." I glance around, my stomach sinking with Deimos's words. "I don't see any . . . corpses."

"They could be buried by the sand, but . . . hold on." He slides his visor back down and taps something on the side of his helmet. After a pause, he does the same to mine, and blue lines race across my visor, outlining the edges of everything near us. He taps it again and the blue lines disappear, filling my vision with reds and yellows and whites, making Deimos appear as if he's made of flame. One more tap and the blue lines reappear alongside the red, white, and yellow blobs.

"It tracks heat signatures for people and objects," Deimos explains. "Which is why I look like I'm made of magma."

I nod and peer across the sands—a few paces to our left, a bundle of tiny yellow and orange blobs with long yellow tails move beneath the sand.

"Cute," Deimos says. "I've always liked *entu*—they have a nasty bite if you're not careful, though."

I smile softly. "I wouldn't know."

"They're useful when you're out in the desert—if you follow them, they'll take you to the nearest natural source of water."

I glance at him. "Do they? I wouldn't have guessed."

"*Shae*, I'm decently sure that's how the nomads survive out here. Of course, I've never spoken to one, but it would make sense given their lack of access to more advanced technology. . . . Do you think Eros would know?"

"Probably. He grew up with them."

Deimos smiles. "Fascinating."

I lift a shoulder and glance over the sands. "So, if we're looking for corpses . . . would this filter pick them up? I can't imagine they'd still be warm unless this just happened."

"They won't be warm, *nai*, but they'll still show up—probably as a dull blue or purple. The filter would recognize it's not sand. I don't see anything, though—which is good." He turns slowly in a circle.

I turn with him, and a small square several paces ahead lights up on my visor with a blue outline. I walk over to the square, pick it up, and raise my visor. "Deimos."

Deimos steps beside me and touches the red strip of fabric. At the top is yellow lettering—but the letters aren't in Sephari.

"Looks like a . . . face scarf? For sand protection?" Deimos says. "But probably rebel owned. I don't suppose you can read the redblood language."

I shake my head. "That means they were here, though. Right in the same area as the explosion."

Deimos nods. "May or may not be connected . . . though given their tendency toward explosives, I'm leaning toward *may*."

"I agree." I crumple the fabric in my hand. "If Eros came this way, maybe the rebels stopped him."

"With an explosion? Drastic, but not impossible, I suppose. Neither of them are here, though, and it's not like we know where their base is."

What did you see, Eros? What did you see?

I bite my lip. "We don't, but . . . I may have a guess."

Deimos arches an eyebrow. "You do?"

I nod. "Let's keep going." I turn back to the bike and freeze.

So do the two *kazim* sniffing our bike.

My heart thunders in my ears as I glance at Deimos and take a shivering breath. I don't have to wonder if these *kazim* are feral or tame—without nanites, any of the formerly tame *kazim* are undoubtedly wild again. In a way, I'm almost glad Iro passed before the nanites failed; seeing him turn against me would have been the worst betrayal of all.

"Where did they come from?" I whisper. "I didn't see them on the scan at all."

Deimos barely shakes his head, his hand steady at his hip, where I hope he has a weapon. "*Kazim* don't show up on the scan—their fur masks their heat signature. They have the perfect camouflage out here."

The *kazim* continue sniffing our bike—more specifically, my bag hanging off the bike. Their long, crimson tails swish lazily as they nudge my bag into the sand. I don't dare move—every breath feels like a risk. I'm unarmed—not that the Asheron guards would have ever allowed me any weapons—but even if Deimos and I were both as armed as soldiers, we wouldn't be able to take on two *kazim* alone.

"Did you pack food?" Deimos asks so quietly I almost don't hear him above the *kazim*'s low growls and purrs, like grinding stone.

I nod.

"Okay. Let's sit. Slowly. Very slowly."

My heart climbs into my throat. "Sit?"

Deimos nods. "We need to make ourselves small, unintimidating, and uninteresting. If they attack us, we're dead."

"Are you sure?" I hiss.

"Sure there's no way we can take on two *kazim*? Absolutely."

That's not what I meant, but one of the *kazim* looks up from my bag and stares right at me. It looks so much like Iro did, from its deep, sand-tinted fur to its piercing eyes. A part of me aches at the memory, but this is not Iro. This *kazim* could kill me.

I move slowly, so slowly my legs burn as I sink to the sand. The *kazim*'s ears flick as it eyes us. Sweat drips between my shoulders. My stomach is a mess of knots. My center is ice. I hold my breath and pray. *Please don't let it eat us. Please don't let it kill us.*

The truth is, I don't know what *Kala* listens to and what he doesn't.

The truth is, I don't deserve saving at all. Not after what I did to Eros and his family and his people. Not after what my failure set into motion.

But deserving or not, the other *kazim* rips into my bag and the food spills out—a couple wrapped fruits and vegetables, packs of dried fruit and meat, and a wrapped pastry. It's enough of a distraction. The *kazim* watching me pounces on the food while the other drags the bag over the sand, purring lowly. The closer *kazim* gathers the bags in its mouth and rolls onto its back, happily chewing through the wrapping.

I glance at Deimos. To the bike. Back to Deimos. He nods. We crawl slowly, slowly. My arms shake beneath me as we near the bikes—and the *kazim* on its back, eating my food just the length of a person away. Deimos had left the bike on standby—which means it's floating and humming softly, ready to go. I just don't know how we'll get on it and accelerate fast enough to get away from the *kazim*, should it startle and attack.

We're close now. The hum of the bike barely masks the thick, slobbery chewing sounds of the *kazim* nearby. I'm shaking so much my teeth clatter—I set my jaw and breathe through my nose.

"Where are we going?" Deimos whispers. "Enjos?"

I'm too shaken to speak. The *kazim*'s tail thumps the sand on the other side of the bike. I just nod. Enjos. Enjos is where we're going if we don't get eaten by *kazim*. It's only a guess, and I could very well be wrong, but it's the only guess I have.

Deimos carefully grabs the bike's steering unit, looks at me, and jerks his head over his shoulder. I crawl backward as he slowly drags the bike away from the *kazim*, cringing as he does, as if he expects them to realize what's happening and attack us.

We double the distance. Triple it. The closest *kazim* keeps eating and rolling in the sand while the other chews my bag to shreds. It's a good thing I didn't have anything important in there.

"Okay," Deimos finally whispers. Sweat glistens on his face and shoulders. "We're far enough. Let's just go while we can."

My voice is still caught in my throat, but I nod and stand, trying not to look at the *kazim* as we throw on our helmets and climb onto the bike.

One breath later—two—Deimos kicks off and we shoot across the sands.

We arrive with the suns high above us and their heat pouring over our shoulders, but that doesn't stop the chill sliding down my back as we pass the bodies of the men I killed. The men Eros helped me kill. The men who would have—

I close my eyes, take a deep breath, and open them again.

"Do you know what happened here?" Deimos asks.

"Those men are criminals," I answer. "They tried to . . . hurt me."

He glances back at me. "*You* did this?"

"Some of it. Eros helped with the last few. But we didn't . . ." I grimace at a split-open corpse. "The animals have taken advantage of what we left behind."

Deimos nods. "Where should we stop?"

"I . . . the temple." Heat flashes over my face at the thought of returning there, but I force the words out anyway. "Let's go to the temple."

Deimos nods, and we move forward. Over the corpses of the men we left behind. To the place I ruined everything with one desperate kiss.

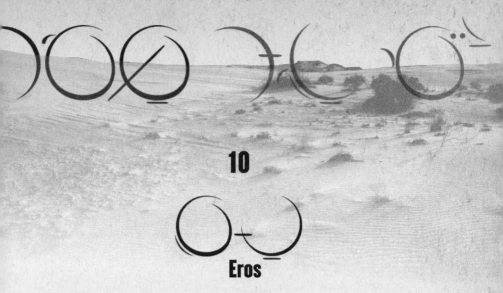

10

Eros

An alarm blares overhead, startling Mal and me out of our beds. Red light flashes through our room, again, again, the sound slamming against my heart, over, over. It's not screaming, it's not screaming, I'm fine, I'm fine—

"Uncle Eros?" Mal yells, slapping his hands over his ears. "What's going on?"

Inhale, exhale. Relax. Everything is fine. We're fine. I take a shaky breath. "Let me find out." I move toward the door, but Mal stumbles toward me.

"Wait!"

I stop and face him. Mal squints up at me, wincing with every scream of the alarm. "What if it's dangerous?"

"I'm sure we're fine. They're armed to the teeth down here. I'll just go find out what's going on—I promise everything is going to be fine."

"You can't promise that. You don't know what's going on any more than I do."

"I don't, but—"

"I'm coming, too."

I frown. Would Mal be safer here, or at my side? The truth is, I'm not sure. I can't be sure of anything down here—I can't trust anyone or anything, not really.

"I'm not a little kid anymore," Mal says. "Let me go with you. I can handle it."

I sigh. "Fine. Let me, um . . . should I hold your hand or something?"

Mal glares at me.

I laugh. "Okay, okay, sorry. Um. Here." I hold his shoulder. "Just so you don't—"

"Let's just go."

We do—I've taken all of one step forward before the door swings open and the guard beckons us out into the hall.

"I can watch the kid, but Commander Jakande needs you," he says.

"I'm not a—"

"Mal's coming with us. Let's go."

The guard hesitates but nods and leads us forward. Five mos later and with my ears ringing as loud as the sirens, we enter the monitor room they brought us to when we first arrived. The door closes behind us, muffling the scream of the alarm, but the sound still echoes painfully in my ears.

"Do you know these two?" Rani points to the screens.

My stomach sinks as a camera zooms in on Kora's face. I grit my teeth. She's here. Probably for me. And I doubt it's to apologize.

No, she's probably here because of Serek's message.

A guy with light brown skin and mismatched eyes and markings stands next to her—Sepharon, dressed in black and red, so not from Asheron, where their colors are black and gold, and not from Elja, where their uniforms are white and red. He doesn't seem to be threatening her, though—they stand side by side, looking at the building we're beneath, while the guy speaks to her.

"So, you were here recently?" he asks in Sephari, his deep voice filling the room.

"Oh, shit." Shaw laughs. "Hold on, we know that chick— that's the one Eros was macking with the last time we saw them. The ex-*Avra.*" He grins at me. "Am I right or am I right?"

Rani looks at me. "Are you still romantically involved with her?"

My face warms and I scowl. "No. Not that it matters."

Shaw snickers. "Trouble in paradise?"

I glare at him then glance at Rani. "She's not a threat."

"And the guy?" Rani gestures to the screens. "We haven't monitored him before."

"I don't know him."

She crosses her arms and frowns at the screens.

"What do you want us to do?" a woman in an armored uniform asks. "Do you want us to take them out?"

My heart jolts. I may be blazed at Kora, but that doesn't mean I want her *dead.* "Take them out? You're not going to— they're looking for *me.*"

"I'm sure they are," Rani answers. "But they've come too close, and if they find you, they find us."

"Then let me go. I don't need to be here."

"That's not happening until you agree to our terms."

My chest goes tight. Kora's *right* here, and my way to Asheron is breaths away. I'll lose it if I miss this chance. I can't stay a prisoner. "I can't help you if you keep me here."

"So you're agreeing to help us?"

I cross my arms over my chest. "No, but—"

"Then there's no discussion. If I let you go without your agreement, we're just as stuck as if we'd kept you here. At least with you here, there's a chance you'll develop some sense and agree before it's too late."

Develop some sense? I swallow back the raging words I want to say and take a deep, steadying breath. "Then at least let me talk to them. They don't have to come down here—I can go to them."

"And reveal our location?"

"They tracked me all the way here; I doubt they're going to just give up now."

Rani purses her lips. "They might if they don't find any-thing. They might think it was a dead end."

"Commander, the male is doing something."

We look at the screen. The guy has put on a red and black sand bike helmet and pulled the visor down, looking at the sand beneath his feet. "Oh." He laughs. "Oh, that's clever." Rani stiffens as the guy gestures to Kora. "Go get your helmet and turn on the settings I showed you."

Kora does, then stands next to him, staring at the sand beneath their feet. For a long mo they're both quiet, then Kora pulls off the helmet and looks around. "If they're hiding underground, there must be cameras somewhere."

Murmurs wash over the room and Rani grimaces.

"They can see us?" Shaw frowns. "Those must be some fancy helmets."

"Probably," the guy on the screen says, answering Kora. "Which means they're likely watching us. Maybe even listen-ing . . . I wonder if they speak Sephari."

"The military sect of Eros's camp did, so assume they do," Kora says.

"Let me talk to them," I say again, turning to Rani. "They know we're here, and they're here for me. Let me talk to them."

Rani bites her lip and crosses her arms over her chest, watching the screens. Kora straightens her shoulders. "I know you can hear us—and we're not leaving until we have Eros."

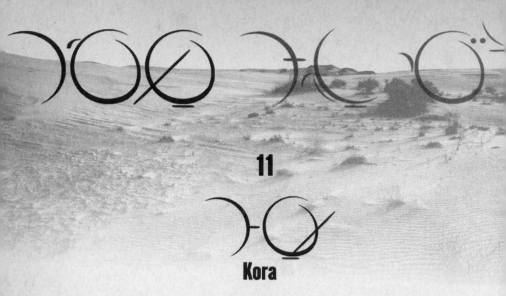

11

Kora

"How did you know?" Deimos asks as we wait for the rebels to emerge. The suns beat down on us, and the angle of the abandoned temple's shadows leave us completely exposed. I try to look at the building as little as possible—I don't want to remember the rough surface on my back, or Eros's fingers scattering embers over my skin.

I especially don't want to remember what I did to him after.

I shake my head, not quite daring to believe we've actually found him until I see him for myself. Alive. I wipe sticky, sweaty hair from my face. "When Eros and I were last here, he said he thought he saw . . . something. At first, I thought maybe he would come back to see what it was, and then when we found the explosion marks . . . " I shake my head. "If I'm truly being honest, I just didn't have any other ideas."

Deimos raises his eyebrows and nods. "That was . . . not much to go on. Are you religious?"

I glance at him and shrug. I'm not sure how to even begin to answer that question. I'd have to know what I believed first.

"Because religious types would probably say that's *so* little to go on, *Kala* must have led you here."

"And what would you say?"

Deimos smiles and looks at the abandoned temple. "I'll reserve my judgment until after we're back in Asheron with Eros in one piece."

We don't have to wait long before the rebels emerge with Eros and one of the redblood boys from his camp who found me in the desert not so long ago. Relief washes over me like a much-needed rain; he's alive, and as far as I can tell, unharmed—at least, not fatally harmed. A large, deep bruise mottles the right side of his bare chest, but I have a feeling that happened long before he came here—during the explosion at the arena, maybe, or in his escape afterward.

Regardless, he's alive, and even though his face is hard and his expression unreadable, it's so good to see him here.

We found him.

A tall woman with skin as dark as Jarek and black hair shaved close to her skull steps beside Eros, her posture strong and confident. She's the one I address first. "Eros needs to return to Asheron. The council is selecting replacements for him as we speak—if we don't hurry, he'll lose his spot on the throne."

"Eros is free to go as soon as he agrees to support us wholeheartedly when he takes the throne," she answers in fluent Sephari.

I frown at Eros; he says something in their language to the woman. She hesitates and answers; he rolls his eyes and gestures to the people who emerged with them—people armed with phasers and likely a host of other weapons.

She sighs, says something that sounds like *fai,* and then Eros and the boy close the distance between us as the red-bloods stay back.

"Hello," Deimos says cheerily. "Good to finally meet you."

Eros arches an eyebrow at him and looks at me. "Friend of yours?"

"Haven't decided yet," I answer.

Deimos places his hand over his heart. "That wounds me. And after all we've been through together!" He turns to the boy and smiles. "I'm Deimos. What's your name?"

The boy doesn't look at him, but mutters, "Mal."

"Great name."

A faint smile echoes over Eros's lips—until he turns to me. And then his smile drops and his expression shutters into something hard and angled. His voice is flat when he asks, "What happened to your wrist?"

I purse my lips. "Roma. I'm fine. It'll take several more sets to heal, but I'll survive."

Eros nods. His eyes are still sharp as a knife blade. "They want me to overthrow the monarchy in place and replace it with something . . . representative. With humans ruling along-side Sepharon."

I stare.

"Bold," Deimos says, and Eros snorts.

"*Bold* is a word for it. *Suicidal* is another."

"Do they not realize the Sepharon would *never* let you do something so drastic?" I ask. "I mean, as *Sira*, your word is law, but not if the people depose you."

"I did try to get that across, but they seem less concerned about that than they are about my leaving without an agreement."

"So agree," Deimos says.

We both stare at him.

"Agree?" I say, my voice a little louder than intended. I step closer to them and quiet my tone. "He can't agree to something so foolish. Can you imagine what an *overthrow* of the world government would cause? Especially now, with everything as fragile as it is?"

"It'd be chaos," Deimos says quietly. "I'm not saying Eros has to do it. But if all they need is Eros's word that he'll work with them . . . well, honor isn't the redblood way, so if he gives his word, we can go and figure the rest out later. We don't have time to play negotiator with them; even if we leave *now*, I'm not sure we'll get back to Asheron in time."

"And you're speaking from what experience, exactly?" Eros asks.

"Ah, right, of course, my apologies." Deimos rests his hand over his heart. "I'm one of the d'A'Sharo *kjo*. So, like Kora, I was raised in politics."

Eros frowns, so I add, "He seems reasonably competent, so far. Though I'm . . . not sure I agree that's a good idea."

"Reasonably competent." Deimos grins. "A bit unenthusiastic, but acceptable, for now."

Eros hesitantly nods. "Well . . . he's right."

"Of course I am," Deimos says, and Eros narrows his eyes at him. Deimos smiles back like a child caught stealing sweets. "My apologies, please continue."

Eros shakes his head, but for just a breath he can't hide his faint smile. "We can't stay here if we want to change anything. But they were the ones who blew up the Arena to save me—going back on my word with a group capable of that kind of destruction wouldn't end well."

"It wouldn't," Deimos agrees, "but we just need time to come up with a way to handle it. For now, giving your word allows us that time."

Eros furrows his brow and glances at me.

My throat thickens; the prospect of giving your word without intending to keep it goes against every fiber of my being. But we're running out of time—we may already be too late—and Eros . . . Eros seems eager to get back to Asheron. To claim his rightful place. Even if I suspect he's angry at me.

I should be relieved, but this isn't right. Your word is your honor, and I never expected Eros to be anything more than reluctant to take such a position of power. But maybe I'm twisting something out of nothing. Maybe I'm worrying too much because I've lost the ability to believe things can go right.

Not everything has to be such a struggle. Maybe, for once, this can be easy, and we can return to Asheron with our *Sira*-to-be before the suns set.

"Okay," I say. "Do what you have to, Eros. Just . . . be careful."

Eros turns back to the rebels. "If you let Mal and me leave right now, and you swear not to follow us, I'll work with you if I take the throne."

The woman lifts both eyebrows; evidently, she was not expecting Eros to agree any more than I was. "You'll support us as *Sira*," she says.

"I'll do everything I can to get fair treatment for humans."

Her eyes narrow. "That's not quite what I said—"

"Your aim is to make us equals," Eros says. "To create a balance so humans and Sepharon can coexist peacefully and on the same societal level. We want the same thing, and I swear to work with you to try to get there."

"Okay," she says. "But I want you to swear to support us. To help us. I want your word you won't turn your back on us—and if you do, I want you to understand we will rip this world apart and make your life a daily torment until we destroy you. I'd hate to have to do it, but you wouldn't betray us without consequences."

Your word is your honor. I glance at Eros. Something like pain flashes across his face—just for a breath, just for a blink. The look he gave me when I turned away from him again and again, when I pushed him away after what we shared here. But he doesn't hesitate, he doesn't say *naï*.

Instead, he nods and says, "I understand. You have my word."

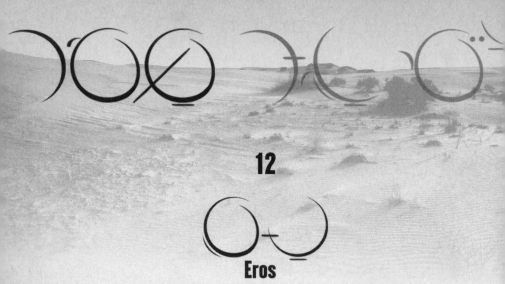

12

Eros

"Former *Sira* Ashen has arrived, and he brought a relative with him: Lejv d'Ona, apparently a cousin of *Sirae* Asha, Roma, and *a'da Kala* Serek. Also, the night of silence is tonight, to honor his passing." The bedroom door closes behind Deimos—the bedroom Mal and I will be sharing, the bedroom that is too large, and even despite the oppressive heat, way too luxurious for either one of us.

Well. Maybe not either one of us. Mal sure seems to be enjoying the layer of pillows on the floating bed. But between the massive, pillow-topped bed, the painted walls, the sheer curtains rustling in front of the window, the decorative statues, a giant glass floating over the north wall twice as long as I am tall, a bookshelf I won't touch, and the plush throw rugs scattered across the deep, stone floor, I'm drowning in luxury. And it's all for me—some thin guy who looked like he smelled something rotten when he looked at me, assigned me this room when I arrived with Kora. That he was so obviously unhappy to see me kinduv makes me wonder if this is supposed to be a lesser room compared to some of the others.

"A cousin," Kora says. "So Lejv has a legitimate claim."

Deimos nods. "He does, though if Eros is who *a'da Kala* Serek says he is—"

"He is."

"—then Eros's claim is superior."

I'm not sure what he keeps saying before Serek—"a" doesn't mean anything on its own, as far as I know, and "da" means "from," but *from Kala* doesn't make sense in context. I'm too tired to try to figure it out. I sit next to Mal and brush his overgrown, fiery hair out of his face. He's exhausted, and asleep—finally—and he has to be terrified here, in a place where people like him are usually slaves or prisoners. But he's safe. Eight sets ago, I never would have imagined it was possible for any member of my family to be here—in the Sepharon world capital, in the palace, asleep on a bed meant for royals, safe.

"I won't let anything happen to you," I whisper.

"So we verify again, that's not a problem," Kora says. Just her voice sets me on edge, skimming over the surface of my broiling blood. Does she realize how much she hurt me when she turned her back on me in the desert? She might as well have told me I'm worth as little as people before her made me believe. Does she even care? "In fact, Niro told me they were already in the process of confirming Eros's claim."

"It doesn't look like they've made any formal announcement yet," Deimos says. "Which means they've probably already verified it's true and just don't want to bring attention to it."

Every muscle in my body is heavy—I want to sink next to Mal and sleep and sleep and never wake up. I can't remember the last time I had a full night's rest—before Dima's dungeon, maybe. Which was how long ago? Seven sets? More?

And to think I kept my mouth shut for her while her brother tortured me.

"So then we need to talk to the Council," Kora says. "Have they gathered yet?"

"Sulten said they're gathered now," Deimos answers. "Everyone expects them to announce they've chosen Lejv as the primary candidate."

I need to sleep, but there's little point in trying—not unless I want to watch Jessa and Aren and Nia and Day and Nol and Esta die again, and again, and again. Not unless I want to hear those screams, not unless I want to dream of the white room, dream of not dreaming and needing to dream, and the pain, and full-bodied exhaustion—

"Eros." I jump—my heart races and everything inside me screams *move*—but it's just Kora. Standing in front of me, arching an eyebrow. She must have just said something. Did she ask something?

"I don't—what?"

"The Emergency Council has gathered; we need to speak to them together to stake your claim to the throne officially, now that you're here."

She's really not going to apologize. She probably doesn't even think she did anything wrong. I swallow fire and press my palms against my thighs. Harder. Forget her. Focus on the conversation. Apologies don't matter right now—these blazing politics do. "The who?"

"The Emergency Council—they're the remaining former *Avrae* and *Sira*. They came down from Dura Kol to oversee the installation of the new *Sira*."

Her words gloss over me, fuzzy and out of focus. Drowned out by the part of me that hates what she did to me. Emergency

Council. Former rulers—and *Sira*? Focus. "So . . . Serek and Roma's father?"

"Your grandfather, *sha*," Kora says. "He's a hard man; I don't expect he'll be happy to see you."

Because stars forbid my Sepharon blood relatives didn't actively hate me down to my cells. "Of course not," I mumble.

"But not like he can do anything to you," Deimos says. "We've already figured if they haven't announced anything about the genetic check, it's because they confirmed what *a'da Kala* Serek said, which means they have to consider your claim seriously."

"So they hate me, and I'm in their way."

"Get used to it," Kora says. "You're not going to be the most popular *Sira,* especially not at first. But that's only natural; it's a big change for a lot of people. They're not sure how to handle you, but they'll learn. We'll teach them together you're the best man for the throne."

Get used to it—as if it were that easy. But of course, it would be, for her. My mind swims with words, with images of thrones and riots, of guards marching toward me and the complete blackness of the dungeons below. Of that fucken throne room with all that gold and black and me.

This is what I'm supposed to do. I'm supposed to campaign for a throne I don't want—I'm supposed to throw myself into proving to everyone I'm the best one for the job, and I'm supposed to believe it.

But I don't believe it. I came here for Mal, and pretending this is what I want might be too much. Maybe it would've been better for everyone if I'd died in that arena.

"I think . . ." Deimos says softly, glancing at Kora. "Maybe he needs some rest. He's had a long couple of sets."

Day would think I'm such a traitor being here. I glance at Mal—does he think I've betrayed them by coming here? By becoming one of them?

I'm not completely one of them, but I have to take on the part of me that is, and I'm not sure I'm ready. I'm not sure I'll ever be ready—I don't want to forget who I am; I don't want to become someone I'm not. But I'm both. I've always been both; I just don't really know what that means.

Kora is arguing with Deimos. Because of course she is. "He can rest when we're done speaking to the Council. They need to know he's here, Deimos. They need to know he intends to hold on to his claim and fight for it."

Deimos sighs. "Right, and I agree—but maybe it'd be better if you approached them first yourself—"

"*Better?*"

"For Eros. He just—he doesn't seem like he's ready to go in there set to kill, you know? And if they see him washed out like this . . ."

"He'll be fine. Right? Eros?" Kora looks at me expectantly—always fucken expecting *something* from me—and I just—I can't focus on this. I can't focus on any of this.

"Mal needs medical attention." The words roll off my lips and stumble into the air. Kora stares at me, and Deimos glances at Mal passed out on the bed. "He's partially blind," I add. "The nanites . . . the Remnant doc thinks it's brain damage from the nanite attack. She said nanites might be able to fix it."

"Did she also mention the nanites are dead?" Deimos asks. "Which is why we're standing here sweating our asses off?"

I suppress a groan. "*Sha*, but—"

"Deimos is right," Kora says brusquely. "Once our medical system is rebuilt, that's something you can discuss with the medics, but right now there isn't much anyone can do."

It doesn't surprise me she doesn't care about Mal, either, because why would she? She only cares about herself. But it doesn't stop my chest from tightening or my pulse from drumming louder. "And how long will that take?"

"A long time, unfortunately," Deimos answers. "Cycles, probably. Part of your job as *Sira* will be figuring out how to fill the gap in the meantime, but . . . you don't need to worry about that just yet. Let's get you on the throne first . . . starting tomorrow."

"Tomorrow?" Kora yelps. "The Council is meeting *now*. We should be there *already.*"

"I agree," Deimos says. "But Eros is clearly not in the right frame of mind to face them now, and if he goes in there seeming weak, it'll only damage his position."

"But—"

"Look," Deimos says a little more forcefully. "I know you think you know what's best because you were formerly an *Avra*, but I was *also* raised in politics, and while no one ever expects I'll rule myself given the number of brothers I have ahead of me, I was taught how to maneuver the courts all the same. How we play this is important—and how Eros is perceived right now will make or break his chance to convince the Council he's the right man for the job. If we mess this up now, he's done."

Kora frowns. "It was one thing when Eros wasn't here—then my representing him alone was the best that I could do. But now that he is, the Council won't take lightly to his refusing to make an appearance. It'll be useless for me to go in there alone."

He crosses his arms over his chest. "It won't. Tell them Eros sent you as his representative—he's had a long journey and he's resting; he'll make his formal appearance tomorrow. But in the meantime, you're there to make sure his claim is considered, because he *is* here and he *is* ready to take the throne." Deimos glances at me and grimaces. "Or . . . so we'll tell them, anyway. We'll handle reality tomorrow."

Maybe I should be irritated they're talking for me and making decisions about me. Maybe it should bother me the way Deimos looks at me with something like pity. But the truth is, he's not wrong—I'm *not* ready for this today. The world is rolling past me like I'm not here, and I can barely focus on their conversation, let alone what I could possibly say to the Council. At least Deimos gets that.

Kora looks at me, supposed concern etched into her furrowed brow, the downward tilt to her lips, the stiffness of her posture. "What do you think, Eros?" she says, softening her voice.

"*Sha*," I say, and my voice sounds tired, so blazing tired, even to me. "I'll face everyone tomorrow."

"I don't like this," Kora says.

"You've made that clear," Deimos answers. "But this is the best we can do with what we have."

Kora shakes her head and turns to the door, but even as it slides open, her words sink like stones in my gut. "I can't help you if you cut me off at the knees, Eros. Remember that."

The door thuds closed behind her. Deimos sighs and runs a hand through his shaggy dark hair. "You look like you need rest but aren't going to get any anytime soon."

I grimace. "Probably not."

"Well I'm starving, and you two likely are as well, so let's find some food, *sha*?"

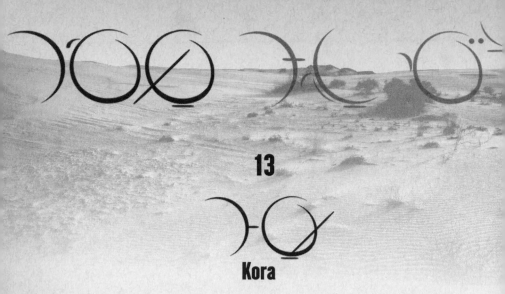

13

Kora

Walking down the cool, stone halls with guards as my shadows, all I can think about is I still haven't apologized to Eros.

And that last argument didn't help.

I sigh and refrain from pinching the bridge of my nose. I can't look worried or stressed with guards on my back—I have to project confidence I don't have. But I should have taken some time to pull Eros aside privately and clear the air with him, and I didn't. I dove right into the task because . . . well . . .

It's easier to think about politics—to argue about politics—than to admit my colossal mistake. It was easier to be irritated by his lack of cooperation than to acknowledge I probably hurt him. Than to admit I don't deserve his forgiveness.

The truth is, I'm terrified I'll apologize and he won't want to hear it. What if my saying I'm sorry confirms it's far too late to make amends? I'm not certain how I would handle that rejection, even though it's exactly what I'd deserve after the way I rejected him.

I need to apologize. But the thought of bringing up the conversation sends my stomach spiraling to my toes.

As I near the gold-engraved doors to the private meeting room, I shake my head. I can worry about when to apologize to Eros later. Now I need to focus.

The five men making up the Council scowl as I enter, not that I expected anything else. Unlike most of the open windows in the palace, the meeting room's walls are a specially tinted glass—smooth and clear, so from the inside it appears as though there are no walls at all and the view into the large palace garden is beautiful, but on the outside, the glass is so deeply purple it's impossible to view inside. The afternoon light filters into the room and reflects off the polished tile floor—every tile a unique, shiny swirl of gold and silver, white, and black. In the center of the room is a long, floating table with a large glass embedded in the middle that can be used to project whatever is relevant into the air. Today, however, the projection is off.

Four of the men here I'd already met—the former *Avrae* who were there the set before, Tamus, Hala, Ruen, and Oniks. The only woman, Lija da Daïvi, must have arrived this morning, along with the man with the most power on this council, former *Sira* Ashen. Like her son, Daven, who I met before everything went to the Void at my lifecycle celebration not so long ago, Lija's eyes are that particular combination of green centers, thick hazel, and dark blue borders. Unlike Daven, however, her long hair betrays her northern roots—it's so light, it nearly appears white, like the purest shade of the *aska* stone that made up the temple back in Elja. Combined with her smooth, light brown skin, she's quite beautiful.

Ashen, meanwhile . . . it's startling how much he looks like Serek. His long, lean figure; the slightly lighter tint of his brown skin, his pointed jaw and chiseled nose—it's clear who Serek took after in terms of appearances. Which is unsettling, given Ashen's reputation for being much closer in personality to his violent son, Roma.

"*Riase*," I say, bowing as I address the former rulers by their most respectful title. "I apologize for interrupting. I'm Kora Mikale Nel—"

"We know who you are, Kora d'Elja," Ashen says gravely. "What's more important is what makes you think you have the right to barge in here uninvited."

I clasp my hands behind my back. "Of course. I just wanted to be certain the Council was aware Eros—the son of Asha *ana da Kala* Serek spoke of—has arrived in Asheron and intends to pursue his right to the throne. He sent me here as his representative, to formally submit his candidacy to the Council here today."

"His right," Ashen says flatly. "He's a half-blood. He has no rights."

I open my mouth to answer, but Lija da Daïvi beats me to a response. "Actually, as you mentioned at the beginning of this meeting, Eros's genetic claim has been verified by Asheron's best geneticists. He is, to our knowledge, the only son of *Sira* Asha, who was taken before his time."

I nod. "Had Asheron been aware of his existence when *Sira* Asha was killed, I don't doubt he would have been installed as the next *Sira* as soon as he came of age, but of course we can't turn back the cycles."

"*Kala* knows what my son was thinking when he chose to . . . procreate with a redblood." Ashen grimaces. "I can't even begin to imagine the circumstances that brought him to believe it was a good—or even merely acceptable—idea. But the fact of the matter is, we don't know what he intended with the half-blood. Whatever it was, however, we can be certain it wasn't to install a halfbreed as *Sira*."

The other men mutter their agreement, but Lija doesn't look so convinced. "I don't believe we can say anything about *Sira* Asha's intentions for certain, as he was killed before he could make any formal announcement."

Ashen pulls his shoulders back, his voice confident and calm. "Had he intended to make the half-blood his inheritor, he would have announced it formally in Asheron the set of the half-blood's birth. As he didn't—"

"*Actually*," I cut in, "before *ana da Kala* Serek was killed, we'd determined *Sira* Asha was killed the set of his son's birth. *Sira* Asha was murdered not far from the capital—it's not a stretch to imagine he was perhaps returning to Asheron to make the formal announcement himself."

"This is nonsense," Hala d'Inara says. "The redbloods don't even understand our calendar—it'd be nearly impossible to determine the set of the half-blood's birth based off their rudimentary capture of time."

"It would have been difficult," I say, "but it was made easier when Eros told us he was born on the last full solar eclipse, over eighteen cycles ago."

Ashen rolls his eyes. "Of course he would make that claim—everyone knows the night my son was murdered by those rebels."

"But Eros didn't—the redbloods have no reason or resource to keep remembrance of our tragedies. He was shocked to learn he was born the same night as *Sira* Asha's assassination."

"Of course he was," Ashen answers dryly. "As shocked,

I'm sure, as he pretended to be upon *discovering* he was sup-posedly next in line for the *Sirae* throne."

"Eros had no idea until the nanites my people injected him with reacted to the ones disguising the true color of his eyes, and we flushed his system to save him."

"How convenient."

"Regardless of whether he was aware of his lineage," Lija da Daïvi says, "*ana da Kala* Serek wasn't wrong when he claimed Eros has a legitimate birthright this Council needs to consider when determining the next *Sira*. In fact, if he wasn't a half-blood, we wouldn't be having this meeting at all—he would have been crowned the moment his genetics were confirmed."

"Which doesn't matter," Tamus d'Ona answers, "because he *is* a half-blood, which all but erases his legitimacy because we have no way of knowing his father's intentions when he chose to have a son with a redblood."

Lija sighs impatiently. "Asha's intentions wouldn't have mattered if Eros's mother weren't a redblood."

"But she was," Ashen says. "Which means my son's inten-tions are the *only* thing that matter—but as we have no way of raising the dead to ask him, we'll have to decide the mat-ter ourselves." He turns to me, spearing me with the golden centers of his intense gaze. "If the boy is so eager to claim the throne, why is he not here to do it himself? Why send a dis-graced girl thrown from her own territory to speak for him?"

Every royal turns to me as my body flushes with prickling heat. I clench my fists behind my back and force myself not to glare, not to cry, not to rage with anger or lose control. I am a royal and today, Eros's representative and his only chance to force the Council not to disqualify him outright.

I can do this. I must do this.

Strength. Power. Respect.

Ah—respect.

"It's true my brother framed me for a crime I didn't commit and forced me to flee my own territory. But I am not disgraced—I am a former *Avra* just like many of you, and I hold a right to be in this room and speak for my future *Sira*. Eros will make his first official appearances tomorrow, but today he's had a long journey and needs to rest. He wants to be his best when he faces the Council, so out of respect to all of you, he has chosen to send me in his stead rather than approach you unprepared."

Lija nods. "A reasonable request; how many of us have at one time or another sent a representative in our stead rather than disrespect our host by arriving exhausted?"

"A suitable representative maybe," Tamus says. "Not a failed *Avra*."

"Perhaps if he'd been here with you, at least," Hala d'Inara adds. "Exhausted or not, if he didn't have a suitable representative, he should have either come himself or approached us with you."

Their words sting, but they're not wrong—I wanted Eros to come with me. I knew they wouldn't take me seriously, not alone, but he . . .

Well. Judging by the way this conversation is going, I suspect the recording I was originally going to use would only further sour the mood. And if I'm being true, nothing I could have prepared with or without him would have likely changed their resistance. Still, I wish he'd come with me so they had one less argument against him.

I can only hope he'll be better prepared to face everyone

tomorrow. Another refusal could spell the end of his campaign before it ever begins, assuming I manage to pull this off at all.

"These circumstances aren't ideal," I say, "but they're not unprecedented either. Eros has the right to choose a representative when he isn't prepared to arrive himself, as was the case. He trusts me, and I him, and tomorrow he'll begin to show all of you why I believe him to be the next *Sira*, just as *ana da Kala Sira-kaï* Serek proclaimed."

"So be it," Ashen says. "But this position will not be *handed* to him regardless of what my son announced globally, and what any genetic test may claim. The test and my son's sacrifice are the only reasons I'm allowing the half-blood to be considered at all, but the throne will go to the best one for the job—and I'm nowhere near convinced your boy even begins to satisfy the credentials for the position."

"I understand." I bow to the former *Sira* and *Avrae*. "Thank you for your consideration in this delicate matter."

But as I turn away and stride back to the door, Ashen's words tumble over and over in my mind, repeating a truth I did not speak, a truth I fear Ashen knows anyway.

If Eros doesn't shape up and start taking this seriously, I'm not certain he'll be the best one for the job, either.

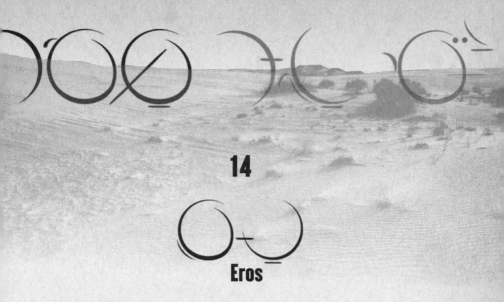

14

Eros

I keep waiting for the point where exhaustion forces me to shut down. Where my scattered mos of rest between staring at the ceiling with a rioting mind, and tossing and turning in my enormous bed—never quite comfortable despite the ocean of pillows—leave me more exhausted than I was before I first closed my eyes. Between the moments when my mind gives in and I snatch snippets of sleep full of blood, explosions, fire, smoke, and so, so much death (Nol—Esta—Day—Jessa—Nia—Aren, bits of people splashed across Jol's arena).

I keep waiting for the moment when my mind says *enough* and forces me into a deep, dreamless sleep, but no matter how much I want it, it doesn't come.

The edges of pink and blue have just touched the horizon when I step outside and breathe in the warm desert morning while touching the edges of Aren's bracelet on my wrist. Some guards follow, but no one questions me as I push one step after another, faster, faster, as my toes dig into the white, gritty sand, so much harsher than the smooth red powder from home, but somehow better than the cold, metal flooring of the Remnant.

This isn't my desert or my sand, but at least I'm outside and despite the guards shadowing me here and there, have the freedom to go where I want, whenever I want. At least I'm under the same twin suns echoing of home.

The palace complex is larger than Kora's was in Elja—there are multiple courtyards and gardens, a library and records building, a museum; shops selling sweets, clothes, shoes, perfumes, books, ports, gadgets, decorative rugs and vases and plants, more clothes, more perfumes, more shoes; a section just for merchant stalls; statues and fountains and perfectly placed plants everywhere; and near the front gate, a line of red tile embedded in the ground, marking some kinduv security sweep always heavily covered with guards.

The palace complex is its own microcity within the city of Asheron. Everything is clean and maintained; the patrons setting up their shops barely spare me a passing glance as I jog by. I'm not sure if it's confidence in their government or duty that keeps them continuing business as usual even when the air is thick with uncertainty, but I can't help but think this is what Vejla should have looked like back in Elja. This is what stability looks like.

I'm about halfway through my first circuit around the perimeter of the enormous complex when someone familiar comes jogging toward me. My body tenses—my breath's stiffer, shallower, my heart pounding harder—and I shouldn't be reacting like this. Deimos has only ever been nice to me. But I can't stop the edges of fear racing through me as he nears with that all-too familiar smile.

It's not him, I remind myself, because I'm not—I'm not freaking out because of him. *It's anyone. It's my brain. It's me.* My hypersensitive, asshole brain making me flinch and setting my heart racing at the slightest thing.

I hate it.

"*Or'denja!*" Deimos says cheerfully, slowing to turn and continue alongside me. It takes me a moment to parse the words from his accent—the vowels drawn out and consonants sharper than I'm used to. *Or'denja.* Good morning.

"*Denna,*" I answer stiffly.

If he notices my lack of enthusiasm, he doesn't show it. "It doesn't surprise me you're a morning runner, too. Always made me the odd man out back home—in A'Sharaf, the mornings are full of merchants and sailors all over the docks, which makes a morning run more complicated and dangerous in theory, I suppose, so most of the royals wait until nightfall when curfew sends everyone inside and the sea breeze tints the shadows. It's very pleasant, actually, if you don't mind how terribly boring it is . . ."

He smiles at me, amusement glinting in his mismatched eyes. I guess we're having a conversation now. "Do you not have a protected complex for royalty in A'Sharaf?" I ask.

"Oh, we do, but as a family we try to make ourselves visible as much as possible so the people get to know us. My brothers frequent local taverns and events, for example, and my parents sometimes shop at the commoner marketplace. Shows the people we don't consider ourselves above them, you know?"

"You don't?"

Deimos laughs. "Well, depends who you ask, I suppose. *I* don't, but I've never had any grand delusions of inheriting the throne, either."

"Even though you're a *kai*?"

"I'm also the youngest of eight."

"Ah."

He laughs breathily. "Traditionally, the people of A'Sharo—royalty included—have very large families. I had a friend growing up who was one of sixteen."

"*Sixteen*?"

"*Sha*, even I agree that's a bit excessive."

The laugh tumbles out of my lips before I register it coming. Deimos grins like he's just accomplished some huge victory, and maybe he has—it's been too long since I was relaxed enough to laugh.

"How about you?" he asks. "How many siblings?"

And just like that, my brief smile slips away.

"Ah, *kafra*," Deimos curses. "I know that look. I'm sorry. You don't have to say anymore."

"I . . . it's okay." I force a sigh. "I had an older brother. He was a good man—I wouldn't be alive without the skills he taught me growing up."

"Skills like . . . desert survival?"

"Well, *naï*, my father taught me that—but Day taught me how to fight, how to defend myself, and to always stay vigilant and pay attention to everything. You never know when a minor detail may tip you off something isn't right."

"Good experience to have, especially in your position."

I nod. We jog in silence for a few mos, our feet pushing through the cool sand. That's another different thing—the red sand back home never got *hot*, but it was nearly always warm unless it got wet. Here, even as the morning heat bakes my skin, the sand is cool under my toes.

"*Ej*, you know, when we're done with this jog, we should spar."

I glance at Deimos. "Sure, I guess. How much experience do you have?"

"I'm a bounty hunter."

I arch an eyebrow. "An *Avra-kaï* and a bounty hunter. Interesting combination."

He laughs. "Came in handy when Kora and I were tracking you down."

"I'm sure . . . thank you, by the way."

He shrugs. "You don't have to thank me. It was the right thing to do—and besides, it was way more interesting than pretending I'm even remotely interested in listening to my brother advocate for a spot on the throne he'll never get."

I snort. "So much faith in your family." But jokes aside, he's making light of a decision that can't have been that easy. Kora mentioned they missed Serek's funeral to look for me. I'd feel bad, but they knew what they were choosing—and in any case, Serek wanted me here. I guess it was kinduv a different way of honoring him. I think he'd get it.

Deimos snickers. "Well when former *Sira* Ashen arrived with his nephew, it was clear to everyone the bidding war was over for them. It'll be between Lejv and you now."

"Great," I mumble.

"I don't envy your position. It won't be easy establishing yourself as a candidate to take seriously, not with all the prejudice and politics working against you."

Not to mention, I don't even know how to establish myself to begin with. Or how any of this will be decided. Are there tests I have to pass? Speeches I have to give? I have no idea, and I'm not sure what he expects me to say—does he think I'll argue or show false confidence? Does he want me to verbally agree to the depressing truth that I'm probably wasting my time here? I don't know, but it doesn't matter—I don't need to say a thing because he's right.

It doesn't take much longer to get back outside the palace, at which point Deimos turns to me and smiles.

"So. How about that sparring match?"

I'm a sweaty, aching mess when I check on Mal, but to my surprise, he's not alone—Kora is sitting on the edge of his bed as they chat quietly. Great.

Mal startles as I open the door and squints at me. "Uncle Eros?"

"Yeah." The door whooshes closed behind me, and Mal grins.

"I could tell because of how you walk," he says proudly. "Kinduv like a soldier but . . . not. It's hard to explain."

I force a smile and don't look at Kora. "That's good. Everything okay?"

"*Sha*," Kora says. "I was just telling him about the sweets they sell in the complex. Apparently he didn't eat last night, so he still hasn't had a taste of real Asheron food."

I blink. "Mal, you didn't eat last night?" How didn't I notice? Deimos had gotten us some food and I was out of it but . . . I'd thought I'd seen him eat. Or maybe he just moved his food around his plate. I guess there *was* plenty left over . . .

He shrugs. "I wasn't hungry—I was too nervous."

I frown. "Okay, well . . . please make sure you eat today."

"Oh, don't you worry," Kora says, "food for *everyone* is first on the agenda. We'll eat in here so we can discuss the plan."

Something twists and twists inside me, like the overtightening of a string. Something that thrills around my heart and clenches tightly in my chest, but I force a smile and say, "Okay. I'm going to get cleaned up. Are you okay, Mal?"

"You don't have to baby me," he says. "I'm lying in a bed big enough for four people with a pretty girl offering me awesome-sounding food. I'm fine."

Kora laughs. "Go clean up, Eros. I've got it handled."

I don't laugh, but I do leave.

This washroom doesn't have an in-ground, filled-to-the-brim bath thing like the room Kora was in last time we were at the Asheron palace, but two, thick, parallel stone slabs about two body-lengths long and wide stick out of the far wall. I'd noticed them when we arrived yesterday but didn't pay much attention until now. The rock slabs are far enough apart that a very tall, grown man could sit on the bottom slab and still have plenty of room above his head. I wave my arm in the space between and jump back as water comes pouring out of the top slab.

Okay.

I try it again, this time resisting the urge to step away as water rains over my arm. And that's what it's like—a heavy, warm rain, like what we get maybe once or twice a year back home. There are more buttons at the back, and I'm guessing they activate soap and what not, so this has to be where I'm supposed to clean up. Which is fine. This is fine. Not a big deal.

So why is my heart racing and stomach clenching?

Deep breath in, deep breath out. I strip out of my sweaty clothes and slide between the two slabs. Water dumps over my head and—

Ice and burning and screaming and pain—

I jolt off the slabs and hit the ground hard, panting, and shivering, and fuck.

Fuck.

I can't—I can't do that. I press my palms against my eyes, and I'm not going to think about that white room, that icy water, those burning cuffs or the screaming, the screaming—I'm not. I'm not.

Inhale, exhale. I force myself up, wrapping my shaking arms around my chest. There's a fuzzy blanket-thing folded near the slabs, so I grab that, wet it, and wipe down. It's not great, but it's something. I'm not using those slabs again.

That done, I change into a new outfit of black and gold pants and the strange, soft, black shoes people wear around here. I pause before the door—deep breaths, don't want to look as edged as I feel so I'll bury it, I can bury this—and walk into my bedroom holding the shirt they'd set aside for me, too.

"I'm not wearing this," I say, holding up the cloth. "The collar practically goes up to my ears, and it looks as ridiculous as it feels."

Deimos laughs as Kora smirks at me. "That's the fashion here," he says. "I like to call them neck braces."

I'm not sure when Deimos got here, but I'm kinduv glad he is. He seems to be a good Kora buffer. "I don't see you wearing one."

"Ah, but I'm representing the much more practical and attractive A'Sharon fashion. It isn't my aim to become the next *Sira*."

"Can I see it?" Mal holds out his hand with a smile. I give him the shirt and he holds it up in front of him, squinting. "It's black, isn't it?"

"Yeah." I smile a little. "Sorry—that probably doesn't help."

"I can kinduv make it out . . ." Mal tilts his head, then sighs and drops it beside him. "But even in the middle between patches where I can see best, it's like trying to see black through black, static-y gauze."

"I had a cousin with similar vision difficulties," Deimos says.

I blink. "You did?"

"Sure," Deimos says. "Genetic defect—he could see sections but had spots of darkness obscuring his vision. He had a tutor who taught him how to use a walking stick. Once you're *Sira*, I'm sure you could get one assigned to Mal."

I sit beside them as Kora hands me a plate of pastries. I still don't look at her. The food looks and smells amazing, but . . . "But that was before the nanite collapse, right? So couldn't they have just . . . fixed it?"

"Nanites can't fix everything," Deimos answers. "The spots of darkness were with the best correction they could give him. Too much tampering with the eyes and you risk scar tissue and a host of other problems. Same goes for other sensitive organs, like the brain—sometimes the 'correction' is more dangerous than just letting the body be."

Deimos pops a pastry into his mouth, chews, swallows, and shrugs. "Besides, not every disabled person *wants* to be cured. My cousin, for example, has told me he's happy with the level of correction he has, and even if he had the option to do more safely, he wouldn't. It's a part of him."

I glance at Mal, but he seems more concerned about the food he's about to eat than his potentially permanent blindness.

"Well I guess there's no point trying to tell these apart," Mal says, picking up a pastry at random.

"Trust me, man." Deimos smiles. "Everything Kora picked out for you is as amazing as *kaf*—"

I clear my throat.

"—*rik?*" Deimos finishes, grinning as he warps the swear into a drink.

But Mal just gives me a withering look. "I know what *kafra* means."

I laugh. "Sorry."

"And fucken."

"Yeah, I—"

"And—"

"Don't baby you," I say quickly. "Got it. Sorry."

He grumbles and takes a big bite of pastry, then smiles as the sweet glaze coats his lips. Kora breaks a flaky roll in half, revealing a center full of some kinduv purple gel-ish filling. She catches me watching her and offers me half. I take it and taste the filling. It's painfully sweet and fruity. I like it.

"So," Kora says, "we need to talk business."

Even though I'd prefer she walked out of this room and never came back, she's right, so I don't argue.

"You need to make an appearance today—during the evening meal formal tonight will be your best opportunity to meet everyone and establish your intention to campaign for the throne. Before that, you have a lot to learn about how to present yourself and face the other royals. You aren't a subordinate, not anymore, so you need to act confident . . ."

Her lecture slips into a low drone; the pressure of a brainblaze wraps around my temples. Her words drift distantly around me; the smoky edges of a bonfire grazing my skin. A fire burning the bodies of my loved ones, lifting their ashes and spirits to the stars. The crackle of flame pops and snaps in my ears; the fire licking at the edges of camp, setting tents ablaze and scorching sand as I stumble through smoke, pressing the headscarf tighter against my mouth and nose as the choked air burns my eyes. I'm running, and Day and Esta and Nol are too far away, and I trip over a body, and I don't look to see who it is, and it doesn't matter who it is, it doesn't matter that I'm running, it doesn't matter that I grabbed a phaser because it won't fire, and Day will look at me, and they'll shoot him right in front of me.

Day collapses again, and again, and again, in every glimpse of a dream, and it shouldn't hurt so much anymore, it should be a dull ache by now but every time, every fucken time hurts like the first.

I didn't save him. I didn't save anyone. I tried again, and again, and every time I slip into a dream, I try to change it but it never changes, it'll never change, nearly everyone I love is dead and—

"Em, Eros? Hold on, Kora, we lost him." Deimos snaps his fingers in front of my face and chuckles when I startle. "You okay, there?"

Heart pounding, deep breaths, muscles coiled and ready to—stars I am *so* edged. "Fine," I mumble. I'm fine. I'm fine. If I say it enough, I might just believe it.

"Did you really start wakedreaming while I'm explaining important information?" Kora asks. She sounds irritated. I don't care.

"I don't think he's slept well," Deimos says. Why is he apologizing for me? I barely even know him.

"It doesn't matter how much he has or hasn't slept," Kora snaps, turning her sharp gaze on me. "You're a breath away from losing the nomination, Eros. They're not going to just hand it to you—you have to fight for it, but you're not trying at all. You'll never be *Sira* if you continue these barely-there attempts. They'll give the nomination to someone else."

The fire churns inside me, bubbling behind my lips. I won't lose it in front of Mal. But—wait, there are crumbs on Mal's plate, but he isn't sitting in our circle anymore. I glance around the room. Where did he go? How long did I lose myself?

"He's not even paying attention," Kora has definitely crossed from irritated into blazed territory. Still don't care. If anything, it's about time; give her a taste of what I've been feeling since the mo I saw her again.

"Where's Mal?" I ask Deimos.

"Washroom." Deimos smiles softly. "He hasn't bathed yet."

"Has anyone showed him how to use it? He can't read Sephari any better than I can—"

"You can't be serious," Kora interrupts. "Eros—I need you to *focus*."

"I need to take care of—"

"*Naï*, you don't. I understand you're concerned for your nephew, but he's not as infantile as you seem to think he is. Let him figure it out on his own; in the meantime, what you *need* to do is listen to me and prepare to face everyone tonight."

I scowl. "He's half-blind—you're asking him to *figure it out* when he can't even see *and* he's never used those blazing things in there."

"*Kala alejha*." Kora presses her fingertips into her temples. "It's like you *want* them to give the nomination to someone else!"

"Maybe I do!" The words explode out of me before I can stop them. I jump to my feet, blood raging like a drumbeat in my ears. "You've never *once* asked me if this is what I want. You've never once stopped to consider maybe I don't *want* to be *Sira*. Maybe I just want to live in fucken peace away from all these blazing politics and people who don't even want me alive, let alone ruling the blazing planet."

Deimos grimaces, but Kora stands and steps right up to me, pressing her finger into my chest. "You really think I haven't considered that?"

"Sure doesn't seem like it."

"It doesn't *matter*, Eros. Of course you'd like to live in peace somewhere, but that's a fantasy you will *never* have. You are a half-blood—worse, a half-blood with birthright to the throne—and I guarantee the first move any of those men would make as *Sira* would be to hunt you down and kill you. So if you want to live, and you want your nephew to live—and I'm assuming you do—then you'll swallow whatever resistance you have to the idea and do your *kafran* job."

The raging in my ears turns to heat spreading across my face and chest and slamming me with an energy that makes me want to scream. But I don't—instead I switch to English and say, "Fuck you."

"I don't know what that means," Kora says flatly, "but unless it translates to '*sha*, Kora, you're right and I'm sorry for being a stubborn child,' I don't care."

Someone clears their throat behind me—I expect it to be

Deimos, but when I turn around, Mal is poking his head out of the bathroom.

"Sorry to interrupt," he says quietly. "I need some help, Uncle Eros."

I don't hesitate—I cross the room in several long strides while Kora curses behind me.

"You are worse than a child!" she seethes. "At least children learn to be obedient!"

I show her how much I care with my middle finger—she probably doesn't know the gesture, but too bad. The door closes behind me, cutting off her tirade, and for a moment—just a moment—I can breathe.

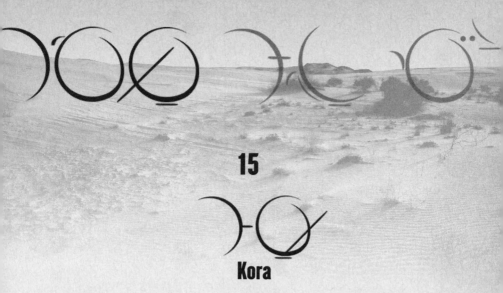

15

Kora

While Eros regresses to the behavior of a five-cycle-old child, I check on the formidable competition. An official announcement hasn't been made yet when I return to the dining hall, which is mostly empty, so I wander until I find the royals lounging in the palace courtyard. The men ignore me as I enter—most notably Niro, who stares at me and then turns to Lejv, who is standing in front of one of two fountains, sharing some story about his travels across the territories, from what I gather. But Aleija looks at me, mutters something to her wife, catches my gaze, and nods to the archway I just came through.

I step back into the hall, and moments later she enters beside me. "Let's walk."

I follow her down the long hallway passing beautifully engraved tiles and potted desert plants—everything from flowers to carefully manipulated cactuses. We continue in silence at first, until the voices and laughter from the men we left behind die away.

"How are things going with Eros?" Aleija asks.

I sigh. "It's been . . . trying. He's overwhelmed with every-thing, I suspect. It's a lot to take in—just a couple sets ago, he

was here about to be executed, and then the nanite attack . . .
I haven't asked, and he hasn't volunteered information, but
his redblood nephew is with him, so I'm assuming they both
lost more family."

"*Kala'niasha*," Aleija says softly, offering her condolences.

I nod. "I'm trying to be patient with him, but we're running out of time. If he doesn't cooperate tonight . . . I don't
know what will happen."

"Lejv will be selected without competition," Aleija says
simply. "And Eros will likely be arrested again as soon as the
coronation is over, if he is unwise enough to still be here."

"And if he isn't still here, he'll be hunted," I add.

"Most likely."

I bite my lip. "I tried to explain that to him, but he just . . .
it's like it doesn't even matter to him."

"Then maybe he's not meant for the position," Aleija
says. "Which is a shame, because he would have had my support. And I think, with some careful maneuvering, he could
have Simos's support, as well."

Now *that* is unexpected. "Truly? I wouldn't have thought
Simos would support a half-blood."

She sighs and touches the edge of her dark braid. "In
most circumstances, he probably wouldn't, but he and Lejv
have an unpleasant history. As they're both from Ona, this
isn't the first time they've crossed circles, and Lejv has been
. . . well, he was less than polite when Simos married Ejren."

I grimace. "I thought most in Ona were accepting of
lijarae."

"Most are. Lejv just isn't one of them."

I shake my head. "Is that the reason you're willing to support Eros, as well?"

"Not the only reason, but it does factor into my decision, *sha*."

I nod. "Well, I haven't given up on Eros yet. He just needs more time to process. *Kala* willing, the time remaining before the formal tonight will be enough."

"*Kala* willing." Aleija hesitates then glances at me. "If not, you may want to leave Asheron with him. It's not a crime to support Eros openly, but you won't be welcome under anyone else's rule."

"I know."

Aleija nods. "I wish you all the best, Kora d'Elja. May *Kala* smile upon you."

I thank her, and we part, but I can't help suspecting I'll need more than *Kala*'s fortune to convince Eros to claim what's his.

I just hope I can manage it before it's too late.

I find Deimos, Eros, and Mal in the hall on the way back to Eros's rooms. Eros and Mal are dressed in casual Ona attire—Eros managed to find a sleeveless shirt without the ridiculous collar so in fashion here—while Deimos proudly wears his A'Sharo skin-tight shirt and Eljan-like loose pants.

"Kora!" Deimos says cheerfully. "We were just about to introduce Mal to the palace grounds. You should join us."

I force a weak smile and glance at Eros. My stomach is in knots. My palms are slick with sweat. But I've been putting this off too long. It's time. "I actually need to speak with Eros. Privately, if possible."

Deimos looks at Eros as Eros glances at Mal. "I can show

him around," Deimos says quickly. "At least, if Mal is comfortable with that?"

Mal shrugs. "It's okay with me."

Eros arches an eyebrow. "It is?"

"Deimos is okay," he answers.

Deimos grins. "I'm okay? What a stunning note of support—maybe after I introduce you to the grounds I'll be promoted to *acceptable*?"

Mal laughs, and a ghost of a smile crosses over Eros's mouth.

"Okay," Eros says. "I'll meet you both out there."

Deimos smiles and takes Mal's shoulder. "We'll see you soon."

The two continue down the hall with Deimos carefully guiding him, and Eros looks at me. I nod back toward his rooms and we walk back in silence. When the doors have closed behind us, Eros takes several paces to distance himself from me and then turns and crosses his arms over his chest.

"Well," he says stiffly, "you have my attention. What do you want?"

I hesitate. "I haven't had the chance to talk to you privately after the . . . the nanite attack. Is your—I know you brought Mal with you, but . . ."

Eros's face darkens and my blood goes cold. "My nephew isn't here with me because I thought it'd be fun."

Something clenches around my heart—I'd guessed as much, but hearing it confirmed . . . I step toward him, but he matches it with a step back. "Eros," I start, but he scowls.

"Is that why you pulled me aside? Morbid curiosity?"

I wince. "*Naï*, I . . . I wanted to apologize—and still do. For earlier today, and for . . . " I take a deep breath. I need to do this—I should have done so the first moment I saw him again. But it seemed the wrong time at the rebel encampment, and it seemed the wrong time on the drive back, and it seemed the wrong time again and again until I had to admit it was never the timing, it was me. I was putting it off. So I'm making it the right time.

Now.

"I never apologized for the way I treated you after our . . . after the kiss. It was wrong—what I did after that moment together was hurtful and you didn't deserve it. You didn't deserve any of it, but I was scared, and I lashed out, and I'm sorry. I'm so sorry."

He stares at me for a long moment before his gaze drifts away. What more is there to say? Is there anything else I *should* be saying? But I've said what I needed to and the words are out and . . .

What if he doesn't forgive me? The thought sits like a cold rock in my gut. Maybe my apology is too little too late. Maybe I irreparably broke whatever we had.

I love him, but maybe rejecting him when he was at his most vulnerable was too much. Maybe I'll regret the moment I allowed fear to corrupt my words and actions into something ugly for the rest of my life.

"Is that all?" he says at last, and my stomach sinks.

The words are sitting on the edge of my tongue: I love you.

But instead I say, "*Sha*," and curse my own cowardice. "It was an overdue apology and . . . probably not enough at this point. But if you'll have me, I'm not afraid anymore. Not of us, not like I was."

A sound almost like a laugh—but colder, hollower— escapes Eros's lips. "*Naï*, of course not—not when I might become *Sira*, right? With a title like that I'm finally worthy of your affection."

Heat snakes up my neck and slams into my chest. "*Naï*, Eros, it's not like that—it was never about worthiness. I was just so afraid of what might happen if we . . . I have real feelings for you, Eros."

Say it. I have to say it.

I swallow the lump in my throat and force out the words, even as they scrape their way up my throat. "I love you."

A breath. My whole body tingles with the edge of panic when he doesn't look at me. When he doesn't speak. When my words hang between us and I can't take them back and I need him to say he forgives me.

"So did I," he says flatly.

Past tense. The words bury hooks into my heart and tear.

"But not anymore," I whisper.

Eros shakes his head. "I don't know anymore. I thought I—I wanted an apology, but . . . " He sighs. "Hearing you apologize and say that should make me happy but I'm just . . . tired. I can't focus on what I may or may not be feeling around you—I guess there's too much going on right now. I really don't know."

My eyes sting, my chest aches, but I bite my lip and nod. It's okay—of course it's okay, of course I can't expect him to be ready to have this conversation, not now, not after everything that's happened. He's right. We have bigger things to worry about now. Our feelings don't matter when the planet is on the brink of chaos.

I inhale deeply. My breath shakes. "Okay. Well, you're right, we do need to talk about more pressing matters, like what you intend to do. If you don't want to do this, Eros, I understand, but then it's not safe for Mal or you here. As soon as the next *Sira* is chosen—"

"I know." His shoulders slump as he turns to the window. He leans his temple against the windowpane and closes his eyes. "If the royals ever doubted I was a threat before, they don't now. Serek made sure everyone on the blazing planet would take my fucken birthright seriously."

I walk to the other side of the window, leaning my shoulder against the wall. "I'm sorry. It must be difficult."

He laughs again, and it sounds almost like a sob. When he opens his eyes, his posture, the shadows beneath his eyes, the pallor of his skin—he's exhausted.

"I . . . also have this." I reach into my pocket and pull out the ring of *Sirae*—the one Serek had taken from Eros for safekeeping, the one I had to take from his corpse moments after he died. The ring that first made everyone realize Eros wasn't just related to any high royal—he was related to the last former *Sira* seen with the ring. To Asha.

I place the ring on the windowsill, and Eros picks it up and sighs. For a long moment, he just looks at it, his eyes full of storms.

"I'll do it," he says at last, but his words aren't one of a man confident in his candidacy—they're the words of a boy too tired to fight it anymore. And I wish I could excuse him from this—I wish I could tell him he didn't have to fight to become *Sira*. I wish I could tell him he could leave right now and live the quiet, peaceful life he's always wanted.

But I can't say any of those things because we know the truth all too well.

Becoming *Sira* isn't a political move for Eros.

It's survival.

16

Eros

I catch up with Deimos and Mal outside, sitting at the edge of one of the two fountains in the palace courtyard, but when I tell them I won't be able to join them for their tour because I need to prepare for tonight's evening meal with Kora, neither of them seem surprised.

"Mal and I will do the tour on our own." Deimos smiles. "Don't worry about it—I'll keep him safe, fed, and entertained while you work."

"Is that okay?" I ask Mal, and he shrugs.

"If you trust him, I guess I do, too. He hasn't been a jerk to me yet, at least."

Deimos smirks. "Oh, is that all it takes to win your approval?"

Mal smiles faintly.

But before I trust him to take care of Mal on his own, there's another question that needs answering.

"Why are you helping me?" I look at Deimos—Sepharon through and through, and royalty. It's in his mismatched eyes, in his height—taller than me, though not by much, and way taller than most humans—in the asymmetrical markings on his skin and the tattoos on his neck and arms. It's in the way he holds himself—confident, unyielding—and the way he walks into every room knowing he could charm anyone he wanted to.

It's also why I never expected him to try it on me with snide comments and winking smiles.

It's been a long time since I've been at ease enough to be attracted to a guy—not because my capacity to be into guys wasn't there, but because letting my guard down around guys at camp was dangerous. Girls maybe looked at me with disgust, but until I learned to defend myself, the men and boys were the ones who taught me impromptu lessons about *my place in the world.* The guys at camp reminded me time and time again that letting my guard down around them could be the last mistake I ever made.

And even away from all that, not so long ago, everything about Deimos would have been a reminder of what I'm not and what I thought I never would be. I've never been able to trust men like Deimos before. But now?

Now I may not trust him completely, but I trust he doesn't want to hurt me. And with that danger out of the way, it's impossible to ignore his magnetic smile and contagious laugh—and he knows it. But still . . .

"Men of privilege like you aren't usually my supporters," I say. "I don't know anything about you—why aren't you out there supporting one of the candidates or placing a bid yourself?"

Deimos smiles weakly. "Well, to start with, I wouldn't wish becoming *Sira* on my greatest enemy."

I grimace.

"Secondly—and more importantly—I believe Serek. He was an honorable man, and he wouldn't have publicly supported your bid, and with his dying breath no less, if he didn't believe you were meant to be on the throne and you'd be good for Safara." He shrugs. "I know the way you've likely been treated your whole life doesn't lend you to believe there are Sepharon who think the mistreatment of humans and execution of half-bloods is wrong. But we do exist, and I'm one of them. So if Serek says you're his nephew and deserve to be on the throne, then that's good enough for me."

Eight sets ago, I never would have imagined I'd get the chance to claim my right to the throne—or that I'd ever want to.

And the truth is, I wouldn't be here if Serek hadn't sent a message to the whole blazing world declaring me the next ruler and asking me to return. But I'm here, and Mal's here, and Kora and some Sepharon prince are standing behind me, and if I turn away now, I'll be turning away the only chance Mal has to get better, the only chance thousands of kids like him have to live a free life.

The only chance we both have to live at all.

This isn't about me—this has never been about me. This is about making the world a better and safer place for Mal. And I may not want any of this, but I can't turn away. Not if we want to live. Not anymore.

"Well . . . I appreciate it," I say. "I don't know what I can do to make it up to you, but—"

Deimos lifts his hands almost defensively, but he's smiling—a gesture I haven't seen before. Must be an A'Sharon thing. "You're already making it up to me," he says, "I can't tell you how long it's been since I've had an entertaining morning exercise partner."

I smile weakly. "All right, well . . . if Mal needs anything, you know where to find me."

"I'm right here," Mal says. "Just because I'm blind doesn't mean you have to talk about me like I'm not standing right in front of you."

Deimos laughs as I cringe. "Spirited." He pats Mal on the shoulder. "You and I will get along just fine."

Mal shrugs, but he's smiling, too, so I guess everything really is okay.

"Go," Deimos says. "Prepare with Kora, and we'll join you later so I can share my pretending-to-be-important wisdom."

And though spending time with Kora is the last thing I want to do, I head back to the room. But unexpectedly, as I walk away, a smile tugs on my lips.

Lying on the floor, the fibers of the red-sand-soft throw rug beneath me, staring at the ceiling, Kora's words drift over me like rain. Harder than rain—supposedly ice falls from the sky sometimes in the north, maybe more like that. Hard, unwanted words slapping my skin and bouncing off.

I don't know how long we've been at it—me pretending not to be blazed and Kora explaining the rules of the Emergency Council and who is on it, and who is here, and where they're from, and what each of them are like, and who is likely to support me, and who is likely to support my execution if I don't win, and what the process is for choosing a *Sira* when inheritance is disputed like now, and, and, and—

"Eros, are you even listening to me?"

Kora is sitting beside me, cross-legged, and her narrowed eyes and stiff posture say as I suspected—she's getting as fed up with this as I am.

"Ashen is the former *Sira*," I say. "The final call will probably go to him."

"Possibly, not probably—it will depend on how involved the priests are, or how close the decision is."

"Which isn't likely to be close at all," I say. "Given I'm a half-blood and most of them hate me by default."

"You have *Avra-saï* Aleija and *ko* Jule da Daïvi's support, and Aleija thinks you may be able to get *Avra-kaï* Simos and *ko* Ejren d'Ona's support, as well."

"Which makes two territories. Maybe."

Kora hesitates. "Well . . . not quite. You'll need the support from former *Avra* Lija and former *Avra* Tamus as well to get full support of the territories. Lija is probable—especially as Aleija is already supporting you—but Tamus is more traditional and would be more challenging to convince."

"So maybe one and a half out of nine. Not exactly encouraging odds."

"Six, not nine," Kora says. "Elja doesn't have a representative, as all of the former *Avrae* aside from me have passed on, and I don't count because I was removed. There isn't a former *Sira* representing Sekka'l or Invino either, though, for the same reason. So you only need to convince five former *Avrae* and the former *Sira* and garner enough support from the territory royals who arrived to run and give their support."

"Which is . . . did you say twelve people?"

"Fourteen, including the spouses."

I press my palms over my eyes. "So you're saying right now I have two out of fourteen."

"Three. Deimos hasn't announced it officially yet, but he's already told me he'll back you."

Nice of him. "His brother won't be happy."

Kora grimaces. "And neither will his grandfather, Oniks, who is on the council. But it doesn't matter—he's permitted to lend his support to whoever he wants, and he's assured me he won't be intimidated out of supporting you."

"So three out of fourteen. Great."

"If you get Simos and Ejren on board, and Aleija convinces former *Avra* Lija, it'll be six, which is nearly half."

"Right, but most of those people won't be on the Council, who have the final say."

"That's true," Kora admits. "They don't get a vote, but they can influence the six Council members who do. So if you get Simos and Ejren to support you, for example, you *may* be able to convince former *Avra* Tamus, as well—and then you'll have two on the council behind you."

"I thought you said Tamus was a long shot."

She shrugs. "He is, but I didn't say it was impossible."

My mind spins with names and numbers and probabilities pointing me again and again to the arena with my head on the block.

"Even with all that, it won't be enough. I need four supporters on the Council to get a full majority—which I'm probably not going to get."

"You may not . . . but that might not matter. The people can lend their support one way or the other, as well, which the Council members take into consideration when making their decision. And as I mentioned before, there's still the priest element, which is more unpredictable—sometimes they get involved with political affairs, sometimes they don't.

The priests can use various methods of choosing a *Sira*, and if they think *Kala* is particularly invested in this decision, then their involvement could change everything because *Kala* overrules all."

"Seeing how I'm not exactly religious, I'm not sure their involvement would help me."

Kora sighs. "Well if it comes to that, Deimos and I will coach you. But for now, let's just worry about getting as much support from the candidates and Council as we can."

My head throbs. I close my eyes and squeeze the bridge of my nose. "Even if everything goes perfectly, this is all sounds impossible, Kora."

"The odds are against you, *sha*, but—"

"It's not impossible, blah, blah, blah, *sha,* you've said that a million times."

Her voice goes tight. "I don't know what else you expect me to say, given how you seem determined to be completely negative about all of this."

I scowl and open my eyes. "The more you explain everything, the more it sounds like I don't have a chance in the Void. Do you really expect me to be confident and happy about all of this?"

"Of course not, but—"

"My life is on the line here and so is Mal's. Trying to claim my birthright is literally my only chance for us both to survive the next cycle, but when that chance looks more and more like it's not a blazing chance at all, you can't blame me for not being positive about it."

Kora leans forward and massages her temples. "I know, Eros, but I don't need you to be positive. I just need you to stop focusing on how impossible this all seems and focus on the information I'm giving you—the information you'll need to stay afloat tonight when the royals expect you to be able to converse like you know what you're doing."

I snort. "Pretty sure the royals expect me to crash and burn."

"Then prove them wrong. Show them you deserve to be here—show them you're a force to be taken seriously."

Heat races through me, setting my nerves on fire. My heart pounds as I sit up, my hands shaking on the soft fibers of the throw rug. "But I'm *not*, am I? I don't know what I'm blazing doing here—I wasn't raised in the Sepharon courts like you were—I barely even know what people in Asheron eat for the morning meal, let alone what they want from a ruler!"

"Which is exactly why I'm here!" Kora runs her hands through her hair and sighs heavily. "Eros, why do you think I'm sitting here trying to teach you? You're not alone, and we're not expecting you to know everything—you just need to focus and try to absorb as much of this as you can."

"Right. Absorb everything I need to be able to pass off looking like I'm not completely over my head tonight in three segs." My head throbs as I stand and cross the room. "I'm taking a walk. I need some air."

"Eros—"

The door slides shut behind me. My bare feet slap against the hard floor as I walk down the long hallway leading outdoors. My head feels like someone is pressing against it on all sides—like if I hear any more about these fucken Sepharon politics, or who expects what, or how I've basically lost before I've even begun, my skull might just cave in on itself.

The truth is obvious: I can't do this, and staying here is suicide.

Doors whoosh open in front of me, and I nearly walk straight into two people coming in as I go out—Deimos and Mal. Deimos steps out of the way and pulls Mal with him as he reaches out and grabs my shoulder. Mal gasps and stumbles a little before smacking back into Deimos.

"Whoa, there—what's going on?" Deimos asks. "Shouldn't you be with Kora?"

"I need a break," I say stiffly.

Mal frowns and squints at me. "Are you okay?"

If I were being honest I'd say no. I'd say I'm not okay, none of this is okay, the only thing playing politics will do is delay the inevitable—my execution and . . . what will they do to Mal? I don't know. I don't want to know.

Instead, I lighten my voice and say, "I'm good." The lie tastes bitter on my tongue, like biting into the inner not-poisonous-but-still-disgusting rind of a prickleplant. "How was your tour?"

Mal shrugs. "It was cool. I couldn't see a lot, but they have a lot of good food out there and everything smelled good."

Deimos smirks. "I may have introduced him to his newest addiction, *kelo*. I'm afraid there's no going back now."

Stars know what *kelo* is, but I force a thin smile anyway. "I'm glad you two had a good time."

The doors slide open and closed behind me. "Eros."

I don't have to turn around to recognize Kora's tired voice. My stomach clenches. I close my eyes and inhale the hot, dry air.

"You know," Deimos says, "Mal, if you're okay with this, I think Eros could use some *kelo* himself and room to breathe. Could you go with Kora and wait for us to get back?"

I open my eyes as Mal shrugs. "I'm tired and kinduv want to lie down, anyway."

Deimos smiles. "Kora?"

"Sure," she says softly. "Just—please don't take long. We're running out of time."

Her words clench around my lungs. Running out of time—running out of hope—breathe, breathe, just breathe.

Deimos throws his arm around my shoulders—it takes everything in me not to flinch even as my face warms at his nearness—and winks at Kora. "We'll be back in a flash." He pulls me down the stone steps dusted with gritty sand. I guess I should've worn those shoes—unlike the red Eljan sand, this desert here has been kinduv grating on my skin. But we're out over the cool white waves, and Deimos still has his arm over my shoulders, and he smells sweet and spicy, and all I can think is this is a mistake.

Coming here was such a big mistake.

"So," Deimos says after we walk several mos in silence. "You look like you're two breaths away from a meltdown. I take it the panic is setting in."

"I don't think I can do this." We walk into the market-place, bustling with people despite the tense, nervous energy in the air. The harsh sand presses into the soles of my feet. The lilt of the Sephari here I hadn't noticed before—slightly faster than the Eljan accent I'm used to and clipped at the edges—surrounds me and whispers what I already know.

I don't belong here. I've never belonged here.

"Of course you don't," Deimos says. "I'd question your sanity if you were confident about all of this."

I frown at him. "What's that supposed to mean?"

"Exactly what it sounds like." He gestures to the market-place around us, the stalls and shops. "Aside from when you were running for your life, you've never been here, *shae*? You weren't raised with Sepharon, you don't know the politics or the people. You're probably the least qualified person on the planet to be the next *Sira*."

A crash to my left—someone dropped a vendor's bowl—and my heart is in my throat. The vendor yells at the culprit and the shouting builds, and builds, and I close my eyes and take a shaky breath and this has nothing to do with me. Bite my lip. Force my eyes open. Face Deimos.

"If this is supposed to be making me feel better, it's not working."

He laughs. "Well I'm not done. What I'm saying is it's nat-ural for you to be panicking right about now because you're a sensible person and you recognize you haven't been ade-quately prepared for this. And it's okay—no one's expecting you to know everything you'll need to rule today."

"So then why am I doing this? Why would *anyone* think making me *Sira* is a good idea when I don't even think sup-porting me is a good idea?"

He shrugs. "You tell me."

"What?"

"Why are you doing this? Why should anyone support you? Why did a rebel group of redbloods go out of their way to abduct you on your way to claiming your birthright here in Asheron? Why does *anyone* want you on the throne?"

"Right now, only humans and you two want me to be *Sira*."

"*Shae*, so tell us why. Why are the . . . *humans* counting on you? What does Kora see in you? Why am I choosing to support you over my brother or anyone else who tries to make a claim?"

Good question. And it feels odd to answer. After living my life until now only visible enough to get shoved and spit on, part of me doesn't believe people will want to back me. That some already do. "The humans are hoping I can make a difference for them. That they'll be able to peacefully coexist with the Sepharon and won't be treated as slaves."

"Good. Keep going."

"They want equality, and they think I can get it for them. But—"

"*Naï, naï*—you have enough naysayers and doubters without piling on your own. Tell me why anyone should support you."

I take a deep breath. Let the hot air settle over my skin and sink into my bones. "Because . . . people like me shouldn't be executed at birth. Because no one should be bought or sold like an animal. Because we all have families, and dreams, and personalities, and we deserve to be treated like people. Because no one should have to run their whole lives just for the illusion of freedom. Because no one should have to live in fear that one day someone will come, destroy their homes, and rip apart their families."

Deimos smiles. "Good—you've got the redb—human support. Now tell me why the Sepharon should support you."

I frown. Why *would* any Sepharon support me? I represent everything so many of them don't want—not only peaceful coexistence between two species, but acceptance and unity. Most Sepharon don't think I deserve to live, so why in the world would any of them want me—or anyone like me—in power?

"Maybe I'll give you a hint," Deimos says. "We're not *all skoi*. Many of us know buying and selling people—human or not—is wrong. Did you know the servant class in A'Sharo is paid? It's not perfect, obviously—not enough people in power have shared the anti-slavery sentiment to abolish it completely, but we *are* moving forward. The pay is a living wage, and the servants have rights to shelter, protection from abuse, and fair compensation. There are Sepharon out there who would support what you stand for. Many are just waiting for someone to push us over and abolish it outright."

I nod. "So you're saying . . . you think some Sepharon would actually be happy to see me in power."

Deimos nods. "Many Sepharon—especially our generation—agree we're way overdue for a change. You might be exactly the change we need as long as you're ready to take on the responsibility."

I run a hand through my sweaty hair. "Equality," I say. "That's my stance."

Deimos nods. "Equality *and* birthright. You'd be surprised the number of people who would support you even if they disagree with everything you say simply because you're *Sira* Asha's son and that's the way it's always been." He blinks and straightens his shoulders. "Actually, maybe that'd help you—have you ever seen recordings of your father in power?"

"Um, *nai*."

Deimos smiles. "His reign wasn't as long as it should have been, but he was a very popular *Sira*. I honestly think Safara would look drastically different if he hadn't been killed all those cycles ago. He spoke about tolerance and changing things for the better—some even say he was in the process of abolishing the law demanding the killing of half-blood babies when he was murdered. Which in retrospect makes sense as he knew you were about to be born."

I frown. "I didn't . . . no one told me that."

Deimos nods. "If we maneuver carefully, maybe we can get *Sira* Asha's supporters to stand behind you, too. Your messages are more alike than you might think. But you need to take the first step—and that means going to the meal tonight and establishing yourself as a real candidate for the throne. Without that, you might as well grab Mal and start running."

I glance at him. "You really think I can do this?"

"I may not know you very well yet, Eros, but I know a force to be reckoned with when I see it. And you, *mana eran*, are a force."

Mana eran—my brother. My mouth moves into a grimace or a smile—I'm not sure which. But somehow, impossibly, with Deimos's words ringing in my ears, I start to believe him. The odds are against me, of course they are, but maybe this is more than the crash of fate stumbling over reality.

Maybe, just maybe, I was meant to be here all along.

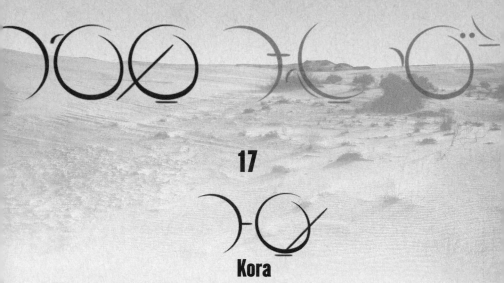

17

Kora

"So," I say, as Mal clambers onto Eros's bed and sprawls out over the plush layer of pillows. "Is there anything I can get you? Food, drink, glass for entertainment . . ."

"*Naï*," he starts to say then cuts off and sits up abruptly. "Wait. Glass? Is that those . . . all-in-one things with everything on it?"

I smile, pick up a glass off the bedside table, and sit next to him, placing it on his lap. "Is that a good place for you to see it?"

He hesitates, and then stretches his legs out in front of him and pushes the tablet until it rests against his knees. "That's better."

"Okay." I rest my palm against the glass and it lights up.

"*Welcome, guest.*"

Mal's eyebrows practically shoot into his bright rust hair. "It can talk?"

I laugh. "It can do all sorts of things. Here." I swipe away the numbers game whoever used it last was playing and tap open the newsfeed, which displays a map of Safara. "This allows you to watch the world feeds—you can pull it up from any territory or station."

"So you can just . . . see what's happening around the world whenever you want just by touching one of the territories?"

I nod. "And it's always running. So, for example, if I touch Elja . . ." I tap my territory and the screen fills with rectangles, each depicting a different newsfeed with images all around the territory. "Then you just choose which feed you'd like to watch."

Mal taps one in the center and the image fills the screen. "Huh," he says, and I smile until I look at the feed he's chosen.

It's not just any feed—it's what's going on in Vejla.

And what's going on in Vejla looks chillingly like a riot.

Shops and homes are on fire; people have taken to the streets with handwritten signs and stormed up to the palace gates—gates that are no longer nanite sealed, gates that are no longer impenetrable. Instead, Dima has stationed his men in front of the gate, holding back the horde with shields, phasers, and charged batons.

Mal frowns at the glass. "That doesn't look good . . ."

I swipe my fingers alongside the edge of the glass, raising the volume. A light voice fills the room: "With more than a hundred dissenters imprisoned and a new tax imposed upon Eljans across the territory—a tax the impoverished people of the territory can't afford—Vejlans have taken to the streets to protest their young new ruler, who it seems was less prepared for the position than Eljans had hoped."

My stomach churns at the images, the screaming, my home tumbling into chaos *again*, but this time there's nothing I can do. I failed to prevent this while I had the chance.

Vejla is burning, and all I can do is watch.

I swipe my shaking hand over the screen, shutting down the feed and opening the central menu again. Mal must sense I'm upset despite my attempts to swallow the tightness in my throat and the stinging in my eyes, because he pushes the glass away and smiles weakly at me.

"So," he says, "while we're waiting for Eros and Deimos to come back, could you show me around the palace? I only know how to get outside and where our washroom is, but if I'm going to be staying here, it'd be good to know how to get around so I don't depend on someone being my guide all the time."

"Of course." My voice is tight and strained. I clear my throat, stand, and force a smile. "Let's get you acquainted with your new home."

The words aren't quite right—I know that as soon as I say it and Mal's smile slips away. My error is obvious: this isn't Mal's home, and even if Eros manages to miraculously win the bid, it may never truly be home to him. Not in a palace where he is the first human to walk these halls freely.

But the words are out and Mal doesn't try to correct me; instead, with my hand on his shoulder, we step into the hall, flashing false smiles to the guards and tucking reality away into the darkest places of our minds.

A place where reality will stay, untouched, for a little while longer.

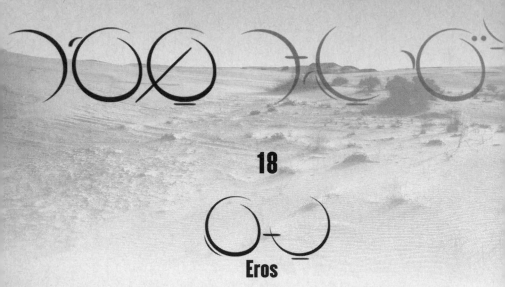

18

Eros

"So, I can't walk in there shirtless, but draping this nonsense over my shoulders somehow makes it okay?" I hold up the scrap of black and gold fabric Deimos handed me out of my clothing room—ignoring that I have a blazing room dedicated just to hold clothes.

"You don't drape it over your shoulders," Deimos calls from the clothing room. "There are arm holes, see?"

"But it has no sleeves. And obviously isn't meant to close over my chest because there's practically no fabric."

Deimos pokes his head around the corner of the doorway and smirks as I glower at the shirt—if you can call it that. "*Sha*, well, I never said Ona fashion was *sensible*, just that I knew what they expected from you." He looks at Kora and Mal, sitting on my bed behind me. "Is he always such an infant over clothes?"

"I'm not an infant."

Kora and Mal laugh. "He didn't protest as much in Elja," she says, "but I also didn't ask him to wear a shirt or shoes."

"Ah, *sha*, how could I forget? Everyone walks around half-naked in Elja."

Kora snorts. "As if you don't enjoy the view when you visit."

Deimos grins. "Well, I never said I *minded* your strange clothing customs."

I roll my eyes. "Are you two done flirting?"

"Whoever said I was flirting with *her*?" Deimos winks at me and disappears back into the clothing room. My face burns as Mal cracks up behind me and Kora suppresses a giggle. I put on the blazing shirt.

Deimos emerges from the room with a gold circular band and what looks like the bottom of a gold shoe with strings attached to it. "Here." He passes me the band and places the shoes at my feet. "Those were the most understated I could find."

I nearly laugh as I run my fingers over the smooth metal band engraved with writing I can't read. "This is pure gold."

"*Sha*."

"As are the shoes."

"Very observant."

I look at him. "And that's *understated*?"

"You've forgotten where you live." He gestures to my extravagant bedroom and the view outside overlooking the courtyard and one of the gold-studded fountains with water somehow manipulated to look like molten gold. "Gold is for royalty, and your mission tonight is to convince a room of racist old men you're just as much royalty as the former *Sira* himself."

"He's right," Kora says. "The clothes he's chosen for you are perfect. The style nods to Elja, your former home, while communicating with Ona fashion. It's regal without being over the top." She looks at Deimos. "Good choices."

"Why, thank you. At least *some*one appreciates my talent."

I sigh and slip my feet into the awkward shoes, but I'm not sure what to do with the band. I frown at it until Deimos plucks it from my fingers and takes my left hand.

"Here." He slides the band over my hand and up my arm, until it rests over my bicep—covering my tattoo from Elja. Bumps rush over my arms as he steps back and nods to the mirror on the opposite wall. "Take a look."

I turn around and face myself in the mirror. With the black pants I'm still wearing from earlier, the black and gold-edged scrap of a shirt, the gold arm band and gold shoes, I have to admit, they're right. I look Onan—and more than that, the gold accents make my eyes impossible to ignore.

I look like Sepharon royalty. And I'm not sure how I feel about it.

"You definitely look the part." Kora steps next to me. "Now you just have to act it."

But the way they're covering my tattoo, like my past is something to hide, sits heavily in my stomach. I'm not ashamed of what happened, and it's not like people don't know I was Kora's servant for a time. So why try to hide it?

I slip the band off and slide it onto my other arm. I don't like the tattoo or what it represents, but it's a part of my story now. And I'm not going to pretend otherwise.

When I turn back to everyone, Deimos is nodding and Kora . . . Kora's worrying her lip. There's something sad in the way she looks at me, brow slightly furrowed, lip twisting. Does she actually feel guilty about it?

Good. She should.

I turn to Mal. "What do you think? Can you see me?"

"Kinduv." He squints at me. "I can see the gold at least. And, um, how you're standing."

"Would it help if I moved closer?"

He shakes his head and scoots to the edge of the bed. "*Nai*, it's okay. You look . . ." he hesitates. "It looks right, I guess."

I smile weakly. "You guess?"

"Yeah. It's just weird seeing you look so . . . them." I grimace, and Mal quickly adds, "But you don't look bad. It fits you."

It's so strange, standing here in the palace, dressed as royalty. Glancing at myself in the mirror, I want to say Mal's wrong and it doesn't fit, I want to say it feels wrong to see myself as one of them, to present myself as Sepharon royalty.

But the truth is it doesn't. I may not have been raised here, I may never have imagined myself here, I may never have *wanted* myself here—but seeing myself like this now, I can almost imagine what Asha must have thought my life would be like. I can almost picture being here all along, with a Sepharon father teaching me how to navigate Sepharon politics and standing proudly behind me even in the face of hate and racism—and a human mother smiling beside me.

I can almost imagine maybe I really was meant to be here. Maybe Asha was right all along.

Entering the dining room is like waltzing into a pack of starving *kazim*. Deimos, Kora, and I are some of the last ones to enter—only Ashen and Lejv have yet to arrive according to Deimos's quick check moments before we entered ourselves.

And now, standing at the entrance in front of twelve royals for the first time, I want nothing more than to turn around, walk right back out, and pretend this isn't happening. But I can't. I have to act like I belong here, like I want to be here, like I know I'm the next *Sira* even though I doubt that'll ever happen. So I walk right up to the place Kora told me to—at the inner crest of the apex, across from where former *Sira* Ashen will sit—because apparently the best way to show everyone I'm serious is to spend my meal sitting across from my grandfather, who has all but said he thinks I'm trash.

In other words, this is going to be a blazing party.

I take my seat on the cushion, sitting back on my heels like Deimos suggested—because even the way I sit makes a fucken statement—while he and Kora sit cross-legged on either side of me.

It's not exactly the most comfortable position—my knees and toes are going to be killing me by the time this is over—but I'll forget about all that as soon as the former *Sira* comes in to glower at me. At least I could save Mal from this uncomfortable posturing—he opted to stay back in my room and relax with whatever food we send back to him. I don't blame him for not wanting to show. I sure as the Void wouldn't be here if I didn't have to be.

A man with dark hair pulled back glares at me from down the table—the guy who assigned me my room. He isn't dressed like one of the royals—his clothes look closer to the uniform the staff wear here—so he must be the former advisor Kora mentioned, Niro, who gave her a hard time before I got here. I stare him down until he averts his gaze.

"Hello, *eran*," Deimos says cheerily to a tall, thin man who's started the glowering game early with a heated look at

Deimos. "Haven't seen much of you the last set or so—have you established yourself as Lejv's favorite enthusiast yet?"

I rush through the names Deimos and Kora taught me today—he said *eran*, which means brother, so this must be Oniks—no, wait, Oniks is the former *Sira*—Deimos's grandfather. I scan the table and find him quickly—a stern man with thick black hair and a trim beard, dressed in customary A'Sharo black and red. So then the thin guy must be . . . Sulten. One of Deimos's many brothers, Sulten.

Sulten's face colors at Deimos's taunt. He scowls. "I should have known you'd be the first duped into the half-blood's ridiculous game."

"This half-blood has a name," I say, centering my gaze on Sulten. "Unless you want me to refer to you as Deimos's ugly brother, maybe you should try using it."

Deimos gapes at me then throws his head back and laughs loudly. I guess I've surprised Sulten, too, because his eyes bug out of his head as his face flushes to a deep shade of purple, and I expect Oniks to be just as pissed, but instead he has a ghost of a smirk on his lips.

Is he actually . . . amused?

Two men with piercings on their faces, dressed in black and silver—Ona's colors—laugh next, one touching his forehead to the other's shoulder as he laughs (Simos and Ejren, I think), and Aleija and Jule—who are easy to remember because they're the only women beside Kora and the older woman, who I assume is Lija, here—join in the laughter, too.

This isn't the first impression I was planning to make, but I guess this works.

"Oh, what's wrong, Sulten?" Aleija croons, grinning at

the furious *Avra-kaï.* "Were you not expecting Eros to speak for himself?"

"You really are your father's son," the Ona council member says—his name is . . . Tamus! Tamus, with the longish brown hair, former *Avra* of Ona, Simos's father. Kora told me something about him but . . . I don't remember what. Doesn't matter. I can talk to him without every detail.

"Thank you." I smile—and for once, for once, it's genuine. I may not know much about Asha, but from what Deimos has told me about him . . . being like my father may not be such a bad thing. "Did you know my father well?"

"Refer to him as 'my father,' not Sira *Asha."* Deimos's suggestion. And one Kora agreed was a good idea: *"Reinforce the notion that you are his son. The more who accept it and see the connection between the two of you, the better."*

"Ashen is a childhood friend of mine," Tamus answers. "I watched all of his sons grow up—and one never forgets their best friend's first born."

Ah, *that* was what Kora had told me—Tamus and Ashen are close, so she didn't think Tamus was likely to support me ever. Still . . . maybe she was wrong?

"Many remember Asha as a young visionary *Sira*—and he was," Tamus continues, "but in private, he was also very spirited."

"Spirited to a fault, some might say," a voice answers behind me. Everyone rises, and so do I, which can only mean one thing.

The former *Sira* walks around the long crescent-shaped dining table, a tall, lean man with long hair tied into a bun following in his wake. Murmurs of acknowledgment ripple around the room as they nod and bow to their former ruler.

Ashen steps to his place directly across from me and looks me over. His gold-rimmed irises are dark—more like Roma than Serek—and something about his cool, dispassionate gaze rolling over me sends a shiver down my spine. His stare catches on my tattoo—or maybe my light, barely-there markings?—and my skin prickles at the pause.

He isn't looking at me like an adversary or even a threat. The slight curl of his lip, the apathetic stare—he's looking at me like he might an animal prepped for slaughter.

The room is deadly quiet—all gazes settled on us. Everything inside me screams *move*, screams *say something*, screams *bow*, but he isn't my ruler and he never was.

Still, he deserves some respect, and shunning him isn't going to win me any friends.

I break the silence. "Good to finally meet you. I've heard much about you both." I glance at Lejv, who watches me with an equally apathetic stare.

"As have I," Ashen says, but his tone is flat, unimpressed. Which is fine. I didn't expect him to try to make me feel important—he brought Lejv to Asheron himself, so I'm the last person he wants to see.

Ashen sits and so does everyone else as Sepharon servants enter the room with plates, trays, and bowls piled high with steaming food. Ordinarily the sight of all this incredibly delicious looking—and smelling—food would instantly make me hungry, but with Ashen sitting across from me and talking to Lejv, and awkward conversations burbling around the table, it'll be amazing if I manage to eat anything.

After the food is served and everyone has a plate full of meats, vegetables, fruits, breads, and a variety of sauces and gravies, Deimos clears his throat and smiles. "So, I imagine the genetic testing results have come in."

Lejv frowns at his plate, but Ashen glances at Deimos and nods. "They have."

"And judging by the fact that no one has attempted to claim otherwise—"

"They verify what my youngest son claimed, *sha*," Ashen finishes.

"Can't say I'm surprised," Tamus says. "Eros looks much like his father. And his eyes speak his heritage clearly enough."

"*Sha*," Deimos adds. "Seems he's the only candidate with an undeniable physical connection to the line of succession."

Ashen's gaze flickers to me, then back to Tamus, but he doesn't answer. Lejv shifts uncomfortably—if he's chosen over me, he'd be the first *Sira* without the iconic gold gaze. Not that it matters in the grand scheme of things, but the Sepharon are big on tradition.

"Some might argue *Kala* has already made his choice," Kora adds. "As the gold eyes originated from *Kala*'s blessing on Jol and his family line."

Two middle-aged men in green—from Inara judging by their colors, if I'm remembering right—glance at each other. I don't remember everything Kora said about the men from Inara, just that they're a year apart and one of them is the former *Sira*—just recently replaced with his fifteen-cycle-old son, Kalan—while the other is his brother. Judging by their reaction to Kora's mention of *Kala*, though, I'd bet they were religious.

"I severely doubt *Kala* intended to put a mongrel on the throne," Ashen says. "But time will tell—we all submit to his will in the end."

My throat tightens and muscles clench at the word—
mongrel. Like some kinduv inbred animal. And as if anyone
knows what their deity wants. This asshole is supposed to be
related to me, and he's sitting there talking about me like I'm
diseased.

Blood doesn't make family. I know that. But that doesn't
make it sting any less.

I take a large gulp of whatever's in my sweating stone
flute—the liquid is cold, but it burns down my throat and
traces a hot path into my stomach. My head is fuzzy for a
blink and I eye the glass. It must be some sortuv brew—which
means the last thing I want to do is drink it quickly in this
company where I need to have my wits about me.

Deimos slides a smaller stone flute toward me and nods
with a smirk. I sip that instead—lukewarm water.

"So, Eros," Lejv says loudly, obviously intended for everyone to hear. "We missed you yesterday—was your journey
from the redblood camp long?"

"Long when you end up without transportation, *sha*," I
answer. Deimos, Kora, and I agreed they don't need to know
what actually held me up—getting abducted by rebel humans
who made me swear to support them isn't exactly the sign of
a strong ruler. And a man who promises humans much of anything isn't someone they're going to want to back. But it isn't
really a lie—I *didn't* have transportation when the Remnant
took Day's bike from me. I'm lucky they gave it back so Mal
and I could travel back with Kora and Deimos.

"Ah, of course. How fortunate the former Eljan *Avra* and
the young *kai* were able to find you out there."

The move is obvious—discrediting my two biggest supporters, which discredits me by association. "I owe a debt to

Kora and Deimos," I say. "One I intend to repay in full when I'm *Sira*."

Deimos smiles. "We're happy to serve our future ruler."

Lejv laughs and a couple around the table join in with him. "Of course you are." He chuckles. "And I suppose you'll serve that redblood he brought with him, as well, in this hypothetical scenario?" He turns to Ashen and smirks. "Can you imagine? A half-blood on the throne and a redblood *Sira-kai*?"

People around the table frown and glance at each other.

"Mal isn't my son, he's my nephew," I say. "He wouldn't be *Sira-kai*."

"That doesn't explain what he's doing here," Lejv says. "Or why you thought it'd be a good idea to bring a redblood into Asheron and treat him like royalty."

"I'm treating him like a person," I answer stiffly. "He doesn't have his own room—he's staying with me, because the nanite attack the former *Sira* was removed from the throne for killed all remaining members of his family."

Lejv purses his lips, but I'm not done—not even close. I lean forward and keep my gaze on him. "I'm not apologizing for bringing an orphan to the capitol—an orphan, I might add, who is a making of the throne I'm inheriting. We destroyed his life—*all* of us—and I intend to make it right for him and for the others whose lives we've ripped apart with our hatred and intolerance."

It isn't a speech I should be making to a room full of bigoted Sepharon royalty, but the words pouring out of me are true. Whether I like it or not, I've been a part of this from the very beginning—my existence wasn't an accident; it was a strategic political move. And no one else is going to make things change, no one else is going to take care of people like Mal, ground into the sand and left to die. No one else is going to change the world for him, and for his children, and for his children's children.

I want Safara to be a better place, a safer place, for people like me, like Mal, like the Sepharon servants bringing us food and drink and disappearing into the background. But no one else is going to do that—no one else is going to try to change a blazing thing.

It's up to me.

I'm the change.

My words echo in the silence of the room; even Lejv and Ashen, glowering at me from across the table, don't have a rebuttal ready.

So I speak for them.

"My father was ready to do the unacceptable—the unthinkable, to many of you—to make Safara a better place for everyone. I'm not here by accident; having me was a deliberate move, and I'm not backing down now."

I sip the brew again and keep my eyes on Lejv and Ashen. But there's nothing for them to say, not really.

I've made my move.

"That was *incredible*." Deimos laughs and claps me on the back hard enough to make me cough, but then lowers his voice so he doesn't wake Mal, who is fast asleep on my bed. "*Kala*, did you see their faces? Lejv looked ready to wet himself."

"You did great, Eros," Kora says with a tired laugh. She

sits on the edge of my bed. "I don't think anyone was expecting you to come in with so much confidence and presence. You held your own."

"Held his own? You more than held your own, Eros—you decimated them. You showed everyone you're a real contender and you're not going to sit back quietly."

I smile and sit on a pile of pillows on the floor—I guess Mal decided there *is* such a thing as too many pillows after all—leaning my head back against the edge of the floating bed. "I'm kinduv impressed with myself," I say honestly. "I was nervous at first, but when Sulten and Lejv started talking me down, I just got really blazed off."

"Blazed?" Deimos frowns. "Is that Eljan slang?"

"Redblood slang, I think." Kora laughs.

My face warms, but I shrug. "It still translates."

"Blazed," Deimos says again. "I like it."

I smile.

Kora smirks. "More importantly, you impressed Tamus. I didn't expect him to take so easily to you, but it looks like you remind him of Asha. He was smiling when you finished and said you weren't backing down."

"Oh, *sha*e, I saw that," Deimos says. "You may actually get him on your side."

"I hope so," I say. "It'll be hard, though, since he's so close to Ashen. He might back Lejv just out of loyalty to his friend."

"He might, but he might not if he thinks Ashen is making a mistake by refusing to acknowledge you," Kora says.

Deimos nods. "Loyalty is important, but loyalty to your *Sira* comes first—and if we get Tamus to believe you're meant to inherit the throne, he might back you against Ashen and Lejv."

"That's a big if," I say.

"It is," Kora says. "And before the dinner, I wouldn't have thought it realistically possible. But now we might have a chance with Tamus—and doubly so if we get Simos and Ejren on our side."

"So maybe it's not hopeless," I say. "It's better than what we were imagining earlier, at least."

"*Shae*, we didn't give you enough credit." Deimos laughs. "*Kafra*, you were amazing out there."

My face warms again, and Kora smiles. "You really were. I'm proud of you."

It's a strange thing to be here, in the grandest palace on the planet, among friends. I've been so used to isolation, so used to everyone hating me, that having two people with no obligation to like me backing me anyway . . .

It's more than I ever expected, and it feels unreal, but it's not. It's here. It's now.

I might actually have a chance at this.

"So what do we actually know about Lejv?" I ask. "Besides that he has Ashen's support by virtue of not being me."

"Well, he's *a' da Kala* Serek's cousin, as you know," Deimos says. "So his claim is legitimate, albeit not nearly as strong as yours. He was raised in politics and was formerly an Ona ambassador, so he's well-versed in"—Deimos waves his hand—"all of this."

Kora nods. "We can't say for certain what his campaign promises will be, but as Ashen is supporting him, I imagine it'll be along the traditional line—prioritization of restoring the nanites, which you should do as well, Eros; continued separation of redblood and Sepharon—"

"Is he like Roma?" I interrupt. "Do we have any idea what his ruling style might be like?"

Kora and Deimos glance at each other.

"The little interaction I've had with him gives me the impression he's stringent," Deimos says. "Very rule-oriented. I imagine he won't try to carve sand with new law proposals."

I nod. All of that is expected, really—I wouldn't expect a traditionalist like Ashen to support someone risky. "And do we know where he stands on the nanite attack?"

Kora looks at the ceiling and shakes her head as she sighs. "If he's the same as everyone else, then he condemns it, but he won't try to make reparations with the redbloods. As far as they're concerned, it's unfortunate and someone should be punished, but they don't feel the need to go as far as make amends."

I scowl as heat creeps up my neck. "Of course not. Because that would mean acknowledging we deserve to live in peace to begin with."

Kora sighs and stretches her arms over her head. "*Sha*, well, unfortunately I don't believe that stance is a surprise to anyone here."

That's true, but it doesn't make me less blazed to hear it. I glower at the mosaicked wall.

"But as well as tonight went, we still need a strategy," she continues. "Even with Tamus on your side—which isn't a guarantee—you're not going to get a majority on the Council. If we want to bolster your chances, Eros, you need the people behind you."

I shake my head. "You really think the people are going to support a half-blood?"

"If you go out there like you just did at dinner, they just might," Deimos says. "It won't be *easy*, per say, but if you show them just how much you are like your father, I think you've got a good chance."

"Go out there?" I glance at Kora. "Go out where?"

"Deimos and I were speaking earlier and . . . we think you should go out into the city and make an appeal to the people in person."

A trickle of ice slides down my throat and into my stomach. Oh.

Deimos nods. "They all know your name thanks to Serek, but most of them have never seen you or anyone like you. You're just a name to them—show them you're a real person, and more, you're ready and able to take your rightful place on the throne."

I run a hand through my hair. "Plenty of them saw me when I was nearly executed in the arena."

"Well, *shae*, but you on your knees in front of the chopping block isn't the lasting impression we want them to have."

"And even then," Kora adds, "most of them only saw your image on a glass—seeing you in person, how you walk, and speak, and hearing your voice—that's what we want them to remember. That will show them you're more than just an image on a glass or a name in the air."

Deimos nods. "You could be their next ruler. Show them you're willing to reach out to them and you won't just shut yourself away in the capitol like so many *Sirae* before you have."

I bite my lip. "But what's the point of appealing to the people if they don't make the decision? Having their support isn't going to help me much if the Council decides they don't care."

"The people don't make the decision," Kora agrees, "but they *do* influence it. Rally them behind you, and the Council will take notice and factor it into their decision."

"Exactly," Deimos says. "And if you don't, Lejv will, and the last thing we want is to give the Council another reason to choose him."

My stomach churns at the thought of going into the city, in front of thousands of Sepharon who cheered at my execution, in front of so many who think I'm worth less than the sand under their feet. And now I have to face them and pretend that isn't the truth, pretend there's actually some chance they would back me as their future ruler, pretend just the thought of speaking to a crowd of thousands—tens of thousands? Hundreds of thousands?—isn't utterly terrifying.

"Do we . . . have to start with a giant speech?" I shift as my skin prickles. "Couldn't we start with something smaller like . . ."

Kora and Deimos look at me expectantly. I have no idea where I was going with that.

"Like . . . I dunno," I mumble.

Deimos smiles kindly. "Ordinarily we could consider starting with small groups on the street, or something of the like. But Lejv isn't going to start small, and we need to expose you to as many people as possible—especially since, as you said, people around the planet only associate you with . . . well . . ."

"Your near-execution," Kora finishes. "We're not going to erase that image with small groups on the street. We need to introduce you as someone powerful to take seriously."

I pick at a pillow as my stomach crawls to my toes. This is my life now. If I'm going all in with this—and I have to, I am—then this is what it means. And if I actually manage to get picked as *Sira*, I'll have to get used to these kinds of public addresses. I can't get by with trying to be invisible, not anymore. Now I need to make people pay attention.

Now I need to make them remember me.

"Okay." My voice shakes as I speak—I take a breath and look at them both, Deimos leaning against the wall across from my bed and Kora sitting several lengths away, gently touching the silky sheets. "I guess I'll—I mean, I don't know what I'm going to say . . ."

"I'll put something together for you," Deimos says. "But just think about what you'd like to get across. You did really well just improvising today, and it's important you say what you want to say."

I try to smile, but it feels like a grimace. "Right. Sure."

"We want to go tomorrow morning," Kora says. "Before Lejv beats us to it."

Tomorrow morning. I have to be ready to talk to a city, in person, with some kinduv enlightening speech tomorrow morning.

Sure.

"Great," I mumble.

"I know it seems like a lot at once," Kora says, "but we have faith in you, Eros. You can do this."

I don't answer. There isn't much to say, besides wishing I had a fraction of their confidence, which isn't what they want to hear right now.

Deimos pushes off against the wall and straightens. "I'm going to get materials prepared. See you in the morning, Eros."

"*Shae*," I say, tasting his A'Sharo slang equivalent for *yeah*. I think he notices, because he smiles before he leaves.

Then it's just Kora and me with Mal's soft snores behind us, and I don't know what to say.

"I suppose I should let you rest." Kora stands and smiles weakly at me. "It's okay to be nervous, by the way. I wouldn't expect anything else."

I look at her. "I don't think I'm ready for this."

"Probably not—but you'll never feel ready, not really. I never felt ready—or wanted, or even remotely qualified—either. But it doesn't matter. You push through it and you do what you must. That's all anyone can ever expect of you."

I don't say what we're both thinking: she never felt wanted as a ruler because she wasn't, and she ruled anyway until they ousted her. Until they nearly killed a *Sira-kaï* just to frame her for his murder and get her off the throne.

Even if I manage to take the throne despite the hate, despite so many not wanting me there, I won't be safe. Neither of us will ever be safe.

Instead, I say, "I'm sorry." Part of me revolts against the words—but she is trying, and I haven't been. And like it or not, what she did doesn't make it okay for me to be a jerk.

Kora blinks. "Sorry? For what?"

I glance out my balcony, where the sheer curtains blow in a gentle, warm night breeze. "I haven't exactly been . . . the easiest to work with lately."

She smiles softly and sits next to me. "*Naï*, you haven't, but I can't blame you given everything, either. You've been through a lot, and I'm at fault for some of it, so I wasn't expecting a warm reception anyway."

I grimace. "It's more than that, too. I mean, *sha*, I was—and am—pretty blazed at you so that hasn't helped, but . . ." I shake my head. "I haven't been able to sleep much, either. I just keep remembering *everything*, and every time I close my eyes, something I want to bury resurfaces and I just . . ." I sigh and run my hands over my face. "That and all the stress with everything else has kinduv fucked with my mood and ability to deal with everything, so I'm sorry for snapping at you and being a jerk in general."

Kora rests her hand on my knee. "I'm sorry things have been so difficult for you. If you ever need someone to talk to about it . . ."

I don't say anything. Because the truth is, I can't trust her with that part of myself again. No amount of apologies will change that.

She stands, but I take her hand before she can walk away. I shouldn't be doing this. But her skin is smooth and warm, and this gentle touch is just . . . nice.

Then I pull her closer, slide my hands to her hips, and she straddles me, and we're kissing.

This isn't like last time—hungry and desperate, clinging so hard it hurt, kissing until our lips ached and breaths came in gasps—this is quiet, slow. This is knowing nothing can come out of this kiss because my nephew is sleeping just a few paces behind me, but not wanting anything to come out of it anyway. This is the touch of lips to lips, the brush of her fingers over my cheeks, her slightly sweet taste sliding over my tongue. This is forgetting, just for a mo, and feeling.

Kora leans forward, and her weight settles on me. She slowly runs her hands up my sides, scattering barely-there sparks over my skin. But something churns in the space between my lungs, and this kiss . . .

I don't know.

It's not the same.

It echoes what we had, but we're reaching. It feels like trying to force what we felt before, like going through the motions and holding on just a little longer, just a little longer to see if it comes back. And it's not like I don't like it, it's not like I don't react to her mouth on mine and her weight grinding into my lap, but it's—emptier. Impersonal. I could be kissing anyone right now and it'd be the same.

It feels like I have to forget she made me open up and then turned away. Like I have to ignore that she reminded me, again, I was beneath her. That I was good enough to mess around with, but not royal enough for her to stick around. And yeah, she apologized, she was scared too and didn't mean to make me hurt, didn't know how deeply that betrayal went.

But it doesn't matter.

We break away at the same time, our mouths slipping apart, and as she looks at me, I know she feels it, too. Something broke between us, and I'm not sure how to fix it. Maybe we lashed out at each other too much, maybe we've just seen more than we can handle and hurt each other too many times. Maybe when she turned away *again*, it was the end, because as much as I'd like to, I can't forget how awful she made me feel. I can't trust her to never turn her back on me again.

Or maybe it's not anyone's fault, but it's not the same because we aren't the same. Not anymore.

Kora slides off my lap and smiles weakly. "Good night, Eros."

She turns away and walks out of my room, and I could stop her with a word or a *wait* or a touch, but I don't.

I let her go.

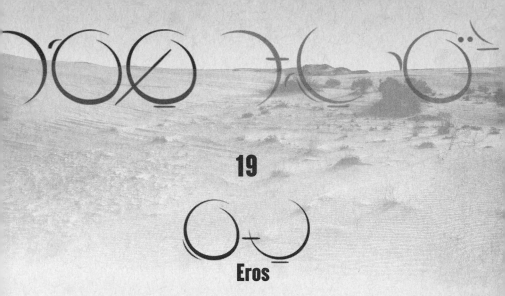

19

Eros

I lie in bed, staring up at the ceiling, listening to Mal sleep and trying not to think—not about tomorrow; not about the kiss; not about what will happen if I lose this campaign; not about ashes mixing with smoke; not about Mal curled up with Aren in his arms; not about screams and explosions and fire; not about so much blood and bits of people scattered on the rubble; not about my cheek against hard, smooth rock and the hiss of shifting sand as the executioner lifts the blade; not about the slippery warmth of another man's blood soaking my hands; not about wanting to sleep so fucken bad in that white, cold room; not about Day, or Nol, or Esta, or how everything could have been different if I didn't live in a world where humans have less freedom and respect than animals and half-bloods are murdered at birth.

I'm tired—so fucken tired. But closing my eyes means reliving everything again, and again, and again, and I can't. I can't.

So I don't.

I slip into the hallway, my bare feet patting against the warm, slick stone. Guards lining the hall glance at me, but

I'm not a prisoner here—and as I'm an official candidate now and Kora's my official advisor, they've finally stopped following us. I don't know if someone ordered that—seems unlikely Niro would have—or they just realized it doesn't matter because guards are literally everywhere anyway, but I'm glad. I can do whatever I want without being followed.

I lift my hand to knock on the door and it slides open automatically—unlocked. Deimos glances at me from his bed and blinks.

"Oh, Eros, *ej*, come in."

I do. Deimos lifts the glass he had on his lap and waves the screen at me. "I was just looking up *Sira* Asha's old speeches for inspiration—have you had the chance to search for them yet?"

"*Naï*," I answer. "And, um, I should add, before you write anything down—I can't read."

"Right, *shae*, Kora mentioned that. It's not a problem—I was just going to put together some clips for you to watch so we can discuss a plan, but this works even better."

I sit next to him and the bed bounces a little under my weight. Deimos places the glass on my lap and swipes two fingers over the image—a tall man with a thick ring of gold in his eyes, skin a touch lighter than mine, and thick, brown hair shaved close on the sides and back.

Something warms inside me as I stare at the image. For the first time, I see why Serek thought Roma would recognize me immediately and why Tamus said I remind him of my father.

Because even if Deimos hadn't told me he was looking up Asha's old speeches, I would have known who he was instantly.

"*Kafra*," I whisper. "I really do look like him."

Deimos laughs quietly. "It's kind of incredible no one noticed before. I mean, your skin's darker and marks are harder to see and your jaw's a little narrower but . . . even before you speak, the resemblance is undeniable."

My eyes sting, which is ridiculous so I rub the sting away. I clear my throat.

"Seems you hardly took after your mother at all, whoever she is," he adds.

Take after Rani? I shake my head. "*Naï,* I don't look much like her. If she hadn't told me we were related, I wouldn't have guessed."

Deimos arches an eyebrow. "You didn't know you were related to your mother?"

"She didn't raise me. I only just met her . . . right before you and Kora picked me up."

Deimos's eyes widen. "She lives with those underground redbloods?"

I grimace. "More accurately, she leads them."

His mouth drops open then snaps closed. He frowns. "Oh, *her.* Huh . . . you're right, I wouldn't have guessed either. Obviously. Though I suppose it explains your handsome coloring."

My face warms as I glance at him. Did he just . . . is he calling me handsome?

Deimos grins. "Don't look so shocked. You are undeniably attractive."

Now my face is on fire, and I'm smiling before I can stop it, but he's—he's flirting with me. He's *definitely* flirting with me. "Um—thanks." I just stuttered. What's wrong with me? I turn to the glass. "So . . . how do we start this thing?"

Deimos laughs. "Right, sorry. Here." He waves his hand over the glass and Asha's voice fills the room as the image moves. I can't tell exactly where this is recorded, but it's outside somewhere, and there's a line of golden statues of stacked letters behind him. Asha looks over what I'm guessing is some kinduv crowd and then speaks.

"Tradition is the backbone of our community—it's what brings us together as a people, what unites us in times of hardship and strife. We uphold tradition with every prayer to *Kala*, with every celebration, with every coronation, and funeral, and birth. It's on our bodies and in our souls, it builds our towns and grows our cities, it weaves us together as a united people of many cultures and backgrounds and makes us strong.

"Tradition is a tenant every one of us honors, but so is progress.

"Dedication to progress is what gave us the nanite technology that strengthens us as a people—the technology that eradicated illness, quickly heals the wounded, and allows us to grow fresh food on even the most desolate land. The technology cools our homes in the southern lands, insulates them in the north, reinforces strength where we need it, and I'm sure it'll do so much more in the future.

"Progress has given us peace through the unification of the territories—it's what established a united government and an integrated system under a single monarch. It's what said enough violence, enough division, and now progress will lead us into a brighter future. Progress will make the world a safer, more loving place for our children and our children's children. It will bring us together in ways this world has not yet seen.

"I love this world and I love my people, but I believe it is progress—not tradition—that will lead us into a brighter tomorrow. We have so much to learn and so far to go, but we will do it together, as one people on one planet. This is our home, and together we will make it a better place for us all."

The crowd off-screen cheers so loudly Asha has to stop. He smiles at the crowd and cameras and nods, lifting his hand as he raises his voice. "Thank you, thank you. Good night."

The image freezes—Asha smiling endlessly at the crowd—and cheering stops. And for the first time, I can almost imagine Asha with Rani—two young people determined to change everything together. I can almost picture a younger, less-bitter version of the woman who calls herself my mother standing at Asha's side. I can almost understand how they thought bringing me into this world would be the catalyst for something bigger than any one of us.

But they were wrong. Because Asha never made it back to Asheron after my birth—he never had the chance to announce my existence and declare me his inheritor. Instead, he was murdered at the edge of the capital and the woman who was supposed to be my mother disguised my eyes so no one would know the truth and left me with the Kits.

And maybe it was easy for her—maybe all I ever was to her was a symbol of a movement, of a change with a real chance to take hold and set the humans free. And maybe when that movement died with Asha outside of Asheron, it was easy to turn away and move on to a new plan.

One of waiting, and violence, and explosions, and blood.

"He was really going to change things," I say into the quiet.

Deimos nods. "He was. He never directly explained what he planned to do—I suspect that was going to come after he announced you—but if you listen to what he was saying, it seems obvious. I'm almost surprised no one expected him to have a son with a red . . . a human."

"Given how everyone treats Sepharon-human relationships like an unthinkably disgusting thing, I'm not that surprised."

"*Shae*. That's true." He sighs and leans back on his arms. "Well, what was and could have been don't matter—what matters is you're here now, and it's your turn to make a change."

"I have to convince everyone to honor my inheritance before I can think about changing anything."

"Well, *shae*." Deimos smiles. "But convincing them to honor your birthright to begin with will be a change in itself—just the act of putting you on the throne spells a new tolerance Safara has never had."

"I guess so."

Deimos nods. "So, tomorrow what you'll want to do is reinforce the connection between you and *Sira* Asha, and show them you're a person who legitimately wants to make things better for everyone, *shae*? No one knows who you are right now, and half-bloods are spoken of like . . . well, you know. But if you go out there and show them you're not as terrifying or monstrous as people have been led to believe, it could be the start of something good."

"Sure. No problem. Just make thousands of people conditioned to hate me like me."

Deimos laughs weakly. "No one said it'd be easy, but I think you can do it."

"You barely know me."

"I know enough." Deimos smiles and looks me over. "Stand up, will you?"

"What?"

"Just humor me."

I frown, slip off his bed, and stand.

"Hmm . . . okay, I have an idea. Hold on." He disappears into his washroom, then after a moment calls, "Come in here, would you?"

What is he blazing doing? I'm not sure I want to know, but I warily enter his washroom anyway. He's pulled a floating flat cushion in front of him—one of the many seats placed along the counters bordering the room. And he's holding something that looks vaguely familiar—a red, thick handle of some kind. It's not a device we had at camp, so I'm not sure where I remember it from . . . did Kora use it once?

"What is that?"

Deimos laughs. "It doesn't bite—come sit. I've done this before, so don't worry."

"Done *what* before?"

He slides his thumb over the handle and it buzzes. That noise—my breath catches as a chill washes down my spine. It wasn't Kora I saw using it; it was one of the guards who prepped me for servitude.

Deimos must see something on my face, because he turns it off and places it on the counter. "What's wrong? You look like I've just asked you to jump out the window. They're just trimmers—you must have used one before, given how short your hair is . . ."

"*Nai*, I—" I take a deep breath and cross the distance between us, sitting on the cushion. "It's fine. Just don't make me bald."

Deimos laughs weakly. "That's not the plan—although I'll bet you probably *could* pull off bald well."

"Deimos."

"Relax, relax." He turns the trimmers back on. I grit my teeth against the buzz and grip my knees. This is fine. This is nothing like before. This isn't a big deal.

Deimos hesitates. "Remember the haircut Asha had in the video?"

Shaved close on the sides and back, short but trim on top. It suited him. "*Sha.*"

"That's what I'm doing. Just to visually connect you two a little more—I think the people will remember and make the connection quickly."

Tension gathers in my shoulders and knots at my spine at the incessant hum of the trimmers, but I bite my lip and say, "Okay."

"Okay. Hold still."

The low, warm buzz hums against the back of my neck and skull as Deimos works. I close my eyes and breathe deeply, in and out, trying not to think about the last time I had my head shaved, trying not to picture the blood dripping down my neck, the low burn of the knife's path under my jaw, the fear and deep-set ache of watching Kora's men kill Day right in front of me.

It was so long ago, but with the hum of the trimmers against my scalp, it feels like this morning. It feels like right now.

But then Deimos rests his hand on my shoulder, and I'm not sure how he knows how uncomfortable something as simple as cutting my hair is, but he must have gathered because he squeezes my shoulder and some of the tension melts away. My skin buzzes beneath his hand, and it's warm, and though my heart pounds harder, I'm not afraid. The iciness of the memory drips down my spine and disappears and I can breathe. I'm all right.

Sometime later, Deimos turns off the trimmer and says, "Done."

I force my eyes open. Deep breath in, deep breath out. Stand and face the wall-to-wall wide mirror.

I've never had a tailored cut, not like this. I touch the soft hair buzzed close to my scalp on the sides—down to my skin above my ears and a little longer closer to the top. He didn't touch the hair on top—even though it's been growing in for sets, it's still short—but with the shaping on the sides and back, now it looks purposeful. Like the length wasn't just hair growing in from getting my head shaved but was meant to imitate a style.

And you know, it looks okay. I look even more like Asha. But also—it looks right on me.

"Suits you." Deimos smiles.

I smile weakly and glance at him. "Thanks for your help."

"Of course. Just do us all a favor and win this thing."

"I'll do my best," I say, and for the first time, I mean it. For the first time I want this—and maybe, just maybe, I believe I can do this one step at a time.

This is what I was born for, and I'm not running from it anymore.

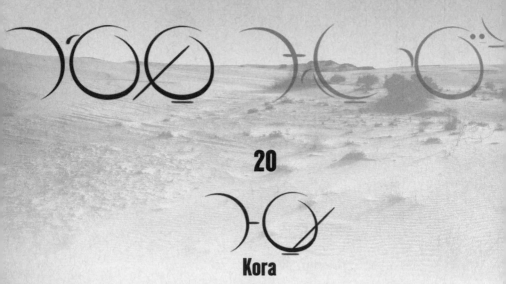

20

Kora

Are Eros and I irreparably broken? It's the question I wake with long before the suns rise—and long before I want to be awake.

Kissing Eros didn't feel like kissing him the first time. It wasn't breathless need and a wave of sparks under my skin—it wasn't wanting more and not caring what it meant for just a breath.

I care for Eros deeply, and it hurts to acknowledge things are changing between us. But I can't deny the truth. This time, kissing Eros felt like kissing a friend.

I run my hands over my face and sit up, grabbing the glass resting on my floating bedside table. Four quick swipes and I've opened Vejla's feed again. I shouldn't be looking at this, not when knowing the terrible truth will eat at me as long as there's nothing I can do. But I can't stay away, either. Elja is my home, and avoiding reality doesn't make it less real.

The feed awakens. The riots are still going on—I don't think I've ever seen so much of Vejla burn. I can't stomach the live footage for long so I find some articles about it and read until my face is hot, my eyes burn, and my breath trembles in my lungs.

Dima imprisoned protesters peacefully speaking out about the nanite attack. And then he imprisoned those protesting their arrest. And now the people want his head.

It should be gratifying to see my brother fail so spectacularly after cycles of believing he'd be a superior ruler. But with my people suffering and my brother walking the edge of a blade, I can't help but think this all would have been avoided if I'd just been a better *Avra*.

The dining hall is empty save for Niro and a couple of Lejv's supporters when Eros, Deimos, and I grab our morning meal after their early jog. It's a bit . . . uncomfortable . . . walking next to Eros and preparing to talk to him like nothing happened. Like we didn't kiss and it wasn't empty.

Eros doesn't look at me much as we fill our plates with food, and I'm not sure if it's because of the kiss, or because he's distracted, or both. I imagine most likely both. But maybe it's better that way—it's important we focus on the task. I may have failed in Elja, but I won't fail here. Eros must be the next *Sira*, and I'll do everything I can to make sure he gets there.

Deimos piles his plate high with fruit, meats, and wraps and encourages Eros to do the same, but even after Eros's plate is full, he barely picks at his food. Niro and the few others seem more interested in us than the food, so we ignore them until they leave.

"You should eat." I nod at Deimos's already half-empty plate. "I know you're nervous, but this meal has to hold you over until tonight."

Deimos nods. "Plus, we both just ran a ton—if you don't eat, you'll pass out midday."

Eros grimaces, but he makes more of an effort to clear some of the food from his plate. Deimos calls a servant over and asks him to bring a plate to Mal in Eros's room. I should ask Eros what he plans to talk about—get him thinking about what he'll say, but he's so anxious already and I don't want him to stop eating altogether, so I wait until he and Deimos have finished their meals before broaching the topic.

"We talked about it last night," Deimos says when I ask. "I showed him a couple of *Sira* Asha's speeches."

"Ah. Thus the new hairstyle."

Eros shrugs. "He thinks it'll help remind people of Asha."

I nod. "It'll help—not that you needed to given how much you look like him already, but it doesn't hurt." I glance over his black and gold clothing—regal, but understated. I glance at Deimos and he smiles.

"What do you think? Did I choose well?"

I nod. "You look like a monarch, Eros."

"Great," he mumbles. "Now I just have to figure out how to feel like one."

"I don't know, *eran*. Seems you've already got it down—anxious enough to toss your food and questioning whether this is merely a bad idea or an absolutely horrendous idea." Deimos looks at me. "Am I close?"

I laugh lightly. "That describes it well, actually."

Deimos grins. "Thought so. My father asked me to give a speech at a party once and I nearly lost my evening meal in front of hundreds of people."

Eros groans and covers his face. "You're not helping."

"I know."

"I'm certain you'll be fine." I touch his hand. Eros glances at me and bites his lip. "Think of it less like a speech and more like a dialogue. You're just introducing yourself to the people and showing them you're serious about inheriting the throne."

"And it'll only take a couple mos," Deimos adds. "It'll all be over before you know it, and we can return to the palace grounds and get drunker than the Star Festival."

"Speak for yourself," I say. "I'm not interested in completely losing my head."

Deimos smirks. "We'll see." He turns to Eros. "Do you want to practice what you're going to say first?"

Eros pushes his half-full plate away and stands. "Let's just get this over with."

We exit the palace grounds together, the heat of the suns warming me from the inside out. Eros is clearly anxious—biting his lip, taking measured breaths, tapping his fingers against his thighs—but to his credit, as soon as we pass the palace gates marking off the end of the complex, he pulls his shoulders back and swallows the nervous energy setting him on edge.

If I hadn't seen him looking sickly all morning, I'd almost believe the anxiety had faded away entirely. But I don't bring attention to it—last thing I need is to accidentally set him off again.

The streets are populated, as usual, but they seem not quite as full as I expected. Last time we traveled through Asheron—albeit before the explosion in Jol's Arena and the destruction of the nanites—the streets were packed with people, so full Serek's port had to slow to a crawl. Today, as we travel on foot, we bump shoulders with a few people here and there, but there's more than enough room to maneuver. Is this because of everything's that's happened, or is something going on? Even when we'd arrived late in the set with Eros and Mal after rescuing them from the redblood rebels, the streets had been more populated.

I glance at Deimos—he's frowning and looking around, too, and he's been out here more than once after the explosion and nanite attack. Which means this is unexpected.

Which means, more likely than not, something is happening.

A voice echoes faintly through the streets, wavering in the suns-burned air. Too quiet to make out at first, but distinctly male, with a confident tenor and a projection that sounds . . . amplified?

We pick up the pace, moving quickly beyond the shops and stalls and toward the city center. The voice grows louder, and the closer we get, the more I am sure this isn't just someone speaking loudly—this is someone speaking with an external amplification. It could be nothing—a vendor, a merchant, a protestor with an amplifier pressed to his throat.

Or it could be something significant.

Something like—

"*Kafra*," Deimos curses. "I know who that is."

Eros looks grim—our quick walk breaks into a jog as we dance around people not interested in the broadcast until we have to stop. Not because we've reached the center, but because a thick crowd of people blocks our way. And we're still nowhere near the city square.

"It's Lejv, isn't it?" Eros presses his fist to his lips. "He beat us to it."

I don't want to confirm until we've seen him ourselves, but my stomach twists all the same. If it *is* Lejv and the people are already gathering like this to see him . . .

It takes all my self-control to keep the hot panic prickling up my throat off my face. "We can't get in there to see. Not unless we want to push through thousands of people for the next quarter league."

Deimos scowls and glances around. He taps Eros's shoulder, catches my gaze, and nods to an alley to our left. "Follow me."

We do. I'm surprised—but also not—by how clean this space between shops is. The alleyways in Vejla were so packed with trash and debris it was dangerous to try to walk through—or, more likely, over—it. But here in Asheron, the black-brick streets are pristine, barely dusty, the stone still shiny under our feet. A warrior stands in the center of the alley and nods at us as we pass—keeping watch, I suppose.

And all the while, the voice that's likely Lejv's drifts over the crowd, still faint at this distance, but enough that I can grasp a few words here and there on the wind.

"Tradition is the backbone . . . a ruler who . . . stronger . . ."

"This way." Deimos pats a silver ladder bolted to the side of whatever building we're standing next to. The solider a few paces away watches us, but he doesn't protest as Deimos and then Eros climb—either this isn't prohibited, or he recognizes us. Probably the latter. I climb beneath Eros, my heart racing as I grip the warm metal rungs.

If this is Lejv like Deimos thinks it is—if he's packed the city center so fully that even here, a quarter league out, the crowd is too dense to pass through—if he's appealing to the people and he wins their favor . . .

This would be hard to bounce back from.

Deimos and Eros reach the edge of the building first, and the slump of Eros's shoulders tells me all I need to know. I stand next to him and grimace at the massive crowd extending to the circle, where Lejv stands on the elevated steps of the Appeals Building. Orb-guides zip past our heads, and Deimos snatches one out of the air. It whirs in protest and Deimos taps its surface.

"Are you in need of assistance?" it chirps.

"How long has Lejv been up there?" he asks.

"Twenty moments," it responds. "Would you like to view the recording?"

Deimos frowns and releases the orb-guide. "Not now."

The orb-guide spins and flies away just as the crowd bursts into applause and cheers. Eros turns away, running his hand through his newly trimmed hair. I tug on the wrap covering my burn scars. More than anything, I want to shout my frustration, but Eros is spiraling—it's in the tension in his shoulders, in the way he shakes his head as he paces a path into the dusty rooftop.

"So now what?" he asks. "That was our plan, wasn't it? Get out there before Lejv does—except he got there first, and now we're fucked."

"*Kafra*," Deimos hisses again.

"We'll just have to come up with another plan," I say, carefully keeping my voice steady. "Lejv got there first, but that doesn't mean you can't make your own appeal later."

"Right," Eros says, "after half the city has cheered at his rally and decided to support him."

"The people can still make their own decision—"

"Eros is right," Deimos says tightly. "The key to this plan

was to get there first so he could make an impression before they've seen anyone else. It's going to be a much harder battle now that they've heard—and evidently love—Lejv."

"Harder, *sha*," I say, "but not impossible."

Deimos shrugs. "Nothing's impossible, but this is a massive setback we can't afford."

And I want to say he's wrong. I want to say we'll make do and find another way to garner support from the people, but the truth is I can't say that, not genuinely.

The truth is, with so much stacked against us from the start, I don't know how we'll come back from this.

21

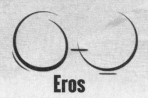

Eros

We wander.

I don't know where we're going—I don't know if any of us do—but I get the impression Asheron isn't too dangerous because no one seems concerned. Or they figure we can take care of ourselves, which we can. I'm not armed, but Deimos probably is, and . . .

And it doesn't matter, anyway. Most of the city is somewhere long behind us, cheering for Lejv and pledging their support.

What am I doing here? Why did I ever think I had a chance—as though anyone would ever support a half-blood on the throne, regardless of my birthright, regardless of my charismatic father, regardless of the blazing world prince declaring me the inheritor.

None of that matters, because no one will ever see past the too-light markings on my skin. My not-round, not-really-notched-and-pointed ears. My impossible-to-hide not-human, not-Sepharon genetics. I can't pretend to be one of them, not completely, not really, because I'm not. It took me nearly two decades to figure out I'm not one of the humans, either. I'm something else entirely, and only one of me exists.

I'm not one of anyone.

We wander deeper and deeper into the city—or maybe farther away. I'm not sure how far this city goes, but I imagine it's larger than we'd ever be able to walk in a set, given the whole *capital of the world* thing. It doesn't matter. With the silence so thick between us, we'd stroll right out of the city just to get away from the sinking sense of failure.

Eventually, the city changes. The streets are still polished here—absurdly so; our reflections glint back at us in the black rock beneath our feet. But the buildings change from gleaming, newly updated shops and shiny floating stalls to what I'm pretty sure are homes. Dull, rectangular buildings climb high into the air, like massive pillars with evenly spaced holes for windows. Here, the people aren't wearing the latest flashy fashion statement—they're dressed better than Vejla's poor, for sure, but their clothes are well-worn, sometimes too big or small, sagging and frayed at the edges. People wear their hair longer here—there are more beards on one street than I'd seen my entire stay at the Eljan palace.

And then there's us. Freshly trimmed, dressed in Ona's—and for Deimos, A'Sharo's—finest. Even without my gold eyes and even without Kora and Deimos's markings declaring them royalty, it's obvious we don't belong here.

And yet, no one looks as us threateningly or with disgust or dislike. No one shouts at us to leave or glares as we walk by.

Instead, we get curious glances. Murmurs of conversation follow us—a few bursts of quiet laughter—my name slipping quietly from their lips, flashes of hesitant smiles.

I've literally never had a Sepharon I didn't know smile at me. And I'm not sure if it's because Kora's here—or, more likely, maybe, Deimos?—but the soft smiles and nods as we pass are undeniable.

And then a man steps out of a building ahead of us, walks past the small group of kids and adults alike sitting on the steps of the entrance, and steps right to the edge of the street, watching us approach with his arms crossed over his chest. His skin is dark, so I almost don't notice it at first, but when Deimos says, "Huh. Interesting," next to me, I look again.

My steps slow. The man's arms are bare—no markings of any kind, no lighter paths of skin every Sepharon is born with, no swirls or lines they call *Kala*'s mark. His ears are round, but his eyes aren't a cloudy gray.

He's human, and as far as I can tell, he's free. Living in the Sepharon capital of the world.

I stop and take a closer look at the crowd—most of them are Sepharon, as I expected and assumed—but the man who caught my attention isn't the only clear-eyed human watching us. I spot a woman, too, holding a small human child against her hip. A teenage girl leaning against a human man I assume is her father. They're here, living among the Sepharon at the edge of a city not so long ago ruled by a man who ordered their execution.

"I didn't realize . . ." Kora starts quietly, then hesitates. "Actually, I guess this makes sense—Serek and I heard screaming from the city when . . . when the nanites were activated."

I grimace. "What's your name?" I ask the man we spotted first.

"Bjeren," he answers and I arch an eyebrow. He doesn't just live among the Sepharon—he has a Sepharon name.

"And you're free?" The words are out of my mouth before I consider how he might take it. Bjeren's eyes narrow. "I'm not questioning it or threatening your way of life," I add quickly. "I just—I had no idea humans lived freely in Sepharon cities anywhere."

"We do. Quietly," Bjeren answers. "It only works in areas where our Sepharon neighbors are accepting, but we're here—and not just in Asheron. The northern territories have a lot more of us. The Sepharon there are more widely welcoming in the right cities."

"And . . . intermarriage?" Kora asks carefully.

Bjeren purses his lips. "Too dangerous anywhere. Especially for any kids that'd come out of it." He looks at me. "But I don't need to explain that."

I shake my head and glance around. "You shouldn't have to hide. Any of you. But it's good to see some humans living here peacefully. I honestly . . . I never imagined this was already happening."

Bjeren nods. "Sepharon rulers would like us to think it can't happen. It's easier to pretend we're lesser and that humans and Sepharon are incompatible when there's no proof of us living peaceably."

"And they know we won't bring attention to it, because the spotlight is too dangerous," the mother with the baby adds. "So we don't talk about it, and they pretend we don't exist and nothing changes."

"Until they tried to kill us." Bjeren scowls. "I'm not going to sit here quietly next time they decide murdering us is the best option."

A Sepharon man near Bjeren rests his hand on his shoulder. "*Sira* Roma's actions were horrific, and many of us support our human brothers. We've had enough inequality and injustice, but nothing's going to change if we stay silent. We have to say *enough*."

A shout of approval across the street encourages another and another. More people come out of their buildings, lining the street on either side, filling in slowly around us.

"And I'm with you, too," I say. I take a breath and look around at the thickening crowd—mostly Sepharon, but human faces, too, watching me with intensity in their gazes and hope on their lips. Seeing them like this—humans and Sepharon side by side, it's incredible. And seeing them look at me with something like expectation fills me with energy. I pull my shoulders back and look at Bjeren, at the Sepharon man standing at his side. "I can't promise any of you I'm going to win this campaign—*Sira* Ashen's choice, Lejv, is on the other side of the city as we speak, promising to take the throne with thousands of Sepharon swearing to back him. The Council recognizes I'm *Sira* Asha's son—that my birthright is on the throne—but they don't care. They don't want a half-blood in the capital and I can't change that.

"But I can promise every one of you I'm going to fight. For you. For my human nephew who lost his whole family—my brother and his wife and most of their children—to Sepharon violence. I'll fight to make sure that attempt at blazing *genocide* never happens again. I'll fight so you can live freely and loudly together, so you can love who you love and start families fearlessly. I'll fight so you never have to look over your shoulder again, so you never have to worry about Sepharon soldiers knocking on your doors to tear you away from freedom and your families. I'll fight so every one of us lives at peace, so we stand together equally.

"We're a divided world, and we're ripping each other apart—but we can be stronger if we stand together. I believe that with everything I am, and I think you do, too."

A cheer like a roar rips through the crowd, surrounding us in a wave. Those orb-camera things whip around us—when did they get here? How long have they been recording? But with the voices of human and Sepharon people falling over me like rain, with Bjeren's smile and the nod of approval from the Sepharon man at his side, I can't stop the smile that washes over my mouth and the lightness bubbling up in my chest.

A feeling I'd almost forgotten; a feeling I'd long given up on; a feeling that tastes like hope.

"*Kafra*, that was amazing," Deimos says with a laugh as we enter the palace. "You might have a shot at this, Eros."

"Might." I wipe sweat off my forehead, but even the built-up oppressive heat indoors isn't enough to leech away my smile.

"It's not quite what we planned," Kora says, "and it won't get you as much initial support as we'd hoped, but . . . this might actually be better than what we thought we needed."

I glance at her. "Really?"

She nods. "If what Bjeren said was true about others like them out there, you may already have more supporters than we accounted for. That's good—the guide footage the Council will review to determine the will of the people will show that. We'll just have to make sure they don't ignore it."

"That's true," Deimos says, "but enough strategy for one set, *shae*? We should celebrate. I, for one, want to see what happens when the two of you get spectacularly intoxicated."

My face warms—the last time I got drunk, I ended up laying a camp girl who hated me for it for as long as I knew her afterward. Until Aryana was cremated with so many others after the nanite attack.

"I'm not sure that's such a good idea."

Deimos blinks at me with false innocence. "*Nai*? Why ever not?"

I shove him lightly, and he laughs.

"I've never been *spectacularly* intoxicated," Kora says thoughtfully. "But I may have to agree with Eros here."

"You two suck the fun out of everything."

We laugh and turn the corner into the hall where our rooms—and Mal—are waiting. But when we walk around the bend, Mal isn't leaning against the wall between my and Kora's rooms. Instead, we find a mountain of a Sepharon man I know all too well. A man who sets my heart racing and turns my blood to ice. And the cold—the burning—the pain and screaming—he nearly killed me. I never expected to have to face him again, but here he is.

Jarek.

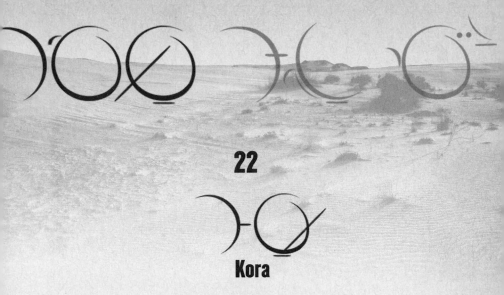

22

Kora

"What are you doing here?" The words are out of my mouth before I can stop them. I haven't seen my brother's partner—the man who is surely the new *Avra*'s second, who has stood at my brother's side since they were boys—since the night I ran from Elja.

And now he's here. And Dima isn't. Or at least, he isn't in the hall with Jarek.

Deimos stiffens next to Eros. "Should I call the guards?"

"*Naï*," I say quickly. "It's fine, I'll handle him. You two check on Mal."

Jarek frowns at Eros and Deimos. "I just need to speak to Kora."

"Whatever you want to say to her, you can say to us," Eros answers stiffly. He looks ill—pale, and are his fists shaking?

"Eros, it's fine," I cut in. "I can handle him. Please—take care of your nephew. Jarek and I will be in my room."

"Kora—"

"He's not an assassin, Eros," I say, exasperated, though it's nice that he actually seems to care. "And you're no longer my bodyguard. I'm fine."

Eros scowls, but walks to his room and doesn't look back when the door slides open before him. Deimos frowns and glances at me. "If you need anything, you know where to find us."

"Thank you, Deimos."

He nods and follows after Eros.

My heart pounds and my stomach churns as I enter my room. Jarek can't be here to hurt me, as he and Dima have everything they wanted and I don't pose a threat, not anymore. It wouldn't make sense for him to come all this way to go after me when I was leaving them alone.

Which means something must be wrong. Or maybe everything is wrong. I saw the riots in Vejla on the feed myself . . . has something happened to Dima?

As soon as the doors close behind him, I face Jarek. "Is Dima okay? What's happening?"

Jarek grimaces. "I . . . assume you've seen Eljan coverage off the feed."

"Not as much as I would like, but I have seen some."

"Then you know about the riots."

"I saw a glimpse of that, *sha*. How long has that been going on now?"

Jarek sighs. "It started in earnest a few sets ago. I'm sure you've heard of the arrests Dima ordered."

I take a breath and nod. "I did."

"That's not the worst of it. The cities of the north have started a movement and are threatening to break from the territory—so Dima increased the military presence there, and violence against the guard has escalated. We're on the brink of civil war, Kora. I'm not sure how much longer Dima will be able to hold off further escalation. Not to mention, the guard is barely holding off the mob. Fortunately, I don't think the people yet realize how easily they could break through the gate with the nanite reinforcement gone."

My heart stills for a breath. I hadn't read that this morning, though it had crossed my mind. "*Kafra*," I whisper.

Jarek nods. "Then there's the matter of what will happen when the new *Sira* is chosen."

I frown. "What do you mean?"

"Dima conspired with Roma, and it was his . . . bending of the truth that led to the nanite attack. It's public knowledge Dima supported Roma fully, which means when the new *Sira* is chosen, with Roma no longer around to be punished . . ."

Something cold slinks down my throat and coats my heart, spreading through my veins with every pump. "You think the new *Sira* will punish Dima in his stead."

Jarek nods. "They would've punished him either way, but I . . . even if Eros isn't chosen as *Sira*, Dima is as good as dead for supporting Roma and catalyzing the attack. The people will demand retribution—and they'll get it."

I sink onto my bed; tears sting my eyes and talons scrape the back of my throat.

For all Dima has done to me—for turning his back on me again and again, nearly murdering Serek and framing me for it to take my place on the throne—it should be easy to turn away from this and tell Jarek to deal with it on his own. It should be easy to say he deserves whatever comes to him, whether imprisonment or execution. It should be a simple thing to turn away at my brother's weakest moment.

But even with everything he's done to me, I can't hate him. Dima was dangerously cruel, but he's my brother. And as much as I wish I didn't, as simple as it would make this if it weren't true, I still love him. I can't just leave him to die—but what does he expect me to do? He *imprisoned* peaceful pro-testors and those who rightfully spoke up against genocide. Elja was fragile and fracturing when I had to run—now my brother is smothering them.

I look at Jarek. "What exactly are you asking?"

"Return to Elja with me. I know you have little reason to trust me after everything, but I swear on my life I'll keep you safe. You can't help Dima from here, but in Elja . . ."

I take a slow breath, fighting against my racing heart. Return to Elja with Jarek—who supported my near-arrest to begin with. To somehow save Dima. Who tried to kill me. I choose my words carefully: "I can't help either of you if I'm powerless."

Jarek bites his lip and nods. "I know. But I'm not asking you to return as Dima's sister—I'm asking you to return as Elja's *Avra*. As *Avra*, you could reinstate order and protect Dima from the people before they break through . . . and I hope from whatever the new *Sira* demands."

My throat tightens. "I'm not *Avra* anymore—Dima is."

"He is, but I'm certain after everything that's happened under Dima's command, the people—and Elja's council—will approve your reinstatement. I think they'll agree you're more suited for the role than one of your militaristic cousins. And I—" Jarek's voice breaks, and he closes his eyes and inhales deeply. "I will support you, as well, with the backing of Elja's military behind me."

Jarek is offering me everything I wanted just a few terms ago—support from my people, support from my military, sup-port from the council who whispered behind my back and probably plotted against me alongside Dima. A few terms ago, their promised support would have made me happier than I've ever been—it would have lifted every worry and erased every hurt from being rejected as *Avra* again, and again, and again.

But today, with the words slipping from Jarek's lips, they only bring me sadness.

"You're going to betray him for me?"

Jarek bites his lip. "I've already betrayed him by coming here. But I'm not . . . I'm not doing it for you, I'm doing it for Elja. And for him. If you can't save him, I don't believe anyone can. But I want to try, and the only way I can think of is to have you back in Elja. As *Avra*."

I snort. "As if my brother would ever let that happen. He'd have me arrested the moment he saw me."

"He wouldn't be able to. When he became *Avra*, he made me head of the guard. I'll keep you protected."

I frown. "If you're head of the guard, why did you allow him to arrest those protesters?"

He sighs and runs his fingers over his beard. "Undermining your brother publicly is very different from privately not allowing him to do something."

It's true. But here's the truth he isn't saying: going back to Elja means leaving Eros when he needs me most. It means turning away from my closest friend and hoping he can handle the pressure of politics, of a world full of poison foreign to him. It's hoping he can learn everything he needs to learn to navigate the realm of royals and political alliances—something most royals spend their entire lives preparing for—in a matter of sets, and hoping he can do it on his own.

Or, maybe not on his own. Deimos is here—and as *Avra-kaï* d'A'Sharo, he's been just as prepared as I was. But can I trust Deimos to take care of Eros and teach him everything he'll need? Can I trust him not to turn his back on Eros if things don't progress the way we hope—if his family pressures him to support Lejv instead?

The truth is I don't know. Deimos seems trustworthy enough, and he's been more helpful and supportive than I ever would have expected of any Sepharon *kaï*, but I don't know him like I do Eros.

But I also don't have much choice. Not really. Not because of my brother, who doesn't come close to earning my turning away from Eros again. But my people deserve better than Dima's violent rule. I failed them once already, and I'll never forgive myself if my territory crumbles while I stood by and did nothing to try to stop it.

"I need to talk to Eros," I finally say. "But I'll go with you, Jarek. Today."

Deimos and Eros are laughing with Mal when I enter the room, and I almost feel guilty for the dark cloud I'm bringing in with me. Their laughter dies away as Eros and Deimos look at me, and Eros stands, his smile slipping off his lips.

"What happened?" he asks. "Why is Jarek here? Are you okay?"

I sigh. "I'm fine. I need to go to Elja." The protest is on Eros's lips in an instant—I raise my hand. "Before you say anything, let me explain, first."

"But—"

Deimos grabs Eros's wrist and pulls him back, forcing him to sit on the edge of his bed beside Mal. "Let her explain." He looks at me. "Go ahead."

And so I do.

When I'm finished, neither Eros nor Deimos speak. Eros has his head in his hands, tension gathered in his tightened shoulders. But it's Mal who is the first to speak. "So, you have to go back to Elja to save your brother."

I nod. "And, with *Kala*'s grace, to save my territory. I owe my people that much."

"Your brother tried to blazing *kill* you." Eros stands, his voice shaking. "He *framed* you for attempted murder."

"Eros—" Deimos starts, but Eros steps forward.

"And even if you don't care about that—even if you don't care how he nearly cost you your life on more than one occasion, he blazing locked me in a dungeon and *tortured* me for six *kafran* sets. And now you're going back there because he can't handle the situation he made himself? Are you serious?"

I frown. "This isn't just a matter of not being able to handle a bad situation, Eros, this is *his life,* and more importantly, my people—"

"It was your life, too, but he didn't care about that when he was trying to take your place as *Avra*."

I close my eyes and inhale deeply. "I know."

"Then why in the Void would you *ever* go back?"

"Because he's my brother," I snap. "And failed *Avra* or not, I am responsible for my people. You would have done the same for yours—in fact, you're here right now at least partially for them."

Eros scowls. "My people aside, my brother never tried to *actually* kill me."

"And if he had? Would you turn your back if his life was at risk? If he needed you, despite everything he'd done? Can you truly say you'd forget about him when he needed you most?"

"He would deserve it," Eros mumbles.

"*Sha,* he would. And Dima does deserve my turning away. He deserves to die, and he deserves to watch the territory he lusted after fall apart because of his foolishness. But my people don't deserve to suffer at his hand—and deserving or not, I won't leave my brother to die."

The following silence is so thick it's suffocating. Eros stares at the floor, Deimos grimaces at Eros, and Mal glances awkwardly between them, and then squints at me and says, "So when are you leaving?"

"Immediately," I answer. "I just wanted to talk to Eros first and . . . well, I don't have a lot of belongings here."

"Mal and I will take a walk." Deimos stands. "Give you two some . . . privacy." Deimos rests his hand on Mal's shoulder, and moments later, Eros and I are alone.

"He tried to kill you twice, you know," Eros says flatly.

I blink. "What?"

"Framing you was the second time. The first was the assassin who broke into your room while I was guarding you."

"How do you . . ." The truth is, I'd suspected as much already—but hearing Eros confirm it aches deeply. "Are you sure?"

Eros hesitates, then nods. "The Remnant leader, Rani, said Dima hired them to send an assassin after you. The pale man was one of them. Dima paid them with credits, weaponry, and tech."

I close my eyes and take a shaky breath before opening them again. "Okay," I say softly. "Thank you for telling me."

Eros opens and closes his mouth. He pauses, like he's considering something, then shakes his head. "But you're still leaving."

"I don't have a choice. I'm not leaving my brother to die and my people to suffer."

"But you're leaving me to figure this out by myself." He looks at me. "Again."

"Eros—"

He stands. "Forget it, Kora. You want to leave, leave. I shouldn't be surprised."

I cross the space between us and hold his arms. "It's not like that, Eros. I'm not leaving because I *want* to, I'm leaving because I have a responsibility to my people. I couldn't live with myself if I left Dima to a probable execution."

He bites his lip and doesn't look at me.

I hesitate. I don't want to say the words, I don't want to acknowledge the reality of the distance spreading between us. It hurts too much to know I'm likely at fault and leaving will make it worse. But pretending not to see it won't help anyone, either. "And . . . it's not like it's been the same between us, anyway, has it?"

Eros's shoulders slump. "I don't know."

"I think you do." My eyes sting as reality wells up inside me. As the feelings I've been trying to ignore spill over my lips. "Just . . . be honest with me. You don't trust me anymore, do you?"

When Eros looks at me, the pain in his gold eyes twists into me like a wound. He takes a shaky breath. "You betrayed me."

I swallow my instinctual denial. When I kissed him and then pulled away to court Serek, I hadn't meant it as a betrayal. I was scared and trying to protect him by drawing attention away from him, and though I knew my feelings for Eros, I hadn't thought it'd ever be possible to pursue them. I'd thought walking away was best for us both.

I was wrong. But I can't undo what I did. And I can't ask Eros to forget my actions and trust me like he once did.

"I understand." My voice aches with restrained tears. "I'm sorry."

He bites his lip. "I know."

I inhale deeply. "We've changed, which is natural given everything but . . . maybe we were never meant to be more than . . ." My throat goes tight. I drop my hands and take a shaky breath. "I think you feel it, too."

"I don't know what I feel anymore," Eros says softly. "I'm exhausted and terrified all the time, and I don't know what I'm doing or how you expect me to navigate this without your help."

"You have Deimos," I answer. "We're both still getting to know him but . . . I think he's genuine. He truly intends to help you however he can."

Eros purses his lips but eventually nods. "I think so, too."

"He's just as equipped to help you with this as I am. Maybe even more so—I was never the best at the charismatic side of things . . ."

He laughs weakly. "Understatement."

"Your faith in me is inspiring."

Eros smiles weakly and touches my cheek. His warmth is a bonfire on a cold night—I want nothing more than to press myself against him and let him hold me for eternity. So when he kisses me, I don't pull away. I close my eyes and taste his soft lips, the warmth of his body, the sorrow of this slow kiss, which isn't starting something new, but ending what we had.

When he pulls away with shining eyes, it's clear he knows it, too.

"We won't be able to have a romantic relationship if I'm *Avra* again and you're *Sira*," I say. "It's strictly forbidden for a *Sira* to be with any *Avra* because it'd upset the balance of the territories. As *Sira*, you can never appear partial to any one territory or monarch. It's . . . it's essential to the peace of the nations."

Eros forces a smile, but the pain is evident on his face. I shouldn't—not now, maybe not ever again—but I kiss him again, quickly, just one last good-bye.

"I'll always love you," I whisper on his lips. "But I want you to find happiness without me. I want you to succeed in everything you do. You'll always have my support, Eros, but this—" My voice catches. I have to finish; I can't leave without closing this door. It wouldn't be fair to either of us. "This is good-bye." I take his hand and trace the oath scar on it. "I release you freely from your oath. You served me well, Eros, but it's time you become your own man, now, free from any bonds or promises. When I see you again . . . it'll probably be political."

His shoulders and jaw are tight when he nods. His voice is hoarse, hurting, when he says, "I wish you all the luck in the stars, Kora. Take back your territory and show that *kafran* brother of yours what a real *Avra* looks like."

I smile and step away. "Thank you, Eros. You are truly my dearest friend."

And I walk away with Eros's gaze on my back and my heart bleeding into my lungs.

23

Eros

"*Ej*, Eros. Eros. Wake up."

Part of me wants to punch Deimos for shaking me awake when I've finally—*finally*—fallen asleep, but most of me is too tired to open my eyes, let alone lift my fist and aim it at his teeth. How long have I slept? It couldn't have been long. It was mostly another thrilling night of staring at the ceiling.

Stars, I'm so tired.

"I know you're awake. Your breathing changed two mos ago."

"Then maybe you should take the hint and leave," I say. "You know how difficult it's been for me to sleep."

Deimos sighs. "*Shae*, and I do feel badly, especially given how relaxed you looked, but the Council called a meeting and we needed to be heading over some time ago."

I groan and force my eyes open. Sit up, try to rub the sleep from my eyes. Mal is still fast asleep next to me—star-shined kid can sleep through anything, I swear.

"Do you have pants on, or do you need me to grab you some?"

"You really think I sleep naked when sharing a bed with my nephew?" I deadpan.

"Good point."

I shake my head and roll out of bed. Walk into the washroom, but hesitate in front of the sink; before the whole torture thing, I'd splash cold water on my face to help wake me up, but . . . better not. I'm not really up for risking another panic attack. I wet a fuzzy blanket and pat my face down instead, then run the damp cloth over my hair for good measure. It'll have to do.

I sigh at my reflection—the water is drying and sweat drips down my back. The suns haven't even risen yet and it's already hot as the stars. And here I thought it might be a little cooler up north. Not that we're really *north* as far as Safara is concerned, but we're still north of Elja. But evidently not enough not to broil to death inside.

Back in my room, Deimos has picked out some clothes for me. "Just get changed quickly. We need to—are you wearing the ring of *Sirae*?"

I blink. Glance at my hand. "Oh, *shae*. Kora gave it back a few sets ago. I put it on again after she left." Putting the ring on again had felt more purposeful this time around. The first time I'd slid it on my finger, under the waning light of the four moons, I didn't know what it meant. I knew it'd been held for me, but I hadn't recognized it as anything more than a nice, probably valuable ring.

This time, when I put it on, I knew the history behind the ring—that every *Sira* up until my father wore it and passed it down to his firstborn son. I was next in line; though Lejv and others, I'm sure, would like to take it from me, the ring of *Sirae* is mine.

Deimos arches an eyebrow. "What was Kora doing with the ring of *Sirae*?"

"I'm guessing she got it from Serek, who got it from me. I guess Asha left it for me when I was born."

"Huh. It suits you." He smiles, but only briefly, then hesitates. "I've been meaning to ask . . . is it night terrors that keep you awake?"

I sigh. Look away. Stare at the wall. "I don't know. I guess. It's memories, mostly—of being tortured, and my family dying in front of me, and wondering if they'd still be alive if I just—if I'd gotten there faster or—"

"Hold on." Deimos lifts his hand and closes the distances between us, gripping my arms and looking into my eyes. "You're referring to the nanite attack, *shae*? You know that wasn't your fault, don't you?"

I bite my lip. He means that, there's an intense earnestness in his eyes. It's hard to look at, so I glance at the swirled, tooth-like markings on his left shoulder, instead. They almost look like mine, except, you know, lighter and easier to see.

"Eros."

I sigh, though my throat is tight and painful. "I-I know. But maybe if I'd gotten there faster—"

"*Naï.*" His voice is firm, demanding. I meet his gaze again. "You can't do that. You can't torture yourself with *what ifs* you'll never be able to change. *Nothing* about what happened was your fault."

I close my stinging eyes and take a shaky breath before I lose it. But he's—he's right. I know he's right. It's not going to be easy to stop asking *what if* but . . . it wasn't my fault.

It wasn't my fault.

"Thank you," I whisper, opening my eyes again. "I guess I . . . needed to hear that."

Deimos smiles weakly, releases my arms, and pats my back. "I'm glad to help. If you ever need to talk, don't hesitate to let me know, *shae*? I'm here for you."

I smile weakly. It's nice of him to offer—I haven't had someone to turn to like that since Nol and Esta died. I don't know that I'll take him up on it, but it's good to know anyway. "Okay. Thanks."

Deimos smiles and nods to the door. "We *do* need to go, though."

A couple mos later, we're walking into the banquet hall, where pastries, breads, fruit, and warm orange *melos*—a sweet, thick dish that's not quite solid, not quite liquid and apparently a common morning dish in Ona—have been set out. The Council isn't here yet, but most of the royals have arrived and are picking at the food. I'm not hungry, but Deimos passes me a thick stone cup with a steaming, frothy white drink inside.

"To help you wake up," he says quietly. "It's good, trust me."

I sip it—it's sweet and spicy and traces a hot path all the way down to my stomach. The warmth would feel better on a cold day, but it tastes good, and after a few sips, I'm actually more awake.

"Do I want to know what this is?" I ask.

Deimos snickers. "It's nothing bad. It's a popular Sephari drink called *ljnte*. I practically grew up on this stuff."

"Good to know," I mumble, taking another sip. The drink is making my head buzz a little, but not in a sluggish can't-think way like with brew. It makes keeping my eyes open and not daydreaming about sleep easier—like alertness in a cup.

I may have to drink this stuff more often.

"*Ora'denja.*" Aleija and Jule sit next to me, filling their own cups with *ljnte* as Jule serves herself a bowl of *melos.*

"*Denna,*" Deimos says cheerily. "Excited to see all our bright and shining faces this morning before the suns rise?"

Aleija laughs. "Oh, *sha*—bright and shining is exactly how I'd describe everyone right now."

"Well *I'm* feeling bright and shiny," Deimos says. "Although that might be my second cup of *ljnte* talking."

Aleija laughs again and even I can't help a smile. Kora's right—he's ridiculously good at the charismatic, social part of royal life.

Aleija looks at me. "I heard Kora left last night with an Eljan soldier—is that true?"

I glance at Deimos and he nods. "It is," I say. "Though she went voluntarily, not because the soldier forced her to."

"Interesting," she says. "Do you anticipate her return?"

I resist the urge to frown and sip my *ljnte.* "*Naï.*"

"Ah. Shame, she seemed like quite an asset."

"She had pressing matters in Elja to take care of," I answer. "Loyalty to her territory first, and all of that."

"Understandable."

I shrug, but Deimos is giving me that *keep talking* look, so I glance at Aleija again—who I guess noticed the ring because she's staring at my hand with a soft smile.

"It's good to see you wear your inheritance," she says softly. "I'd wondered what happened to the ring."

"I'm proud to wear it." I touch it with my thumb, and Aleija nods. "Um . . . how is Daïvi doing these days?

"Very well, thank you for asking. The people are happy with my sister's rule, and everyone's excited about the upcoming royal wedding."

"Royal wedding—who's getting married?"

"My little brother, Daven." Aleija smiles. "To his boyfriend, Zek. He's lowborn and they met by chance but have grown to care for each other deeply. It's all very romantic." She grins and I can't help but smile. It feels like so long ago when I met them in Elja—Daven came to court Kora but made it obvious his heart wasn't in it. He and Zek were delighted when Kora told them she'd be choosing someone else.

"That's good to hear," I say. "Daven and Zek seemed happy together when I met them."

Aleija arches an eyebrow. "You've met my brother?"

"I worked at the Eljan palace before I came here. I was there when your brother came to court Kora."

"Ahh, *sha*, I remember now. I was relieved when Kora turned them away."

I smile softly. "So were they."

"*Sha,* they were." Aleija smirks and sips her drink then turns and kisses Jule on the cheek. The two begin talking quietly so I turn back to Deimos.

"Not bad," he appraises quietly. "Now you just have to do it again with everyone else."

"Wouldn't count on it," I say. "That only worked because I happen to have met her brother. I don't have that connection with everyone else."

But Deimos shakes his head. "*Naï*, that happened because you found a point of connection. You can repeat it with the others—you just have to dig a little to figure out what the connection is."

"Easier said than done when half the people here hate me."

"*Sha*, well, I never said socializing with everyone would be easy."

I sigh. "This is all so complicated."

"Once you get accustomed to it, it's not as complicated as you think. You just need some time to grow into it."

Grow into it. Sure. The doors slide open behind us and the patter of footsteps hushes the quiet conversations. I don't need to look back to see who's come in—the Council is here.

And Lejv walked in with them like he's one of them.

Deimos scowls. "So much for impartiality," he mutters.

"They were never pretending to be impartial," I answer quietly. I'm impressed with how calm I sound, even though I'm anything but.

Deimos glares at them, and maybe their blatant favoritism should bother me, but unlike Deimos, I never expected anything less. I'm used to being overlooked and underestimated. Maybe, just once, I'll be able to use their low expectations to my favor.

Or maybe I'll crash and burn and be on the run again, this time with Mal at my side, his life equally at risk. But I can't worry about that, not now. I run my thumb over the smooth black and gold ring on my finger. I'm meant to be here. I am.

The Council members take their seats on the inner rim of the crescent table, former *Sira* Ashen across from me once again. This time when he glances at me, I meet his eyes and hold myself confidently. Shoulders back. Gaze firm. He breaks eye contact first, and even though it's nothing, it feels like a small victory. A group of two men and two women stand tall behind them, gazing over us.

These four are unlike any Sepharon I've seen before—they have white writing inked into their marks, not black, and there's something wrong with their eyes. Each of them have the multicolor rings all Sepharon have, but the colors look bleached—so light their irises look almost colorless, leaving only their pinpoint dark pupils. They all wear identical flowing robes, with layers of fabric over layers of fabric—they must be baking under all that clothing but somehow they don't seem bothered.

I glance at Deimos, but he doesn't seem concerned—his shoulders are relaxed, and he even has the echo of a smile on his lips.

I'm not sure who these people are or what it means that they're here, but if Deimos doesn't seem worried about it, then maybe I shouldn't be either.

Of course, Deimos might just be hiding his nervousness, since this is politics, and everything—even your blazing facial expressions—is a calculated move.

I try to keep my face even as I look over them again. I'm not sure it's working, but better than not trying, I guess. I know how not to react to even the shittiest situations.

"The Council has deliberated this delicate situation," Ashen finally says. "With Eros's genetic tests confirmed as former *Sira* Asha's son, the Council recognizes his bid for the throne must be taken seriously. By the same token, the Council agrees in this unusual situation that with a candidate completely unprepared for a role of such magnitude, we must take another more qualified candidate into account with equal consideration. Guide footage has been reviewed thoroughly and both candidates have already received support from the people—Lejv, in the main square amongst thousands of Asheron's own, and Eros, amongst the . . . commoners."

While I'm glad they've seen the footage, it takes everything in me not to scowl at the way Ashen's lip curls when he says *commoners*. As though their support somehow means less because they're poor.

"Therefore, the Council has agreed to take both Eros d'Elja and Lejv Isak d'Ona as true candidates for the throne. Furthermore, the Council has agreed to accept the High Priest's request to be involved in the decision-making process, to ensure *Kala*'s will ultimately influences the final decision."

No one speaks, and no one looks especially surprised. I probably shouldn't be surprised, either—the Sepharon as a whole err on the religious side.

I'm just not sure what this means for me. How is *Kala*'s will determined? Could they use this as an excuse to pick Lejv even if I perform better than expected? Who verifies the will of a deity who may or may not actually be real?

"As such," Ashen continues, "the High Priest will examine both Eros and Lejv in three sets' time to determine *Kala*'s first judgment of the character and devotion of both candidates."

I'm not supposed to react to this, but my shoulders tense before I can stop them, Ashen's words sinking into my blood and seizing my muscles.

A priest is going to determine my character and devotion.

Devotion to a religion I'm not a part of—to a god I don't believe in—to make a decision that could overrule the whole Council. Which means one thing.

I'm fucked.

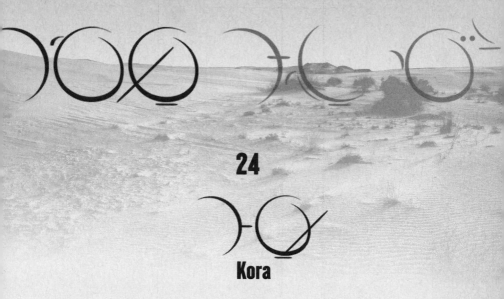

24

Kora

Trying to get through the front gates of the palace grounds is impossible—and dangerous to attempt—because it would require fighting through the mob of more than a five hundred strong and opening the gates the guard are working so desperately to keep closed. Sitting in Jarek's transport, I slink back away from the window, silently grateful no one can see into the tinted windows as we glide past the edge of the crowd, far from the gates. They aren't protesting me— not anymore—but that doesn't slow my accelerating heart or calm the hum between my lungs.

I close my eyes and take a steadying breath. This was, potentially, a catastrophically bad idea. What's to say the people won't be just as furious to see me as they are Dima? I doubt they know Dima framed me, even if they know now that I wasn't at fault for Serek's poisoning. How do I know they won't want *both* of our heads? And can I really trust Jarek not to feed me to them?

I glance at Jarek as he runs his thumb over the steering unit and takes us down a quiet side street. His lips are tight, shoulders stiff, dark brown skin glistening with sweat thanks to the transport's broken cooling system. Or maybe nerves. Or both.

Kala, I hope I made the right decision.

We don't go through the front gates—instead Jarek takes me to a private, closed off sand garden behind one of Vejla's many temples, past a guard who nods us through, and onto the intricately moved sands that probably took some priests several sets to put together. Swirls and detailed spirals and turns weave through the red sand, turning the fine powder into a work of art.

A work of art Jarek is digging through with his bare hands.

"We're ruining their work." I grimace as Jarek lifts sand by the handful, digging a hole to *Kala* knows where. "Why are we even here?"

"Just wait." Jarek drops to his knees as he digs deeper into the sand. "Or, better, help me dig."

I frown, but kneel across from him and begin digging with my uninjured arm through the flour-soft sand. "Are we looking for something?"

"A door. But we're not looking because I know where it is—we just need to move this sand out of the way."

"A . . . door?" I frown. "I don't understand—it's not like there are any secret entrances into the palace complex."

Jarek grunts and keeps digging.

My eyes narrow. "Because if there *were* secret entrances into the palace complex, important figures, such as, say, *ken Avra*, would know about them."

Jarek mumbles something that sounds suspiciously like *they usually do* and I stop digging. Heat races into my face as my heart drums in my chest. He isn't saying—they couldn't possibly—

"They usually—were you *purposefully* keeping information from me when I was *Avra*?"

Jarek sighs and wipes sweat off his forehead with the back of his hand. "*I* wasn't keeping information from you—your father was. Before your coronation, he ordered certain things not be disclosed to you until your twentieth lifecycle celebration."

"Oh, of *course* he did," I hiss. "I imagine the same stipulation was not made for my brother."

Jarek continues digging in silence, which is answer enough. I curse under my breath, my hand shaking as I single-handedly dig deeper. My father wasn't pleased about my taking the throne—he never hid his irritation that I, not Dima, was born first and thus would inherit his position as *Avra*. He openly favored Dima—he mentioned repeatedly I'd never live up to the same kind of leader my brother would be had I not been born.

It took me a long time to realize I didn't want to be the same kind of leader as my brother. I wanted to be better.

But even with the favoritism, even with my father's undesirable comments and the never-ending judgement in his gaze, I never imagined he'd sabotage my efforts as *Avra*. I never imagined he would set a tone of distrust to my guard, my Council, my court before I had even taken the throne.

I never expected resolute support from my father, but apparently setting the bar above *not sabotaging your daughter* was too much to expect from him.

My fingers jam into something hard—I curse and glance at Jarek. "Found it."

Jarek nods. "Do you feel the handle?"

I press my palm against the smooth surface and push sand out of the way, sliding along the door until— "*Sha*, I have it."

"Pull the handle up, then grip it and turn it left. If it's too heavy for you to pull up with the sand on top, I'll help you."

I do as he says—pull the handle up, grip it tightly, turn left, and something thunks beneath us. Jarek moves out of the way and I stand, stepping back as I pull on the handle. The hiss of shifting sand whispers beneath me as the door lifts a bit and sand races over the edges—but Jarek is right, this is really heavy, especially as I'm only using one arm to lift it.

"*Sha*," I say, my voice tight and strained. "Your help would be appreciated."

Jarek steps behind me, slips his hands over mine, and together we yank the door open. Sand rushes into the newly uncovered tunnel as lights blink along the edges and down the tunnel wall, lighting a path along metal rungs of a ladder.

And it hits me all at once why this is familiar—I may have not entered the rebel base in Enjos, but . . . could this explain where the rebels were hiding in Enjos? Is it possible they had access to tunnels deep under the sand like this?

Did we build the underground network in Enjos and then leave it ready for the taking when the city was abandoned?

"Come," Jarek says. "It's safe, I promise. Just pull the door closed after you as you descend and lock it by turning the handle right."

"What about the sand? Won't it be obvious to anyone else who comes by?"

"The guard who let us in will cover it again, and the priests will etch a new design in the sand to discourage anyone from disturbing the garden."

My face warms. "The priests know about this, too? Is there *anyone* who doesn't know about this?"

Jarek just sighs.

After I lock us into the tunnel, we descend in silence. Though I've avoided using it, my arm is almost healed now, so while putting weight on it stings a bit, it's manageable. The tunnel is longer than expected, and I can't help but feel a little grateful Jarek went first—it'd be a long fall if I slipped and he wasn't there to grab me.

Eventually we reach the bottom. Lights flicker to life as we walk, revealing the tunnel before us one piece at a time. There are several turn offs—much more than I expected—but Jarek must have traveled these tunnels before because he takes the turns without hesitation. After a few moments, the ground inclines until we reach a set of twisting, gradual stairs, which leads to a shorter vertical tunnel with a ladder. Jarek goes first, and soon we've reached another door. He unlocks it and then pounds on the door twice.

"Lower your gaze." Jarek glances down at me. "You don't want to get sand in your face."

I look down. Breaths later, the door opens and sand pours over us. Washing all of this off later is going to be wonderful.

We emerge behind the Grand Temple within the palace complex. The deep red sands, the white stone pathways, the glistening temple under the twin suns—it all washes over me in a wave and grips the back of my throat. My eyes sting as I breathe in the smooth desert air. I never expected I'd be able to return here—not to Elja, not to Vejla, and certainly not the palace complex. Not over the smooth red sand I love, surely not on the glistening white streets I played on as a child.

And yet, not quite half a term since I ran, here I am.

I'm home.

The guards tell us Dima is in his rooms, and they say it with a wary gaze that sets a chill down my back. Jarek and I walk quickly, Jarek's shoulders tight with tension, his frown heavy as he worries his lip. My heart thrums as we wind through the palace, closer and closer to my brother's bedroom, closer to seeing the boy I haven't faced since he framed me for attempted murder and tortured my friend.

The boy I grew up with and confided in until it wasn't safe for me to do so anymore. The boy I loved even after he was twisted by jealousy, even after he could no longer look at me as just his sister, his friend. The boy who plotted against me behind my back, who didn't stop when his plan could have gotten me killed.

Who may have even executed me himself had Eros not allowed me to escape.

Eros is right—I should hate Dima. I should feel no pity for him, not an ounce of love anymore. But love doesn't disappear just because someone has hurt you, just because someone has betrayed you, just because they turned their back when you needed them most.

So maybe what Eros and I had was too fragile, too young to be love. Maybe our feelings, real as they were, hadn't had the chance to grow into a bond that can withstand shattering mistakes. Maybe we didn't protect it long enough before exposing it to hurt, and mistrust, and fear.

Maybe it was my fault, or maybe it was just what we both went through, or maybe it was both. But that the moment we had together slipped away from us like sand through our fingers, tells me maybe it wasn't meant to become love at all. Because love is resolute, and even though Dima doesn't deserve it, even though he's done everything in his power to try to kill it, I still love my brother as much as I did when we were children. I couldn't change that even if I wanted to.

It just hurts a lot more now.

A nearby crash startles me out of my thoughts. Jarek and I pause for just a breath before racing down the hall toward Dima's room. Jarek doesn't knock or check if the door is locked—he races to the bedroom door and rushes inside. I follow after him, sliding to a stop just a couple steps from the doorway.

Dima is sitting on the edge of his bed, staring at Jarek wide-eyed. Deep shadows almost look like bruises under his eyes, and his skin has the sickly pallor of way too many glasses of *azuka*. Seeing him like this is a kick to the stomach.

My brother and his partner stare at each other for a few breaths.

"Jarek?" Dima croaks.

Jarek crosses the room, side-steps a broken glass several paces from Dima's bed—the crash we heard—and pulls my brother into his arms.

And Dima sobs against Jarek's chest.

"Shh," Jarek whispers, rubbing Dima's back. "I'm sorry. I'm here."

"You *left!*" Dima wails. "You just *left*, and—"

"I know. I'm so sorry, but I had to—I need you to trust me, Dima."

My brother still hasn't looked at me. I'm not certain he's even seen me yet. But he looks up at Jarek, sniffling, his eyes red and bleary from tears and drink.

And then he looks at me.

The following silence as Dima stares at me, blinking slowly, taking in that I'm here, not dead, not in Asheron, but here in his room. The realization that Jarek must have brought me, because Jarek just arrived and so did I.

I can't breathe. I'm not sure what I'm supposed to be feeling right now, and I can't breathe.

"Dima," Jarek says slowly, "I think we all need to discuss the situation . . . preferably when you're sober again."

"Kora," Dima breathes.

"Hello, Dima," I answer carefully. I open my mouth to say it's good to see him, but truth be told, it's not. Brother or not, I would have been perfectly happy never to speak to him again. Not to mention, he doesn't exactly look thrilled to see me either, and this could go badly quickly, and he looks terrible. So instead, I say, "It's been some time."

Dima looks at Jarek. "You . . . brought her here?"

"As I said," Jarek answers, "we'd be better off discussing this when you're sober."

"What—*kafra*!" Dima yanks away from Jarek. "Are you—is she here to—is this a *coup*?"

Jarek grimaces. "We'll discuss this when you're sober."

"We will *not* because she—guards!"

My shoulders stiffen and my heart slams against my chest. Jarek won't let them arrest me again . . . will he? Was it a mistake to trust him?

But Jarek glances at me and shakes his head. Pounding feet of the summoned guards do not follow the call—no one bursts into the room. Come to think of it, most of Dima's guards are likely outside trying to contain the crowd, anyway.

Dima is shaking as Jarek stands in front of him, hands raised to try to calm him, not that it seems to be working. Dima's gaze darts from his boyfriend to me and back again, face red and . . . I know that look all too well.

Terror.

"Dima," I say softly. "You're my brother, and despite everything, I love you. I want what's best for you and our people . . . and we can discuss it more when you can think clearly. For now, nothing has changed except I'm here." I look at Jarek. "I'm assuming I'm free to go where I please?"

"The guards won't bother you," Jarek says. "They're aware you're—"

"*Nai*," Dima spits, turning on me. He begins crossing the distance between us, but I stand firm. "I won't stand for this. I didn't spend my entire *life* in your shadow just to—"

"Dima," Jarek cautions.

My brother spins to face Jarek. "Don't you even speak to me! How *dare* you bring her back here? You think I don't see what this is? You think I don't know what you're trying to do?" Dima pivots around—his fist—I duck, step back just enough as my brother staggers forward.

Then I kick him in the temple. Hard.

Dima hits the ground and doesn't get back up. Jarek rushes to my brother's side as I stand over him, shaking with adrenaline, with the echo of what I've just done coursing through my veins.

"He's fine," Jarek sighs. "Just unconscious."

I nod and take a shivering breath. "He isn't going to just give up his position."

"He will," Jarek says. "When he's sober, and when we talk to him together. He doesn't have a choice, and he'll realize that soon enough—with the nanite coating strengthening the gates destroyed, the guard can only hold back the mob outside for so long. And if the people get in here, we're all dead."

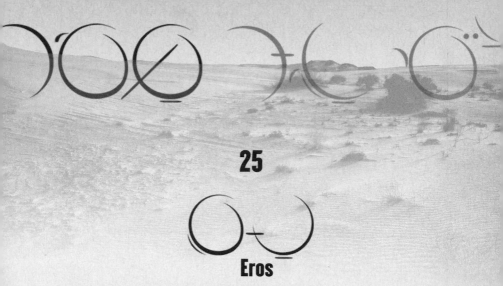

25

Eros

"Stars, Deimos. There isn't a fucken chance I'm going to remember all of this."

I lie on the floor, my palms pressed firmly against my closed eyes, trying to push back the edges of a brainblaze wrapping around my skull. Sands and stars know how long we've been locked in my room while Deimos explains the tenants, and message of *Kala*, and this religious rule and that restriction, and who the priests are, and how they're seen by the general religious public, and more information than I can take in.

And I'm supposed to learn everything in two sets. I'm supposed to be able to pretend I'm a devout follower, that I believe in their god, that I think some deity put us here and left us to our own devices, which apparently is a good thing even though as far as I'm concerned we've fucked things up royally, but never mind that.

Devout follower of an unfamiliar religion. A religion I don't believe in. And somehow, *devotion* is going to be used as some judge of my character, as some marker of whether I'm meant to rule. Because *Kala* would never put a heathen on the throne, stars, no.

"This is ridiculous." I sit up. "And it has nothing to do with being a ruler. How is knowing the stories of *Kala*'s eight prophets going to help me be a good *Sira*?"

"It's not." Deimos shrugs. "But that doesn't matter. What matters is the people think you're a follower so you can set a good example."

"I don't see how being religious automatically makes me a good example of anything except how to be religious."

Deimos runs a hand through his hair. "I'm not disagreeing with you, but that's the way it is. The Sepharon have always been a religious people, and when Jol created the unified monarchy system, this religion was established as The One Way. That's just how it is."

"I'm not going to be able to learn enough of this in two sets to pretend to be a devout follower."

"I can help." Mal walks over, running his hand along the wall until he moves to the center of the room and sits next to Deimos, who's sitting across from me. "It's easy to remember if you just do memory tricks with it."

Deimos arches an eyebrow. "Memory tricks?"

"Ma . . . I learned a while ago. Like, you said the eight prophets are Telos, Henna, Alura, Nidos, Kenja, Mika, Ora, and Malkus, right?"

Deimos grins. "Impressive." He looks at me. "He's good at this."

"Great," I say. "If only he could take the test for me."

Mal snickers. "Yeah, I wouldn't do that even if I could, but you know how the kids at the Remnant base called their mas *mom*?"

"Uh . . . did they?"

He nods. "I heard them. Anyway, thank mom." He says the last two words in English and Deimos stares at me.

"What does that mean?" Deimos asks.

"Thank *mamae*," I translate, then look at Mal. "I don't get it. What do you mean thank mom?"

"That's what the prophet's name spell out: Telos, Henna, Alura, Nidos, Kenja . . ."

"Mika, Ora, Malkus," I finish. "Huh."

"Oh," Deimos says. "That's . . . pretty clever."

Mal grins. "You can do that for the tenants, too, probably, but I don't think it'll spell out an English word . . ."

"We can probably do it with Sephari words, too," Deimos says thoughtfully. "Though if you don't know how to read Sephari, will you be able to memorize that, Eros?"

"If it's basic like Mal's English one was, maybe . . . but then again I don't even know the Sephari alphabet. At least I know that much in English." I shake my head. "Okay, but hold on, now I'm going to have to memorize nonsense words *and* religious facts?"

"The nonsense words will help you remember the religious facts," Mal says. "Trust me. It's how I remembered all of da's rules at camp."

I smile softly. Day *did* have a fuckton of rules.

And so we work together—first establishing the main things I need to memorize to pass on a basic level, then how to arrange them into easy-to-memorize English and Sephari words—after Mal helps Deimos work out the English letter equivalent of the words. Rather than take a break and join everyone for dinner, we get food sent up to the room, and Deimos reads aloud passages of their holy book (the *Jorva*—I need to remember that) as Mal and I eat the rice and meat stew in a rolled-up wrap the way Deimos shows us.

The passages are interesting, at least—it's not just a rule book like I expected; it's full of stories of the prophets, and given that it's a holy book, there's a lot more sex and violence than I expected. When Deimos starts reading about Malkus getting it on with his boyfriend, I nearly choke on my food.

"Hold on. There's *lijarit* sex in the *Jorva* and yet half of the Sepharon think the *lijarae* are *wrong*?"

"*Shae.*" Deimos smirks. "We call that hypocrisy. Also, there's a whole sect of Sepharon who believe Malkus's sections were added in afterward and he's not *really* a prophet— which is *skola*, but *shae*. They argue he shouldn't be counted because he was the last of the prophets, but everyone knows they only take an issue with it because accepting Malkus's passages means accepting the *lijarae*."

"And . . . the priests that are here? What do they think?"

"Depends who you talk to, but the High Priest, Arodin, is the only one who matters and he'll be interviewing you himself."

"Okay. And does he accept Malkus's passages?"

"Given he has a husband himself, I think it's safe to assume *sha*."

I arch an eyebrow. "The High Priest has a husband, and there's a whole sect of Sepharon who think it's wrong but who accept him as their priest anyway?"

"Remember what I said about hypocrisy?" Deimos laughs. "There's a whole realm of religious politics we're not going to get into, but let's just say the High Priest's time in his position has not been uneventful. There are plenty who'd love to see him replaced with someone else."

"Someone not *lijara*."

"Naturally." Deimos shrugs. "But it doesn't matter, because Arodin is who we have so bigots have to accept it."

I smirk, and Deimos keeps reading. And for a time, with Mal lying next to me, eyes closed as he listens to Deimos read, with delicious food and a quiet night, and even with the edges of that stubborn brainblaze buried behind my eyes, something settles inside me. Something cooling my nerves and breathing into my lungs, deep and steady.

For a time, I'm not afraid. And it's nice to be able to breathe again.

When we finally step out for the informal evening meal, two men are waiting in the hall, and they smile as I walk over with Deimos and Mal. Ejren says something to Simos, who nods as we approach.

"Eros," Simos says, "it's good to see you. Would you mind sparing us some time?"

Deimos nods and smiles at me. "Mal and I will get food and bring it back to the room, *shae*?"

I hesitate, then nod. "*Shae*, but keep an eye on him."

"Of course." Deimos guides Mal down the hall with his hand on Mal's shoulder, leaving the three of us alone.

"Studying up?" Simos smiles.

I sigh and run a hand through my hair. "Understatement, but s*ha*, you could say that."

Ejren nods. "We'd assumed you didn't learn much about our faith when living with the nomads."

"But I wouldn't worry about it excessively," Simos adds. "Lejv isn't known for his renowned faith, either."

I smile weakly. "Good."

Simos nods. "At any rate, we've spoken with Aleija and Jule, and we wanted you to know you have us behind you. I can't promise my father will follow suit, but we'll certainly work on him."

I sigh and smile—that gives me four definite backers. It's nowhere near a majority, but it's a start. And honestly, it's more than I would have guessed I'd ever get a few sets ago. "Thank you. I appreciate your support."

"Of course." Ejren smiles. "It'll be good to see some positive change, for once."

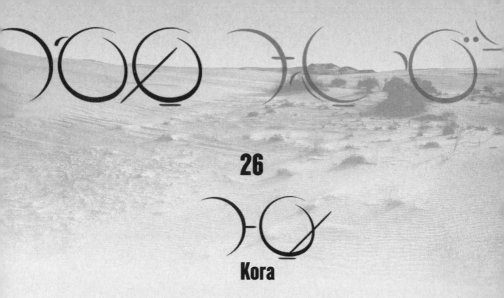

26

Kora

It takes several sets for my brother to sober up and finally, *finally* agree to meet me, and during that time, I reacquaint myself with home. I walk into my room, left untouched since the moment I ran, and for a breath I can see it as it was the night I had to leave. With Eros by the opened garden doors, a knife in his hand and something hard and fierce in his eyes. With Iro by my side, his fur bristling as the guards advanced. With Jarek watching dispassionately as Dima ordered my arrest, as my brother betrayed me in the worst way possible.

Did Jarek know it was a setup, or did he believe I'd attempted to kill Serek? If he was unaware, was he angry when he learned the truth? Or *has* he learned the truth? Does he still believe I attempted to murder the man I'd agreed to marry? Did he cross the deserts anyway with that lie established as truth in his mind, believing there was no other way to save Dima?

I never thought to ask on the journey over what he believed of the events that took place. It hadn't even occurred to me he didn't know the truth by now, even though it hasn't been long since the night I had to run. Seventeen—*naï*, twenty sets. Not even half a term.

My brother has been *Avra* for less than a term and the territory has all but crumbled around him already.

But even if I were to ask Jarek, would I believe him? How am I supposed to trust either of them? And what happened to Anja? I'd expected to see her by now—I wanted to hear her account of what happened, to know how deeply this betrayal went. Did Anja know what she was giving me when she painted my lips with poison and handed me the antidote? Or did my brother use her innocence to get his way?

Where is she? Why isn't she here?

I run my hand over the smooth sheets on my bed. My earring from Mamae is waiting for me where I left it, on my bedside table the night of my lifecycle celebration. Life was so different last time I sat here, terrified my betrothed had just died right in front of me. The world was different, Eros was different, and so was I. It may not have been so long since that night, but we've experienced so much since then.

I feel like I've aged ten cycles.

But for as different as I am, as much as I've learned, and hurt, and survived—a part of me is still the same. A part of me is still scared about what will happen when I become *Avra* again. Now that they've had a taste of my brother, will my people still despise me? Maybe they'll want a new ruling family altogether. Maybe they'll blame me for my brother's failure, for his ever taking the position to begin with.

And yet, as nervous as I am to see how they'll react, I can face it this time. I can face *them*. I've defended myself against raiders and survived in the desert without resources. I've stood up to arrogant Asheron officials, faced former *Sirae* and royalty of the world, brought Eros back to Asheron from rebels, and walked into the city with the future *Sira* at my side and smiled proudly as he spoke to the people there with more power than even he realizes.

And now I've faced my brother again—the man who nearly had me killed and threw me from my territory.

I'll face more dangers and struggle with new challenges yet. But this time, I'm ready for them. This time I'm stronger than I ever believed. This time I won't let anyone get in my way.

A knock at the door startles me out of my thoughts. I almost laugh at my surprise—being asked permission for someone to enter the room is how it *should* have been when I was *Avra* here but rarely was the case in practice.

Few people at the palace respected me enough for even such a small thing.

"Come in," I say, and the door slides open.

Jarek smiles weakly at me from the doorway. "Dima's sober. He's ready to talk."

I sigh. "Is he really?"

"I've . . . prepared him for the conversation. He's not thrilled with either of us, naturally, but he'll listen."

"Time to get this over with, then."

Jarek grimaces.

My bare feet pat over the warm stone as the hot, dry air bakes my skin. My heart beats steadily as we weave through the halls, and up and down a set of stairs, and beyond the library and our personal training room, past so many doors opening into the courtyard outside or the palace complex streets, and back to my brother's room. Smoke reaches into the horizon with shadowed fingers. A dull, distant roar hums endlessly, washing over the sands; the protests of the people beyond the gates. The protests that will only get worse if we do nothing.

Now or never.

Dima is sitting on floor cushions at a small circular table on the far side of his room, a glass resting in the center of the table. Jarek sits next to him, and I kneel across from them both, sitting on my heels for a little extra height.

"Jarek tells me you want your position back," Dima says dully. "As if I couldn't have assumed as much myself."

"Actually," I say, "I would have been happy to stay in Asheron and help Eros rather than return here unwanted. There are benefits to not ruling a fraught territory—freedom to do whatever I want, for example. And the companionship of my friends, rather than self-imposed isolation here. Had Jarek not asked me to return, I'm not certain I ever would have."

Dima purses his lips. Jarek frowns at me, but I continue. "I'm not here because I want to be, or because I'm lusting after your position—even though you *stole* that position from me. But I'd lost, and I'd accepted it and wasn't going to fight it."

"Evidently that's not the case," Dima says bitterly, "as you're here."

"Because you need help, Dima—and more importantly, our people need help. Because neither Jarek nor I want you executed—which is what will likely happen if you continue down this path." I swipe my hand over the glass, waking it, then open the city feed and enlarge the footage of the palace gates.

People screaming and throwing stones at the shielded guards holding the crowd back. Fires burning in the distance, clouding the purple sky with thick, black smoke. People chanting "out with the tyrant" as they scream and rail against the guards.

Dima runs his hands over his face. The deep, purple shadows under his eyes, the thinning of his face—he looks exhausted. "They weren't happy with your rule, either."

"They weren't, *naï*, but at least partially because they thought you would be a better ruler as you're a man."

"So you're saying I failed."

I shake my head. "I'm saying you've gone down a dangerous path, but it's not too late to reverse it."

"By declaring myself a failure and installing you in my stead."

I glance at Jarek. He nods and takes Dima's hand.

"By telling the people you're stepping down from your *temporary* position as *Avra*, as the charges against me have been cleared and I've returned to Vejla," I say.

Dima frowns, but Jarek squeezes his hand. "The people won't know you planned to keep the throne—we'll tell them you never intended to make your position permanent; you just needed to take over while the investigation was underway."

Dima's frown deepens. "There was a coronation. They won't believe it."

"They will, because it's not unprecedented. Historically, even our temporary rulers were crowned—traditionally in Elja, it was a requirement of *anyone* who served as *Avra*, even if only for a set."

"So I lie," Dima says flatly. "Not exactly honorable."

I hold back the words I want to say: that what he did to me wasn't *honorable*, either. "You don't have to lie," I answer. "We won't talk about your intentions at all—just that you served as *Avra* while the charges against me were tackled and now that they've been cleared, I've returned to reclaim my position. All of which is true."

My brother sighs and looks at the feed still playing on the glass.

"Besides," I add, "you didn't have a problem lying to Roma about Eros when it served your purposes."

Dima looks away.

"About that . . ." Jarek says hesitantly. "When the new *Sira* is chosen—"

"I know," Dima whispers. "My sets are numbered. I made a bad bet."

"I'll do everything in my power to protect you, but I'm not going to protect you from the inevitable trial. You *should* be tried," I say. "You've done too much to avoid one. I will, however, do everything I can to make sure the outcome isn't your execution. But first you need to return me the authority to be your shield. I can't help you if I'm not *Avra*."

"You probably can't help me even if you *are Avra*."

"Let me worry about that. With me reinstated, you at least have a chance—you won't be able to defend yourself as a guilty man, especially one whose own people are protesting. But I wasn't involved in your crime, and as *Avra* I can influence how it proceeds."

Dima presses his face into his palms and takes a long, shuddering breath. "This is all I ever wanted," he whispers, his voice choked with emotion. My heart breaks at his pain, even as part of me screams *this is all his doing, he deserves every bit of misfortune*. But deserving or not, my love for my brother won't just go away—and as Jarek slips his arm around Dima's waist and pulls him close, the words come to me.

"It's not the only thing you ever wanted." I nod to Jarek. "You have someone who loves you more than you even realize. Jarek would do anything for you, and no one can ever take that from you."

Jarek smiles softly, but Dima shakes his head. "I can't have him, either, not really. The people won't accept us together here in Elja. As though they didn't hate me enough already—I'll be a total outcast if the Eljans ever learn about us."

"It won't be easy," I concede, "not at first. But I will support you both wholeheartedly—and publicly when you're ready—and the people will come around. Besides, our generation is much more accepting than the last—and we outnumber our elders." I smile. "The world is changing, Dima, and we can be a part of it together. We each have a role to play and yours isn't over."

"But your role as *Avra is* over," Jarek says. "Or, it should be. This will be better for everyone, including you."

Dima runs his hands over his face—something he's always done to try to stop himself from crying, even as a child. But he leans into Jarek, takes a shaky breath, and nods. "Okay," he says hoarsely. "I'll support you, Kora. You can take back the throne."

A wave of relief washes over me like a cool rain. "Thank you, Dima." I hesitate. "There's one more issue we need to discuss." Jarek frowns at me—I hadn't discussed this with him, but I believe he'll agree it's necessary. "After we announce my reinstatement, I'll be putting you under watch. You aren't to leave the palace, not even to explore the grounds—both for your safety, and so the people know you're being monitored and won't run before your trial. I'm sure you can understand the necessity."

Jarek grimaces and Dima stares at the floor. "So, I'll be a prisoner."

"You'll be restricted," I amend. "You have to lose *some* privileges, or the people will think I'm overlooking your crimes."

Dima purses his lips, but nods. "So be it." He hesitates. "And I'm . . . sorry. Truly, for everything. I could have gotten you executed and I—" He closes his eyes, inhales deeply, and looks at me again. "I would have gone through with it, had I had the opportunity. I'm so sorry."

"I know." And though the apology can't erase what he did, though I'm not likely to ever trust him again, I won't turn away from him either. Not even now.

For the first time as *Avra*, I have my brother's support. And as we stand to prepare to head outside to address the people together, I can feel it in my bones.

This time will be different.

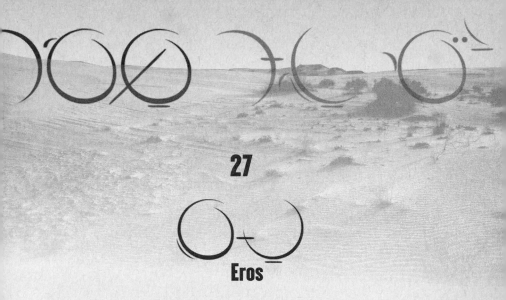

27

Eros

"I'd insist you eat something," Deimos says, picking a pastry off my plate, "but seeing as you look like you might lose last night's dinner at any moment, I'll just help myself to your morning meal instead."

I push my plate toward him and try not to glance at Lejv and his supporters at the other end of the courtyard. We're standing outside the blindingly shiny, white Grand Temple, waiting for the black, gold-inscribed stone doors to open—which none of us can touch because we're not rulers or priests (I guess I've retained some of Deimos's religious lessons over the past three sets after all). We're also waiting for the priests to emerge and come summon us. Summon me. And Lejv. Everyone else will wait out in the suns with the food and water.

I wish I could stay out here with them under the oppressive heat of the suns. I don't even care we've gone well beyond the comfortable heat index to dangerous heat index, and I don't care the sand is gritty and white and not like home. I just don't fucken want to go in there.

But it doesn't matter for a mo what I want, because I have to prove to religious fanatics I'm not a total heretic automatically unfit for the throne I'm trying to inherit.

My stomach churns. My hands are cold and shaky. Every breath shudders in and out of my lungs. And Deimos is right—I'm not so sure I'm going to make it through the set without emptying my stomach. I was surprised I'd even made it through our jog this morning without tossing up.

If Kora were here, she'd probably try to reassure me with stuff that isn't actually reassuring, like how the priests don't decide *everything* or . . . something. What is she doing right now? I hope she made it to Elja okay. I'm not sure I would've trusted Jarek to keep her safe from Dima, in her place. No, fuck that, I definitely wouldn't have trusted Jarek in her place. But she made her own decision. She's gone.

I'll have to ask Deimos to show me how to check the feed for her later or something. After this is over. I need this to be finally over.

Stars, I'm so fucken nervous.

"*Ej,* Eros." Deimos waves a hand in front of my face. "Relax, would you? You're making the kid nervous."

"I'm not nervous," Mal says quickly. "I just don't like this sand—it's not as soft as the red desert . . . plus it's kinduv hurting my eyes."

I frown. "The sand is hurting your eyes?"

"It's too bright." He squints at me. "It's like . . . washing out the little bit I *can* see."

Deimos frowns. "Do you want to go inside? I can take you back to Eros's rooms so you can relax."

Mal snorts. "So I can be bored, you mean. I'm okay. I'll just . . ." He glances at his chest, then smiles, takes off his shirt, and drapes it over his head so it shields some of his eyes but doesn't block them completely. "There." He laughs.

I rest my arm on his shoulders to pull him into a hug, but he groans and ducks out of the way. "Way too hot for that. Sorry."

"I can help with that." Deimos grabs a water cube off the table, holds it over Mal's head, and presses the release so it splashes onto him.

My stomach clenches and my heart freezes—pain and screaming and no, no, *stop*. Stars, I have to get a grip—that water wasn't even on *me*. Relax. Nothing is wrong. No pain, no screaming, no nothing. I'm fine. We're fine. I slip my fingers under Aren's bracelet and grip it and breathe.

Mal gasps and jumps out of the way, laughing. "Hey!" He pauses. "Wait, actually, do it again."

I force a laugh. Deimos grins at me as he pours more water on Mal's head. "There we go. Finally, a smile."

"*Naï*, don't point it out." Mal smirks. "You'll scare it away."

I snicker, and this time I don't have to force it. "Blaze you both."

"I still don't understand what that means," Deimos answers. "*Blaze*. Like a fire?"

I shrug. "Like the suns, I guess."

"So you're telling me to go into the suns?"

"Basically."

"I like it." Deimos grins. "So it'd be the equivalent of—"

"Maybe let's not teach my nephew new Sephari swears just yet."

"Awww." Mal laughs. "Oh well, I already know the worst one, anyway."

I smirk. "*Sha*, you've shown us."

"*Kafra*," Mal says. "It's kinduv fun to say."

Deimos snickers. "*Shae*, well, we *are* standing in front of the holiest temple on the planet, so maybe we shouldn't say it here."

"*Kafra*," Mal whispers. "*Kafra kafra*."

Deimos squirts him with more water, and Mal laughs again. I smile as Deimos turns to me, and even though I'm still so blazing nervous my insides are vibrating, the distraction is appreciated. I never thought I'd say this about a Sepharon—let alone a guy—but Deimos is . . . kinduv sweet. He goes out of his way to help me even with the ridiculous things, like pre-testing nerves. Even if it's just to make me laugh, I'm glad he's here; I'm more at ease with him by my side.

Until the men on the other side of the courtyard erupt with laughter, and I glance at the thick temple doors and want to hurl again.

I can do this. Maybe. Ugh.

"Aaaand I'm losing you again." Deimos rests his hand on my shoulder. "Look, Eros, it'll go well or it won't. You're understandably nervous, but it's going to go the way it's going to go, *shae*? And whether it goes well or disastrously, we'll handle it together."

I sigh. "I know."

Deimos nods. "For what it's worth, you've worked really hard, and you're in the best position we could reasonably expect you to be in. The rest is up to *Kala*."

I glance at him. "You believe in that stuff?"

He shrugs. "Enough. He *did* save you during your almost-execution."

"Sure as sand that was the Remnant rebels."

"Why can't it be both?"

I shrug. "Just seems fake to give credit to things people do to a god you've never seen."

"That's fair," Deimos says. "I guess it's just a matter of how you view the world."

"Maybe," I sigh.

"But for the sake of today—"

"Better I pretend to believe otherwise. I know. Not that I see the point when it's obviously unrealistic to assume I believe a religion humans are known *not* to believe in when I was raised by humans."

"*Shae*, well . . ." Deimos kicks at some sand and sighs. "Even if you don't convince them you believe it wholeheart-edly, it might be enough just to show them you're open to it and you've made the effort to learn about it."

I look at him skeptically. "You really think that's going to be enough?"

He shrugs.

"Nothing I say is going to be anywhere near enough, because it's coming from me."

Deimos frowns. "Maybe. But maybe not—the third tenant is—"

"Balance. *Shae*. I remember."

He smiles. "And in a world where there are both Sepharon and—*humans*, what's more balanced than someone who is both?"

"Somehow I doubt they're going to see it that way."

"You never know. No use in giving up before you've tried."

I look at him. "I wouldn't be here if I was giving up."

"That's true." Deimos glances at something behind me and nods. "Well, here we are. Too late to back out now."

I glance back—my stomach lurches and a rush of cold and then hot races over me. The temple doors are opening.

"Stars fortune," Mal says quietly. "We'll be waiting for you."

"And praying *Kala* cuts you some slack." Deimos smiles and pats me on the back. "You can do this. And no matter what happens—"

"We'll get through it," I finish quietly. "*Shae*. Thank you."

"No need to thank me. Just do your best."

The four priests we saw the other set step out into the sunlight. Deimos said none of them are the High Priest—he'll probably be waiting somewhere inside the temple. Which isn't at all terrifying.

Deep breaths. I'll be fine. Hopefully.

"Eros." One of the priestesses nods at me. "Lejv." She turns to my opponent, who must've walked over when the doors opened. "It is time."

The Grand Temple is dark and cool inside. Lejv and I walk silently down the aisle between rows of pillow-like mats built into the floor, where people kneel during a service or prayers. Thin, slit-like windows let in slices of sunlight, but it's not enough to light the enormous auditorium. I'm not sure why they like to keep it so dark in here. I don't think that was part of what I'd learned . . .

Or maybe I'm already forgetting things. Which—not going to think about.

Our bare feet pat quietly against the smooth stone as we follow the four priests through the auditorium and past a long, gold statue made of writing I can't read, but I'm pretty sure says *Kala*—it's against their beliefs to depict their god because that's considered idol worship, so they represent *Kala* with his name instead.

At least I'm remembering some things. Hopefully with three sets of cramming, the information that stuck will be enough to get me through this. Whatever this is.

Past the statue, the priests take us beyond a long, dark purple curtain—chillingly close to the color of Sepharon blood—that drapes from the ridiculously tall ceiling all the way down to the floor. The curtain is thick and heavy—so much so it takes two priests to pull the edge back enough for us to get through.

It hushes closed behind us with a low *whoosh*, like the kinduv forced exhale you get when someone punches you in the stomach.

Back here it's even darker than the front room, and it takes a moment for my eyes to adjust to the shadows. It's a smaller section of the room—maybe a sixth of the size of the much larger auditorium. A table floats against the west wall, eight bowls float against the northern wall, and there's a closed door on the east wall. A book lies in the center of the table—I'm assuming their *Jorva*—alongside a metal bowl filled with what looks like herbs and dried flowers attached to a chain with a handle and eight neatly stacked cups.

The priest who said my name earlier takes two of the cups and passes them to one of the guys, who then takes the cups to the bowls and dips them into each bowl. Meanwhile, she lifts the handle portion of the bowl-chain thing as the other woman comes over with a match and crystal strike stick. She strikes the match and drops it into the bowl, where it burns the herbs and flowers inside.

The smoke is a weird blue-gray color, and as the priest wafts it toward us, it fills my head with a sweet, thick smell; my head buzzes. Then the priest with the cups comes over and hands one to me and one to Lejv.

"Drink," he says.

I glance at the cup. The liquid inside is shiny and purple-gray, like water mixed with metal and . . . something chalky. I have no idea what this is, but Lejv tosses it back like he doesn't want to taste it. The priest frowns at him and then looks at me expectantly.

I drink it slower. One of the tenants—the fifth, maybe?—is about savoring life so . . . I don't know. The priest just seemed annoyed Lejv drank his so quickly, so I take my time. Whatever this stuff is doesn't taste awful, thank the stars—it's thick, but also weirdly slippery, so it's not hard to swallow. It's spicy and sweet and warms my throat on the way down, filling me with liquid heat.

I'm fucken glad it's cool in here, or I'd be a disgusting, sweaty mess right now.

The priest nods and takes my cup and Lejv's. All four of the priests walk to the closed door, the woman with the burning herbs in the lead. Together, they press their hands against the door and it slides open. They gesture for us to follow, so we do.

Beyond the door are stairs and a dark corridor lit by burning sconces. The stairs go down, and down, and down, and the deeper we descend, the cooler it is. But since the corridor is so narrow, it also fills with the smoke from the burning incense, and combined with the warm drink we had, my head is buzzing a ton and I feel light, like with every step lower I might just float away.

I'm hyped. They got us fucken intoxicated before this interview test thing. Like, *really*, intoxicated, or at least I will be by the time we get to wherever we're going because stars, that smoke stuff is really fucken strong. I kinduv want to laugh about it, but everyone's being *so* serious and somber, so I screw my face up into my super serious face, which probably doesn't even look super serious, but oh well, doing my best.

At least I'm not nervous anymore? Not even sure what I was nervous about to begin with. I mean, they started this whole thing by giving us a drink and filling us with relaxing smoke so how bad could it be?

Lejv giggles behind me. I bite my lip because his giggle is kinduv contagious and I have to force myself not to smile, but this is all super serious, so serious, so I'm not gonna laugh, I'm not.

I really do want to, though.

We go down, and down, and down, and down until we've descended into the core of the planet—except not really because then we'd be dead—but that's how deep it feels we've gone until finally the stairs open into a room.

A large, dark room like a replica of the auditorium way way above us, except darker and fire-lit. There's a curtain in this room, too. Smaller curtain, because the ceilings aren't nearly as high in this room. But probably as heavy—at least, it looks as heavy.

Oh, and there's a guy here, too.

He looks kinduv like a stick. Really tall, and really, really thin—like, dangerously thin. No hair, white markings all over his face and head and down his neck, into these thick, purple robes that look like he wrapped himself in a fancy blanket. It's kinduv funny, but I don't laugh. I'm good at not laughing. Way better than Lejv, who's giggling again.

He needs to get it together because it's a lot harder not to laugh when he's giggling like a delighted little kid.

"Remove your clothes and enter the pool," the skinny priest says.

Pool? Oh, there—how did I miss that? In the center of the room, a long body of water so still it almost looks like glass. Missed it because it's dark in here and also I was staring at the skeletal priest. Water bothers me—usually I'd definitely *not* want to go in there, but . . . what was the big deal? Not like it'll hurt or anything. This might be fun.

I'm halfway through taking my pants off when it hits me I'm getting naked in a room full of people. Well, not *full*, but there are six people other than me and this is weird. It's weird, right?

Lejv is already naked, which is way more of him than I wanted to see, ever. Not that he has a bad body, he's fit enough, I guess, though I'll bet Deimos is probably way fitter but—okay, anyway, pants. I strip and step to the edge of the pool, next to Lejv. My toes touch the water—it's warm, at least, which is good because it's a little on the chilled side in here. Not unbearable though. Not like last time I had to be naked in a room full of people and they were blasting the coolant and they shaved my head and—

I close my eyes. Deep, sweet, smoky breath in. Out. Open them again. The priest is watching us. Did he notice my almost-panic? I hope not.

A low hum fills the room, and it takes me a mo to realize it's not the room humming itself—it's the four priests who walked us in here. They're each standing at a corner of the pool now. What is the humming for? It doesn't sound bad, at least. It's a little creepy, though, this low, monotone hum like a machine, but not a machine.

"Walk slowly through the pool," the skinny priest says. "Don't stop until you've reached the other side."

We step into the pool, but it's not like a step like a stair. It's a gradual entrance, like what I guess a lake or the ocean would be like, except the sides are straight and wall-like. But the entrance and exit are this gradual thing and the floor is slanted, so each step brings me a little deeper, a little deeper, a little deeper. To my knees. To my hips. My waist. Chest. Neck. I take a breath (sweet, smoky, head buzz), another breath for good measure (my head is buzzing so bad—good?), then the water reaches my lips, my nose, eyes, I'm under.

It's quiet down here. The humming of the priests is distant, like leagues away, though it echoes faintly almost like a pulse. I throw my arms out to the sides as I force my feet to stay on the floor. The water is warm, and walking through it is like walking through a full-body hug.

Aside from that one bath back in Elja, I've never been completely underwater before. Not like this—bathing in camps was quick, a splash of water here, a spray there. But this, even with my arms extended to either side, there's nothing but water, water, water. I can almost imagine it goes on forever.

Hopefully Lejv won't giggle down here, or he'd probably drown. Which would be funny—wait, no, not funny.

. . . a little funny?

The water lowers to my ears, my lips again, my neck, and I can breathe. The coolness of the air is extra-cool now, as the warmth of the water slips lower and lower and then not at all.

Lejv and I are standing side by side, shivering, as warm water drips over us. One of the guy priests gives us fuzzy blankets. I rub it over my body, soaking up the cooling water, and then glance at Lejv. He's wrapped the blanket around his waist, which is a good idea, so I do the same.

It hangs around my waist like those skirts the Asheron guards like so much. Except not as fancy and a blanket.

"We'll start with Eros," the skinny priest says, startling me awake. Well, not awake—I wasn't asleep—but at attention? "He's the only person who's spoken since we entered the temple." I was starting to think we weren't allowed to speak in here or something.

"Lejv, you will wait here."

Lejv nods, but doesn't speak, so maybe we're *not* supposed to speak except for the skinny priest who I'm pretty sure is the head priest. Did the *Jorva* say something about this? We're supposed to be quiet and *in a contemplative state of mind* or whatever, but quiet doesn't mean silent, does it?

How am I supposed to answer questions if I have to stay silent? I'm overthinking this. I must be. I don't remember anything about mandatory silence in the temples. Just quiet and contemplative. Which I've been doing. I think.

The skinny priest turns away and two other priests—one of the men and the woman who was holding the smoke stuff before—follow. So do I. When we reach the thick curtain, the two priests step in front of the head priest and part the heavy curtains together. The High Priest enters and I follow, but we don't enter another room—instead, there's another heavy curtain. The two priests part it again, then again at the next curtain, and finally we're through.

The room back here is small and bare, with two kneeling mats placed on the floor. The priest kneels on the far left, and I kneel on the one across from him, so we're facing each other. The High Priest nods, so that must be right. The other two priests stand sentry by the curtain, watching us in silence.

"You've come a long way," the High Priest says.

I hesitate. If he's speaking to me, that must mean I'm allowed to talk. So I do but keep my voice low just in case. "You could say that."

"Many wonder what you're doing here, Eros. You weren't raised by Sepharon—you don't know our culture and our ways. You may be a half-blood, but you're much more red-blood than you are Sepharon."

"I thought that once," I say. "Before I came to Vejla and lived with Kora for a while, I rejected the Sepharon part of me. I thought I had to in order to be accepted by the humans, but even then most of them didn't accept me. Even then I was too Sepharon to be seen as human, as one of them. I was ashamed of my Sepharon side—I *hated* being associated with them. But recently I realized I didn't have to be ashamed of what I was. Sure, people still hate me—for being part human this time—but I can't change who I am and I don't want to anymore."

The Head Priest nods. "Well answered."

I smile. I'm kinduv impressed I came up with all of that, to be honest. My head is so fuzzy and I'm smiling in front of the Head Priest and the words slide out so easily—I barely think them before they spill over my lips and gather on the black floor between us.

"What did you give us?" I ask. "I mean, I don't *mind*, it's kind of nice and fuzzy, but I'm definitely drugged, which is an unusual way to do an interview."

The Head Priest smiles. "The drink is *ufrike* and the herbs are a combination of *zeili* and *araban*. Together, the combination helps open you up to Kala, and to the truth."

"So . . . like a drunk truth potion."

The Head Priest smirks. "Something like that. Don't worry about your inhibitions—I'm here today to look into your spirit and interpret what Kala plans for you."

"Because *Kala writes on all of our beings; the truth of the stars is written on our souls*," I recite, impressed I remembered that, too. Maybe this drunk truth potion stuff is good for memory, too. Or maybe I just remember it because Deimos must've said it like at least five fucken times.

"That's right," the Head Priest says. "So you've read the *Jorva*?"

"Deimos read it to me—it's interesting. And surprisingly violent and sexual." And I just said that out loud. To the Head Priest. Okay.

"The *Jorva* doesn't shy away from any facets of life. It is a reflection of who we were then, who we are now, and who we'll be to come."

"Deimos said that. He said the character of every Sepharon who was, who is, and who will be is already written. Not literally, because that'd be impossible, but through the poetry of the *Jorva* itself."

"It sounds like Deimos is very knowledgeable."

"*Shae*," I say. "He's a good guy."

The High Priest nods. "I'm guessing it's safe to assume you hadn't read the *Jorva* before your sessions with Deimos."

"Well, I can't read at all, so."

He arches an eyebrow. "You're illiterate?"

I shrug. "Reading wasn't a top priority for survival at

camp. Some can read enough English to mostly get by, though I never learned much, but none of us could read Sephari. It was too complicated—and not like we came across much Sephari writing anyway, so it wasn't a problem."

"Interesting. But your Sephari is fluent—I'm assuming you must have been familiar with our language before meeting Kora, otherwise you're an exceptionally quick learner."

"I was. The human military speak Sephari, but as far as I know, few people know how to read it."

"Fascinating. So the *Jorva* and our beliefs are all new to you. Unless the redbloods also believe in *Kala*?"

"It's new. Like, as of the last several sets new."

The Head Priest purses his lips and nods. Maybe I shouldn't have said that. There were things I wasn't supposed to say, wasn't there? A strategy I was supposed to take, to make them think . . . something.

What was the plan? We had one, didn't we? My head is foggy and lighter than air, like it might float off my shoulders and bump against the ceiling. But the Sepharon respect the truth and lying is, like, against their honor or something, so maybe it's okay I forgot the plan. Because the plan probably had some lying in it. Or at least careful truth-telling, but isn't that the same as lying?

"It is," the Head Priest says.

I stare at him. "What is?"

"Careful truth-telling is equivalent to lying."

I blink. And blink and blink. Blink again. "Can you read minds?"

The High Priest laughs. "*Naï*, but you just spoke your mind freely, which I encourage. Nothing should be hidden here, not while I read your spirit."

I . . . spoke my mind freely?

Fuck.

I said everything out loud, didn't I?

"*Sha*, you did. But don't worry—as I said earlier, it's important everything is out in the open during our . . . interview, as you called it."

"I'm saying everything I'm thinking out loud," I say.

"You are. It's one of the effects of *araban*. Completely natural, don't worry."

"Okay," I say, and just like that I'm not worried. I wish it was always this easy not to be worried. Maybe I should take this stuff more often. Then again, saying literally everything that comes to mind probably isn't the best in the long term . . .

"I would imagine not." The High Priest smirks. "Tell me, Eros—this is all so new to you, I'm finding it hard to believe you became a believer as soon as you heard our ways. Not that I would ever question *Kala*'s ability to turn even the most resolute denier into a believer at the simplest thought, but as that's not something that happens every set, I'd like to hear how you feel about all of this. Do you believe *Kala* is the one true god and our ways are the best way to honor them?"

"Them?"

The High Priest smiles. "Many refer to *Kala* as a male, but *Kala* is *Kala* and has no true gender. Thus, I and many others refer to our god in neutral terms."

"Oh." I pause. "I don't know. I've never been religious—even the nomad beliefs at home just seemed like a nice way to look at the world without giving up, you know? I guess life would be easier if you believed in an afterlife and some force giving purpose to everything. Because if you don't believe that, then you have to believe there's nothing after you die, and you weren't born for any purpose which . . . can be kind of depressing."

"True. So you don't know what you believe?"

"Not really. I like the idea of believing in something, and after losing so many people . . . I *want* to believe in something, in some other world where I'll be with my family again and they aren't gone forever. But it just seems like people blame everything, good or bad, on this being with no proof of anything. Like more of a coping mechanism than something real."

"I can understand why you'd feel that way, *sha*. So you're saying you don't believe in *Kala*."

"I'm saying I don't know. Maybe the Sepharon are right and *Kala* exists, or maybe the nomads are right and our collective spirits become one with the stars and look over the world and our loved ones after we pass. Or maybe you're both right, or you're both wrong. I'm not sure how to prove it one way or the other."

"Well, that's the thing about faith," the High Priest says. "It wouldn't be *faith* if there was tangible proof. The whole concept of faith is believing in something you can't see with your own eyes. If there was a way to prove it, it would be *knowledge*, not belief."

"So there isn't a way to ever know who's right and who isn't."

The High Priest shrugs. "We'll certainly know after we pass, but there's no coming back to share the findings one way or the other."

I grimace. "Believing in anything is hard."

"*Sha*," the High Priest says. "It certainly is."

28

Eros

"Well, I completely fucked that up," I say while Deimos helps me crawl into bed. As he adjusts the pillow behind my head, his bicep brushes against my cheek. He has nice arms. Nice face, too. Nice everything, really.

Deimos sighs. "*Shae,* you may have mentioned that two or three times on the way over."

"More like six or seven times." Mal tilts his head back and squints at me. "You are *really* blazing."

I snicker because it's true. I am.

Deimos arches an eyebrow. "Blazing can be used in that context, too?"

"Blazing can be used in any context," Mal says. "But this time I mean he's super hyped."

"So hyped." I rub my hands over my face. The whole room blurs and refocuses. I do it again—blur, refocus. This is kinduv fun.

Deimos frowns and pulls my hands away from my face. "*Kala*, you're worse than a child on this stuff."

I laugh. "You should have seen Lejv—he was giggling when we had to strip and walk through the water bath-thing."

Deimos smirks. "Well, at least he was just as affected as you were."

He was *definitely* just as affected. Maybe more affected. Either way, it's good news for me. Probably. "*Shae*. Too bad you weren't there."

"You want to see me intoxicated?"

"*Naï*." I grin and Deimos arches an eyebrow at me and it looks kinduv funny with one eyebrow higher than the other and then I'm giggling and Mal says, "Oh, *gross*" and then I'm *really* laughing and so is Deimos.

"What I'm wondering," I say, when the laughing dies away, "is how the priests weren't affected. I mean, they were all breathing the same smoke stuff—though I guess they didn't take that *ufrike* stuff first . . ."

Deimos groans. "No wonder you're so affected."

I smile. Why am I smiling? Something about Deimos groaning and saying *affected* is just funny I don't know. "Why? The *ufrike*?"

"*Shae,* you're going to have quite the next set experience tomorrow. Or later today. I should get you some water . . ."

"Well now that I've told the most religious person on the planet I don't believe the religion he bases his entire life on, I guess we should probably start packing."

Deimos sighs and sits on the edge of my bed. "I wouldn't say that, necessarily—I heard some of the men talking while we were waiting, and they seem to think Lejv isn't particularly religious either. If he admitted his lack of faith like you did, then you may not be out by default."

I laugh. "So no matter what, the next *Sira* isn't going to be religious, even with the High Priest involved in choosing who it is?"

"If we're lucky." Deimos smiles softly. "My guess is if Lejv isn't religious, he spilled just as much as you did and the High Priest knows. So we'll see what happens."

"But he's still not a half-blood. And he knows a lot more about the faith than I do. And he has way more supporters."

Deimos grimaces. "That's all true."

"So, I'm probably fucked either way."

"Unfortunately not literally, but *shae*."

I laugh. It's not funny, because nothing about this situation is funny, but I laugh because I feel like I should laugh even though everything about this is unfunny, but damn, this is one blazing amazing drug.

Or, I guess I should say, two drugs. Three? Because the drink and the smoked herb stuff.

Deimos smirks. "I'm glad you found that funny."

"He'd find anything funny right now," Mal says.

"It wasn't funny," I agree, but I'm smiling, and it *is* sortuv funny that I'm smiling when nothing is funny and no one is happy.

"Is there anything you can give him to make him stop being so annoying?" Mal asks.

Deimos snickers and shakes his head. "It'll pass, he just needs to ride it out."

"Why'd they give him drugs anyway? I thought it was supposed to be an interview."

"It *was* an interview," I say. "They just . . . said it'd make me . . . open or something."

"To make sure he told the truth," Deimos says. "I should have thought of that when we were preparing—it didn't occur to me they would drug them up for the interview. I thought that was something they mostly did to train the priests . . ."

"The priests get hyped, too?" I laugh. Now *that's* funny. It *is* funny, right?

"They say it opens them up to *Kala*'s influence or something. Extended use of the *araban-zeili* combination as well as some nanite serum they use changes their eye color permanently, even if they stop taking it, which is why all of the experienced priests have super light eyes."

I snicker for no reason then snicker because I'm snickering and this is getting kinduv exhausting.

"It's weird." Mal frowns at me. "I don't like him like this."

"Don't worry. He'll be back to normal in no time."

I run my hands over my face and sigh. "No time is right," I mumble. "If that went as badly as it probably did . . ."

Mal bites his lip and looks at Deimos. "What will happen if Uncle Eros loses?"

Deimos sighs and runs a hand through his hair. "I'm . . . not sure. But I'll make certain Eros and you get out of Asheron safely, no matter what."

"So if we lose, we run," Mal says.

"*Sha*," I say softly, and even I don't find any of this funny or worth smiling about. Will the Remnant come after me for losing? I don't want to find out. I can't imagine they'd ever let Mal and me live in peace if we tried to go back to them—not that I'd ever really consider going back anyway.

If we lose, we run.

And if we don't find somewhere safe quickly, we die.

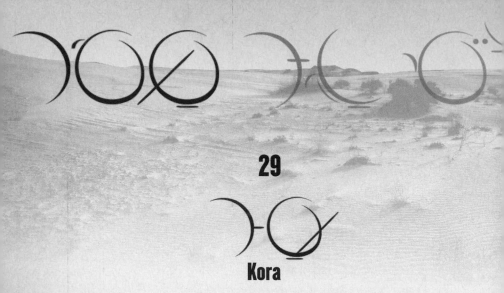

29

Kora

It's been some time since I've stood before the council, but it feels different doing so with my brother at my side. The council is smaller than the Emergency Council in Asheron. The Emergency Council is meant to represent one from each territory and the capital, though with Invino, Sekka'l, and Elja's representatives unavailable—by which I mean dead— there are six, instead of nine. Here, there are four men all old enough to be our parents or grandparents. I'm not entirely sure how four was chosen—perhaps because it's half of the sacred eight?

It doesn't matter. There are four men and they all hate me, but for once in my life, I'm not afraid. Unlike the Emergency Council, the council here in Elja are just meant to guide—they can't overrule an *Avra*'s decision.

I just pray Dima keeps to his word and agrees to reinstate me as *Avra* without Jarek in the room.

The original council meeting room is small, but with beautiful, floor-to-ceiling windows that allowed for a gorgeous view onto the palace grounds. The nanite screen kept out the sand and made it impossible to see into the room from the outside. But now the nanite screen is destroyed, and the room is unusable, a security risk, and probably filled with sand.

We meet instead in a private room in the library. The room is a little too pristine and sterile for my liking—it's a recent addition and built to match the modern minimalistic metal architecture that's become popular in the cities. It feels out of place in the traditionally built palace, with its mosaicked walls and engraved doors, but the architecture of palace renovations is hardly my biggest concern.

"Kora," the eldest council member, Roek, says. His silvering hair is cut short and severe—like his personality. "How unexpected." His voice mirrors his eyes—flat. Decidedly unimpressed. Depressingly, it reminds me of my father.

"More unexpected, I think, to see the two of you standing here together," Torven adds. Torven was father's closest friend since childhood but paradoxically has always been the kindest to me out of all the council members. Which is to say he at least attempts to appear unbiased with his council.

"It's unexpected to me, as well." Dima glances at me and lowers his gaze. "Though . . . overdue."

I nod. "With Jarek's help, Dima and I have come to an agreement that we hope will help calm the riots."

"Have you now?" Roek's voice is still flat, though he lifts an eyebrow. "Well, perhaps our two young rulers will act their position yet. Go on."

Dima flinches at the reprimand, but it doesn't bother me. I'd heard far worse from the council during my short time as *Avra*.

"I've . . . agreed to reinstate Kora as *Avra*," Dima says. His voice is tight, shoulders stiff—saying the words aloud is probably physically painful for him. But he isn't hesitating, at least, not yet. "We'll tell the people my time as *Avra* was only meant to be temporary, while the investigation surrounding *ana da Kala* Serek's attempted murder was completed."

The eyes of all four council members widen. Torven's mouth even drops open a little. I bite back the smirk nipping at my lips.

Torven is the first to recover. "While we're on the matter, what *was* the conclusion of the investigation?" The way he's looking at Dima, eyes steady and fingers drumming on the table, tells me he already knows the answer.

The back of my neck prickles, hot. I glance at Dima as a purple flush creeps up his neck. If they know Dima set me up—would they actually hold him accountable? They aren't usually permitted to interfere, but this *was* a criminal action. Against a *Sira-kaï*, no less.

Do I want them to hold him accountable?

"Kora . . . is innocent," Dima says carefully.

"*Sha*," Torven says smoothly, "she is. Tell me, Dima, why is she innocent? What was the conclusion of the investigation?"

He definitely knows. Dima glances at me, eyes sparked with panic, sweat glistening on his forehead, but I'm not saving him from this. I don't know what the council will do, but I want to hear it from his own mouth. I didn't know I needed to hear it until this moment, but watching him with the silence of the room smothering him, the need steels my fists and keeps me looking right back at him, strong, unblinking.

I want to hear my brother admit he framed me.

Dima takes a long, shivering breath and rolls his shoulders back before meeting Torven's gaze again. "It was me. I made it appear Kora attacked the *Sira-kaï*, knowing our medics would be able to save him and the repercussions would mean Kora losing her position. I wanted to be *Avra* so I . . . I took what wasn't owed to me."

Something releases in my chest. I close my eyes for just a breath, let his words sink into my bones. He admitted it. And not just to me, but to the council. I don't have to pretend it didn't happen, I don't have to pretend it was acceptable, or forgivable. The truth is out and I can breathe.

The council members nod. None of them look remotely surprised, which makes sense, given the investigative guard would have reported to them.

"You realize you'll have to answer for this alongside inciting the nanite attack with your deception," Roek says. "There must be a trial, and when Kora is *Avra* again, she'll have no choice but to hold it so you can answer to the people, and to *Kala*."

"I understand," Dima says.

Roek looks at me and I nod. "I understand as well."

"Good." Roek looks at the others and they all nod. "Then we're in agreement. Announce it to the people—but understand, Kora, you weren't a particularly popular *Avra*, either. There's a good chance they won't be any happier to have you return than they are right now with Dima on the throne."

I purse my lips. "I know."

"And have you determined what you'll say to convince them to give you a second chance?"

"I have."

"Then so be it." Roek folds his hands. "May *Kala*'s fortune smile on you both. We'll be watching."

Dima, Jarek, and I walk beyond the red sands to the gates. Every step should be terrifying. Every step brings us closer to the screaming, to the people's chanting, to their anger and pain and fear. But every step on the warm, white stones of the pathway, slightly chalky on the soles of my feet, brings me closer to a feeling I know too well.

With every breath closer to the gate, I'm shedding my old skin—the scared girl I was had no place on the throne. She was too tied into her own grief to see the needs of the people; she was too terrified of betrayal to focus on what mattered.

That girl died somewhere out there in the desert. That girl was never fit to rule, but she wasn't truly me.

The gates are still untouched, thanks to Dima's men pushing back the crowd with their shields when the people surge too close. They carry buzz batons and wear helmets and red and white armor; it's almost surreal seeing them so militarized.

I've only seen our guard like this once—when the people were at these gates protesting my rule. But before that, they rarely needed to be ready for battle.

Two guards are manning the gate, and their eyes widen as we approach. They bow, and I nod and say, "Open the gate."

The men stare at me then look at Dima. My brother nods. "Do as she says."

They do. The gates open almost silently, with the whisper-thin hiss of shifting sand, not audible at first over the dull roar of the crowd. But as the gates open, the crowd quiets and the orb-guides whir to face us. Good—their recording should stream live to the rest of the territories.

And then I step through with Dima and Jarek and the crowd explodes with voices again.

"*Avra*!"

"Traitor!"

"Tyrant!"

"How does it feel now, coward?"

"Release our people!"

I raise my hand and wait. Slowly, surely, the crowd quiets again, until all that's left is the shift of bodies and whisper of breathing.

And so I speak.

"My name is Kora Mikale Nel d'Elja. You know me as your *Avra*, and you know after *Sira-kaï* Serek fell dangerously ill within my walls, an investigation prompted me to temporarily step down while my brother ruled in my stead. But my name has been cleared, and I have returned to my home, my people, and as of this moment, I am resuming my position as *Avra*."

The crowd murmurs, voices rising like a wave, but I raise my hand again and they quiet once more.

"I understand many of you will have mixed feelings about this—I made many mistakes as *Avra*. I overlooked the pain of my people; I didn't understand just how much so many of you are struggling to get by in the city that should be the most prosperous in the nation. But right now, Vejla is weak. As *Avra*, I will do everything within my power to make our home strong again, to restore it to the days of my grandfather, and his father, and his father before him.

"It won't be easy, and it won't be quick, but I am here, and I'm listening. I see what I failed to see before, and I won't let you suffer in silence anymore."

The crowd hums with murmurs again, but no one is outraged, at least. I take a deep breath and look at Dima. "I understand my brother imprisoned some citizens of Vejla during my absence. My first act as *Avra* again is to release those people. All of them."

This time the crowd isn't quiet—cheers fill the air as they lift their fists and clap and shout in celebration. I smile, and my chest is light—this is the first time I've heard them actually support a decision I made. Not that I didn't expect them to support it, but seeing them happy is incredible.

I nod to Jarek. "Make certain they're released immediately."

Jarek nods. "I'll lead the men myself."

"Thank you." I turn back to the crowd and let the smile linger on my lips. "My second act as *Avra*," I say loudly, and the crowd quiets again. "Thank you. My biggest mistake as *Avra* before was losing sight of the people. I never want that to happen again, and to ensure it doesn't, I want the people—you—to choose a representative who will work with me closely as my official advisor."

Gasps ripple through the crowd and Dima stiffens beside me. I didn't mention this part of my plan to him—or the council for that matter—but the truth is, I didn't have to. I am *Avra* now, and I don't need to confer with anyone to make my decisions—certainly not my brother, who brought Vejla to its knees in the short time he was in power.

But though I don't doubt he thinks this is a terrible idea, Dima stays silent beside me.

"You'll have two sets to decide," I say. "And I want it to be a mutual decision. Choose someone who you feel can best represent your needs, someone you can trust to bring what Vejla most needs to my attention. I will return this time in two sets to welcome your representative.

"The decision is in your hands. Choose wisely."

And then I bow to them, and the crowd goes silent. This isn't an arbitrary move—an *Avra* never bows to anyone "except the *Sira*," and an *Avra* never bends. But those were the old ways, and the ways that made me overlook my people's needs. Those were the ways that taught me I was above the people and should hold myself as such, but the truth is, I'm not.

I'm not above them. I'm one of them, and *sha*, I was born into power, but we're not so different. My people deserve respect, and with this bow, I'm showing them they have mine.

When I straighten again, my heart skips a beat and my eyes sting. Because my people aren't protesting, aren't screaming, aren't demanding someone rule in my stead.

They're bowing on their knees—the greatest show of respect.

My vision blurs, but I smile and I don't cry. And this time, with my people backing me, the change hums in the air.

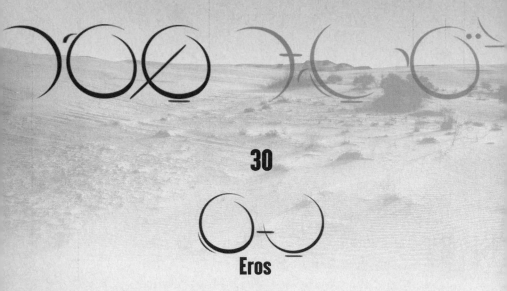

30

Eros

I wake with the world's worst brainblaze, a churning stomach, and Mal hugging me in his sleep. I grimace against the early morning light and press a pillow over my face, blocking out the light, pushing into the dull throb behind my eyes.

Not five mos later, the hiss of my doors sliding open cuts through the quiet, and Deimos's laugh fills the room. "The suns are awake and so should you be!" he announces cheerily.

"Shut up," I mumble into my pillow.

Mal shifts beside me and rolls away, muttering something that sounds like "five more mos."

"You can have all the mos you want, Mal," Deimos says a little more gently. Then the pillow rips away from my face and he grins at me. "*You*, however, need to get ready for the set. Come with me. A wash will help with next set syndrome, and so will this." He passes me a cream-colored square with black flecks in it.

I sit up and frown at the square. It's kinduv hard, but squishes slowly when I press on it. "What is this?"

"*Tenna*. Chew it—trust me, it'll help. And it doesn't taste too terrible, either."

"Reassuring." I pop it in my mouth and chew on it. It's cold and sortuv spicy, but also sickly sweet. I'm not sure I like it, but as I chew, it softens in my mouth—and gets even sweeter, and spicier, and it gets this weird salty taste, and I definitely don't like it.

My lip curls as I resist the urge to spit it out. "This is awful."

Deimos snickers. "You'll get used to it."

I stand and keep chewing even though I want to spit it out and chug something else to wash the flavor out of my mouth. But the coolness spreads down my throat and into my stomach, and up into my skull, calming the brainblaze already. As awful as it tastes, Deimos is right—it *does* seem to be working.

"See? You look better already. Now let's get you cleaned up, *shae*? You have to look presentable at the morning meal today."

I sigh. "We're having the morning meal together?"

"By request. I think the High Priest is going to talk about last night's results and the decision from the interviews."

Oh. Great. I ignore the icy chill dripping into my gut. "Should I be packing already?"

"Mal and I packed some things for you both after you passed out—in case you need to run. I think he's starting to like it here—he even explored on his own a bit, so hopefully running won't be necessary."

Mal's been exploring the palace on his own? And he helped pack? I frown. "I should have helped."

"Don't worry about it—it wasn't difficult, as you two don't own all that much. It was mostly just food, unperishable supplies, some water, and clothes that technically aren't yours."

My frown deepens. "I don't want to steal from the palace—it'll just give them another reason to come after us."

"If it comes down to it, I'll leave enough credits behind to cover the clothing before we leave. It'll be fine."

I glance at him. "We?"

Deimos blinks and smiles softly. "Well, *shae*, I'm not going to just abandon you if you don't win this."

"Deimos—"

"*Naï*, Eros, listen to me." He places his hands on my shoulders and looks at me intently—something about the closeness and the intensity in his gaze fills me with heat. "I consider you a true friend, and I don't just abandon my friends if they aren't as successful as I'd hoped. I'm a bounty hunter; I can help you both get far away from here without leaving any tracks. And maybe I can't take you to A'Sharo, but I *do* know places where you could lie low until everything calms down."

"You'd be unnecessarily endangering yourself," I say. "You really think they aren't going to notice you disappeared the same time Mal and I did?"

Deimos snorts. "Of course they'll notice. But once you're both safe, I'll return home and tell anyone who asks that I escorted you out of the city—like the orb-guides will show—then we parted ways and I went on a job."

"You'd lie for me?"

Deimos smiles and lowers his hands. "If I had to lie, I would—I'd do anything for you, Eros. But in this case, all I'd have to do to make it the truth is take a quick job on my way home." He shrugs. "Simple enough."

I guess he has a point, but those words—*I'd do anything for you*—swirl warmly around my heart and stick in my mind.

He probably doesn't mean anything serious by it—I shouldn't read into it—but still. It's nice. "Smart."

"I like to think I am, *sha*. Handsome, too."

I smirk—but he's not wrong. "And modest."

"Well, let's not get out of hand."

I laugh. "Oh, before I forget, can you show me how to look up, like, video feeds of Kora? I think you can on the glass thing, right? I just want to make sure she made it to Elja okay."

Deimos nods. "I can show you how to work one later. I saw some footage before waking you, though—she had quite an impressive display this morning where she announced taking back the throne *and* told the people to select a representative to work with her."

I blink. A representative for the people? "She . . . really?"

"Impressive, isn't it? The people loved the idea—the riots have stopped and they even bowed to her. I think she'll be fine."

I smile. It's good to hear Kora's doing as well as I know she can. She may be stubborn and a little irritating—well, a lot—but she takes her position seriously, and more importantly, she cares. She's made some terrible decisions with serious consequences that can't be overlooked, but it sounds like she's finally progressing.

Deimos pats my shoulder. "All right, with that update, we have enough time for a quick jog, then you really *do* need to clean up and make yourself presentable."

"I think I can manage that."

"I know you can."

Our running path around the complex is so familiar I don't have to think about it anymore. Deimos and I run side by side, our steps and breaths in sync, in an all-too familiar rhythm. It reminds me of the morning runs I used to do with Day. It reminds me of nothing but hot, dry air and miles of endless powdery red sand. If I close my eyes, I can almost pretend it's Day, not Deimos beside me, but then—I don't want to.

I loved my brother and miss him terribly, but I don't need to pretend Deimos is someone else to enjoy these moments together. I've never had a closeness like this that wasn't required by family—I've never had such a close friendship with a guy outside the Kits, and I definitely never imagined I'd have one with a Sepharon guy, no less a Sepharon *prince*.

But here we are, running side by side. Here we are in perfect rhythm, our steps, our breaths, our path burned into our minds by countless revolutions. And yes, the white sand is harsh on our feet, and yes, the buildings and stalls, and fountains, and statues and everything else is so far from home, so foreign to the camp I used to know, but I don't hate this newness either.

Deimos nudges me with his shoulder and grins. I pant out a breathless laugh and nudge back, and something about this—us, this togetherness—it's so natural. I can imagine doing this for cycles to come. Running around the complex in the morning hush with Deimos until our muscles won't take us anymore.

I can almost imagine a future here with Deimos at my side.

Sometime later, I'm freshly blanket-washed and changed into what Deimos calls *Asheron's best*, which is apparently a black and gold (of course) sleeveless shirt that isn't meant to seal in the front (I don't know), and dark gray loose pants that cinch just below the knees, with gold embroidery all over the soft, shiny fabric, and gold sandals.

I doubt I'll ever get used to the fashion here, and normally I wouldn't care enough to bother trying, but Deimos is always well-dressed so I just let him choose my clothes for me. By the time we're done, Mal's awake and announces he's going to walk around a bit before strolling out the door, his hand trailing along the wall. I almost stop him, but Deimos touches my shoulder; sparks scatter over my skin.

"It's a good thing—he's getting more comfortable here and getting used to his surroundings. Let him go, he'll be fine."

The thought of Mal walking around the complex on his own sets me on edge—what if something happens? But Deimos is right; if he's confident enough to do it, I'm not going to stand in his way. He's not a baby.

Despite Deimos's earlier spirit, though, as we head to the banquet hall, he seems more anxious than usual.

"The Head Priest will be there, along with everyone else. I'm not sure about the other priests, but that doesn't matter—they aren't important," Deimos rambles. "They didn't elaborate on what they'll be announcing, just that some kind of decision's been made, so either they picked one of you or there'll be another test, or . . ."

"Hold on," I say. "There's a chance they'll interview us again?"

Deimos shakes his head. "Not an interview, *nai*, but if they're undecided, they might have you both do . . . something else. Possibly. Or they may have already made a decision."

"Something else like what?"

"I don't know." He frowns. "I'm not a priest, so I'm not sure what all of the options are."

I frown.

"But it'll be okay. Whatever happens, I'll ensure you and Mal are taken care of."

"Thank you."

"Sure." He sighs and rakes his fingers through his hair. "Sure, sure, sure . . ."

Dammital. Deimos's nervousness is catching—as though I wasn't already anxious enough. Deep breaths in, deep breaths out. I drum my fingers along my thigh until we cross into the dining room—then Deimos and I pull our shoulders back and walk like we have nothing in the world to be worried about and I almost laugh at how synchronized the whole thing is.

I guess I really am getting used to life here.

Deimos and I aren't the first ones to enter, but we're not the last, either. Simos and Ejren nod at us as we enter the quiet room, and Aleija smiles when we sit next to her and her wife.

"Fully recovered?" she asks with a quiet laugh.

"Recovered enough," I answer with a small smile.

"Good. That *ufrike* and *araban-zeili* combination can do a number on you."

"*Sha*, Deimos forgot to mention to me they'd be drugging us for the interview."

"I didn't realize!" Deimos laughs. "Though, in retrospect, it makes sense. I probably should have predicted it."

I smirk. "Probably?"

"Hush."

Aleija laughs. "To be fair, I only knew because it's especially common in Daïvi for any religious ceremony of remote importance. I imagine it's less so in A'Sharo."

"I honestly wouldn't know." Deimos shrugs. "My brother Olen does nearly all of the religious ceremonies in private, and he doesn't talk about them. And as the youngest son, the priests there don't care if I participate in the annual rituals, so I haven't participated since I was fourteen."

"Ah," Aleija nods. "And they don't give the substances to the children."

Deimos smirks. "I would hope not."

A burst of laughter and talk behind us announces Lejv's entrance with his many supporters. Men sit at their respective places around the crescent table, piling their plates with food I forgot was there.

I guess we're here to eat while we listen to the verdict, even though my stomach is anything but hungry right now.

Deimos slides a large serving spoon portion of wiggling white squares onto my plate. I grimace. "What are you doing?"

"You want to try that," he announces, and I'm not sure if he's joking. I mean, the food is *moving*—food isn't supposed to move. But then he serves himself a heap of the stuff so I guess maybe it's not terrible.

"What is it?" I frown at the quivering squares. "And why is it moving?"

Deimos snickers and passes me one of their weird utensils—I still haven't mastered how to use these, but at least I know what *not* to do now, I guess. "It's called *istel* and the movement is just the texture—every shake of the table makes it move, but it's not alive, I promise. And it's good. Trust me."

I look at him skeptically, but then he pokes one onto his utensil and eats it. I frown at the thick white squares, but poke one with the stick thing they eat with like Deimos did and put it in my mouth. It's cold, and sweet, and the texture is kinduv wet and slimy, which I don't love, but when I bite into it, it's thick—and I have to admit—tastes pretty good.

"Your food is so weird," I mutter.

Deimos snickers. "It's your food now, too."

We eat with everyone but the former *Sira* and the High Priest, and the initial quiet grows into an endless murmur of voices, spattered with bouts of laughter and louder conversation. The more I eat, the easier it is to focus on the food rather than my nerves, so I manage to fill and clear my plate.

"We'll have to bring some of this back for Mal," I say.

"Already had some sent to his room." Deimos smiles. "I talked to the staff this morning before waking you up."

I blink. I shouldn't be surprised—Deimos has gone above and beyond when it comes to making sure Mal gets what he needs throughout our time here. It's the first time I've seen a Sepharon treat a human as . . . well, *human*. "That was . . . thanks."

"Any time." Deimos takes a large bite of some kinduv meat mix I haven't been brave enough to try because some of the meat is *purple* and some of the other meat is gray, which . . .

Another time.

When almost everyone has just about cleared their plates and no one is reaching for more, Tamus enters the hall in his customary Ona black and silver. I expect him to go to his usual place across the table, but instead he walks right up to me and nods to the door.

"Can I have a word?"

Deimos raises his eyebrows and my stomach flips, but I nod and stand. "Of course."

We step out into the hallway and far enough from the doors that they slide closed, shutting out the chatter inside the dining hall. The air vibrates in my chest as I try to swallow my nerves.

"My son and his husband have spoken highly of you," Tamus says.

I smile softly. "I'm glad to know them."

Tamus nods. "I've been paying close attention to both Lejv and your evaluations and have reviewed many of your father's archived speeches. He was a visionary, and the more I consider what we know—from your birth to your genetics and possession of the ring and the mysterious circumstances around his death—the more I'm convinced your being here is not an accident."

Tension rolls off my shoulders and something thrills inside me—if this conversation is going where I think it's going . . . do I actually have Tamus's support?

"Unfortunately, most of the council doesn't see it that way."

And just like that, the thrill dies. I don't know why—it's not like I thought anything else; I *knew* most of the council didn't support me. But hearing it from Tamus stings nonetheless.

"I . . . expected as much."

Tamus nods. "Lija da Daïvi also supports you, as I'm sure you may have guessed, and there are a couple others who are undecided. But I wanted to warn you, because much of the council is positioned against you, and I can't imagine it will go well for you or your nephew if Lejv takes the nomination."

Cool air breathes down my spine and ice settles between my lungs.

"I wanted you to be aware," Tamus says, "both that you have support from Lija and me, but also that you need to tread carefully in the coming sets. I can't tell you what the High Priest decided, and it's not a hopeless situation, but there's still much that needs to be done to garner you enough support, even if the next sets go well for you."

I take a deep breath and nod. "I appreciate the warning. Thank you."

Tamus nods and we return to the dining hall. Deimos nudges me as I sit and leans close to whisper in my ear. "What was that about?"

His warm breath washes down my neck and I shiver. "Later," I answer quietly.

Not two mos later, Ashen enters with the High Priest. The air goes cold and my stomach churns—maybe I shouldn't have eaten so much after all. I wipe my hands on my thighs under the table and inhale deeply through my nose as Ashen kneels at his place across from me. The High Priest doesn't sit—he stands behind Ashen and looks around at everyone.

Deep breaths in, deep breaths out. I'll be fine. Everything will be fine.

Stars, I hope everything will be fine.

"Thank you all for joining us," the High Priest says. "As I'm certain you've heard, my fellow brothers and sisters have discussed at length the results of the examination of our two candidates, Eros d'Elja and Lejv d'Asheron. Both men spoke freely and truthfully, and their words and spirits were considered. Together, we prayed to *Kala* and listened to their word, and we unanimously agree on the message we heard from The Glorious One Above."

The room falls to a stillness barely disturbed by breathing. The words that come could change everything. They could be a death sentence for me and Mal, or not. They could mean more waiting, and testing, and awful, tense moments like this one with the next verdict.

Deep breaths in, deep breaths out.

Please be fine. Please please please let everything be fine.

"Eros and Lejv are well matched," the High Priest says. "*Kala* agrees both men are well-qualified upon examination, and so *Kala* has elected to make the decision directly." The High Priest lowers his head, as though bowing in reverence. "This is their decision, and we are but their vessel. And so it has been decided."

Then he bows and takes a step back. What does that Voiding mean? How can a god decide *anything* directly? It's not like religious deities come down from their thrones and visit the planet from time to time—it's not like any of us have ever seen *Kala*, or ever will.

So what in the Void does *Kala making the decision directly* mean?

I glance at Deimos. His eyes are wide and he's chewing his lip. Fuck. He's worried. If he's worried, I should be worried.

Something's wrong. What does this mean?

"The match will be tomorrow at the rising of the suns, in the courtyard," Ashen says. "It will be broadcasted live to all, and the world will watch as Lejv and Eros fight before *Kala* to determine the final decision."

My breath catches and I glance at Lejv. Fight. We're fighting?

I can fight. How well prepared is Lejv for hand-to-hand combat?

It doesn't matter. I can fight, and I'm anything but out of practice—Deimos and I spar almost every day, and I've trained for this my whole life. Something like lightness rises in my chest and wraps around my heart.

Is it possible things have actually gone my way? It is possible I'm really one sparring match away from securing safety for Mal, for myself, for humans around the globe?

"Tomorrow, one man will become *Sira*." Then Ashen looks right at me and the lightness turns to ice. That look—pure malice. Something is wrong, something is wrong, something is wrong.

And then he says the words, and everything is wrong at once.

"One man will become *Sira*. And one man will die."

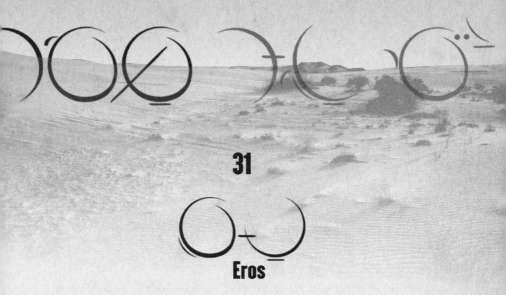

31

Eros

"You're holding back." Deimos glares at me as I catch my breath, sweating under the suns, hands on my knees.

"Sure," I pant. "Holding back. That's why I need to break to catch my breath."

"You could have better connected that kick."

I roll my eyes. "We're sparring, not really fighting. I'm not trying to *actually* hurt you."

"*Shae*," Deimos says. "But you won't be able to hold back during the match tomorrow."

I stand up straight. Kick off my shoes even though the sand is course under my feet—but it's harder to get a grip on the ground wearing them. The courtyard is a wide, sandy space with statues marking off each corner of the square. Two fountains trickle gold-tinted water endlessly on either side of the square, and the three corners of the palace marking off the north end aren't shading the square anymore.

I walk to the nearest fountain, take a breath to brace myself for the inevitable, and dunk my head under. The water isn't as cool as I'd hoped, and the shock is a lightning bolt to my system—I pull my head back up quickly before the memories hit. But when the water drips down my shoulders, and my heart beat slows, I close my eyes and take an easy, deep breath. I'm cooler now. Worth it.

"You realize that's probably a holy fountain or something of the like." Deimos smirks.

I open my eyes and snort. "*Naï* it's not. We're nowhere near the temple."

"True, but dunking your head in is *probably* frowned upon."

"Too bad." I sigh. "It's way too hot for me to care." I sit on the edge of the fountain and Deimos rests next to me.

"You heard what I said, though, *shae?*"

"*Shae,*" I mumble. "Can't hold back tomorrow."

"I mean at all. One of you is going to die, and it can't be you."

I press my face into my palms. It should be easy to say, *sha, of course, I'll do what I have to.* It should be easy to agree that as much as I don't like it, tomorrow's match has to end in a death. And it's not like I haven't killed before—multiple times. It's not like I hesitated before killing those men who attacked Kora or killed Day and my parents. It's not like I've ever hesitated to do what's necessary when faced with an enemy, with life or death.

But I'm tired. I'm so tired. I don't want to add to my personal death toll; I don't want the list to grow. I don't want to dream about another life I've taken, and I don't want to relive it again, and again, and again.

I have so much blood on my hands already and I don't want more. I don't, I don't, I don't.

But this time, like every time, I might not have a choice. This time, like every time, it'll be me against him, my life or his, and losing my life will mean more than dying.

If I lose, so does Mal. So do humans across the globe. And maybe I'd be able to live with letting everyone down, maybe I'd be able to accept humans will continue to lose again, and again, and again, because I wouldn't be around to see it anyway. Maybe I'd be able to accept that.

But what I can't accept is leaving Mal in danger. What I can't accept is my thirteen-year-old nephew running for his life—and probably losing it eventually anyway. What I can't accept is his best-case scenario would be becoming some-one's servant, because there's no way he'd make it back to a camp—or even The Remnant, for that matter—alone.

His life is in my hands, and tomorrow, it might cost another life. The life of a man I care nothing about, the life of a man who represents everything I'm fighting against. But a man nevertheless.

A life.

"Look," Deimos says softly. "I know . . . it's not easy. They're asking so much from you—"

"I'm not sure you do know, actually—"

"But if this doesn't go the way we want it to, I want you to know I'll take care of Mal."

I blink. Stare at him. "What?"

Deimos frowns. "If . . . if you lose, I'll protect your nephew. It wouldn't be perfect—and he'll probably never be respected, but I can ensure no one else takes him. I can make sure he'll grow up healthy, and strong, and not as someone's servant."

I frown. "You can do that?"

Deimos nods. "He might . . . if anyone questions it, I may have to call him *my* servant, but I swear to you it won't be true. He'll be his own man—or at least, as much as a human can be in Sepharon society. And when he's grown, I'll let him leave or stay, whatever he wants. He'll be free to make his own choices, I promise you."

I nod. I pinch the bridge of my nose and I try not to feel, but this is real. I might be dead in a set.

"Thank you." The words are tight and shake on my whisper. "I don't know why you're . . . but thank you."

"Because I care about you both," Deimos says. "And because you both deserve so much more than *Kala*'s handed you. I may not be able to change the world alone, but I can make his easier, and if things don't go well . . ." He grimaces. "If things don't go well, I can only hope keeping him safe will be enough."

I run a hand through my sweaty, wet hair and inhale deeply. "Have you seen him fight?"

"Lejv? *Naï*, but at the very least he's not as physically prepared as you. Of the eight sets you've been here, I've only seen him run once, so I'd guess his endurance isn't as refined as yours. If he turns out to be a good fighter, you can outlast him if you're smart."

I nod. "Is it likely he's a good fighter?"

Deimos hesitates. "It's . . . not *un*likely. I'm sure you've noticed most Sepharon take care of themselves—the fourth tenant—"

"To take care of the body *Kala* gave you, *shae*, I remember."

Deimos nods. "And most Sepharon royalty I've met—the men, at least—have done some time with their territory's guard. And those men are all skilled at hand-to-hand combat."

"Great," I mutter.

"But it's not a guarantee. Maybe *Kala* will smile on us and Lejv won't be as skilled at fighting as many royal men are."

I look at him skeptically. "Because *Kala*'s been *so* nice to me, so far."

"Well." Deimos laughs weakly. "Still worth hoping, isn't it? Hoping while planning for the worst."

Hoping while planning for the worst should be my life's motto. "I'm assuming they know I can fight."

"Everyone knows you were Kora's bodyguard before you came here, which obviously requires a very particular skill set."

"Right." I shake my head. "So I'm going to walk out there blind and he'll already know what to expect."

"*Naï*, you'll walk out there expecting him to be a master of fighting arts, and if you're wrong, all the better."

I sigh, fighting off the edges of a brainblaze pressuring my skull. "Can I ask you a random question?"

"Right now?" Deimos laughs. "Need a break from heavy topics?"

"I do."

"Go on, then."

"How did you become a bounty hunter?"

"Ah." Deimos smiles, and something about the amused twist of his lips is catching—I find myself mirroring a ghost of his grin. "Well. Fortunately, all of my elder brothers took the boring, official jobs—you know, *future ruler*, medic, priest, captain of the guard, diplomat, that sort of thing. So I wasn't pressured to do anything but show up at official events and be my naturally charming self."

I smirk. "Naturally."

"Don't tell me you disagree—it'd break my heart."

I glance at him, and my smile breaks into a grin because he's pouting ridiculously. "I don't disagree. You're . . ." Deimos is a lot of things: addictive, unfairly handsome, hilarious, magnetic. He's the guy friend I've never had—the prince who went out of his way to help me when he didn't have to, who has woven himself into so much of my life that I don't want to imagine a set without him. He makes me happy when I shouldn't be and hovers in my thoughts long after we've said good night.

But I go with the word least likely to tempt me to spill my every thought about him: "captivating."

"*Captivating.*" Deimos grins and my face warms, despite myself. "I like it. *As I was saying,* I more or less could be anything I wanted, and I knew I wanted to travel and have an exciting job, and also, I'd learned early on I was a talented fighter. I didn't immediately know how to combine those into a job, however, so I began with traveling. I went all over—up north to Inara and then around Ona and Elja. I saw the endless ocean on the Northern and Southern shores, the peaks of Daïvi, and Invino, and even spent some time in Sekka'l though that was . . . less enjoyable. And then, during my travels, I was cornered by two, shall we say, *unsavory* individuals? But they underestimated me, and I subdued them and brought them to the authorities—who then *paid* me for my service, and thus the idea was born."

I laugh. "That's incredible."

Deimos beams. "Why thank you. You're rather incredible yourself." And now I'm blushing again, which must encourage him, because he leans closer and smiles conspiratorially. My heart pounds at his nearness and my skin prickles—I can almost taste his breath, he's so close.

"You know I mean it, *shae*?" he says. "I really admire you. You're truly one of the most amazing people I've ever met, and I'm honored to call you my friend." He hesitates. "And . . . sometime after you've won the match and your life isn't in immediate danger, maybe we can be something more?"

My heart beats harder at his words. *Something more* could mean a lot of things: closer friends, maybe, or maybe he means . . . could he be hinting at something romantic? I don't *think* I'm reading too much into it—he's been flirty practically since the moment we met. And I'm not completely sure which he's trying to say, but the way he's biting his lip and looking at me makes me think it could be the latter. Maybe.

Of course, I've never had a guy show this kinduv interest before—stars, I've never known a guy who wasn't family who didn't think of me as *lesser*. Until Deimos, I avoided other men and boys for my own safety, as much as I wished it could be different. So I don't know how this kinduv relationship starts—how two guys decide they want to be more than friends. But whatever Deimos means, I want to try.

He's not asking for now, because this timing is obviously fucked. But this open-ended potential for *something more* sounds like exactly what I need right now: something purely good to hope for.

"*Shae*," I say, adopting his word with a smile. "I'd like that."

Deimos's face lights up like a sunrise, and he stands and offers me his hand. "Well, we've had a break enough, *shae*? Ready for round five?"

Mal wants to walk around the grounds with me—*just* me—so Deimos goes off to relax or whatever while I take Mal's shoulder and we wander. He walks the halls expertly, his fingertips just grazing the smooth walls as we move, his head held high and proud. I smile. It's good to see him confident like this, even in a place where people like him aren't usually welcome.

I can't say for sure one way or the other, but seeing how the servants were always Sepharon here, Mal may be the first human to walk these halls.

"So where are you taking me?" I ask.

"Garden," Mal answers. "I found it a couple sets after we got here. I like it. There aren't usually a lot of people there and it sounds really calming. Smells good, too. I've been hanging out there when you and Deimos are gone and no one bothers me."

"Good. You know if you ever have an issue—"

"I'll tell you and Deimos. I know, but it's okay—I think most people would rather just pretend I don't exist." He shrugs. "Works for me."

We step off polished stone onto the gritty, white sand. I don't think I'll ever get used to the roughness of the desert here. I miss the blanket-soft red powder of home.

Outside, Mal switches to my other side so he can keep his hand against the wall as we turn right. It's opposite the direction I usually go in, since Deimos and I usually run in town, but I think the courtyard is somewhere this way. The reflection of the suns off the sand makes it feel twice as hot. I don't mind it, though—I know heat like I know air.

We walk next to the pathway so Mal can use the walls as his guide. It's quiet back here, mostly empty except for the ever-present guards standing at attention every couple measures. The polished black and gold stone pathway is bordered by silver trees with gold and bronze leaves, shiny and almost metallic. They remind me almost of the trees back in Elja, except those were white with silver leaves, and these look like they were made entirely from flakes of precious metals. Everything here is perfectly spaced out and organized—there aren't even any random plants and brush back here, like you see spread over the sands.

Eventually we turn a corner beside a path bordered with more of those metallic-y trees, but spaced out between flowers and decorative bush-things. The flowers are bright colors—purples, blues, greens, oranges, reds—and the bushes are striped with white and a blue so deep it looks black. And Mal is right, the air is sweeter back here, almost fruity.

In the center of the garden is another fountain, but this one is unusual. The center of the fountain looks like one of those silver trees—except carved of completely white stone. Water pours off it into the large white base below, and the whole thing is carved to look like—I think it's supposed to be Asheron. Maybe it's supposed to mean something.

Mal and I sit on a stone bench opposite the fountain and I nearly leap out of my skin—we're not alone. I mean, we're never alone because the guards are everywhere, but sitting on a bench on the other side of the fountain isn't a guard.

It's Lejv.

"What do you think?" Mal asks, and Lejv looks up, I guess noticing us for the first time, too. It's all I can do to keep my voice calm as my heart beats a little harder. I'm not afraid of him—it's not like he's going to attack me in broad sunlight—but relaxing is hard when I've got a living reminder of what I have to do tomorrow sitting just paces away.

But Mal doesn't know Lejv is here. He can't see him.

"It's nice," I say. "I see what you mean about it smelling good."

Mal nods. "I like the running water sound, too. I've fallen asleep out here a couple times." He laughs, and even with the guy I'm supposed to kill tomorrow watching us across the way, hearing Mal laugh is enough to make me smile, just a little. It's good he can find something to laugh about today. Stars know I wish I could.

Lejv stands and starts crossing the garden toward us. I stiffen, and Mal must feel it because he lowers his voice and asks, "Are you okay?"

"It's fine," I answer quietly. "We're just not alone."

Mal sits up straight just as Lejv rounds the fountain and nods at me. "We've never really been formally acquainted."

Formally acquainted? I guess he means we never introduced ourselves to each other, which, no, was pretty unnecessary given everything. I know who he is, and he knows who I am. What do we need a formal introduction for?

"Guess not," I answer carefully.

"You must be Mal." Lejv smiles at my nephew. "I've heard you enjoy exploring the palace grounds."

My eyes narrow. Why are people gossiping about Mal? Should Deimos and I have been more careful with him? Should I have asked him to stay in my room? It didn't seem right making him more of a prisoner than he already is here, but I'm not sure I like that people have been talking about him, either.

Though I guess they'd probably talk about him if he were locked in my room, too.

"*Sha.*" Mal raises his chin. "You must be Lejv. I've heard you're going to try to kill my uncle tomorrow."

I choke on words as Lejv's eyes widen. He glances at me then laughs uncertainly. Mal just smiles.

"Ah, well . . . there is a match tomorrow, unfortunately, *sha*."

Unfortunately. Does he mean that, or is he just being polite because Mal is here? I think I'd rather he didn't mean it. I'd rather he wanted me dead, because it's going to be hard enough to fight to the death without either of us having second thoughts. Not that either of us have a choice anyway.

Lejv turns to me. "I wanted to say I'm . . . sorry for the way this has unfolded. When Ashen came to me and suggested I was the next in line to take the throne, I never imagined it would come to this. I'm . . ." He hesitates. "I'm not sure I would have agreed to claim my blood right had I known it would end like this."

What is he trying to say? Is he just coming forward because he's afraid he'll lose? Did he actually imagine I'd roll over and let him take the throne without a fight? Or maybe he thought I wouldn't attempt to claim my birthright at all—which, I mean, I didn't even know I was going to at first but . . . why would he say that now?

"If you really think that then maybe you should bow out," I answer.

Lejv presses his lips together. "I think we both know I can't do that."

"Why not?" I stand. "I don't love the idea of fighting to the death over the throne either, but I never imagined they were just going to *give* it to me, and I'm prepared to do what I have to. If you don't want to fight, then don't. You know my claim is stronger than yours. Walk away."

Lejv's face shutters and he looks me in the eye. "I'm not walking away, and I'm not afraid to fight you, Eros. I, too, am prepared to do what I must." He shakes his head and turns away. "I just wish I didn't have to."

We eat our evening meal in my room. There's no point trying to make nice, not anymore—not when we'll be killing each other in a set. And not when we've made it clear neither of us are walking away.

Still, what Lejv said hangs in my head, an unwanted echo. It was easy to imagine having to kill someone who wanted me dead, who was happy to fight. It's another thing entirely to know he's just as reluctant as I am to go out there. To know he doesn't want to fight either.

To know it doesn't matter what we want, because tomorrow we'll fight to finally end this anyway.

Mal is uncharacteristically quiet. He sits so close to me our hips are touching, and he barely eats the stew and flat noodle mix of tonight's dinner.

I nudge him with my elbow and nod at his bowl. "You should eat. It's good—a lot of meat and vegetables in there."

Mal stares at his bowl. "I'm not hungry."

"Too many snacks?" Deimos asks, but we both know the answer—the plate we left him to snack on throughout the day is still full of pastries and fruit. It doesn't look like he touched it at all.

"I don't want you to fight," Mal says.

My stomach sinks. I put my arm over his shoulder, pulling him closer. "I'll be fine," I say with confidence I don't have. "You know how well trained I am—you've seen . . ." My chest aches—I almost said *you've seen me spar with your dad.* I try again. "You've seen my training. You know I can fight."

"Yeah," Mal says, switching to English. "But so can all the Sepharon. That's, like, the first lesson in camp guard training—expect all the Sepharon can and will kill you. They've been just as trained as you are—maybe even more."

Deimos looks at me questioningly. I grimace. "It's true he's probably trained," I answer in Sephari, "but I've killed Sepharon men before. If anything, I have better odds than I've had before—I'm only fighting one man this time. All I have to do is beat him and this will be all over."

Mal stares at our food. I sigh and hug him. "I can't promise I'll be fine; the truth is I don't know how well he is or isn't trained. But I'm as prepared as I can be, and I'll fight for us both. My chances are good—in a way, I've been prepping for this my whole life."

"And," Deimos adds, "on the off-chance things don't go our way, you won't be alone. I've already told Eros I'll take care of you if anything happens. I'll make sure you grow up free, and healthy—and *kafra*, I have a very nice home, if I say so myself." Deimos smiles and Mal frowns at him.

"Don't you live in the palace in A'Sharo?"

Deimos laughs. "I did, but *naï*, I got my own place on my fifteenth lifecycle celebration. And it's a great place, with a swimming center, and privacy, and a view of the mountains—and there's more than enough room for us both."

Mal nods and looks at his food again.

"Either way, you'll be taken care of," I say. "So don't worry, *shae*? We're ready for every possibility."

"I'm not," he says softly. "I don't want to be prepared for the possibility where you're dead, too."

I bite my lip. My breath shakes as it slips from my lips. "I don't want to be, either."

When Mal squints up at me again, his eyes are teary. "Just swear you'll fight your hardest."

I don't hesitate—not for a breath. "I swear. You have my word."

And so we eat in silence. And I don't think about how tomorrow, my morning meal may be my last.

I don't.

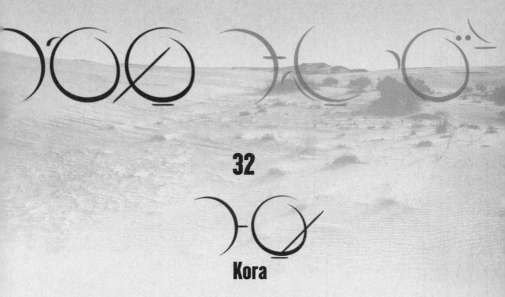

32

Kora

Standing in front of Dima's bedroom door the next set, an echo of another time washes over me. A time when Eros was at my side, and I was covered in a layer of sand from going out into Vejla for the first time in too long, and I was angry Dima never respected my privacy by announcing his entrance before bursting into my room time and time again, so I did the same to him.

I walked into his room without announcement or invitation, and I found him in bed with Jarek.

The echo twists painfully inside me—not because seeing my brother romantically entangled with his closest friend was in any way hurtful, but because my violating their privacy hurt Dima. More than hurt—it ripped him apart. I'd never caused him so much pain, not like that, and though it wasn't my intention, intentions don't matter when you've hurt someone. And it was too late to take it back.

This time, I knock and announce myself. "Dima, it's me. May I enter?"

A shuffling sound and the low murmur of voices leaks under the door before it slides open. Jarek nods me inside, respectfully lowering his head as I enter.

Dima lowers his head, as well, and it shouldn't be, but the gesture coming from him looks so foreign. I'd never seen my brother show me genuine respect—every bow and murmur of my title was once infused with bitterness and rage.

But this, this is quiet. Humble. Real.

"It's good to see you," I say to my brother. "I thought I'd confirm you're doing well."

Dima shakes his head and sits on the edge of his bed. "I wouldn't say well, but I'm fine, *sha*. You don't need to worry about me."

"I always worry about you. I'm your sister; it's impossible for me not to worry about you."

Dima closes his eyes like I've hurt him, and I don't understand. I replay my words in my mind. How could what I said be hurtful? I glance at Jarek, but he just looks grimly at my brother. His arms are crossed over his chest, and when Dima opens his eyes again, Jarek arches an eyebrow at him and tilts his head toward me.

Is he expecting something?

"You're too good to me, Kora," Dima finally says.

I frown at him and open my mouth to answer, but he lifts he hand.

"Please, just . . ." He takes a shaky breath and grips his knees. "I . . . did not treat you as a brother should. We were close once, as children, but . . . my jealousy corrupted what we had, and I'm sorry. I'm so sorry. I framed you for Serek's attempted murder as I admitted in front of the council. I tricked Anja into giving you the lip paint—I told her it was a gift, and I gave her the antidote and said it would calm your nerves. She had no idea what she'd done, and when she figured it out . . . she couldn't handle the way I'd used her to hurt you, and her blood is on my hands, and I'm sorry."

My eyes sting as my brother slides off his bed and onto his knees at my feet. And there is the answer to the question I'd been too afraid to ask—if her blood is on his hands then she . . . she must have . . . I press the side of my fist to my mouth.

"No number of apologies will ever be enough," Dima rasps. "I'm a failure—and worse, I betrayed my own blood to take a throne I was never meant to have. *Kala* didn't choose me to rule—he chose you. I can see that now, and I wish—you don't know how badly I wish I'd seen it sooner." Dima's shoulders shake, and then he's crying, and I'm crying, and we're on our knees together and Dima is hugging me. His arms are wrapped around me and he sobs into my shoulder and says, "I'm sorry, I'm so sorry," over and over, and these are words I never expected, not from him, not ever.

"I know," I whisper, then clear my throat and try again. "I know. And I accept your apology, but Dima . . ." My voice catches and I inhale deeply. My brother pulls away and wipes at his face, but his body still trembles with unshed tears. "I don't know that I'll ever be able to trust you again—not like I did when we were children. You're my brother, and I'll protect you however I can, but I can't return a high position to you again. As it is, there are some who think I should keep you in the cells."

Dima bites his lip and nods. "I don't expect my position back, not ever, and . . . " He takes a shaky breath. "If you want to keep me in the cells, I won't fight it."

"Hold on—" Jarek starts, but I lift my hand and he quiets.

"I'm not going to keep you in the cells. Not if I can help it, and right now, at least, I can. But it's good to know if . . . things intensify, you'll cooperate."

"I brought you here to keep him safe," Jarek says. "Not to treat him as a prisoner."

"And I said I'd do my best." I look at Jarek. "I don't want to put him in the cells, and for now, I can refuse. But if the demand becomes too high, I may have to give in—and he may end up safer locked up than outside. But I need to temper the will of the people first—without their support, I am nothing."

Jarek frowns, but nods. "You should be able to avoid it, at least until a new *Sira* is crowned."

I nod and look at Dima. "Once a new *Sira* is chosen, who-ever they are may choose to call for your prosecution."

"After everything that happened, I . . . wouldn't expect anything less."

"Okay." I squeeze him one more time, then release him, and stand. "Thank you for apologizing. I may not be able to trust you, but I hope we can rebuild our relationship over time."

"I hope so, too." Dima takes a shaky breath. "And for what it's worth, I think you're a great *Avra*. I always have."

My eyes sting and my vision blurs anew. But I stand tall, and when I leave my brother and his partner, the buzz of something new rings in my bones, even through the pain of knowing my friend, Anja, is gone forever.

A hope for something better.

The meal table feels empty without Iro curled up at my side and Anja nearby. I sit at the apex of the curve, as always in Elja—or always since my coronation, anyway—with Dima across from me and Jarek to his right. The table is large enough to seat dozens of others, but without the council joining us, and they rarely do, the wide room feels empty.

I was sitting in this very spot with Anja at my side when Eros burst through the doors with Jarek and Dima on his heels, and collapsed on the floor, screaming—

I close my eyes and inhale deeply through my nose. Things are so different now. Eros is in Asheron, poised to become *Sira*. Anja is dead. My brother got what he always wanted and nearly ran Elja into the ground with it. And tomorrow, the people will choose someone to represent them, for the first time in Elja's history. And I will work with them.

I don't know what to expect. I just hope whoever they choose is someone reasonable. But this is the right decision—I feel it in my bones. I think Eros would agree.

"Guide," I call. My voice is too loud in the empty room, and Dima and Jarek watch me curiously as an orb-guide floats from the wall opposite us to my side.

"May I be of assistance?" it chirps.

"Turn on the world feed."

The guide twirls and the screens across the table hum to life as I retrieve a glass held on the underside of the floating table—one for each seat.

"Checking on Eros?" Jarek asks.

I nod and scan the article headers on the glass. "I didn't get the chance to check last night. Have you heard anything?"

Jarek's silence makes me look up. He and Dima are looking at each other with an expression I don't like—as though they're having a silent conversation.

My back prickles with cold. "What is it? Is Eros okay?"

"For now," Dima says carefully. "We assumed you already knew."

I open my mouth to tell him to get to the point, but Jarek beats me to it. "The High Priest and council have decided to allow *Kala* to make the ruling directly."

My heart withers in my chest. "You mean . . . through a fight."

"To the death," Dima confirms. "*Sha.*"

There's no question that Eros can fight, but this—this is different. One wrong move and he'd be killed for all the world to see on the feed. He has a chance, and a good one at that, but I . . . I didn't want to have to see him fight for his life.

Then again, he's been doing just that all along. I just hope this fight will be the last he'll ever have to be part of.

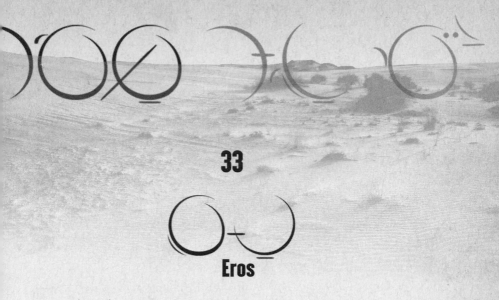

33

Eros

I need to sleep.

It's not a question. If I'm not well-rested tomorrow, it could kill me. Insomnia tonight is the last thing I need—but I can't remember the last time I've had a full night's rest, and tonight, of course, is no different. Even if I need the sleep more than ever. Especially because I need the sleep more than ever.

I listen to Mal breathing beside me, keep my eyes closed, and try to let it lull me to sleep. I synch my breaths with his, try to focus on darkness, on nothing at all, but through the darkness comes whispers. I touch Aren's bracelet and run my thumb over the smooth black and gold ring on my hand. This might be the last time I lie awake in bed, listening to Mal fast asleep beside me. This might be the last time I struggle to sleep, because tomorrow sleep may be eternal.

Tomorrow might be the last fight of my life. I wish I could pretend otherwise, but the truth is I don't know what to expect, not really. Deimos and I could only guess at how well Lejv may fight. We don't know what weapons he'll choose or even what weapons will be available to us. We don't know if there will be a weapon I'm familiar with, or a weapon Lejv is familiar with, but everything tells me the odds will be stacked against me. Again. Because they don't want me on the throne. Because this world wasn't built for me, and the Sepharon never fail to take the opportunity to remind me I don't belong here.

Except Deimos and Kora. But they aren't on the Council, and neither of them can help me tomorrow.

At least Mal will be okay. At least, whatever happens, Deimos will take care of him and keep him safe. I trust he meant that promise. I trust he won't break it.

I don't know when it happened, but I trust Deimos more than I do Kora. I trust him not to turn his back on me—or Mal—when things get difficult. I trust when he gave me his word, he'd rather die than break it. Kora broke that trust with me too many times, but something tells me Deimos never would.

I wish my mind would let me rest; I wish the nightmares suffocating me in death, ash, torture, and blood would leave me alone. Because if I didn't have the same paralyzing nightmare tape smothering me every time I manage to sleep, I think I would dream about Deimos. I think I'd let myself imagine what *something more* might mean. I think I'd kiss the spot on his lip he bites when he looks at me; I think I'd lie under the moons with him in a dream world far from reality.

But I know my mind and what those sets in Dima's dungeon did to me. What watching people die again and again while I couldn't help them imprinted into my dreams. And tonight, with my thoughts racing and tomorrow looming overhead, sleep couldn't be farther away.

Eyes open again. I drag myself out of bed, and head outside. My brain can't rest, so maybe a run will calm me enough to collapse into bed. Or hopefully wear me out enough, at least, so when I pass out, I won't dream at all.

I don't have any other ideas, but I desperately need sleep, so it's worth a try.

The complex looks different at night—the deep black-purple sky paints the white sands light purple. Three of the four moons are visible tonight, scattered across the sky, shining among the stars. Our jogging path is on the edge of the complex and isn't as well-lit as the sparkling white streets of the inner city, but I'm not worried. Deimos and I have gone around our track enough that I could do it in my sleep.

I run through the shadows, past the silent buildings, my bare feet slipping through the course, cool sand. I run across the night, my breaths settling into a familiar rhythm, every step closer to tomorrow, to the fight I never want to have. I run into the black, the stars gathering on my shoulders and sinking into my blood, whispers of lost loved ones settling between my lungs.

I don't know what Nol would tell me to do, but he'd hate to see me fight for my life. He'd hate to see me become this person with blood on his hands and lives in his throat. He'd hate this violence, this coldness, this *kill or be killed*. That was never Nol's way. That was never what he taught me.

Fighting to survive was Day's method of living. Bloodshed was Day's necessary sacrifice. Violence broiled in his bones, not because he wanted it, not because he liked it, but because we were being hunted. Because the Sepharon decided we didn't deserve to live free. Because he'd never spent a set when he wasn't running, wasn't scared for his life, for his family. Violence wasn't Day's nature, but it was what this world demanded from him. It was the only way he could see out of the ever-looming threat. It was the only way he knew to live another set, see another sunrise. Fight. Fight for air, for food, for water. Fight for the life they don't want us to have—take freedom from their mouths and watch life bleed from their eyes.

Nol told us if our lives demanded blood, we'd have to sacrifice our own. Nol told us infusing violence into our souls meant racing into blood-soaked deaths. He said ask for violence and you'll get it—he said our only hope was to separate ourselves from brutality.

In the end, he was right. But he was also wrong. Because Day died violently, but so did he, and so did Esta, and so did so many who never asked for this, who never wanted violence. So did the young and old, the sick and healthy, the dreamers and fighters.

In the end, it didn't matter if they'd vowed to fight for their lives—it didn't matter if they'd shunned violence from their hearts or embraced it to their cores. In the end, there was pain, and blood, and screaming, and crying. In the end, everyone became ash, and ash rose to the stars.

In the end, there was Mal, and me, and the haunted faces of survivors who will relive those nights for the rest of their lives. In the end, everyone bled, everyone hurt.

In the end, it didn't matter who you were or how you viewed the world. There was no escape.

Tomorrow, it won't matter if I want to fight or not, it won't matter if I'd rather do anything else than take another life. It doesn't matter if the weight of people I've killed, the people I couldn't save, drags me down a little more, makes me feel more like a monster, an animal. It doesn't matter if I never wanted to be this person, this guy who has to fight for his life again, and again, and again. It doesn't matter if I didn't want politics, if I didn't want power, if I didn't want anything but to live in peace with my family on the red sands of my home.

No one cares what I do or don't want. No one cares I'm dreading this fight because no matter how it ends, I'll lose. It doesn't matter if victory, to me, will never taste like blood and death, like sweat and struggle, like one last gasp under the suns. Not for me, not for my enemy.

I'm so tired of fighting. But it doesn't matter. It will never matter.

Sweat drips down my temples, my back, my chest. The clean scent of the desert air—too dust-tinted to be home, too sweet for the crimson sand. I'm about halfway around the track, and the rhythm of running is sinking into my muscles— the low burn, the steady pounding, the tart taste of just a little farther, just a little farther, just a little—

Gasping a mouthful of black—

On my back, head throbbing, throbbing, throbbing like—

Warmth trickles between my eyes and down the bridge of my nose. It smells like rust. It feels like agony. My visions swims in and out of darkness as I sit up, and black figures block out the moonlight, and the world spins to the left, spins to the left, tilts, and tilts, and tilts, and—

I'm staggering backward and on my feet and something— someone—has my arms pulled back until my shoulders burn and my back is against someone's chest. I've been here before. I threw Jarek over my shoulder and ran, and ran, but not now. Now blood pours over my lips, and I blink, and pull—

Screaming. Coughing. It's me. Something hard slams into my chest again, and I can't see through the stars, and I'm on my knees. I'm on my knees and every breath burns through me, and it's so dark, and I spit blood, and everything tastes like rust, like death, like fire licking through my lungs and the dull throb between my eyes. Someone—probably several someones—is attacking me and everything hurts.

I'm in the room again, and Dima is wedging a knife behind my jaw. And my mother is screaming, and I'm frozen, and burning, and let me sleep, let me sleep, *please* I just need to—

The back of my head bursts with a blow into a starry night sky and the sleep I've wanted swallows me whole.

34

Eros

"*Kafra, kafra, kafra*—you are *not* dead, you're not *kafrek* dead. I swear to *Kala* I will destroy you if you're dead. Wake up. Wake *up*. Eros—"

"Shut up," I groan. Everything hurts. Not everything. My head, and my face, and my ribs. Everything above the waist, then, and every breath flames across my chest and burrows behind my eyes. "*Kafra*," I whisper.

"Open your eyes. I just—Eros—"

"Relax." I open my eyes. Squint into shadow. Deimos is huddled over me, his eyes wide, bathed in silver moonlight. You'd think he was the one just attacked in the middle of the night, with the way he's looking at me.

To be fair, I probably look bad. I think my nose is broken. And maybe my skull. And definitely some ribs.

"Can you get up?" Deimos asks. "I can call some medics, but I don't want to leave you here . . . *kafra* where are those orb-guides when you need them?"

"It's fine." I start to sit up—hiss. That fucken hurts. Moving above the waist at all hurts like a—

Fuck.

"Here." Deimos gingerly touches my back. "Is this okay? Did they get your back?"

"*Nai*," I mutter. "Just my ribs, the back of my head, and my fucken face."

Deimos tries to laugh but it sounds strangled. "Good news is you'll still be handsome as Jol when your nose isn't a disaster."

"Thank the stars. I was worried. As long as my looks haven't suffered, I guess everything's fine."

We look at each other. Then Deimos laughs and so do I—but I stop because laughing feels like ripping my ribs out of my chest—and then I'm pretty sure Deimos is crying. Seeing him so upset almost hurts worse than my throbbing body.

"Deimos," I start, carefully, "correct me if I'm wrong, but *I'm* the one with the broken ribs, *shae*?"

"*Skel.*" Deimos presses his palms against his face and laughs weakly. "I'm sorry. You're right. I just—*skel*, you scared me there for a minute."

"My face looks that bad, huh?"

"Stop joking," he says, but when he lowers his hands, he wears a weak smile for all of a breath before it fades. "*Kafra*. Those *skoi*. C'mon, let's get you inside—I'm going to destroy Lejv first thing in the morning, I swear to *Kala*."

I grimace. "I'm not sure who did this. I didn't get a good look at anyone. But it was two men. And I thought you said Lejv played by the rules."

Deimos slips his arm around me and carefully helps me to my feet. It still hurts, but I bite back a groan. "That's what I thought, but . . . *Kala* knows. Even if it wasn't Lejv, it was obviously some of his supporters. We'll get the council to delay the fight until you're recovered, but this is—what cowards."

"I guess this means Lejv isn't a great fighter," I say through a wince. "If they felt the need to sabotage me before the fight."

"I suppose not," Deimos answers. "But that's not good news when you have broken ribs and a cracked skull."

"*Naï* . . . but it will be when I recover."

Deimos sighs. "After he's had more time to prepare, but *sha*. I'm so sorry, Eros—*kafra*, you should have found me if you wanted to run."

"I didn't think I'd need a bodyguard. I didn't want to wake you up unnecessarily."

"Evidently it wouldn't have been unnecessarily, but I wish you had. I wasn't sleeping anyway."

"I obviously didn't know that."

"I know." Deimos frowns at me. "If they hadn't destroyed the nanites, this wouldn't even be a problem. The medics could have mended your bones in a segment."

"*Sha*, and they probably wouldn't have bothered if the nanites were functional, because they'd know how quickly it could be healed."

"Cowards," Deimos says again. "*Kafrek* cowards, every one of them."

"It'll be fine," I say. "You'll talk to the council, and they'll postpone the fight until I've recovered. That's only fair, especially when it's obvious this was a sabotage attempt from Lejv's side."

But Deimos doesn't look convinced, and to be honest, I'm not sure I believe me either.

35

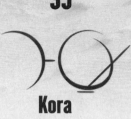

Kora

After missing the news about Eros's upcoming match, I set my glass to collect any mention of Eros in the news. Naturally that means more articles and feeds than I need, because few news sources on Safara are *not* talking about the half-blood that may become the next *Sira*, but I scan through it a couple times a set nevertheless. I don't want to miss anything again.

Now before the suns rise, I sit in front of my mirror, putting my hair up with a wrap and double-checking the covering on my scarred arm and shoulder. It still feels strange to do this alone, though it's been nearly half a term since Anja helped me prepare for the set, but she taught me well how to strategize my presentation, from the way I wear my hair to the color of my arm wrap.

Today I will meet the people and their choice of representative.

Today I will start in earnest my new rule with an aide at my side. Something that's never been done, not in Elja, not in any of the other Safaran territories. Some opinion writers think I'm foolish, but the Eljan feeds at least seem cautiously optimistic, which is all I care about.

I meet my gaze in the mirror and roll my shoulders back. I keep my chin up and inhale deeply. Strength. Power. Respect. I am *Avra*, and this time I won't fail my people. This time I will show Safara why I, not my brother, was meant to rule all along.

This time I'm ready.

It's still far too early to go out and see everyone though, so I sit on my bed and pull my glass onto my lap to check the news collected for me overnight. The list is longer than usual—and my heart jolts at the first headline: Eros Attacked Night Before Match.

Oh, *Kala*. I can't breathe—if Eros was hurt, or worse—

A fist in my throat, I splay my fingers to open the short article.

"Unverified reports indicate the half-blood contender for the *Sira* throne, Eros d'Elja, was attacked during a night jog by unknown assailants. Guide footage of the attack is conspicuously absent. If the reports are true, it is yet unknown if the match will go on as planned today, but sources indicate Eros is still alive. Updates to follow."

Other, longer articles all say the same. That the attack is unverified, that Eros is alive, that no one knows whether the match will be delayed. Some call it convenient, as though Eros didn't want to get this nightmare over with. Others call it an "interesting" update, as though this attack were a form of entertainment.

It doesn't matter how it's presented—the thought of Eros getting attacked in the middle of the night makes me sick to my stomach. The cowards.

I'd refrained from messaging Eros because I didn't want to distract him, but I need to know he's okay. As *Avra*, I have access to the personal glasses of other royals. Eros doesn't have his own assigned to him yet, but Deimos does. I find his name in my list of contacts quickly and send him a short video message.

"Deimos, I've seen the reports this morning of Eros's attack. Please let me know he's okay—I—" My voice cracks. I press my fist to my mouth and take a deep breath. "I just need to know he's fine. I'll keep an eye on the feed for updates on the match. Just please tell me he's okay."

I turn off the recording, send it, and stare at the ceiling with stinging eyes. The match was always going to be dangerous, and I was ready for that. But this attack beforehand and the reminder that he could die this evening—that he could have died last night—

It hurts.

It's terrifying.

And for this to happen just before I face the people—it's a bad omen.

I take some time to compose myself before the suns rise. Deimos, to his credit, responds quickly with a written message saying Eros is injured, but alive, and they're going to appeal to the Emergency Council to get the match postponed. It's a precarious situation, but hearing there's still hope, is what I need to swallow my fear and fill my lungs with the confidence to face everyone.

I leave my room just after the suns rise.

It's a surreal thing to be here again, back in a position of power. But it's so different from before; before, walking the halls was terrifying and facing the people more so. Before,

I looked at every corner for a threat, glanced at every guard knowing it was only a matter of time before someone—maybe one of them—turned against me.

And I was right; I just had never expected that someone to be my own brother.

But walking the halls now, I don't feel as though the armor of strength, power, and respect I wear is fake. I don't feel like a little girl playing pretend, like a child wearing a crown always too heavy for her to bear.

Today I feel like an *Avra*, truly, for the first time. And I'm not afraid. Not anymore.

The people are gathered at the gates when I emerge under the suns and walk over the home sands. Dima and Jarek don't join me this time—I haven't seen much of my brother since he officially returned my title to me, but Jarek told me he'll be fine, he just needs some time to process. Which is fine. Dima can process all he wants; I have work to do.

"Open the gates," I tell the guards manning the entrance. They don't hesitate—the gates pull back and I step in front of the crowd.

For this moment, everything is so quiet. A warm, gentle breeze wisps past my cheek, almost a caress. The people watch me with expectancy, with a strength in their gazes that looks, feels, and tastes like respect. They hold their heads high and they nod and bow, and no one is afraid, no one is angry, and everyone is here. There are more people gathered than I've ever seen at once in Vejla—they extend into the horizon, deep into the city, farther than I can see.

And, truly, I am not afraid.

"Thank you all for gathering here," I say. "It's wonderful to see so many of you. Have you chosen a representative?"

A murmur washes through the crowd, and a young man near the front steps forward. His face is scarred—the mark of a burn I know all too well spreads in a streak from his forehead, over his left eye, and down his jaw and neck. The burn mars the skin of his left shoulder, where it disappears into his shirt. His left leg ends just above the knee—the rest is a stylized white and red metal prosthetic, made to look like a mechanical leg, provided by the territory. Interesting that he chose to go for a replacement that's clearly artificial, rather than one of the seamless, pseudo-skin nanite-built replacements.

Then again, I suppose if he had, he probably wouldn't have a prosthetic at all right now.

My shoulder prickles as I look him over—I don't need to ask where he received his scars. I wasn't the only one left marked from the explosion that ended my coronation and killed my parents. But something about him is different: he doesn't wear his scars like something to hide. He doesn't cover his shoulder or try to hide his leg—even the scars on his face are left unpainted, for all to see.

Meanwhile, I cover my scarred arm down to my fingers. I leave it uncovered for nothing—even just glancing at the shiny, mottled skin reminds me endlessly of the set I'd do anything to forget.

"Very well," I say. "What is your name?"

"Uljen d'Elja," he answers smoothly. "I'm honored to be chosen by the people."

Uljen. His name ripples through the crowd, repeated quietly over and over into a blanket of voices.

"*Er or'jiva*, Uljen." I smile. "I look forward to working with you. Please, come with me."

"Not yet." Uljen pulls back his shoulders and lifts his chin. "The people of Elja have chosen me, but not as your second."

Though the morning suns beat down on me, a cold chill whispers down my spine. Men near the front of the crowd cross their arms and nod. The guards beside me stiffen.

"Oh?" I say carefully, ignoring the part of me that knows exactly what this is, exactly what is coming. "If not as my second, then what?"

Uljen smiles, and all the stars in the universe couldn't thaw the ice that washes over my blood. "The people have spoken: they want me to rule in your stead."

36

Eros

"An act of *Kala*?" Deimos repeats, bristling. "I refuse to believe you're this willfully ignorant. This isn't an act of *Kala*—this is an act of Lejv!"

My head throbs with the tenor of Deimos's outburst. The medics gave me some sortuv painkiller—a drug administered through the same prickly gel patch thing Serek used to sample my DNA—and it's taken the edge off the worst of the pain at least, so I can breathe without wincing and my skull doesn't feel like it's on fire. But the throb is still there, and it'll stay for a while.

Good news: they were able to reset my nose (which felt like anything but good news) and my skull isn't cracked—my brain is just bruised.

Bad news: I look like I've been run over by a pack of *kazim* and feel about the same. And now Deimos has called a gathering in the private meeting room, and the Council is calling it an act of *Kala*, because of course they are.

"Deimos," former *Avra* Oniks—Deimos's grandfather—cautions. "Show respect to your elders."

"I'm sorry, *ta'nahasi*, but surely you can't support this. *Kala* didn't ordain this—this is clearly sabotage. Just look at him!"

Seven gazes focus on me again and I grimace.

"He's in no shape to fight," Deimos says. "The *honorable* thing to do would be to postpone the match until he's recovered enough to fight evenly."

"The date of the match is set," Ashen says. "To move it would be disobeying the High Priest's order—and, by extension, *Kala* himself."

"*Kala* wouldn't want such an important fight to be so clearly uneven!" Deimos shouts. Ashen's eyes narrow and I touch Deimos's shoulder.

"It's fine," I say. "They've made their decision. Let's just go."

"But—"

"Thank you," I say loudly, speaking over Deimos, "for your consideration. I'll be at the match shortly."

And with that, I grab Deimos's arm and pull him out of the room, even as he swears the whole while—and we walk right into Lejv.

Deimos's face goes from purple and furious to scowling and murderous in a split breath. I grip his arm tighter in case he gets any ideas, but at this point I wouldn't really care if he attacked Lejv. Not like he wouldn't deserve it.

Lejv's eyes widen, as though he knows what I'm thinking. Or maybe my fucked-up face is just that attractive.

I scowl. "Get out of our way."

"Eros, I—" He shakes his head. "You have to understand, I never—I didn't want this."

I laugh, cold and empty. "Of course not. Just like you didn't want the throne, right? You just don't *not want it* enough to do anything about it."

"There's nothing I can do. The Council has made their decision—"

"Listening outside the doors, were you?" Deimos spits at his feet. "If you were a truly worthy leader, you would have gone in there and told them to postpone the match out of *honor*. Instead you sat in the hall and let this abuse go in your favor like a coward."

Deimos pulls his arm out of my grip and steps in front of me, so close to Lejv that the asshole steps back. "I don't care if it was you who attacked him, or some of your friends. I don't care if you knew about it, or wanted it, or not. You condone it all the same with your silence. And why? Because you know you couldn't beat Eros in a fair fight." Deimos crosses his arms over his chest. "Whatever happens later, you've already lost. The people will never respect a *Sira* who had to cheat his way to the throne."

Lejv stands silent and stiff as Deimos and I walk past him. And though Deimos's arm around my shoulder is mostly unnecessarily, I don't stop him.

I just wish I could believe he's right and Lejv has lost either way.

Mal leans against my shoulder as Deimos paces the room back and forth in front of us. We have maybe a seg before the match, and my body hurts, and I'm not sure how I'm going to be able to fight like this. Will the painkillers numb the pain enough for me to punch? I'm going to have to fight defensively, that much is obvious; even one hit to the wrong place could end me.

It's the worst kinduv scenario, and if I'm being honest with myself, I can't win like this. Even if Lejv is entirely untrained, even if he's never held a blade in his life, my weaknesses are obvious and not difficult to reach.

I'm probably going to die out there.

"You have to concede the fight," Deimos says at last, turning to me. "You have to go out there and appeal for your life. Or we can run now—together. We'll have a head start and—"

"I'm not running." I look at Deimos and pull back my shoulders, grimacing at the ache in my chest. "And I'm not begging for my life, either."

"Then you're a fool." Deimos scowls. "You can't win like this."

"Probably not."

"Then? Do you *want* to die?"

Mal cringes and pales.

"Obviously not. But the Council won't give me mercy— they'll execute me on the spot. And if we run, we'll never stop. Our lives will always be in danger—we'll never live a day without looking over our shoulders. I won't live like that— not anymore, and I'm not going to condemn Mal to that life, either."

Deimos shakes his head. "*Naï*, you'll condemn him to the life of an orphan, living with a Sepharon man he doesn't even know."

"He knows you well enough. And I trust you—you'll take good care of him. You swore to me you would."

Deimos presses his palms against his eyes. When he removes his hands, his eyes are red and shiny. "*Kafra*. You are *throwing* your life away. Do you not realize that? Going out there won't be a fight, it'll be a *slaughter*. You might as well slit your own throat!"

"Deimos—"

"*Nai!*" His shoulders shake as tears gather in his eyes. "If you insist on throwing your life away, you'll do it alone. I'll have no part in this—I can't—I won't watch them *execute* you."

I stand and cross the room, resting my hands on his shoulders. Deimos shivers and looks away, sniffling as tears slide down his cheeks. And I'm not sure if it's just because it's Deimos, or because I'm terrified too, but seeing him like this makes my throat ache and my eyes sting.

"I'm sorry," I say. "I wish I could change this—"

"—you could *run*—"

"—but this is the only way Mal will be even remotely safe. I'm fighting, and you may have given up, but I haven't." I'm not sure if that's true, but saying it, somehow, makes it feel more real. I squeeze his shoulders and look into his mismatched eyes. "I know my chances are beyond slim, but I'm going to do this. And you don't have to support me, but I need you to be there for Mal."

"I need some air," Deimos whispers, and then he turns on his heel and walks away.

And as much as I hate to admit it, some part of me aches as he leaves me behind.

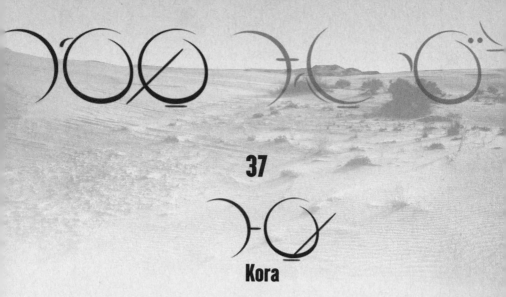

37

Kora

In another life, where I didn't spend most of my sets trying to justify my birthright against a boy unfit for the throne, the suggestion that a man who has never been prepared to rule should become *Avra* in my stead would almost be amusing. In another life, I would laugh, because the notion would be that preposterous, because of course no one could *truly* expect a common man with no preparation whatsoever would be better fit for the position I have spent my entire life training for.

Instead, I'm here, the people are completely serious, the air is thick with potential violence, and nothing about this is funny.

You can't be serious, I want to say, but he is, and suggesting otherwise would insult the people. As would any insinuation I'm not taking this as gravely as the dead.

I go with firm clarity instead: "Absolutely not."

The crowd ripples with murmurs as their faces harden. Uljen frowns, but I step forward before he speaks.

"I understand why the people are putting this request forward—by declaring the reinstatement of my rule, I'm asking all of you to trust me to do better than I had. I know it's not a simple thing, truly I do, which is precisely why I've invited the people to choose a representative to work *with* me. But what I've lacked in understanding what the people need, I make up for with a lifetime of experience and preparation to rule—experience you, Uljen, don't have."

Uljen nods calmly, but the people don't share his serenity. Their whispers grow louder, filling the air with a hiss like an ocean of static. The back of my neck prickles; this tension is far too familiar. We're maybe moments away from an explosion of fury, and all I have to temper it are promises they might not accept.

"I don't except all of you to immediately trust me," I say loudly, speaking over the crowd's increasing rumble. "But I do expect you to trust I'm equipped for my position, and I wouldn't have invited you to choose a representative had I not intended to be a better *Avra* than I was. Together, we can rebuild Vejla and the rest of Elja along with it—but I need your cooperation to do it. Whether we continue with more violence and bloodshed, or with a mutual agreement of cooperation, is up to you."

My breath shakes in my lungs, but my voice is steady. The people take in my words, but before they can respond, Uljen steps toward me and then faces the crowd. "*Avra* Kora is right," he says, and it's all I can do to smother the shock that'd be obvious on my face. "We don't need to lose any more of our children. We can move forward together and build a stronger Elja—and I swear to you to always keep the people's interests centered."

He raises his left fist to his right shoulder and bows—a military movement of highest respect. Was he once a guard? I don't remember an Uljen—but then again, I didn't know most of my guards' names. If he was, I'm not surprised they released him after his injuries.

The crowd returns the gesture, then someone shouts his name. Then another, and another, until the crowd thunders with his name, cheering as Uljen steps beside me and we enter the grounds together. My mind spins as the roar of the crowd washes over me; my heart still beats with terror. The cheering continues as the gates close behind us and we walk deeper and deeper into the complex. But all I can think about is that I nearly lost my sovereignty—again.

Who is this man beside me? I know nothing about him, but he must be all too aware he—not I—is the reason the people didn't revolt. He could have so easily had me ousted, or at least seriously threatened my rule, with just a turn of phrase. And something tells me that was exactly why he challenged me—to show me he could.

When we're far away enough that the cheering doesn't drown out everything else, I turn to Uljen. "If you ever attempt that kind of public power play on me again, I'll have you executed faster than you can say *Avra*." Despite my shaking fists, my voice is steady.

Uljen glances at me and nods. "Understood."

"Good. I'm happy to work with you to make Elja a better place, but I won't stand for even a whisper of sabotage against me again."

"I expected as much, but when I was chosen, the people demanded I put forward the suggestion. I don't think any of them expected you to agree, but I had to show them I was at least willing to try to fight for them."

I'm not sure I believe that, but I've made my point. If I'm going to work with him, we need to move forward, so

I change the subject. "Were you once a guard here at the complex?"

Uljen grimaces. "I was in training—I was sixteen when the rebels attacked your coronation."

Which means he's a cycle older than me—Eros's age. I nod. "I'm sorry you suffered."

Uljen shakes his head. "All of Elja suffered when the explosions went off. All of Elja suffers when any one of us suffers. But it wasn't your fault, and you don't have to apologize for it."

Heat nips down my chest and gathers around my heart. "It was my coronation that attracted the bombers."

"*Sha*, but that doesn't make you responsible for someone else's atrocious actions." He shrugs and glances at me. "You have enough to answer for without adding the events of that set to your ledger."

I purse my lips but nod. As much as I'd rather not think about it—as much as I'd rather move on without looking at the past, I must acknowledge my mistakes if I'm to be a better *Avra* in the future. Uljen's right. While plenty wasn't my fault, including much of my own suffering, plenty also was.

"Are you hungry?" I ask. "Thirsty?"

Uljen laughs weakly. "I live in Vejla. What do you think?"

His answer doesn't surprise me, but it stings. Uljen was chosen by the people, so he must be relatively well known, but he was suffering alongside them—it's a harrowing testament to my failures. I have so much to fix and make up for—but at least I'm starting to right my wrongs. "We have a lot of work to do. But we'll do our best work when we're at our best, so let's eat and discuss."

Uljen agrees, so we do.

I'd already asked the cooking staff to ration our portions the night before—we're in a desert, and our crops were nanite-dependent and largely flash-grown. We need to prepare for the inevitable famine, so today's meal isn't a feast. Instead, the staff prepares us individual portions paired with ripe fruit that will probably be overripe soon—the fruit doesn't last as long without the nanite-provided cooling system.

Uljen listens to all of this in silence then lifts his *ljuma* and examines it. "How many do we have of these? Or any fruit, for that matter?"

I hesitate. "I'm not sure, but I could ask the staff."

Uljen nods. "And how many staff do you have? How many people do you feed every day?"

"The staff makes food for the guard, my brother and me, and themselves." I hesitate. "They number at about forty, and I'm not certain about the guards' numbers, but I could ask Jarek."

"You should." Uljen bites into the *ljuma* and sighs as blue juice drips down his chin. He eats thoughtfully before looking at me. "These will only last a couple more sets before spoiling, and if you have as much as I suspect you do, I doubt you'll finish the full supply before it rots, even with the staff and guard taking their fill."

"That may very well be true," I say. "So, supposing you're right, you're suggesting we give it away, *sha*? How would you propose we do it?"

He nods. "There's no use in keeping food you can't eat when it won't keep. So you take note of the excess, make an announcement, and bring it to the city square where your men can distribute it in an orderly manner. Depending on how much you have, you ration it out so each family can get some."

I nod. "Good idea." I gesture to server standing near the kitchen door. He comes over and I nod to the fruit. "I need an accounting of all our perishables, as well as how close it is to spoiling."

The server bows and disappears into the kitchen.

"I'll talk to Jarek about the number of men we're feeding, too," I say to Uljen.

He smiles softly and nods. "Good. Thank you."

"You don't need to thank me, Uljen. I meant it when I said I wanted to be a better *Avra*—and I truly believe together we can better serve the people of Elja."

"I'll admit I was skeptical how much you'd actually listen to me but . . ." He smiles and lifts a shoulder. "You might just be right."

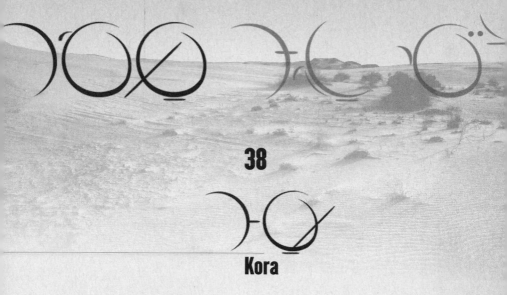

38

Kora

Sitting in my garden later that set, the suns paint the violet sky with shades of pink and blooming, deep reds. Orange lights the underbellies of thick, white clouds, setting them ablaze.

It is now the evening of Eros's match. The set when he will duel his opponent to the death for the title of *Sira*. The set I will watch, a hundred leagues away, while my friend fights for his birthright. For the throne he should have had all along. For his life.

Red bleeds into purple into orange. Morning light blossoms curl and turn away from the sunset, white and pink petals shuddering as they take in the fading light. It feels so wrong to be here when Eros is facing possibly the last segments of his life. I wish I could be there, speak to him in these moments before everything changes. I could contact him through the glass, I suppose, but if I'm being honest with myself, what Eros needs right now is to focus—not have me remind him how worried I am and how worried he should be in turn.

Today, Eros will either die or become *Sira*. And all I can do is wait.

"Quite the setting this evening."

I blink and meet the voice—Uljen leans against the decorative gate closing off the edge of my garden—a new addition erected in my absence. I'm not sure how I feel about it.

"I apologize if I startled you." He smiles. "I was walking the grounds and noticed you out here."

My skin prickles; after what he attempted this morning, I still don't know what to make of him. But I need this partnership to work, so I nod. "It's fine. You're welcome to enter."

"Thank you." He opens the gate and steps inside, then sits on an empty cushion next to me. "You seem distracted this evening."

"Just thinking about the match," I answer. "In Asheron."

"Ah, *sha*, for the throne. Concerned for Eros?"

I sigh. "Eros is excellent at fighting . . . but I don't know what to expect from Lejv. So many men have served in their respective guard—I wouldn't be surprised if they were evenly matched."

"Evenly matched still bodes well for Eros, doesn't it? If that's the worst-case scenario, it seems as though you have little to worry about."

I smile weakly. "Perhaps . . . but Eros was attacked last night and now he's injured. I'm not sure how serious his injuries are, but I imagine they'll affect the way he fights."

Uljen purses his lips and rests his hands on his knees. "That's unfortunate." He hesitates. "There were rumors you two had a friendship. Is that accurate?"

I hesitate—but I suppose it's not damaging to admit, especially now that Eros could very well become *Sira*. "It is."

"Then it makes sense. You care for him, and it's a dangerous situation. Only natural that you worry. You'll be watching the feed when it begins shortly, *sha*?"

I nod. "Nothing could keep me from it."

"I imagine most Safarans feel the same. We've never had an event of this global scale in our lifetime."

"That's true." Neither of us say what he's probably thinking—that Eljans will be watching, but in this traditional territory, few will want to see him survive. He may be technically from Elja, but he's a half-blood all the same. To the traditionalists, that's all that matters—though maybe things are different with the younger generation. I hope so. I don't know how Eljans will ever come to fully accept me if not even my generation is willing is try things differently. I sigh. "I pray things go as well as I want them to."

"And if they do? What then?"

I frown and glance at him. "How do you mean?"

"If Eros becomes *Sira*, how will affect us here in Elja? It's well expected whoever takes the throne will seek reparations for Dima's decisions as *Avra*, from lying to the *Sira* to instigating genocide. Even without the crimes he committed against the Eljans, most expect whoever is *Sira* will demand some sort of recourse. As he should."

I sigh and nod. "*Sha*, I expect something, as well. Particularly as . . . Dima didn't treat Eros well while he was here, either."

"Ah."

"There may have been . . . torture involved."

Uljen's eyes widen. "Then you don't expect Eros will show him mercy."

I tilt my head as I craft my response. "I don't know what to expect, to be true. Eros and I have a friendship, and I believe he'll respect that . . . but I can't expect him to overlook what Dima did, either. Those same crimes you speak of lead to his near-execution and the deaths of some of his family members. He has no reason to show my brother mercy."

Uljen nods. "As we're speaking openly, I don't believe your brother deserves mercy, regardless."

I weave my fingers together and purse my lips. He's not wrong—what Dima did, the acts he instigated and the crimes against Eljans—he doesn't deserve mercy. If he were anyone else, I would have locked him in the dungeons and prepared for his execution. But he's not anyone else. He's my brother—and the only family I have left. I haven't lived a set on Safara my brother didn't also share, and to lose him now would be devastating. Even with everything he's done. Even with all the hurt he's caused. Even with the ways he turned against me.

"The people feel the same," Uljen says. "His rule was short, but vicious. There were citizens brutalized in the street under his orders. Two boys barely of age were executed in the center square because they dared to shout at him during an address to the people. The people won't forget what he did—and they're not going to forgive, either. They want his head."

The heat of Uljen's words tears open an ache deep between my lungs. "I know," I whisper.

"If you refuse them, you may risk them rising against you. You can't show partiality just because he's your brother. He can't be treated differently than any other criminal."

I close my eyes and inhale deeply through my nose. The back of my throat tightens, but this isn't the time, this isn't the place, and I force myself to breathe. "I know. And I don't intend to pardon him without trial. That would be . . . it wouldn't be right."

Uljen nods. "So you intend to have a trial."

"I do. Here in Elja. But it'll wait until the new *Sira* is crowned, because I'll use it as a negotiating point. I imagine the new *Sira*, whoever it is, will want to speak about Dima and settle the matter quickly. By preparing for a trial here in Elja, we can ensure it is *our* people who settle the matter. After all . . ." I take a shaky breath. "Even after everything, he is Eljan. He deserves to be tried by his people."

"I agree," Uljen says. "And I think the people will as well."

I sigh. "Good."

He nods and stands. "For what it's worth, Kora, I'm sorry for all the hardship you've faced and will continue to endure in the coming sets. It can't be easy to be separated from your friend on such a dangerous evening, nor will it be easy to prosecute your own brother."

"It's not," I answer. "Thank you."

Uljen nods, bows, and leaves the garden. I touch the morning flowers settling in for the night and breathe in their smooth, sweet scent as the suns slip toward the horizon.

And I pray to *Kala* for safety, and mercy, and strength to Eros a hundred leagues away.

Today, everything changes.

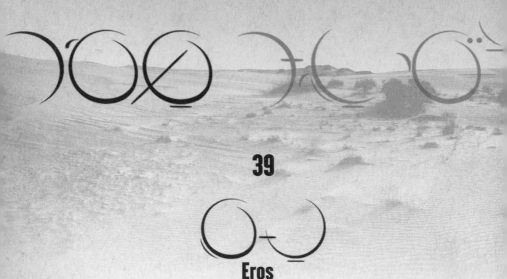

39

Eros

In the end, Deimos doesn't leave me to *throw my life away* on my own, as he called it. He and Mal stand on the edge of the courtyard, Deimos's hands on Mal's shoulders, watching me in silence. He went out of his way to tell me he was there for Mal, not because he's changed his mind and wants to see me fight, but it doesn't matter. He's here, and Mal isn't alone, and that's all I care about.

The courtyard is surrounded by people and orb-guides recording the whole thing. The royals stand on the edges, watching with grim faces as we wait for the High Priest to arrive with the weapons, and Lejv is laughing and chatting with his supporters as though this were the opening to a performance rather than a fight that'll leave one of us dead.

I guess they're all sure which one of us won't be leaving. I'm not convinced they're wrong; a big part of me thinks they're right.

But this isn't the first time I've prepared for slaughter. This isn't the first time I've stood on the course white sands and felt the warmth of the suns on my shoulders and knew it might be my last. But what makes this time different is I have a chance. A terrible chance, granted, but a chance nevertheless. This time, if I go down, I'll go down fighting.

I'll take that over resting my head on the chopping block and waiting for the sword to fall any set.

The crowd parts in front of me, and the High Priest steps through carrying a black slab of smooth rock like a tray. On it are three weapons: a thin stick-looking thing about the length of my forearm, a knife with a silver handle, and a black, sharpened stake with a handle sticking out at a right angle. Lejv chooses the stick-thing and I take the only weapon I know how to use—the knife.

I toss the knife in my hand as we move to opposite sides of the courtyard. It's well-balanced, so if I had no other option, I could throw it, but given this is my only weapon, that would be a last resort.

Then we face each other and the courtyard is deathly quiet. Lejv bows, as do I, and the priest says, "The rules are simple: one man will live to rule and the other will die. May *Kala*'s favor shine brightly on the man best suited for the throne."

Deep breath in, deep breath out. How am I going to do this? I've never had to fight while so injured before. But whatever they gave me is working—the pain is a distant hum.

I can do this. I have to.

"Begin."

Lejv whips his stick out and it extends, sliding open into a long staff that he smacks into place. My heart stills for a breath. Shit. I don't know how to fight with a staff, but if anyone should have grabbed a ranged weapon, it's me. Lejv smiles because he knows it, too—not only am I injured, but it's going to be twice as hard for me to get close enough to hurt him with a knife now that he's armed with a staff.

This mistake could be the last one I ever make.

We circle each other slowly. My pulse throbs in my ears as I hold the knife ready and keep an eye on that fucken staff. I need to disarm him if I want a chance at winning. Lejv swings—I duck—the staff cuts the air just above my head. He swipes again and I jump out of the way—my ribs throb with the movement. Another slash—I lean out of range and warm air whooshes past my arm.

A long-range weapon is only useful if I stay at a distance—I need to get closer.

We keep circling. Sweat slips between my shoulder blades as I watch Lejv for tells. His mouth twitches—I move—the staff slams the sand beside me. I lunge forward, the staff slashes up—hot pain rams into my leg, just below my hip. I grunt and jerk out of the way, my leg smarting. That'll bruise, but better my leg than my ribs again.

Facing each other again. Breathing the hot, desert air in quick bursts. Lejv strikes for my head—I duck under and rush forward. Lejv spins and a flash of black races toward me—I throw myself back into the sand and block my face with my arms—

Pain. My wrist screams and I'm not holding the knife and I'm in the sand and *get up get up get up.* I roll just as the staff slams into sand. Jerk up to my feet, take two quick steps back, out of range. Even the tiniest movement of my fingers sends flames up into my elbow. My knife hand is useless and my knife is in the sand, out of reach. I hold my injured wrist against my chest and bite back the pain. I'm hurt—again—and disarmed, and Lejv still has the fucken staff and I haven't even been able to touch him.

I need to get closer. It's my only chance, but getting in

range could be the end if I don't move fast enough—and so far, I haven't moved fast enough. Every quick movement rips into my ribs—a dull, deep tear—and it's slowing me down. It's slowing me down, and I can't afford to be slow, not today, not here.

I'm unarmed, and injured, and never had a chance in this fight, not really. But Deimos is whispering to Mal and Mal is crying and I'm not giving this up, I'm not losing hope, not even now. I have to do this. I have to survive. I have to.

Lejv leaps forward and the staff flashes out—I duck, scream, and slam myself into him. The impact rams into my whole body—my chest burns and my wrist is agony—but we crash into sand and something snaps and the top half of the staff whips over my head and disappears. Something hard slides under my good hand—I grab it, press it against Lejv's neck, and—

The staff has ripped in two, leaving a sharp, splintered edge, which I'm pressing into Lejv's neck with my good hand. I'm sitting on his chest, my feet buried in sand, my body aching, but here, right here, I have the edge.

I've pinned him under his own weapon.

It's over. I've won the fight and Lejv knows it—he stares at me wide-eyed and his neck bobs with his final breaths.

"Make it quick," he whispers.

And slowly, with sweat dripping down my back and agony coursing through my veins, everything clicks into place. I'm holding an unarmed man under the point of death. All I have to do is shove the staff shard up into his neck—break through skin and muscle and sever the artery and watch his dark purple blood pour into the white sand.

All I have to do is murder a defenseless man in cold blood and the throne is mine.

But this isn't me. I'm not a murderer. I kill to survive, when we're evenly matched and have to move fast to live. But not this—not a man who can't fight back anymore, not when there's nothing more he can do to fight for his life.

This is wrong. This isn't a fight anymore. This is an execution.

The rules were clear: kill to win. But this is supposed to be a match for *Kala* to decide—this is supposed to be under the name of fulfilling *Kala*'s wish. But I can't imagine serving a god who demands death to *prove* their ruling.

I can't, I can't, but I have to, and I—

I scream, lift the shard, and slam the unbroken side against his temple. Lejv grunts and stills beneath me, unconscious. And it's over.

I stagger to my feet as the crowd explodes around me. People rush into the courtyard, and I'm shaking under the twin blazing suns, and someone slams into me, and wraps his arms around me as I stagger back, and Deimos is holding me like his life depends on it.

It hurts, but I wrap my arms around him, too, and he's crying and cursing into the crook of my neck and I close my eyes. My whole body aches with the force of his grip, but I don't care, I don't care—I'm shaking like the suns are a million leagues away and the fingers of my good hand slip into Deimos's thick, dark hair, and then he looks at me and my heart forgets how to beat.

Then I meet his eyes and my heart jolts to life again. My fingers brush softly against the hair at the base of his skull, and we're so close we're breathing the same air and Deimos's nose is almost touching mine. And I know this louder than the beating of my pulse, stronger than the force of his grip:

I want this, I want us, I want *him*, and we're so close all it'd take is moving a breath forward and making it real.

The truth is undeniable: I need Deimos like I need air. Not just like a friend, like *mine*. I want to kiss him and hold him through the setting suns and rising moons. I want night and light to fold around us and wrap us in stars. I want to taste the laugh on his lips and never let go again. I want him by my side as my partner, as the prince I know better than myself.

But I hesitate. And maybe Deimos notices and maybe he doesn't, but he doesn't kiss me. Instead, he rests his forehead against mine, grips the back of my head, and his thumb rubs against the buzzed hair there. I shiver. Our noses touch and my fingers tighten in his hair, and we close our eyes and breathe together. Inhale. Exhale. Like one body. Like one person.

And it feels so good, so incredibly good to be so in sync with someone. Not just someone. Deimos.

"You're okay," he whispers. "*Kafra*, you're actually okay."

"*Shae*," I croak. "Somehow."

I'm not sure how long we stay like that—too long to go unnoticed, probably, but not as long as I'd like. But I'm sure as sand our hearts are beating together, and as much as my body aches just holding myself upright, I need this moment, this relief—whatever this is, I need it. I need him.

Then Deimos steps back and he's smiling, and I'm smiling, and Mal hugs me and kicks my shin.

I laugh. "*Ej*! Maybe you haven't noticed, but I'm injured and very fragile."

"Shut up," Mal says, wiping his teary face with the back of his hand. "Deimos told me you dropped your knife."

I grimace. "I did."

He kicks me again. I laugh and Deimos smirks. "I was ready to jump in there and strangle you myself when you dropped it."

"In my defense, I'm pretty sure my wrist is broken."

"Hold on." The voice comes from behind me—glancing back, Niro is crouched next to Lejv, touching his neck, probably feeling the pulse that's still there. Because I made a decision, and the decision wasn't what they wanted. "He's still alive," he says as Ashen approaches.

"Speaking of your wrist," Deimos says, "let's get you wrapped up. There's no reason to stay here—any official announcements will come later."

I glance at the rapidly growing gathering around Lejv—Niro has stepped away, but he's smirking and the whole Emergency Council is discussing. But at this point, short of walking over and killing an unconscious man—which I'm not about to do—there's nothing left for me here. So I turn away and we walk back together into the palace.

Alive.

"You probably should have killed him." Deimos wraps my wrist with a tight, stretchy bandage. It aches deeply, but at least it'll remind me not to move it while it heals. "Just to be sure, *shae*? But I understand why you didn't. He was disarmed."

"It would have been an execution," I say through gritted teeth.

"I know. At any rate, it doesn't matter—you won the fight, and no one can pretend otherwise. You made it impossible for him to continue the match."

"I thought when the match was over, they were supposed to declare you won," Mal says from across my bedroom. The low hum of voices projected through the glass fills the room, but I wasn't paying attention to what Mal had playing.

"They should," Deimos says. "Why? Are they making an announcement?"

Mal crosses the room and places the glass next to me. "It sounds like Ashen's voice, but I can't see his face."

I glance at the screen. Ashen stands in front of a large crowd outside, addressing the people, I guess. "It's him."

Deimos swipes his hand over the glass, raising the volume as Ashen's voice fills the room.

". . . and while Eros clearly outmatched his competitor, as we all witnessed, both men are still breathing, so he did not complete the match as the rules dictate. Only one survivor, traditionally, emerges from such a fight, but Eros chose to ignore tradition and left Lejv unconscious in the sand instead, humiliating him. As such, the Council has decided we will choose who we feel is most worthy for the throne instead, taking Eros's decision to disregard tradition entirely and humiliate his opponent into account, as well as Lejv's failure to defeat the half-blood in the fight for the throne."

Ashen bows and the feed goes quiet. The room goes quiet.

And then Mal whispers "*kafra*," and something hot, and ugly, and full of fire and energy rears inside me and gathers in my throat and sets my mind ablaze.

"They're going to pick Lejv." The words sound strangled and foreign—not mine. Not from my tongue, not from my lips. "I won, and they're going to pick Lejv, who'll be pissed at me for *humiliating* him." Louder this time, harsher, with edges that cut and leave my tongue tasting rust.

"*Shae*," Deimos says, and his voice is nothing like mine. His is quiet and far away—the sound of a man who knows he's lost.

Because I have.

It's over.

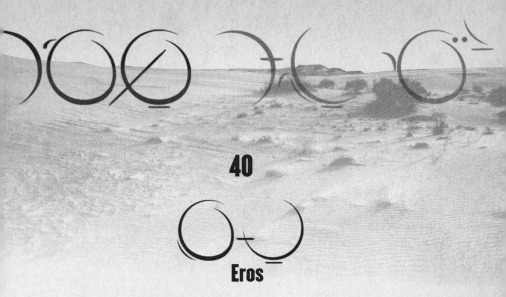

40

Eros

Mal and Deimos leave my room when I ask them to, which is good because the door has barely closed behind them when I lose it.

The scream breaks from my lips and rips out of my lungs. It tears from my spirit and pulls, and pulls, and pulls. It drags me to the ground and says *enough*. It says *I'm so tired,* it says *I deserve to live.* I punch the wall—the pain hits me all at once—*your wrist is broken, genius*—and I'm on the ground, holding my arm to my chest, and crying at my stupidity, screaming at myself for ever believing I had a chance, ever thinking any part of this competition would be fair, ever hoping life would go my way even just once.

I'm a half-blood. Half-bloods don't get happy endings; I've known it my whole life. But this half-blood dared to dream. This half-blood dared to think maybe he'd suffered enough, maybe things would be different this time, just this blazing once, and he was wrong. I was wrong, and it doesn't matter that I did what I needed to, it doesn't matter that I fought and won against all odds. It doesn't matter that this is literally in my blood, that I should have been here all along.

Half-bloods don't get happy endings, and I'm no exception.

"Eros."

Deimos is crouching in front of me. I'm not sure when he got there. All I know is my throbbing wrist, and my burning ribs, and the dull ache of my face, and the agony of losing not because I screwed up, but because I was never meant to win. This was never going to be a fair decision.

I should have known—no, I did. I just dared to hope it might be different and it wasn't. Again.

"You still have a chance," he says, "There are people on the council who support you, and even those who don't would be hard-pressed to argue you didn't win that match. *Shae*, you broke with tradition and didn't kill Lejv, but you're a break in tradition to begin with. It might be okay. It might not—"

"Just stop." I push myself up with my good arm. "I lost, Deimos. They aren't going to choose me. We've been pretending long enough, but it's over. I'm done."

"Eros, you were meant for this—"

"It doesn't matter!" I shout, turning on him. "Don't you see? It doesn't matter *Sira* Asha was my father, it doesn't matter there isn't an accidental pregnancy with the Sepharon, it doesn't matter he must've planned to have me, it doesn't matter I won the match that was supposed to fucken decide who is the next *Sira*—none of that matters because Asha is dead so the Council gets to pretend they don't *really* know what Asha was thinking and *maybe* he just wanted a half-blood as a fucken pet, who knows? We can't know because Asha is dead, and he can't speak for himself, and no one will fucken speak for me. No one will pick me when they can pick a *real*

Sepharon instead. Fuck this. Fuck all of them. I'm done—I'm so *done*—"

Deimos grabs my left hand. I start to pull away—"what're you . . ."— but then he slips the ring off my finger and holds it up. "This is Asha's intention. He didn't give this to you by accident. It isn't a coincidence you happen to have the ring of *Sirae*."

"They don't care," I say dully. "As far as they're concerned, the only thing it proves is humans killed him."

"But this is—"

"*Deimos*." I grab the ring with my good hand and scowl at him. "Don't you get it? Logic doesn't matter. It's not a coincidence I have it and I'm his son—I fucken know that—but they don't care. All they care about is making sure a half-blood doesn't sit on the throne, and they'll break as many rules and traditions as they have to so they can justify choosing Lejv instead."

Deimos purses his lips. "This is wrong. If you just—"

"If I just *what*? This isn't up to me, Deimos! I've done *everything* I was supposed to—I've passed all their fucken tests and it. Doesn't. Matter!" I throw the blazing ring, and it slams against the wall and thuds against the stone floor in pieces.

Oh, shit.

Deimos's mouth drops open. "Please tell me you didn't just—"

We race to the ring and drop to our knees, and the ring is now three rings. A black strip, a gold strip, and another black strip.

My face is flaming and heart is racing and I can't believe I—I didn't think—

I broke the blazing ring of *Sirae*.

Deimos and I snatch up the pieces—I grab the black bits and he grabs the translucent gold. "Does it fit back together again?" My voice is high-pitched, and panicked, and I just broke a fucken priceless artifact, stars above and sands below, and *dammit*al—

I am so dead.

"This is ridiculous," I say, "it can't just—why is it so blazing fragile?"

Deimos runs his fingers over the smooth gold circle, his brow furrowing deeper and deeper. He stands abruptly and grabs the glass. "Come here."

I do. Deimos rests the glass on my bed and looks at the golden circle again. "Did they tell you anything about the ring when . . . whoever gave it to you?"

"The guy who handed it over didn't even know what it was," I say. "The man who was originally holding it for me was Nol, but he . . . he died before he could pass it on."

Deimos nods, bites his lip, then places the circle in the center of the glass. The glass lights up and a voice chirps, "Verify identity."

I blink and the door whooshes opens behind me. "What's going on?" Mal asks.

"Everything is fine," Deimos answers. "Come on in, Mal. Eros, put your hand on the glass."

I shake my head. "What is this? Why is the glass—does it always do that when you put stuff on it?"

"*Nai*," Deimos says, "but I believe it's meant for you. Put your hand on the glass."

My hands are shivering and my pulse is roaring in my ears, but I do as he says. Text I can't read flashes above my fingers, then the voice says, "Welcome, Eros d'Asheron," and Deimos pulls my hand away.

And I can't breathe.

My father is looking at me through the glass, and he's smiling. "It's good to see you, Eros." My breath catches. I look at Deimos. "He can't actually . . .?"

"I think it's a recording." Deimos nods at the screen. "Look."

I turn back to the glass. My father is still smiling, but it's a sad, soft smile. A knowing smile. "If you're watching this, it's because something has happened to me and I'm not with you as I should be. For that, I'm sorry. Your life will be difficult enough even with support systems in place—without them, I can't imagine the hardships you must have endured. But you're here, and you're alive, and for that I can't thank *Kala* enough."

"Is that your dad?" Mal whispers.

"*Shae*," I choke out quietly. "That's Asha."

"He sounds like you."

"I imagine without me there, the Council will do everything within their power to try to stop you from claiming your birthright," Asha says. "And so, as a precaution, I'm recording this message to confirm what my intentions have been from the start. The world will call you a half-blood, Eros. They will demand your life and call you impure—but they are so, so wrong. You, my son, are a bridge. You're everything this world could be; you're a manifestation of the unity between Sepharon and humans. This world is so divided, but I believe we can be united, I believe we can knit this world together, and it starts with you.

"I had you, Eros, with the love of my life—a woman who is human. You are my firstborn, and in case my intentions weren't clear—in case choosing to have you, a son, and giving you the ring of *Sirae* wasn't enough—you, and only you, should inherit the throne after me. Your mother and I chose to have you, Eros, because we believe no one will be better equipped to bridge the divide between the Sepharon and human than someone who is both. Someone who can empathize with both sides, someone who has seen everyone's pain and lived amongst human and Sepharon alike.

"Eros, you are the true *Sira*, and you are the only one I want to inherit my throne.

"When I finish this recording, I'm going to find your mother, who is having you right now on the night of the full eclipse. You have a bright future ahead of you, Eros, and I truly believe you will change the world as we know it and be a better *Sira* than I ever could be.

"I can't wait to meet you, son. I love you already."

He smiles once more and the recording ends. My face is hot and my body is shaking and this—

I was wanted. He wanted to have me, and he wanted me to be *Sira*, and this is everything I needed to hear and everything I thought I'd never hear.

My dad was a *Sira* and he only met me once, but he loved me before he ever saw me for himself.

Someone sniffles beside me, and Deimos flushes when I look at him. "Shut up," he laughs, "you're crying, too."

I can't deny it because I am, but I'm smiling, too.

"So, that was cool," Mal says casually. "Now can we go show the Council?"

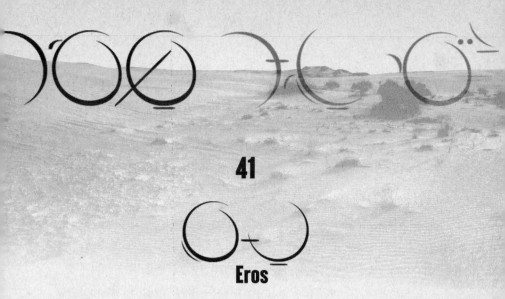

Eros

We don't knock. The Council has gathered in the dining room, as they always do when about to announce a big decision, but this time orb-guides have been permitted inside to broadcast their decision to the nation. When the doors swish open and Deimos, Mal, and I walk in, Ashen looks like he's just about to speak, and the orb-guides whir as they spin in the air to capture our entrance.

"How kind of you to join us," Ashen says drily. "As I was saying, the Council has deliberated and—"

"Wait," I say loudly. The orbs whir to face me again as I walk around the long, curved table full of royals and march right up to Ashen. "The Council doesn't have all the information it needs to make the decision."

Ashen arches an eyebrow. "The Council has looked over *all* of the information available to us—"

"Except this." I hold up the golden core of the ring of *Sirae*. Ashen frowns at it, and Deimos taps a guide hovering beside my head as I lift the glass and place the ring on top.

"Amplify the glass," Deimos tells the guide.

The orb hovers over the glass as I place my trembling hand on the surface and it verifies me again. Light bursts from the guide and it projects the image into the air in front of Ashen and me, for all to see.

Asha's smile fills the room, and quiet gasps scatter through the air. Ashen's eyes widen at the image in front of us.

And so the recording begins, broadcasting not just to the room, but to the whole world as the guides relay the feed. My whole body vibrates with my father's words; my clenched jaw does little to stop my chattering teeth as everything changes.

They won't be able to fight this. I know it with everything inside me, with every shuddering beat of my heart, with every tremble of my cold hands. I know it like I know my father's smile, like I know the words hushing the room, the words burning into my spirit and weaving into my cells. The answer was with me all along—it was sitting on my finger; it was my father protecting me before I was even born. Before he'd ever met me.

He didn't know me for long. He must have found me briefly—held me long enough to give my birth mother the ring. I wish I could remember what it felt like to have him hold me; I wish I could remember the words he said to me that night.

But maybe even though I don't remember the details, even though I'll never unbury the memories of my first night, maybe I haven't forgotten everything because his voice feels right. It reverberates inside me, and even as I stand beside the man who'd do anything to see me fail, even as I face a room full of royals and the world, even as my father's memory declares me his successor, I'm not afraid.

There's no question now: I was always meant to be here.

The recording ends. The projection disappears. A held breath; the silent plunge; the hush before a thunderclap—

The roar of voices erupts around me—an explosion of cheers, and shouts, and anger, and joy.

Deimos beams at me and laughs—and me?

I stand before the chaos and smile.

Glossary/Pronunciation Guide

Note: /r/ is rolled (similar to a Spanish /r/) and /j/ is closer to an English /y/.

Sepharon (SEH-fah-rohn, as pronounced by Sepharon; SEH-fur-on, as pronounced by nomads): the native species of Safara.

Safara (SAH-fah-rah): the planet the Sepharon and nomads live on; in a separate solar system from Earth.

Sephari (SEH-fah-ree, as pronounced by Sepharon; SEH-fur-ee, as pronounced by nomads): the language all Sepharon speak.

el/ol Avra (el/ohl AH-vrah): my/your majesty; Avrae are rulers of the eight territories.

el/ol Sira (el/ohl SEE-rah): my/your high majesty; the Sira is the high ruler who all Avrae must submit to.

Avrae/Sirae (AH-vray/SEE-ray): plural forms of Avra and Sira

ko (koh): a ruler's spouse; ranks directly under the ruler.

kaï (KAH-ee): prince

saï (SAH-ee): princess

kjo/sjo (kyoh/syoh): plural forms of kaï and saï

Kala (kah-lah): God

ve (veh): sir

ken (kehn): the

sha (shah): yes

naï (NAH-ee): no

kazim (KAH-zeem): wildcat

[City] ora'jeve (oh-RAH-yeh-veh): [City] greets you (all)—the equivalent to "Welcome to [city]."

or'jiva (ohr-YEE-vah): greetings (to one person)

orenjo (oh-REN-yoh): honor that is earned.

naïjera (nah-EE-yeh-rah): relax

ljuma (LYOO-mah): a tangy fruit.

azuka (AH-zoo-kah): a powerful drink, somewhat equivalent to alcohol.

zeïli (zeh-EE-lee): a leaf that's dried and smoked for a relaxing and mood-boosting effect.

lijara/lijarae (lee-YAH-rah/lee-YAH-ray): umbrella term equivalent to queer people (lijarae is the plural form)

el ljma si... (el LYEH-mah see): my name is...

alaja (ah-LAH-yah) and **nejdo** (NEY-doh): stringed instruments

ulae (OO-lay): a traditional uniform worn by Ona's military men since before the Great War.

ikrat (EE-kraht): death

kata (kah-tah): a flat food wrap, similar to a tortilla

ushri (OOSH-ree): a savory orange spread

ana da Kala (anah dah kah-lah): literally "Kala's heart," meant to indicate even Kala is mourning when someone revered or well-loved dies

ko (koh): used to refer to spouses of Avrae and Sirae (often as Avra-ko or Sira-ko)

balaika (bah-LIE-kah): a modern A'Sharan style dance

keta-mel (keh-tah mehl): an A'Sharan special; a spicy meat stew often served on a flat wrap over a layer of rice

mana eran (mah-nah EH-ran): my brother

shae (SHAY): A'Sharan variation of "sha"; equivalent to "yeah"

ora'denja (OH-rah den-YAH): good morning (to you)

denna (dennah): literally "a morning"; response to ora'denja

kafra (KAH-fra): a swear word, similar in intensity to "fuck"

entu (EN-too): small furry desert animals with long tails; known as "fetchers" to the nomads

aska (askah): a white stone that reflects subtle colors, like opal; often used to build temples in the Southern territories

riase (REE-ah-seh): most respectful title used to address former rulers

Kala alehja (KAH-lah ah-LAY-ha): God above; phrase used to express exasperation

Kala'niasha (KAH-lah nee-AH-shah): literally "prayers to Kala"; phrase used to express condolences

kelo (keh-low): a cold, sweet dessert

sko/skoi (sko/skoy): a swear word used to describe someone who is a jerk (skoi is plural)

ej (ey): kind of like "hey"

melos (meh-lohs): a sweet, thick, orange dish that's not quite solid, not quite liquid

ljnte (LEEN-teh): hot, white, sweet and spicy energy drink

Jorva (YOR-vah): Sepharon holy book

ufrike (oo-FREE-keh): an intoxicating drink

araban (ah-rah-BAHN): herb combined with zeïli for powerful intoxicating effect. Araban in particular is used as a sort of truth serum.

tenna (ten-nah): a hangover cure chew. It doesn't taste great, but it works.

istel (EE-stehl): a white, partially solid food, somewhat similar to Jell-O.

skel (skehl): another curse word, basically the equivalent of "shit"

er or'jiva (er OR-yee-vah): I welcome you; greetings to one person.

ta'nahasi: grandfather

General terms:

breath: (in terms of time) second

(sun)sets: equivalent to a day.

term: month (50 sets)

cycle: year (8 terms)

mo: moment: minute

Nomad slang:

brainblaze: migraine

blazing: somewhat equivalent British English "bloody."

blazed: angry/ticked off

throwing sand: freaking out

junker: an old, beat-up transportation vehicle.

port: some sort of transportation vehicle, usually equivalent to cars or vans.

Acknowledgments

Writing a sequel has been one of my bucket list items for something like a decade, but I wouldn't give myself permission to do it until the stars aligned. To say that I'm thrilled the stars shifted in all the right ways is an understatement.

Said alignment didn't happen on its own, though, and I have a team of truly incredible people to thank for making this dream come true:

First thanks will always go to my *Kala*, my Creator. I'm so beyond grateful to have my dream career now with not one, but two books to share with the world. I'm more delighted than I can say.

To my incredible agent, who never fails to make me feel like an absolute rock star, Louise Fury, thank you for keeping me grounded enough to navigate this confusing and awesome career, but daring enough to dream big. Your encouragement and guidance means more to me than you know.

I have all the gratitude in the universe for my truly excellent Sky Pony team. My lovely editor, Nicole Frail, thank you for believing in Eros and Kora's continuing journey and pushing me to make it the best it can be. My equally lovely assistant editor, Kat Enright, thank you for the excitement, cheering—and especially those awesome reaction GIFs. Sammy Yuen, thank you for *Into the Black*'s stunning cover that I seriously can't stop fawning over; Joshua Barnaby, thank you for yet another blazing amazing interior design masterpiece; and Ming Liu, thanks for helping me get this book into the hands of the right readers. You guise are the best.

To my awesome CP duo, Laura and Caitlin, I'm unendingly grateful for your support, enthusiasm, and, of course, invaluable thoughts on those early, raw drafts. And to Mark, Kelley, and Julia, thank you so much for your careful readings and wonderful feedback. Your insight truly means the world to me.

Shout out to my Tia and Aya, for reading my books and telling *everyone* about them. I will never tire of answering all of your excited publishing questions or hearing about the latest person you've shared my words with. ¡Te quiero muchísimo!

To my wonderful Twitter friends and Community of Awesome, your support, kind words, excitement, and perfectly random GIFs make my heart sing. And to you, reading this book right now, it's hard to express how grateful I am to you for following me along this journey and spending time with my words. You guise are the reason I do this, and the reason I can continue making this dream-like career a reality. Seriously—thank you.